Romantic Suspense

Danger. Passion. Drama.

Baby On The Run
Hope White

Colorado Mountain Kidnapping
Cate Nolan

MILLS & BOON

BABY ON THE RUN
© 2018 by Pat White
Philippine Copyright 2018
Australian Copyright 2018
New Zealand Copyright 2018

First Published 2018
First Australian Paperback Edition 2024
ISBN 978 1 038 91076 9

COLORADO MOUNTAIN KIDNAPPING
© 2024 by Mary Curry
Philippine Copyright 2024
Australian Copyright 2024
New Zealand Copyright 2024

First Published 2024
First Australian Paperback Edition 2024
ISBN 978 1 038 91076 9

MIX
Paper | Supporting
responsible forestry
FSC® C001695

Published by
Harlequin Mills & Boon
An imprint of Harlequin Enterprises (Australia) Pty Limited
(ABN 47 001 180 918), a subsidiary of HarperCollins
Publishers Australia Pty Limited
(ABN 36 009 913 517)
Level 19, 201 Elizabeth Street
SYDNEY NSW 2000 AUSTRALIA

Cover art used by arrangement with Harlequin Books S.A.. All rights reserved.

Printed and bound in Australia by McPherson's Printing Group

Baby On The Run
Hope White

MILLS & BOON

An eternal optimist, **Hope White** was born and raised in the Midwest. She and her college sweetheart have been married for thirty years and are blessed with two wonderful sons, two feisty cats and a bossy border collie. When not dreaming up inspirational tales, Hope enjoys hiking, sipping tea with friends and going to the movies. She loves to hear from readers, who can contact her at hopewhiteauthor@gmail.com.

Visit the Author Profile page
at millsandboon.com.au.

Be careful for nothing; but in every thing by prayer and supplication with thanksgiving let your requests be made known unto God.
–Philippians 4:6

DEDICATION

Many thanks to expert mums
Stephanie Christanson and Cassy Patterson,
along with Deputy Sheriff Ryan Sherman
and FBI special agent Mike Johnson,
for their patience in answering my many questions.

Chapter One

"You need to protect little Eli."

Jenna North studied her friend. "What's this about, Chloe?"

Chloe gazed at her eighteen-month-old son as he clutched a small white polar bear in one hand and ran a wooden train across a coffee table with the other.

Paperwork had kept Jenna late at the Broad-lake Foundation, where she worked as development manager, when she received Chloe's frantic call. Jenna offered to stop by Chloe's house on the way home, but Chloe rejected the idea. Instead, she came straight over to the school-turned-community-center where the foundation leased space. Jenna hadn't expected Chloe to bring Eli with her, not at this hour.

"I've made some bad choices," Chloe suddenly confessed.

Haven't we all? Jenna thought. "God forgives,

remember?" The words tasted bitter rolling off her tongue. "Chloe, what's going on?"

The young mother shook her head.

"Come on. I can't help unless—"

"I'm scared!"

Eli looked up at his mom with rounded eyes. She pulled him into her arms and rocked slightly. "I'm sorry, sweetie. I'm sorry." She eyed Jenna. "Promise me you'll protect him."

A chill ran down Jenna's spine. Could she truly make that promise considering she'd been unable to protect her own son?

And even herself?

"Please," Chloe begged.

Jenna nodded. "I promise."

Chloe sat back down, clinging to her son. Eli had other ideas. He squirmed against her, so Chloe put him down and he squatted to dig for another toy in his diaper bag. He pulled out a second train and waddled back to the coffee table. Tears formed in Chloe's eyes as she watched him.

Frustrated, Jenna wondered whom to call for help. Perhaps Chloe's counselor? Chloe had admitted to struggling with depression in the past.

"Have you called Rosalie?" Jenna asked.

"Why, you think I'm crazy?" Chloe snapped.

"No, I'm just not sure how to help you."

"You already have."

"Are you sure there isn't someone else?"

"Yes."

A few moments of silence passed between them.

"As long as he has Bubba, his bear, he'll be fine." Chloe handed Jenna a piece of paper. "If anything happens to me, keep Eli safe and find this man."

Jenna glanced at the note and slipped it into her pocket. "Who is it?"

"My cousin Marcus Garcia. He lives north of Missoula, in the mountains. Don't trust anyone else with Eli, okay?"

Jenna nodded. That wouldn't be a problem since trusting people was a skill she'd lost years ago.

"Marcus is the only family I've got," Chloe said, wistful.

"What about Gary?"

Chloe sighed. "I was so naive when I married him. I thought he was my Prince Charming."

Jenna knew that princes only existed in fairy tales.

"But he *is* Eli's father," Jenna said.

"Gary is a selfish man," Chloe said in a firm tone. "He doesn't care about us."

"Chloe—"

"He's dangerous." She pinned Jenna with intense eyes. "Gary is a monster."

Prickles skittered across Jenna's nerve endings.

Keep it together, Jenna.

"Dangerous how?" Jenna pressed.

Chloe stood suddenly. "I'm going to be sick. Watch Eli." She rushed across the office and disappeared into the hallway.

"Chloe!" Jenna wanted to go after her, but couldn't leave Eli alone.

"Mama?" he said.

"She'll be right back, buddy."

He clung tighter to his bear. Jenna kneeled beside the table and struggled to smile at Eli. Her own son would have been a little older than Eli now.

I'm sorry, baby Joey.

"Stop," she whispered and turned her attention to the toddler. "Choo-choo, choo-choo," she said, running a small wooden train across the table. Eli grabbed another train and mimicked her action.

As she watched him intently move his train back and forth, she couldn't help but smile. There was something so pure about a child. Most of the time, when she was around kids, she was able to revel in that innocence instead of being pulled down by sadness. Sometimes it allowed a slight ray of hope to pierce through the darkness of her own grief, grief that drove her to start a new life in Cedar River, Montana.

The sound of shattering glass echoed down the hall. Jenna sat straight up.

"Let me go!" Chloe's voice echoed.

Jenna automatically rushed across the room and snatched the canister of pepper spray out of her bag. She peeked into the hallway...

Two men were escorting Chloe to the exit: an unusually tall man wearing a knit ski cap, and a husky, broad-shouldered guy in a leather jacket.

Heart pounding, Jenna pulled out her phone to call for help. Her petite stature was no match for two thugs, even with her self-defense training and the pepper spray clutched in her hand.

"I won't let you hurt him!" Chloe shouted.

As Jenna's trembling finger pressed the 9-1-1 buttons, a male voice said, "What's going on?"

She peeked around the corner and spotted Police Chief Billings.

For once she was relieved the cops had arrived.

"Stop it!" Chloe squirmed against the tall man's grip.

"Release her," the chief said.

Jenna was about to announce her presence when the chief grabbed Chloe, spun her around and put her in a choke hold.

Paralyzed with fear, Jenna watched as Chloe struggled against his firm grip, kicking and thrashing.

The thrashing slowed.

Chloe's body went limp.

She fell to the ground.

Jenna darted out of sight. The floor seemed to tip sideways beneath her feet.

"Put her in the trunk," Chief Billings said.

No, this can't be happening. *Please, God, help me.*

He'd never listened before. Why should He start now?

"And find her son," he said.

"You think he's here?" one of the men asked.

"It's worth checking. Go room by room," he ordered.

Jenna's mind struggled to come up with an explanation for what she'd just witnessed, but there was none. Her fight-or-flight response kicked in.

Use it to your advantage, she'd been taught after leaving Anthony three years ago.

Doors opened and closed down the hall. She had seconds to figure this out.

She softly locked her office door. Adrenaline rushing through her body, she considered her options. If only she could make it to the north lot where she'd parked her car.

Eli waved a wooden train. "Choo-choo!"

She snapped her attention to the little boy. As the men got closer, they'd surely hear the child's enthusiastic voice. She dashed through the adjoining closet into the classroom next door and yanked the fire alarm. The sharp squealing sound pierced through the air. She rushed back to her office and quickly but gently tucked Eli into his snowsuit. The wail of the alarm drowned out his wails of confusion and fear.

Focus. It's all about focus.

Is this why Chloe chose Jenna to protect Eli, because she sensed Jenna's dark past, her determination never to be a victim again? The word *victim* sent a surge of panic through her body.

Stay calm, she coached herself.

She couldn't wait for the fire department. She'd be dead before they got here.

You need to protect Eli.

She set the toddler down and put on her jacket, tucking the pepper spray in her pocket for easy access. Eli stumbled a few feet away, arms flailing, trying to get away from the shrill alarm.

Across the room, the doorknob twisted right and left.

In an almost disassociated state, Jenna unlocked her desk drawer, removed the false bottom and grabbed her stash of emergency money.

One at home, one at work. *Be ready for anything.*

Money tucked safely into her pocket, she shouldered the diaper bag, picked up Eli and handed him the polar bear. Clutching the bear, he continued to cry, so she unclipped a pacifier from a strap on the diaper bag and offered it to the little boy. He took it and instantly quieted, his eyes rounding like saucers.

Flinging her messenger bag over her other shoulder, she headed again for the storage room. Since the building had once been a school, it had connecting classrooms that would give her access to the north exit, closer to her car.

As she passed through the storage room, she noticed a few car seats they used when taking children on field trips in the van. She grabbed one and forged ahead.

She was a woman on a mission, a warrior who was not going to lose this battle. Not this time.

The wail of sirens echoed from outside. Good. That should chase the intruders away. Violent men connected to local law enforcement—not a surprise to Jenna.

She finally made it to the north end of the school. This was it. She actually might get away safely.

There was no *might* about it. She'd made a promise to protect Chloe's child.

Jenna would not fail.

Clinging to Eli, she pushed open the door to the outside. Floodlights designed to discourage trespassers lit the playground all the way to the secondary parking lot. A strong gust of wind slapped her cheeks as she headed for her car.

What if the men were right behind her?

Traumatic flashbacks replayed in her mind like a video on accelerated speed. She quickened her pace, as if running could get her away from the images.

He can't hurt you if he can't find you.

She approached the corner of the building.

Only a few hundred feet from the parking lot.

Her car.

Freedom.

★ ★ ★

Matt Weller had been on a break, eating a sandwich in the custodian's office and listening to the hockey game on the radio, when he'd heard a woman scream. He thought he'd imagined it at first and checked the closed-circuit video feed. Two men were dragging Mrs. McFadden to the exit. Just as Matt got up to help her, Chief Billings entered the building.

And strangled Mrs. McFadden.

Matt's first reaction was to get his weapon.

As he sprinted across the playground, the fire alarm rang from the building. Why would the perps lure the fire department to the scene? That made no sense whatsoever.

He approached the truck and considered his next move. They would have surely taken Mrs. McFadden's body away by now, removing the evidence.

But Matt knew there had been more than one woman in the building tonight. The lovely Jenna North had been at the center working late, as she often did.

The building was so peaceful when she was there, one of the reasons he liked the night shift.

Until tonight.

Matt climbed into the front seat and took a

calming breath. He needed to be smart about this, needed to protect his cover and Miss North at the same time.

Something caught his eye across the lot—Jenna North carrying a child and a car seat. Hang on—he knew she wasn't married and didn't have kids.

Then Matt saw them—the two perps heading straight for her on the other side of the building.

The woman was going to get herself killed.

Matt shoved his truck into gear and drove slowly toward the building where the innocent Miss North was about to walk straight into trouble.

He couldn't let that happen, no matter the risk.

As Jenna approached the corner of the building, Matt sped up. All it would take was an effective block. Yes, he'd innocently pull up between her and the men and play out his role of night janitor by warning them to leave the premises due to the fire alarm.

He stopped the truck, got out and motioned for Jenna to get down.

Instead, she whipped out a canister of pepper spray.

Matt put out one hand in surrender and pointed around the corner with his other hand.

Her green eyes widened.

He motioned for her to stay low, and then went around the back of his truck to confront the men.

But there was only one guy. Not good. Where was the other perp?

"Get away from the building!" Matt shouted. He had to play his part, although his navy blue custodian's uniform should make it clear who he was.

"My wife is in there!" the guy, midforties, wearing a knit ski cap, shouted.

Yeah, his wife.

"Have to wait for the all clear from the fire department!" Matt shouted.

The man nodded and turned away. Good, an easy fix.

Then Knit Cap Guy snapped around and took a swing at Matt. He dodged the blow and slugged the man in the stomach. He doubled over, coughing. With fisted hands, Matt readied himself for another assault.

The wail of sirens grew louder. The perp jumped to his feet and took off. Matt the FBI agent would chase after him; Matt the janitor would not.

He went back to the other side of the truck to help Jenna.

But she was gone.

He scanned the playground, the surrounding woods, the nearby parking lot. Knit Cap Guy's partner couldn't have gotten to her in the thirty seconds that Matt had been engaged in a fistfight.

Matt needed to find her, protect her.

He climbed into his truck to get his weapon and slammed the door.

A squeak echoed from the back seat.

He froze as he reached for the glove box and spun around. The little boy was sucking on a pacifier, eyes wide and curious, clutching a white stuffed animal.

"Are they gone?" Jenna said from the seat directly behind Matt.

He glanced in the rearview mirror. It seemed like her eyes had grown a brighter shade of green since he'd seen her earlier this evening.

"I think so," he said. "The little boy, is he Mrs. McFadden's?"

"Yes. I promised to protect him."

She studied Matt as if trying to make out his

character, figure out whether he was good or bad. A little of both, he mused.

She needed good right now, very good, and committed. Which wasn't Matt. He wished it could be different. There was something about Jenna North that always made him smile. It was her way with staff members—with everyone, come to think of it. She was gentle and kind, yet persuasive enough to get the job done. The Broadlake Foundation thrived in part because of her fund-raising efforts that supported the operating budget.

He hoped she knew nothing about the cartel's money-laundering scheme, that she was only an innocent bystander.

"My friend, Mrs. McFadden, she…" Jenna's voice trailed off.

He waited.

"She's dead."

Yes, Matt knew because he'd seen it happen.

And now, because she'd also witnessed the homicide, Miss North's life was in danger, as was the child's. Anger simmered in his chest. This couldn't be his problem, not today. He'd get Miss North and the child to safety and get back to his assignment.

Acting like the innocent bystander she assumed he was, Matt said, "We should report this."

"To whom? The police? They're involved."

"Why do you think that?"

"Chief Billings killed Chloe."

Great, not only had she been asked to protect the child, but she knew of the chief's involvement. This put her life at an even higher risk.

"Matthew, may I ask a favor?"

"Sure."

"Can you keep this between us, that you helped me, that I have Eli?"

"Only if you'll do me a favor in return."

"What?"

He had no choice but to protect her. She was in too deep. "Stay here until I deal with the fire department. Once they're gone, I'll come back and give you a ride to wherever you want to go. Okay?"

"Thank you, but my car isn't far."

"They'll probably be watching your car, right?"

She nibbled her lower lip for a second, an adorable gesture. He snapped his attention out the front window of his truck to the parking lot in the distance.

"I guess you're right," she said. "But…you

should know that helping me could get you into trouble."

"I'm okay with that." Matt offered her the truck keys. "If I'm not back in twenty, take off."

He flung open the door and headed for the front of the building. He half expected to encounter the two perps, maybe even the chief, but they were nowhere in sight.

The glass windows on one of the community center doors had been shattered, which must be how the men had gained access to the building.

Motioning to the fire response crew, Matt led them inside. They spread out, looking for smoke. A fireman turned off the alarm and nodded at Matt. "Are you the night custodian?"

"Yes, sir."

"Please wait outside until we clear the building."

Matt did as he was ordered and called the police. He had to. It would look suspicious if he didn't alert the authorities to the break-in. As he was making the call, a squad car and the chief's car pulled into the lot.

A patrolman Matt recognized as Kyle Armstrong exited his squad car. Chief Billings and Kyle approached Matt.

You're only the janitor, he reminded himself.

"I was just calling you guys," Matt said.

"Hey, Matt," Kyle greeted him.

"You two know each other?" Billings asked.

"We attend the same church," Kyle said by way of explanation.

Church was no doubt a foreign concept to a guy like Billings. A dirty cop. A killer.

"This is Matt Weller, the night custodian," Kyle introduced.

Billings extended his hand. "Nice to meet you, Matt. Have any idea who pulled the alarm?"

"No, sir. Apparently some guy broke in." He pointed toward the broken window.

"Some guy? Not mischievous teens?" Billings asked.

Matt opted for sticking to the truth as much as possible. "No, it was a man, sir." He looked directly at Billings, whose eye twitched ever so slightly.

"Can you describe him?" Kyle asked, pulling out a small notebook.

"About five-ten, a hundred and eighty pounds." He directed the rest of his answer to Kyle. "He wore a black leather jacket and knit cap. I'm thinking he was pushing forty?"

"Wow, how close did you get to this guy?" Kyle asked.

"Pretty close. He took a swing at me."

"Are you injured?" Billings said with mock concern.

"No, sir. I grew up the youngest of five boys so I'm pretty good at defending myself."

"The knit cap perp was inside the building?" Kyle pushed.

"Actually we got into it outside, back by the playground."

Kyle looked up in question.

"I went out to my truck to get something, and that's when I encountered the man," Matt said. "The alarm had gone off—not sure what that was about. He claimed his wife was in the building."

"His wife?" Kyle said. "But the center was closed."

"That is correct," Matt said. "I thought I convinced him to leave, but then he went all Rocky on me."

The fire crew exited the building. "It's clear," the shift captain said.

"Thanks." Billings turned to Matt. "I'd like you to walk me through what happened tonight. Step by step."

Of course he did. He wanted to figure out if Matt was telling the truth or creating a story to protect himself, Jenna and the little boy.

"Sure, this way." He led Kyle and the chief into the community center. By the end of this story, they'd be at Matt's truck. He hoped they wouldn't decide to search it, but why would they? Matt wasn't a suspect. If Jenna stayed down and the little boy didn't cry, Billings wouldn't find her.

She'd be hiding right under his nose.

"I was in the back office on break, listening to the hockey game," Matt said.

They got to his office and the cops poked their heads inside.

"Closed circuit?" Kyle asked, eyeing the monitor.

"Yep. For security." Matt curled his fingers into his palm to keep calm. "It gives me a view of the main hallway."

"You didn't see the suspect break in?"

"No, he probably accessed the building while I was at my truck." He feigned panic and looked at Kyle. "Man, I hope I don't lose my job over this—I mean for not preventing the break-in."

"If he was determined to get in, nothing would have stopped him," Billings said.

Matt nodded. Was that subtext? A subtle warning?

"Continue," Chief Billings said.

"So about ten thirty I went out to the truck." He led them to the back door and swung it open. The three men ambled outside. "It wasn't parked this close originally, but kids were finishing up basketball when I arrived at six. I figured as long as I was out here I'd repark closer to the building."

"Besides the basketball league, who else was here tonight, Mr. Weller?" the chief asked.

"A yoga class, line dancing for seniors and the knitting club. They were all gone by nine."

"Anyone else, perhaps employees working late?" Billings pushed.

Matt wondered if he'd seen Jenna North's little blue car parked in the overflow lot. He had to play this just right, be as truthful as possible.

"I might have seen Jenna North earlier. She works for a foundation that leases space here."

"I'll look into it," Kyle said.

Chief Billings eyed Matt speculatively, and he broke eye contact in his effort to act submissive and nonthreatening.

Innocent.

That's when Matt noticed the back window of his truck was cracked open. Matt needed a quick redirect to get them away from Jenna and the child.

"We got into a fistfight over here." Matt led them to the other side of the truck. "Actually, there was one other thing about the knit cap guy."

Billings's eyes flared.

"He had a scar above his eyebrow here." Matt pointed to his own forehead.

"That could help," Kyle said.

"I yelled at him to stay away from the building. He yelled back that his wife was inside, which made no sense. Then he threw a punch. That's about it."

"That's a lot," Kyle said, jotting notes furiously.

The chief kneeled, analyzing something on the ground.

"What is it, sir?" Kyle asked.

"Found a cigarette butt. I'll bag it."

Except Knit Cap Guy hadn't been smoking, which meant Billings was trying to throw the investigation off course.

"Can you tell us anything else, Matt?" Kyle said.

"No, sorry. I'd better go fix the front door, and I should probably call Mrs. Harris, my boss."

"If anything else does come to mind, please

call me directly." Billings handed him a business card.

"Will do. Thanks."

Matt led the cops back to the front of the building, and the knot in his gut uncoiled as they got farther away from the truck, from Jenna and the little boy.

He called Lucinda Harris and explained the situation as he watched the fire trucks pull away. She was worried about Matt and told him to finish cleaning up the mess and leave early. A good thing, since he was desperate to check on Jenna and the child.

The chief and Kyle were still out front, assessing and speculating.

Matt went inside and found a piece of wood from the storage area to cover the broken window. He secured it in place and swept up the mess. He wanted to play the role of night custodian a little longer, until the cops left the premises.

And then he needed to get to Jenna and the child. Let her know everything was okay.

He started flipping off main lights. Through one of the community room windows, he noticed the two police cars pulling out of the lot.

After jogging to the back of the building, he

got his jacket out of the office, locked the building and headed to his truck. He grabbed the door handle, but it was locked. Fearful of being found, Miss North must have locked the doors. He tapped twice, blowing on his chilled hands, and glanced over his shoulder out of habit.

The door unlocked with a click. He climbed into the front seat. "They're gone."

He felt the barrel of a gun pressed against the back of his head.

Chapter Two

Jenna's hand trembled as she aimed the gun at the janitor's head. Of course there was no way she could pull the trigger, but she didn't know what else to do.

I might have seen Jenna North earlier, he'd said to the chief.

The man who'd killed her best friend.

Matthew might as well have opened the truck door and handed Jenna and Eli over to the guy.

"I know you're scared—"

"Drive," she interrupted.

"Please put the gun down."

"Now." She tapped the barrel against his head, not hard, but hard enough.

With a nod, he started the truck and pulled out of the lot.

She still couldn't believe what she'd found when she'd gone through his glove box looking for a tissue.

Zip ties, duct tape and a gun.

Who was this man? Had she run from one killer directly into the arms of another?

The trembling intensified, running down her arm to rock her entire body. No, she would not let the trauma of the past consume her; she would not fall apart.

This time she'd save the child.

She had considered fleeing in his truck, but that would have meant driving past the killer police chief.

"I can explain," Matthew said.

"Just drive."

"To where?"

Good question. The mall was closed at this time of night, yet she needed a very public place to regroup. And then what?

One step at a time.

"I-90 truck stop." It was very public and not far away. She wouldn't spend a minute longer than necessary with this creep. Once away from the janitor, she'd call someone for help. But whom? Patrice, the woman who'd helped Jenna escape Anthony?

Wait—she remembered the slip of paper Chloe had given her with the name of her cousin. That's it. She'd call Marcus to come get her.

"I don't know what you're thinking, Miss North, but if I'd wanted to do you harm I would have turned you over to Chief Billings."

"Then you wouldn't have the pleasure of hurting me."

He shot her an intense look through the rear-view mirror. "I would never hurt you. I want to help."

"Stop talking," she ordered as the past taunted her.

I want to help you get better.

She'd believed her abusive husband. Only after she'd left Anthony did she understand how his words had been an insidious and powerful manipulation.

"At least let me call someone for you," Matthew said.

You need help.

She almost told the janitor to shut up again, but decided to speak the truth instead. "Stop pretending to be my friend. I heard you tell Billings that I was at the center tonight."

"I had to. Your car was a hundred yards away."

Her car. She'd never get it back. They'd impound it, making it harder for her to flee the city.

Which meant she'd have to rely on strangers for help until Chloe's cousin could rescue her.

No, you don't need rescuing any longer.

The janitor turned left.

"Where are you going? I said take me to the truck stop." Fear skittered across her shoulders. Was he going to try to overpower her? In front of Eli?

"We're being followed," he said.

She snapped her gaze out the back window. Headlights shone through the dark night. "That could be anyone."

"They've been behind us since we left the center."

"Just get me to the truck stop."

"Yes, ma'am."

As he drove through town, she scolded herself for trusting him in the first place, but Matthew had seemed like an innocuous sort of man. She'd heard he'd moved to town after serving in the military and that he'd even joined the local church. That in and of itself would have made most people trust him.

Yet Anthony had been a church leader, a pillar of the community—and behind closed doors, he was a monster.

Like Chloe's husband?

Like the man driving the truck?

Why did Jenna attract violent men? Maybe her stepfather had been right when he'd branded her a stupid and weak girl, a lost cause.

"No," she ground out.

"Ma'am?"

She snapped her attention to him. "What?"

"You said something?"

She clenched her jaw. This was not the time for the past to taunt her. Making bad choices when it came to romance seemed to be a habit for Jenna, starting with Mike in high school, and then Anthony. It had taken two years and a miscarriage to get away from her abuser. Tonight, three years after her escape, she found herself right back in the eye of the storm.

This time she'd get it right. She'd protect her friend's little boy.

Her friend. Chloe.

The image of Chloe collapsing on the floor flashed across Jenna's mind. Still in shock about the loss, Jenna had had no time to process or grieve. Chloe wouldn't want her to be distracted; she'd want Jenna to put all her energy into saving Eli.

Chloe was a young mother who'd become Jenna's best friend in town after they'd met on the development committee for the foundation. They'd joined an exercise dance class and regularly gone out for pie afterward. They had the same sense of humor, the same view on life.

It seemed they had other similarities as well— their bad choices in men.

The janitor made a right turn, heading in the opposite direction of her requested destination.

"Hey." She tapped the barrel of the gun against his head.

"Look, trust me or don't trust me. I don't care," he said. "At least let me lose the tail before I drop you at the truck stop."

"You can drop the knight-in-shining-armor act. I'm not buying it."

"Then shoot me."

She snapped her gaze to the rearview mirror. He pinned her with fierce blue eyes.

"Shoot me or let me lose them. Your choice," he said.

She glanced nervously at Eli. She couldn't pull the trigger with a baby in the car.

Who was she kidding? She couldn't pull the trigger, period.

But this creep didn't have to know that.

"Fine, lose them," she said.

"Yes, ma'am."

He sped up, and she jerked back in her seat. She glanced beside her at Eli. The motion hadn't disturbed him from his restful slumber as he sucked on his Binky and clung to his bear.

The janitor navigated down side streets and back up an alley. She clutched the gun grip to stay grounded, but wished it were something else, something spiritual. Her fingers automatically went to the base of her neck, remembering the dove charm she'd worn as a child, a charm that symbolized the Holy Spirit.

A charm she'd ripped off and thrown away as a teenager after she'd lost faith in an absent god.

She thumbed the silver ring on her right hand instead, the braided knot given to her by Patrice, who'd taken Jenna in and helped her heal after she'd left Anthony. The interwoven strands of silver represented connectedness, a reminder that Jenna was never alone, that she could always call on Patrice and the guardian network for support.

Matthew pulled onto the expressway. They were leaving town and heading in the right direction.

"We're good," he said.

"Hardly," she muttered.

"Listen—"

"Don't speak!" she said, louder than she'd intended.

Eli's eyes popped open and he started to cry. "Shh, I'm sorry, little one," she said, fearing she was the wrong person to be caring for a child.

To appease him, she sang a song, one her mom had sung to her when she was little. The little boy's eyes widened with curiosity, and then his eyelids blinked slowly and finally closed.

The car grew eerily silent as they left town and continued on the expressway. She liked the silence, embraced it. It gave her time to think.

About fifteen minutes later, the janitor exited the expressway, pulled into the truck stop and parked.

She removed the gun magazine and pocketed it, opened the truck door and hurled the gun into the snow-covered field bordering the lot. Shouldering the diaper and messenger bags, she unbuckled the car seat.

"You sure you'll be okay?" he said.

She ignored his mock concern and lifted baby Eli out of the car. The little boy still clung to his bear for comfort.

Whether Chloe's cousin came to pick her up

or Jenna called a taxi, she'd need the car seat for Eli. She grabbed it with her other hand.

"For what it's worth, I'm a cop," he said.

She froze and glared at the back of his head.

"Not local," he continued as if he anticipated her fear. "I'm undercover FBI."

"Sure you are." She shouldered the door shut and marched away from the truck. Did he think her that gullible?

Thick, wet snowflakes swirled around her as she crossed the parking lot. There were a dozen trucks and cars in the lot. Good, the more people around the safer she'd feel.

Once inside, she placed the car seat by the door. She considered what to do with the magazine of bullets. Maybe she should have kept the weapon to defend herself and Eli. She'd learned how to use a firearm after she'd escaped Anthony.

No, the thought of shooting someone made her nauseous, and it didn't feel right disposing of the magazine in a public place where it could end up in the wrong hands.

Instead, she decided to ditch her cell in case they could track it, and tossed the phone into the garbage can. She carried Eli to a nearby pay phone and called Chloe's cousin, but it went to voice mail.

"You've reached Marcus. I'm not here. Leave a message."

"Hi, Marcus. You don't know me, but I'm Jenna, a good friend of your cousin Chloe's. She told me to call you. There's been an emergency and I need your help. It's about Chloe's son, Eli. Anyway, I'm calling from a pay phone, but I'm not sure how long we'll be here. I guess I'll keep calling. Thanks."

What a message to leave a stranger. Would he even take her seriously?

She couldn't worry about that now.

As she headed into the twenty-four-hour store, a list of what to do next formed in her mind. First, she had to change her appearance. She bought a local football team knit ski cap to cover her dark hair. She'd tuck it up into the cap until she got the chance to color it.

After making her purchases, she would take her contacts out and replace them with her thick-rimmed glasses to further mask her identity. But what about Eli? Her gaze drifted to a pink child's ski cap. Disguising him as a girl would certainly throw someone off at first glance. She bought some cheap makeup, something she rarely wore, and scissors for cutting her hair. She wished they had hair dye, but that would have to wait until she found a drugstore.

Her panic about not being able to protect Eli was subsiding. She'd made it safely away from the office, away from a corrupt killer cop.

She was proud of herself for getting this far.

Thanks to Matthew the janitor.

"A guy with zip ties, duct tape and a gun in his glove box," she muttered.

I'm undercover FBI.

She briefly wondered if he was being honest and her trauma had blinded her to the truth. No, why would an FBI agent keep duct tape in his car? He'd tried to explain, but she hadn't let him.

Peeking out the store window, she spotted Matthew talking on the phone as he picked up his weapon from the snow-covered field.

Movement suddenly drew her attention left.

The two men from the community center got out of a black car. She gasped and ducked behind a display of snacks, clutching Eli securely against her chest.

What if they came into the truck stop and saw the car seat by the door?

Seconds stretched like hours.

Stop hiding like a coward!

With a fortifying breath, she went back to the counter and peeked out the window.

The cashier stepped up and blocked her view. "May I help you?"

Jenna glanced around her into the parking lot.

The twentysomething cashier with long blond hair also glanced outside. Just as…

The two thugs from the community center jumped Matthew.

"Whoa," the girl said.

"I need to use your phone."

"There's a pay phone—"

"I'll give you twenty bucks."

Matt couldn't leave Jenna North at the truck stop without knowing she'd be okay.

He called in to give his boss an update. "She's a part of it now."

"You don't know that," his supervisor, Steve Pragge, said.

"Billings is after her."

There was a pause, then, "Not our problem. You need to get back to town and be ready for your shift tomorrow."

"And leave an innocent woman and child at the mercy of a killer?"

"If you're that worried, I'll send someone to bring her in."

"I doubt she'll go willingly."

"Then you bring her in. As long as you're back at work tomorrow night."

"I'm not sure she'll come with me either."

"What's the problem?"

"She doesn't trust cops."

"I don't know what you want me to say here, Weller. This woman is a complication. You've got a job to do."

His boss ended the call, and Matt considered the subtext to Pragge's words. He expected Matt to stay on task, return to Cedar River and leave Jenna behind.

Not happening.

Matt wondered what had made Jenna do the about-face from trusting Matt to being terrified of him. The way she'd threatened him with the gun...

The gun. She'd retrieved it from his glove box. Since she probably had little if any experience with firearms, he could only guess what conclusions she would have drawn about someone who casually carried a handgun in his vehicle.

He went into the field to search for his gun

and realized he wasn't angry that she'd tossed it. In fact, he respected her for the move if she thought him dangerous.

Scanning the area with a flashlight, he wondered how to convince Jenna to accept his help. He couldn't arrest her, because she hadn't done anything wrong—although technically she had kidnapped a child. Instinct told him to keep her out of the system, or the chief would find her for sure.

He found the gun, shoved it into the back of his waistband and turned.

Something smashed against his head.

He fell to the cold, hard snow, and blinked to clear his vision.

He was being dragged across the parking lot toward the Dumpster.

As they released him with a jerk, two men started kicking Matt. Was this a random mugging or had the chief's men found him? Did Billings suspect Matt knew more than he was saying?

"Where is she?" a man asked, delivering a kick to Matt's stomach.

"Who?" he gasped.

A solid boot jammed against his neck. He grabbed the guy's ankle and yanked.

The guy went down.

Matt scrambled to his feet.

The second guy snapped a cord around Matthew's neck, cutting off air. After surviving two tours in Afghanistan, dodging IEDs and defending innocents, he was going down like this?

God, if I'm done, I'm okay with that. But please protect Jenna and the child.

With a sudden release, he was shoved headfirst into the metal Dumpster, then yanked back and thrown onto the pavement. Drifting in and out of consciousness, all he could think about was Jenna, her colorful green eyes and lovely smile.

"Jenna North," the husky guy said, his face close to Matt's. "Where. Is. She?"

"Hang on, he's calling," the other guy said. "Yeah… Where? On our way. Let's go."

"What about the janitor?"

"Forget him. We've got a location on the woman."

On Jenna? They knew she was inside? Matt struggled to get up. One of the guys kicked him twice in the ribs for good measure.

Matt coughed and clutched his chest. With blurry vision, he watched the men cross the lot.

He had to get to her. Had to warn her.

Struggling to get up, his head spun and he collapsed on the pavement. He coached himself to breathe, to think past the throbbing headache long enough to help Jenna.

An innocent woman protecting an innocent child.

"Matthew?"

He looked up. Vivid green eyes sparkled down at him. Jenna.

No, they'd find her; they'd kill her. "You need to…"

What? Be taken into FBI custody? Why? He was in no shape to protect her, and by the time backup arrived, the thugs would have surely found her.

"My keys." He dug into his jacket pocket and fished them out. As he offered them to her, they slipped through his trembling fingers. "Take the truck. Get out of here."

He heard the keys scrape against the pavement. Good, she was taking his advice. Looking out for herself and the child.

A few seconds passed, maybe minutes—he couldn't be sure. What he did know was that if the cops found him, they'd ask questions, risking his cover.

Then again, he could tell the truth, to a

point. He'd been jumped and beaten, and when he regained consciousness, his truck was gone.

"Open your eyes."

It was Jenna's voice.

He blinked a few times and found himself looking up at her beautiful face.

"You need to go," he ordered.

"Can you get up?"

"The men—"

"They're gone. Come on—stand up."

"Gone?" he said as she helped him to his feet. He groaned, clutching his ribs.

"They left. I called 9-1-1 and told them I was at Scooter's Pancake House in Cedar River."

"What about…the little boy?"

"He's in the car."

He blinked to clear the stars from his vision, but it didn't help much. Safe to say the chief's thugs had gifted him with a doozy of a concussion. When he reached his truck, Jenna led him to the passenger side.

"I'll drive," he said.

"You can barely stand. Get in." She glanced nervously over her shoulder. A few people inside the truck stop were watching from the window.

As he started to argue, he realized how right

she was. Matt was in no shape to drive and they needed to get out of here, quick. The concussion was messing with his judgment. He'd have to rely on Jenna's acumen for the time being.

Once inside the truck, he closed his eyes. He heard her get behind the wheel, but she didn't start the vehicle.

He cracked open his eyes. "What…what's happening?"

"I need to take my contacts out." She dug through her bag.

"Do it when we're safe."

"I'll do it now, thank you very much," she snapped.

He'd made her angry. Why? He was trying to protect her, get her away from danger.

She pulled out a small container, and before he could say Miranda rights, she'd removed her contacts and was transformed with the help of large, dark-rimmed glasses. Her auburn hair had been tucked into a ski cap.

"Okay, let's take care of you. Where's the first aid kit?" she said.

"I'm fine." As he said the words, he found himself drifting into that dark place—the place between consciousness and sleep, the place where time didn't exist. Distant memories flooded his brain, memories of laughter, then anger...

A casket being lowered into the ground.

Sarah.

A gentle hand pressed a gauze pad against the side of his head. "Shh, hold still."

It was a firm voice, tinged with sweetness and concern. Who was it again? He'd distanced himself from relationships because of his work, his dedication to the job.

He'd attempted commitment with Sarah. And she was dead.

His fault.

There wasn't a day that went by when he didn't pray for forgiveness.

Shutting down the romantic part of his life was what had made him a good agent, an agent willing to devote all his energy into nailing criminals, men who pretended to be heroes, when they were actually...

He was falling again, floating like a leaf dropping from a tree. Where would he land? Back at her funeral? His remorse strangling him as he pleaded with God for forgiveness?

"It's okay. You're okay."

"Sarah?" he said.

"Almost done."

"I'm sorry."

An hour later, Jenna glanced at her passenger and wondered if she should take him to a hospital. His skin was pale and he groaned in his sleep every few minutes. Plus, he'd been having delusions back at the truck stop when she'd bandaged his head wound.

He'd whispered the name *Sarah*. His girlfriend? Wife?

"Stay focused," she said softly. She couldn't afford to be distracted by her passenger's nightmares. She needed to strategize what to do next, other than to distance herself from Cedar River.

"Stay back," Matthew muttered in his sleep.

Jenna suspected he had a concussion and knew the best treatment for that was sleep. She'd learned as much when she'd ended up in the hospital after one of her "falls."

She clenched her jaw. This was not the time, nor the place, to be thinking about the past. She had two people to protect—Little Eli and…an FBI agent. Which begged the question, why was he working undercover as a janitor at the community center?

"Medic," he said. He jerked awake, eyes wide, breathing heavily.

"Hey, you're okay," she said.

He glanced at her with a dazed expression.

"Just a bad dream," she said.

He snapped his attention away, as if embarrassed, and directed his gaze to the road ahead.

"Best thing for a concussion is sleep," she offered.

A moment later he closed his eyes. Wow, that surprised her. She thought she'd get more of an argument, or a lecture about how she should have left him back at the truck stop.

Why didn't you abandon him, Jenna?

Because of the vulnerability in his dulled blue eyes. She couldn't leave a semiconscious man lying on the cold, wet ground. After all, once the thugs figured out Jenna had diverted them from her true location, they would have returned to the truck stop and done even more damage to Matthew. He was in no position to defend himself.

She'd been in survival mode back at the office, driven by the trauma of her past. The chief's actions solidified her opinion of law enforcement, and her cautious nature had made her draw the conclusion that Matthew was a serial criminal, not a cop. Even if he was a cop, she knew they had their own code, and the normal rules of civility didn't apply to them.

Which left her in that same, familiar spot: alone and afraid.

And she couldn't afford to be afraid, not while Eli was in her care.

If only she had a burner phone to call Marcus again, get Eli safely to his cousin. Deep down, Jenna feared she was the absolute worst choice to protect Eli. She'd failed miserably before. What made her think this time would be different?

Her brain started clicking off options. What about… She glanced at her passenger. Could she risk getting help from the FBI? No, they'd force her to return Eli to his father, a man Chloe had called a *monster*. She shook off the thought.

The word *monster* taunted her, reminding her that although she was legally free of him, there were days she still felt like she was under Anthony's thumb, especially when she'd come home to her Cedar River apartment and find things out of place. She'd be yanked back into the past, experiencing Anthony's wrath over her unacceptable housekeeping skills. She'd try to shake it off, reminding herself she'd been in a hurry to get to work in the morning and had forgotten to put things where they belonged.

But the fear of punishment was quite real.

Move on, she coached herself.

She needed to think her way out of this current crisis, not be paralyzed by the past. Who could she go to for help? Jenna had been estranged from her family ever since she'd married Anthony, and had never reunited with them after she'd escaped his abuse. Distancing herself from everyone, past and present, had been the best way to put the horror behind her and live a safe life. She was willing to do whatever was necessary to achieve that goal, and starting a new life where no one knew her seemed like the only way.

A new life where she could be a different person. A stronger person.

She reconsidered calling Patrice. The middle-aged woman was devoted to helping victims flee dangerous situations. No, she had already put herself in enough danger for Jenna, although maybe Patrice could offer some advice.

The flash of blue and red lights sparked

through the truck's rearview mirror. Jenna's heart leaped into her throat.

They'd found her.

Chapter Three

"License and registration, please," a deep male voice said.

Matt forced his eyes open. He was in the passenger seat, and a uniformed officer stood at the driver's window.

"I'm sorry, Officer, was I speeding?" Jenna asked from behind the wheel of Matt's truck.

Jenna North was driving his truck?

"No, ma'am, but your left taillight is out," the cop said.

"Oh, thank you for letting us know."

"You're welcome. I'd still like to see your license and registration."

Jenna nodded at Matt, who read fear in her green eyes.

"Honey, can you get the registration?" she said.

Honey? Why was she calling him honey? And why did his head feel like someone had used it as a soccer ball?

"Sir, are you all right?" The cop aimed his flashlight into the vehicle.

Matt put up his hand to block the piercing beam. "My head," is all that came out.

"We're on the way to the hospital," Jenna said. "He was mugged and has a head injury."

The cop nodded, speculative. He started to aim the beam into the back seat.

"Please don't wake the baby," she said.

The baby? *What have you gotten yourself into, Matt?*

"I still need to see your license and registration," the cop said.

She pulled her license out of her wallet. Matt dug the registration out of the glove box and passed it, and his license, to the officer.

"Did you file a police report about the mugging?" the officer asked, scanning the registration.

"We will, Officer, but I wanted to get him checked out first," she said in a frantic tone.

Jenna North, development manager of the Broadlake Foundation, was worried about Matt.

What had happened to him?

His mind drew a blank. He'd obviously lost the past few, what, hours? Days? The amnesia had to be related to the headache clawing its way across his skull. He was suffering from a concussion. But how had it happened?

Bigger question—why did he have an urgent need to protect Miss North and...a baby?

He looked over his shoulder. There was a sleeping child in the back seat. Whose? Jenna's? No, she wasn't married, didn't have a boyfriend or even date, if you believed the locals. She was a transplant from Tulsa with a generous heart, a woman who used her social and financial talents to raise money for the Broadlake Foundation.

"Please wait here," the cop said and left them alone.

Jenna turned to Matt. "They're going to find us. What do we do?"

She could tell him what was going on, for starters.

"Matthew?"

The way she spoke his name made it sound like they were close, like they knew each other outside of working in the same building. Sure, he might have imagined dating some-one like Jenna, a lovely woman determined to help people. Only he didn't remember ever grabbing coffee with her or chatting outside of work. He was on the job and, even if he weren't, he'd made a promise to himself to avoid romantic entanglements.

"What's he doing?" she said, eyeing the rear-view mirror.

"Patience," he said. "He's running the registration. It's procedure."

He closed his eyes, fighting back the anxiety taunting him. He'd have to confess his condition because he needed her help to navigate through the temporary amnesia. Matt sensed she needed his help as well.

"Aren't you worried?" she asked.

He opened his eyes, but couldn't admit the truth: that he was terrified because he'd lost a chunk of time.

"No, of course you're not worried, you're FBI," she muttered and studied the rearview.

She knew the truth? Which meant what— that she was helping with the investigation? Was that possible? Because he didn't remember her being ruled out as a suspect.

He needed to remember.

"He's coming back," she said, sitting straight.

The officer, who Matt realized was a state trooper, stepped up to her window and passed her the licenses and registration. "The closest medical facility is St. James Healthcare. I'll escort you."

"We wouldn't want to take you away from your duties, Officer," she said.

"You're not. Follow me."

She closed the window and sighed. "Now what?" she asked Matt. "Should I ditch him?"

"Ditch him?" he repeated in a sarcastic tone.

"Bad idea, huh?"

"Pretty bad, yeah."

"What if he called Billings? What if he's on their payroll? What if they're waiting at the hospital? What if—"

"Slow down, speedy. You're making my headache worse."

"Sorry, sorry." The squad car passed them and she followed. "I wish I could get ahold of Marcus."

"Who's Marcus?"

"Chloe's cousin. He's supposed to help."

"Ma'am?"

"What?" She shot him a quick glance.

"Chloe...?"

"Mrs. McFadden," she said. "You remember."

Mrs. McFadden—sure, he knew her. She was on the development board and helped with fund-raising events. All roads to the money-laundering investigation led to Mrs. McFadden's husband, Gary, but they didn't have enough to build a case. They'd even considered that his wife might be involved.

"Matthew?" she said.

"Yes, ma'am?"

"What's going on?"

"I'm having some…memory challenges."

"Oh."

He heard the disappointment in her voice, as if she'd been relying on him to protect her and the child. But that hadn't been his assignment. His assignment was to work as a custodian in the foundation office, be invisible and gather information. Keep an eye on nighttime activity, determine if they were not only laundering money for the cartel but were also distributing drugs out of the community center.

"Blows to the head can do that," she offered. "Don't freak out. It's usually temporary."

"How would you know that?"

She shrugged. There was more to it, but she wasn't sharing. Why would she? She was stuck with a helpless man and…a child.

"So, the child is Mrs. McFadden's?" he asked.

"Yes."

"Where is Mrs. McFadden?"

She gripped the steering wheel with white-knuckled fingers.

"Miss North?" he prompted.

"Jenna, call me Jenna," she said, with slight irritation in her voice.

"Okay, Jenna. Why is Mrs. McFadden's child in my truck?"

"She asked me to protect him."

"I don't understand."

"Chief Billings killed Chloe," she blurted out in a pained voice.

He glanced out the passenger window and fisted his hand to stop his fingers from trembling. Men like Matt didn't tremble, and they didn't let fear run rampant. Yet this was the first time he'd awakened with a chunk of his life missing, like it had never happened, and he was forced to rely on a stranger to fill in the blanks.

Well, not a complete stranger. He'd done a background check on all the foundation employees to help identify which ones were the most likely to be involved in the money-laundering activity. Matt still couldn't wrap his head around the fact that all roads led to the small, quaint town of Cedar River, Montana, known for its world-class scones and snow sports, headquarters of the international and altruistic Broadlake Foundation.

His supervisor had gotten Matt a job as the night custodian, and during the day he continued surveillance at the hot spots in town. They suspected money was being filtered through the foundation in the form of donations, only they couldn't determine who was orchestrating the mystery deposits into the accounts. Everyone had been suspect, even the town's police chief, who was on the governing board.

If what Jenna said was true, it confirmed Chief Billings's involvement. Matt didn't remember seeing the murder, but Jenna had.

Which meant she was a key witness—and her life was in serious danger.

He'd always sensed wariness about Jenna, even though she covered it with a bright smile and polite manners. His job required him to pay attention to the little things, the way her shoulders jerked at unexpected sounds and how she'd clenched her jaw when a drunk, homeless man wandered into the center and refused to leave. Matt had come to her rescue that night, escorting him outside and waiting for Kyle to take the belligerent man into custody.

Something had happened to Jenna North that

didn't show up on a routine background check. Yet it seemed like she'd lived an unremarkable life before moving to Cedar River.

He tapped a closed fist against his knee. How could he remember details about Miss North's background but couldn't remember what happened to him in the past...what? How much time had he lost?

"Can you please tell me what happened tonight?" he said.

"What's the last thing you remember?"

He closed his eyes. "The Avalanche were winning. I was in my office listening to the game."

"You don't remember Chloe screaming?"

"No, ma'am."

"Or finding me outside with Eli?"

"No. I need to figure out how much time I've lost."

She recounted what happened in the last hour, starting with her friend being strangled, Jenna asking Matt to drop her at the truck stop and then her coming to his rescue after he was assaulted in the parking lot.

"That's pretty much it," she said.

Not quite. "I left you at the truck stop when

I knew you were in danger? That doesn't sound like me."

"A misunderstanding." She hesitated. "I thought you were a serial killer."

He shot her a look of disbelief.

"What? You had a gun, zip ties and duct tape in your glove box."

"The gun and zip ties are for work. I used the duct tape to fix a broken hose."

"Oh, okay. Sorry," she said.

"Trusting doesn't come easy for you, does it?"

"I trusted Chloe," she said quietly.

Silence stretched between them.

"Why were you working undercover at the community center?" she asked.

How much should he tell her? He knew she needed enough information to make good decisions.

"We think a drug cartel is laundering money through the foundation," he said. "By taking a job at the center and assimilating into the community, my goal was to discover who's involved."

"Assimilating into the community?"

"Through work, volunteering, attending church."

"That seems hypocritical, to pretend to attend church."

"I wasn't pretending. I enjoy church."

"Whatever."

He'd upset her but wasn't sure why. He'd figure that out later. In the meantime, he'd call for backup. He searched his pocket for his phone but came up empty.

"Your phone's in the console," she said.

He looked at her.

"You dropped it when they attacked you."

"Thanks."

"And here, you'll probably need this." She pulled his gun magazine out of her pocket and handed it to him.

He took it, trying to figure out why she had it.

"I thought you were a serial killer, remember?" she said.

"Right." He pulled the gun out of his waistband, shoved the magazine in place and put it in the glove box.

"You're not keeping it on you?"

"It'll raise questions in the hospital and I don't want to jeopardize my assignment."

"Oh, right."

Matt called his supervisor, pressing the heel of his palm against his temple to ease the pain. It went to voice mail. "It's Weller. I was assaulted and need backup. Send an agent to St. James Healthcare in Butte. I'm with a woman and child who need our protection." He pocketed his phone and leaned against the headrest.

"You don't have to take care of us," Jenna said.

"Excuse me?"

"We're not your problem."

"No, you're not my problem. You're my responsibility."

She smirked and looked away. Why? She didn't know anything about Matt. She didn't know how he'd failed Sarah.

"I'd like to find Chloe's cousin to help us, not be taken into FBI custody," she said.

"I'm trying to keep you safe."

She shook her head, unconvinced. Man, what had happened to this woman?

A few minutes later they exited the highway, and she turned into the hospital parking lot. "Do you want me to drop you at the main entrance?" she offered.

"No, we should stick together until help arrives."

She found a parking spot, turned off the vehicle and tried to hand him the keys.

"Keep them. Just in case."

"I can't take your truck."

"For my peace of mind."

With a curious frown, she got out of the car and retrieved the sleeping child. His head rested on her shoulder as she carried him through the parking lot.

"Want me to carry him?" he offered.

"You've got a concussion. You shouldn't be carrying anything."

Good point, which just went to show that his brain was muddled. As they approached the hospital, the state trooper joined them. "I've gotta go. When you're done being treated, call this number." He handed Matt a business card. "They'll send someone to take your statement."

"Thanks," Matt said.

The cop turned to Jenna. "Ma'am, don't worry. They'll take good care of your husband."

When Jenna didn't correct the "husband" remark, Matt glanced at her. She looked like she was about to burst into tears. Why? Because she was worried about Matt's condition? No, something else was going on.

"Thanks again, Officer," Matt said, and motioned Jenna inside.

Once they were seated in the waiting area,

he noticed her hand trembling as she stroked the little boy's back.

"It'll be okay," Matt offered. "Help's on the way."

No reaction. She didn't nod, shrug or even roll her eyes. She continued to stare straight ahead with a dazed look on her face.

"Jenna?"

She seemed lost in another world, as if she was having a flashback, and not a good one. He touched her arm that held the boy against her shoulder. She didn't look at him. The child was asleep, sucking on a pacifier and clinging to his stuffed bear.

Matt slid a chair in front of her and blocked her view. "Jenna, look at me."

She blinked, and her wounded green eyes connected with Matt's. It felt like he'd been slugged in the gut.

"You're okay," he said.

"I… I don't like hospitals."

"What happened?" he asked.

"I'm sorry?"

"To make you not like hospitals?"

She took a deep breath, opened her mouth and closed it again. Then she said, "I got hurt."

The way she articulated those three words reminded him of a little girl who'd fallen on the playground. But Jenna wasn't a little girl, and he suspected she'd suffered a lot worse than a skinned knee.

"You're not hurt now," he said, gently squeezing her shoulder. "You're A-okay."

She was more than okay in Matt's eyes. This woman was strong, smart and determined to do the right thing, to protect her friend's child.

"I won't be okay until this little boy is safe with his cousin." The fear in her eyes turned to anger.

"I understand, but I need to ask you something. What about the boy's father? I mean, at this point you could be accused of kidnapping."

"His mother begged me to protect Eli, especially from Gary. What would you have me do, hand him over to an abusive father?"

"Of course not, but there are laws and procedures for cases like this."

"What about the law for murder? Or does that not apply to cops? The police are obviously involved, so excuse me if I don't have much faith in the law."

"If Chief Billings killed—"

"If? You don't believe me?"

"I do, but we need more than your word. In

the meantime, we have to protect you and the little boy. My people can help."

"Cops won't help me."

"The chief is one bad cop out of what, twenty on the Cedar River Police force? That doesn't mean they're all bad." *That I'm bad.*

"Chloe's husband is wealthy. I'm sure he can make them bad by throwing money at them."

"You're awfully cynical for such a young woman."

"Well, at least I'm not dead."

That comment stopped him cold. Was she referring to her friend or herself? Had someone threatened Jenna's life, putting her in the hospital?

"Mr. Weller?" a nurse said from the examining room door.

He put up his hand, indicating he'd heard her. Matt studied Jenna. "Will you come in with me?"

She looked at him but didn't answer.

"I don't want to leave you and the child alone," he said.

With a nod, she stood and accompanied him into the examining area.

Jenna managed to keep Eli comfortable and asleep, Bubba the bear wedged firmly between the child's cheek and Jenna's shoulder. As the doctor put a few stitches in Matthew's head wound and examined his other injuries— bruised ribs and a reddened cheek—she struggled to distance herself from the situation. Not easy when she was surrounded by the smells, sights and sounds that triggered violent memories.

Her left eye swollen shut.

Pain piercing across her torso every time she drew a breath.

Knowing that she'd lost her baby, even before the doctor had told her.

As she rocked with Eli in her arms, she decided she had to get out of this hospital before she completely lost it and burst into uncontrollable tears.

Snap out of it. Stop thinking about yourself, and focus on the little boy.

"Want me to hold him?" Matt asked.

She glanced up. They were alone in the examining area. The doctor and nurse had left and she hadn't even noticed. She must pay more attention to her surroundings.

"Are you ready to go?" she said.

"Not quite. The nurse is getting me an ice bag and ibuprofen to take home." He shook his head. "Home? What am I talking about?" he muttered.

"How's your… Did you tell them about your memory?"

"No. Didn't want to give them a reason to admit me."

"Maybe they should do a CT scan."

"Not necessary. You're not the only one who's suffered a concussion before."

She sensed his comment was meant to be an opening for her to share more about herself. But that was not happening. Ever. The shame would choke her before the words passed her lips.

"It will be okay," Matthew said.

He was offering comfort because he sensed how stressed she was, how nervous and maybe even terrified about what would happen next. The list of options flashed across her mind—she'd be arrested for kidnapping; Eli would be handed back to his abusive father and Jenna would be imprisoned for trying to save a child; or worse—she'd be found by Chief Billings.

The image of Chloe's lifeless body dropping to the floor sent shockwaves of fear all the way to her fingertips. The little boy sighed and stirred against her shoulder. It gave her strength.

She stood. "I'm glad you're okay, Matthew."

"I hear a *but* at the end of that sentence."

"I need to find Chloe's cousin Marcus."

"We can help with that."

"But you won't, will you? You'll be required to place Eli back with his father."

"As I said, if you have proof that he is harming the child—"

"Chloe's word is enough for me."

"I understand, but it may not be enough for the law."

"The law." She couldn't stop a sardonic chuckle from escaping her lips. "I don't care about the law. I care about protecting this little boy."

"I can't let you leave." He shifted off the exam table.

Panic shot through her body. Not again. She couldn't deal with another domineering man.

You'll never leave me.

Her mind whirred with options as she clung tighter to Eli. Why had she trusted Matthew?

"Jenna?" he said.

She stared across the room at an IV stand, planning her escape. He placed his hand on her shoulder. She nearly jerked away, but didn't want to upset the child.

"Don't touch me," she ground out.

He withdrew his hand and studied her.

"I'm trying to help," he said. "I don't want you to be arrested for kidnapping."

She was about to fire back a retort when the nurse returned with an ice bag and pain reliever. "Everything okay?" she asked, glancing from Matthew to Jenna.

No, it wasn't okay. She'd been trapped in a cage again, unable to break free.

"We're good," Matt said.

"Someone's asking for you out front," the nurse said to him and left.

As he headed for the door, he turned to Jenna. "Wait here."

What did that mean? That he didn't trust his own people—the agent who was asking for him?

The moment he left the examining room, she grabbed the diaper and messenger bags. There was an exit on the other side of the room. Perfect.

Was she overreacting? No, Matthew's comment about custody and giving this precious child back to his father had strengthened Jenna's resolve to keep Eli safe and away from that monster.

A monster like Jenna's ex.

I can't let you leave. Matthew's words came back to her. Did he belong in the monster category as well?

Holding Eli against her shoulder, she went to the door and cracked it open to determine the positions of Matthew and the agent. The waiting area was empty. Strange.

"I can't help you, sir," a receptionist said. There was something in her voice...

Fear.

Jenna cracked the door a little wider. She spotted two things simultaneously—Matthew on the floor, and a man, wearing all black, pointing a gun at the receptionist.

Jenna snapped out of view. It wasn't one of the men from the community center. Which meant there was a whole army of thugs looking for her and Eli?

Struggling against fear that threatened to consume her, she rushed to the other door, swung it open and started down the back hall. She had to get away. Find Marcus. Get this child into the hands of someone who could protect him.

Guilt snagged her conscience. She'd brought danger into a hospital full of innocent staff members and patients.

The minute she and Eli were safely away, she'd call police about the gunman in the lobby.

"Stop right there," a male voice demanded.

Chapter Four

Jenna froze, her heart pounding in her ears.

She gripped Eli tighter, whispering against his knit hat, "I'm sorry, sweetie."

No, don't you dare give up.

"I'm sorry, but I can't let you leave," the man said.

Did he just say *I'm sorry*?

She turned and was relieved to see a hospital security officer walking toward her.

"There's a man with a gun—"

"Take it easy." He put out his right hand as he approached, like he was calming a wild stallion. His left hand rested on a club at his hip.

"In the lobby—a gunman is threatening your staff."

In a placating tone he said, "I need you to come with me."

Her gaze darted toward Matthew's exam room. Any second now the thug would figure out Jenna was close, and he'd come bursting through the door.

"Please, ma'am," the security officer, a gray-haired man in his midsixties, said.

Every inch of her body screamed to get out of here. If she ran she wouldn't get far, with two bags strapped across her shoulders and clutching a toddler in her arms. The security guy would chase after her, probably sound the alarm, drawing even more attention to Jenna and Eli's presence.

"Why do I need to come with you?" she said.

He sighed and took his hand off the club resting at his hip. "I received an informal request to keep an eye out for a young woman and a child who went missing from Cedar River."

"That's not me."

"Then I'm sure we can clear it up quickly. Please, I need you to come to my office."

The problem was, his office was in the same building where a kidnapper—probably more than one—was looking for Jenna and Eli.

"Let's go," he said.

Refusing would make her look guilty. All she needed to do was act innocent and agreeable, and once he went to check on the situation out front she'd sneak away.

With a nod, she walked alongside him, fearing he'd pull out cuffs, but he didn't. Of course not—he wouldn't cuff a woman carrying a child.

As he led her down the hall, her instincts remained on full alert, and her mind calculated options, solutions. When they made a left turn, she spotted an exit up ahead. Not wanting to give away her thoughts, she turned her attention to Eli, whispering sweet words against his cheek, acting like a loving mom.

A sharp pain lanced through her chest and she shoved it aside. She had to convince the guard she was Eli's mother, not some crazy woman who'd kidnapped a child.

He opened the door to his office and motioned to a chair beside his desk. "I'll be back shortly."

"Aren't you going to call the police about the gunman out front?"

"I'll check it out."

"No, he's dangerous, he's—"

He shut the door on her protest. Foolish man—he wasn't capable of dealing with these violent criminals.

She grabbed the doorknob and twisted. It was locked.

Shaking her head, she fought the frustration welling up inside for letting herself be caught, locked up. For all she knew, the request to keep an eye out for her had come directly from Chief Billings with a generous finder's fee attached.

She needed to get out of here. She needed help.

Grabbing the office phone, she found an outside line and called 9-1-1 to report the gunman because either the guard was an accomplice, or he was making a dangerous mistake by confronting the man.

Then she called Patrice.

"Hello?" the older woman answered.

"It's Jenna." She put it on speaker.

"What's wrong?"

"I'm sorry to be calling."

"You never have to apologize to me. How can I help?"

"My friend was murdered and I'm watching her little boy, and now they're after him too, after us, and—"

"Take a breath."

She paused, inhaled a deep breath and exhaled.

"If you want to think clearly you need to be calm, lower your heart rate and get grounded, remember?"

"Yes."

"What's the immediate danger?"

"I'm locked in a security guard's office at a hospital and I can't get out."

"Yes, you can. Look for paper clips, something to use on the lock."

"If I get out of here—"

"When you get out of there?"

"When I get out of here, I may need your help again."

"There's always room for you at the cabin, Jenna, you know that. Now look for paper clips. Who knows, you might find a spare office key in his desk drawer."

She did her best to one-handedly search drawers, thankful that Eli was sound asleep against her shoulder.

"You're caring for a little boy?" Patrice asked.

"Yes."

"How old?"

"Eighteen months."

A knowing silence filled the line.

"I'm okay," Jenna assured her friend.

"Where is he now?"

"I'm holding him."

"They have these nifty baby carriers that you strap to your body. The motion soothes the child and it would make carrying him a lot easier. You can pick one up when you get out of there."

"Okay."

"What's his name?"

"Eli," she said, sifting through a top drawer. "He's a super good boy." She found a tray of paper clips. "Do you really think I can—?"

Someone rattled the doorknob.

Jenna spun around. "They're trying to get in."

"Can you find something to defend yourself with?"

Jenna grabbed scissors and hit the off button on the phone, not wanting Patrice to hear what might happen next. Because Jenna would surely die before handing this innocent child over to killers.

She swallowed back her fear, gripping the child with one arm while clutching the scissors with her other hand.

The door unlocked with a click.

"Jenna, it's me," Matthew said before entering the office.

He opened the door...

To the sight of Jenna wielding eight-inch scissors in her hand.

He anticipated she'd be panicked, which is why he announced himself. He also knew she'd probably commit assault in order to protect the child.

"Let's go," he said, ignoring her terrified expression and the white-knuckled grip of the weapon.

She didn't move at first.

"We've gotta get out of here, and I mean yesterday." He motioned with his hands. "Is the baby okay?"

That seemed to redirect her attention. She glanced at the child leaning against her shoulder. "Yes, he's fine."

"Good, then let's go."

She started toward the door.

"I don't think you'll need the scissors."

She glanced at her hand.

"Unless you want to bring them, which is fine. We've gotta make tracks here, Jenna."

"Right, of course." She dropped the scissors on the desk and followed Matt. "I saw you on the floor. That man with a gun, and then…" She glanced at him with a question in her eyes.

"I was able to neutralize him."

"So the security guard wasn't working with him?"

"No. I flashed my ID and told him the

woman and child who accompanied me to the hospital were being taken into protective custody."

They reached the exit and she hesitated.

"What?" he said.

"I won't let them take Eli away from me." She took a step backward. "I won't return him to his father."

"I know, and I understand. Right now I need to get you and Eli safe. That's all I'm concerned with. I'm not sure I can trust my own people at this point. But you and me? We have to trust each other. What do I need to do to make you trust me, Jenna?"

"You won't take him back to his father?"

"No."

Matt had just made a promise, one that might require him to break the law. He didn't know what compelled him to say it, but he had to get Jenna and the child out of here. He doubted the guy out front was alone.

She studied him with that contemplative look of hers. "Fine. I'll try trusting you."

"You'll try?" he said, pushing open the door.

"I haven't had much success trusting people."

He guided her through the back lot, his gaze

assessing, searching for signs of trouble. "Have a little faith."

"Haven't had much success in that department either," she said softly.

He couldn't look at her, didn't want to see the devastating sadness he knew would be reflected in her eyes.

"Was that guy working for the chief?" she asked.

"That would be my guess."

"And you think someone at the FBI gave him our location?"

"I can't rule it out. You have my keys?"

"You sure you should drive?"

"I'm better now, thanks."

She passed them to Matt. The brief contact shot warmth up his arm.

They walked in silence—a good thing because he wanted to evaluate their surroundings and the danger that could be waiting for them. Three squad cars were speeding toward the hospital. He shifted her behind him and hesitated. "That should keep everyone busy so they don't see us leave."

"Where are we going?"

"Someplace safe."

Without looking at her, he gently placed his

hand on her arm, and this time she didn't pull away. He guided her toward the truck.

Officers rushed into the ER entrance, where he hoped they'd arrest the gunman, whom Matt had fastened with the security guard's cuffs to a desk. Matt still wasn't sure how he'd found the physical energy to subdue the guy.

But he didn't need to wonder for long. He was focused on Jenna and the little boy, on making sure they were safe.

Jenna quickly buckled Eli in his car seat and climbed into the passenger seat, and Matt pulled out.

Neither of them spoke for a good ten minutes, almost as if they were both still holding their breath, waiting for the next attack.

"What happened back there?" she finally asked.

"The gunman had everyone cornered and ordered me down. It didn't look good. Then the security guard showed up, distracting the gunman, and I tackled him without incident."

"With a concussion and bruised ribs?" she said with awe in her voice.

"Once I cuffed the guy, the guard said you'd told him about the shooter, that you were locked in his office. I assumed it was for your own safety."

"No, the guard said someone informally requested he keep an eye out for a woman who'd kidnapped a child from Cedar River."

"At least it's not an official BOLO," he muttered.

With a nod, she gazed out her window. She looked so…lost.

"You were smart to try to escape once you saw what was going on in the waiting room," he said, trying to offer encouragement. He glanced at her, but she didn't look proud. She seemed ashamed. "What's that look?"

She shook her head.

"Jenna? We've got to trust each other, right?"

"The moment you left the examining room I was planning to escape."

"I don't understand. You didn't know—"

"I was scared of you."

He gripped the steering wheel tighter. "Scared. Of me?"

"Yes." She fiddled with a silver ring on her right hand.

"You're going to have to explain that. Please."

"As you've probably guessed, I have a rather tragic past."

Tragic. The word conjured all kinds of images, images he struggled to ignore.

"I've made some foolish choices I wish I could take back, but I can't."

He waited patiently, wanting her to feel comfortable enough to share her story at her own pace.

"The last time I was in a hospital," she said with hesitation, "my ex-husband put me there."

Things started to make sense: her anxious behavior and the wariness in her eyes. Especially around men.

Even around Matt.

Regret whipped through him.

"I would never hurt you, Jenna."

"Well, whenever I'm in a situation that reminds me of Anthony, I get sucked into the past and feel those same feelings."

"Does that happen often?" he asked.

"No." She glanced at him. "But it's happened a few times since Chloe's murder."

"Understandable. What did I do at the hospital to make you want to run?"

"You stood up to overpower me."

He glanced at her, but she wouldn't make eye contact. Was she still afraid?

"I… I'm sorry," he said.

"What?"

"I'm sorry if my behavior upset you. That was not my intention."

"You said…you said that you wouldn't let me leave."

He had spoken those words, but because he wanted to protect her. Still, he knew that arguing with her wouldn't help to develop the trust he wanted to cultivate between them.

"And that reminded me of Anthony, the things he used to say to me."

"Like what?"

"That's personal."

"If I'm to avoid upsetting you, I'd like to know where the land mines are."

She hugged herself and sighed. "He'd say that he loved me so much he devoted his life to being a good husband. Then it turned into he devoted his life to protecting me, mostly from myself because of my bad choices. After a while you start to believe the lies. One night I'd finally had enough and stood up to him."

Matt could tell she was reliving the incident. "What happened?"

"He grabbed my shoulders and shook me until I could hardly think, then he threw me aside." She glanced at Matt. "That was the last time I ended up in the hospital."

"The last time? You mean there were other times?"

She hugged herself tighter, but didn't answer.

"Didn't you call the police?" he said.

"Why? He donated to the police chief's political campaign to run for mayor. He was friendly with a few of the local detectives. It was pointless to reach out to them for help. Besides, Anthony always had this way of promising it would get better. He went to anger management therapy, and for a while he'd be the loving husband I thought I'd married. It never lasted."

"So you got a divorce? You escaped?"

"With a lot of help. A woman came to see me in the hospital. She challenged me to stand up for myself. That's when my fight for freedom began."

"How did you get away?"

"There's a group that helps women like me. I can't share the details. They need to remain anonymous."

"I understand."

"Do you? You're a man in a powerful profession. You can take away someone's freedom, question their backgrounds, their decisions."

"It's my job to protect—"

"Funny, that's what Anthony used to say. It was his job to take care of me. His job to protect me."

Another awkward silence stretched between them. Matt didn't think it wise to point out he was nothing like her former husband. Post-trauma triggers weren't always rational, but they were definitely painful, and all too real.

"I'm glad you got away from him," he offered.

"I'm not sure I have."

"What do you mean?"

"Here I am on the run again, fighting for my life, and the life of a little boy."

"This is different."

"Whatever. I guess I have to accept the fact that I will repeat my mistakes and will end up living under a cloud of violence. That's just my fate."

"Don't talk like that. You're in this situation because you're doing an honorable favor for your friend."

"Why would Chloe pick me? She had plenty of other friends she could have chosen."

"Maybe she didn't think they were as strong as you, or as nurturing."

When she swiped at her eye, he figured she was fighting back tears.

Way to go, Weller. Make the woman cry.

He redirected his attention to the dark highway, struggling to come up with what he should say to ease her pain. He didn't consider himself an expert at finding the right words to comfort someone, to encourage hope. Maybe if he'd been better at listening and offering compassion, Sarah wouldn't have left.

She wouldn't have driven so fast that she'd ended up dead. He should have been there for her. He could have saved her.

But he didn't.

And now the Lord had given him another chance, this time to save an emotionally wounded, yet strong woman—an innocent woman and a child.

Thank you, Lord, for entrusting me with this responsibility. I will not fail.

Trust.

As Jenna gazed out the window into the darkness, she considered the word and all its meaning. It certainly meant relying on someone, believing they had your best interest at heart.

Trust.

For Jenna, *trust* was like a muscle that had atrophied after years of nonuse. She couldn't remember the last time she'd trusted anyone, especially a man.

She'd trusted the members of Gloria's Guardians, the team that helped her escape Anthony. It had been the right choice. She knew if she'd stayed with her abusive husband—mostly out of fear—she probably wouldn't have made it to her next birthday.

The Guardians set everything up, including the plan to shut down Anthony. It started with the discussion she had with him at the hospital about the loss of their child. She'd recorded every word. It didn't take much to enrage him. It never did.

She hadn't expected him to say she'd deserved to be thrown down the stairs, which was basically a confession to fetal homicide. Just when she thought he might hit her again, two hospital security guards and her lawyer entered the room to intervene.

They had enough evidence to bring charges against Anthony. She didn't want to go through an ugly, painful trial, although she'd pretended to be up for the fight. Fearing she'd make a sympathetic witness, and knowing his own recorded admission would get him convicted, Anthony took a plea deal of three years and agreed to a quick divorce. He didn't want his sterling reputation to be tarnished, and apparently explained to friends that, although innocent, he'd spend the time in jail if it would help his fragile wife heal from the loss of their child.

What a master manipulator.

The Guardians had found her a powerful attorney to defend her pro bono, and even hired a security team to make sure Anthony couldn't intimidate or hurt her while out on bail.

Once he'd signed the divorce papers, the change of identity and relocation efforts began. For all intents and purposes, Anna Marie Brighton had vanished, never to be seen or heard from again.

At first, losing Joey had destroyed her.

Then it had given her incredible strength to fight back.

"How long ago?" Matt said.

She glanced at him. "I'm sorry?"

"When did you divorce your husband?"

After he committed murder.

"It's been a little over two years."

"In Tulsa?"

"No."

"But your background check—"

"You did a background check on me?"

"We were looking into everyone's backgrounds for links to suspicious activity at the Broadlake Foundation."

"What did you find out about me?"

"Other than that you're from Tulsa? Not much."

Her initial panic was quickly tempered with appreciation for the system that had saved her. If he thought she was from Tulsa rather than her true location, a suburb north of Chicago, then even federal agents couldn't see past her newly minted identity into her dark past.

"Who did that for you?" he asked. "Changed your background?"

She shot him a raised eyebrow.

"No, not so I can arrest them."

"I should hope not. There's nothing wrong with wanting to live a safe life away from your abuser."

"I agree."

"They only used first names to protect their identities, and those names could be pseudonyms. That reminds me, I should let my primary guardian know I'm okay. I was on the phone with her when you found me in the office. Wait, and there's another call I should make first. Can I use your phone?"

"You don't have one?"

"Thought it would be best to toss it."

He offered her his phone with a steady hand. Matt's recovery amazed Jenna. He'd been beaten up back at the truck stop, yet in the hour spent at the hospital, he seemed to have recovered quite well. She wondered if that meant he remembered anything about Chloe's murder.

"How are you feeling?" she asked.

"Frustrated."

"I mean physically—your head, your ribs?"

He shrugged. "Ibuprofen helped."

"And your memory?"

"No, I'm sorry." He seemed as disappointed as Jenna.

She found it interesting that even though he hadn't seen the murder, he trusted Jenna's word that it had happened.

Jenna called Marcus, but again it went to voice mail. "Can I leave him your number?" she asked.

"Sure." He gave it to her, and she repeated it on the message.

Then she called Patrice, who also didn't answer, so Jenna left a message. "Hey, it's Jenna.

Sorry about not calling sooner. Things got a little crazy, but I'm okay. Thanks for being there, and keeping me sane. I'm using a friend's phone in case they've got a trace on my cell. I'll pick up a burner and call you tomorrow. Be well."

She ended the call and placed the phone on the dash holder.

"Sounds like you and this woman have become good friends."

"We have," she said. Even though Jenna sincerely wanted to trust Matt, she would never expose the team of mostly women to whom she owed her life.

To think, if she hadn't survived, she wouldn't be here today to protect baby Eli. She glanced into the back seat. He was sound asleep.

"He's a remarkably good boy," she said.

"Yeah, wait until he wakes up hungry. Then he'll let us have it."

"You have children?"

"No, but my brothers have a couple of kids. Is there food in the diaper bag?"

Jenna grabbed it off the floor and searched inside. "Cereal, crackers, fruit, a bottle and dry formula." She glanced at Matt. "Chloe was ready for anything."

"Or maybe she was planning to run."

They shared a look.

"That will get us through the morning. We'll pick up more supplies tomorrow," he said.

"You still haven't told me where we're going."

"There's a couple that offers their home to young women who are in trouble."

"You mean...?"

"Victims of abuse, human trafficking. They stay at Nancy and Ed Miller's farm for protection and to learn skills to help them move on."

"Kind of like the team that helped me."

"Yep. There are a lot of folks out there willing to help people who, by no fault of their own, have become victims."

She wondered if that was a not-so-subtle hint on his part that his motives were honorable.

"Are you sure the farm's a good place to take Eli?" she said.

"These women are victims too, Jenna," he said.

"I know, but aren't we putting them in danger by going there?"

"No one knows the location of the farm except for law enforcement, and the locals are good at protecting Nancy and Ed's altruistic work. Right now they only have one guest, so they've got plenty of room."

"You've spoken with them?"

"Texted. They'll leave a key in the planter box so we can let ourselves in."

His phone rang and he glanced at the number but didn't answer.

"Who is it?" Jenna asked.

"My boss. I'll call him back once we're safe."

That sounded like he wasn't one hundred percent sure they were out of danger.

Shivers trickled across her body. It wasn't until just now that the magnitude of the past few hours landed squarely on her shoulders.

She was still in danger. On the run. And this time it wasn't just about her.

A child depended on her—another innocent child.

"Jenna?" Matt said.

She glanced at him.

"I will protect you."

An hour later Matt's words still echoed in the silence between them. Jenna had gone quiet since he'd uttered the promise…again. He didn't know how many times he'd have to say it to convince her of his integrity and his goal: protecting Jenna and Eli.

Jenna, a witness to murder, who was on the run with another woman's child.

A dead woman's child.

Why couldn't he remember? He had to have seen something at the community center. He wanted desperately for the memory to return, but until the swelling went down in his brain, he was at the mercy of his injuries.

And the men who seemed to be constantly right behind him.

It was almost as if Billings's men knew where he was going to be before he got there. Nah, that was his concussion messing with him. He was overthinking things, acting paranoid, even a little confused.

But he wasn't confused about Jenna. She'd shut down, turning her face to the window as if to signal there was nothing more to talk about.

As if she didn't believe him when he pledged to protect her, and she wanted him to stop saying it.

Well, she'd better get used to it, because he'd keep repeating the promise until he read acceptance in her eyes.

Could he blame her for being cautious after everything she'd been though with an abusive former husband? He needed to be patient and offer more compassion.

He glanced in the rearview mirror for signs they were being followed. The road was empty for miles behind them. Then he caught sight of baby Eli. He hoped they could get him in the house and resettled without disturbing the child too much. Nancy would be thrilled to wake up tomorrow with a little one under her roof, since her youngest grandchild was in his teens.

Confident they weren't being followed, he turned onto the dirt road leading to the Millers' farm, the refuge for young women who'd been used and abused, a lot like Jenna.

He clenched his jaw, wondering what kind of jerk would abuse a lovely woman like Jenna North. A bully, no doubt, a man who had to pick on others to make himself feel strong.

"I'm sorry," he blurted out.

"What?" She turned to him.

"About your ex-husband, what he did to you."

"Me too."

"What happened to him?"

She crossed her arms over her chest. She clearly wasn't ready to share the details.

It was a defiant, determined gesture. He'd need that determination, along with a solid plan, to keep her safe. Tonight he just wanted to settle in, take time in a safe environment to strategize his next move.

They pulled up to the side of the house and parked. "Just give me a minute."

"It's kind of hard to trust you when I think you're going behind my back and saying who knows what to the people inside."

"I'm sure they're asleep, Jenna. I'm being extra careful and want to go in first to make sure it's safe."

"Oh." She fiddled with her silver ring.

"Same rules apply. If something happens to me, take the truck and get out of here." He left the keys in the ignition and shut the door gently, not wanting to wake the little boy. As he climbed the back porch steps, he noticed a soft glow coming from the kitchen and wondered if Ed had waited up for them. He peered inside, but there didn't seem to be anyone around.

Matt tapped softly on the door. Waited. When no one answered, he assumed his con-

siderate hosts had left a lamp on so Matt and
Jenna wouldn't have to enter a dark house.

He had just turned to retrieve the key from
the planter box when a shot rang out across the
property, and he instinctively dove for cover.

Chapter Five

Jenna sat straight up in her seat.

Was that a gunshot? She scanned the porch. But she didn't see Matthew.

He'd just been standing at the door, then turned…

And went down.

If something happens to me, take the truck and get out of here.

Jenna clicked into autopilot, climbed over the console and got behind the wheel of the truck. How on earth had they found them out here, in the middle of nowhere, at a safe house that no one knew about?

Adjusting the seat, she turned the ignition, shoved the truck in gear and hit the accelerator. Spinning the wheel, she whirled around and headed back out on the dirt trail, all the while waiting for another shot, for the shattering of glass. They'd no doubt shoot at her next, right?

Calm your breathing.

She kept her head low in anticipation of the next shot.

It never came.

As she distanced herself from the house, cautious hope tempered her panic.

The blink of the truck's headlights caught movement up ahead, but it wasn't a man waving a gun. A young woman in light blue pajamas was racing through the snow toward the main road. She wasn't wearing a jacket, and her feet were bare.

Jenna couldn't just drive by and do nothing. She lowered her window and called out to the girl. "What happened?"

The woman shrieked and stumbled, falling on the ground. Checking the rearview mirror for signs of danger, Jenna slowed to a stop and got out. She could do this quickly. She could save an innocent young woman.

Even if she'd been unable to save herself until it was too late.

She rushed to the woman, who was a teenager, she noticed as she got closer, one who was casting a worried glance over her shoulder.

"Come on, we've gotta go," Jenna said.

"Don't hurt me. Don't hurt me!" the girl cried, her eyes pinched shut.

"I'm here to help you."

And that's when she noticed the gun in her hand.

"Why do you have a gun?" Jenna automatically reached for it.

The teen scrambled away, clutching the gun with a deadly grip. She didn't aim it at Jenna—not yet anyway.

"It's okay," Jenna said.

"I saw him—he's here! He's never going to let me go!"

"Who, honey? Who's after you?"

"That's why I fired the gun, to warn him to stay away."

"Good, you did good," she encouraged.

If this young woman had fired the weapon, it meant the immediate danger had nothing to do with Billings's men who were after Jenna and Eli.

"I won't go back, I won't," she said with a wild look in her eyes.

She seemed irrational, crazed. Jenna wondered if she'd had a traumatic nightmare that drove her out into the night. Jenna had experienced plenty of those.

"I'm Jenna. What's your name?"

The young woman's eyes darted from Jenna to the truck to the surrounding property.

"Please? What's your name?" Jenna tried again.

"Emily."

"I'd really like to help you, Emily."

"No one can help me."

"That's what I used to think. I was married to a very bad man."

Emily blinked her tear-filled eyes at Jenna.

"Come on, it's cold out here, and you're barefoot." Jenna took a step toward her.

Emily scrambled to her feet and aimed the gun at Jenna.

Her heart pounding, Jenna put out her hand. "Please put down the gun. I suspect you had a nightmare that triggered bad memories."

"It was so real!"

"I know. I've had them too."

The wail of a child drifted from the open truck door. Eli had awakened, probably hungry with a wet diaper. Jenna strategized how to protect the child from a hysterical woman with a gun.

"That's…that's a baby," Emily said, lowering the weapon.

"Yes, a little boy named Eli."

"I had a baby," Emily said.

"Babies are wonderful."

Emily dropped the gun and fell to her knees. She buried her face in her hands. "I didn't mean it. I didn't mean it," she sobbed.

The sound of a car engine roared in the distance. Help was on the way.

Jenna couldn't wait. She couldn't risk Emily reaching for the gun again. She trudged through the snow, picked up the gun and tossed it out of reach. Emily didn't even notice. She was rocking back and forth, apologizing. Jenna suspected Emily had lost her child, just as Jenna had lost baby Joey.

It was surreal to be caught between the traumatized, crying young woman that reminded Jenna so much of herself, and baby Eli crying from the truck.

Jenna crouched beside Emily. "You're going to be okay."

"It was so real." Emily looked up, her face wet with tears. "I was so scared."

"I know." Jenna wrapped her arms around Emily. That's the only thing that had worked for Jenna when she stayed with Patrice, the only thing that quelled the terror. "He's not here now. And baby Eli needs us."

A car door slammed, then a second door.

"Jenna?" Matt said in a strained voice.

She glanced up at his worried expression. An older gentleman stood next to him. She assumed it was Ed Miller.

"We're okay," Jenna said.

"Eli...?" Matt glanced at the truck.

"He's fine. We're all fine."

"I'm sorry. I'm so sorry," Emily whimpered.

"Let's get back to the house," Matt said.

He took a step toward Jenna and Emily. Emily cowered, still clinging to Jenna.

"I'll ride back with Emily," Jenna said.

Matt hesitated, as if he were going to argue with her.

"Can you take care of Eli?" Jenna asked.

"Of course."

"She had a gun. I tossed it over there." Jenna pointed toward the field.

"I'll find it," Matt said.

"I don't understand what's going on here," Ed said.

"Please forgive me. I'm so sorry." Emily's muffled voice repeated the apology over and over.

"I'll explain everything back at the house."

Jenna helped Emily stand. As they headed to Ed's truck, Matthew stopped her by placing a gentle hand on Jenna's shoulder. He didn't speak, but she read the relief in his eyes.

"I know," she said and offered a slight smile.

An hour later baby Eli was fast asleep in a downstairs guest room that he and Jenna shared. Matt had changed him, made him a bottle and soothed the child into a deep slumber, all while denying the intense emotions that ripped through him like a tornado over the Great Plains. It wasn't only the fear of breaking his promise to protect Jenna that threw him into utter panic, but something else, something he didn't want to consider.

He was developing feelings for Jenna North. Inappropriate feelings. What else could explain the tightness in his chest when he and Ed had pulled up behind his truck and he noticed the open door? For a second he thought Billings's men had found her and violently ripped her from behind the wheel of the truck.

Thankfully, Ed saw movement in the snow about fifty feet away.

It was Jenna, on the ground, comforting

someone. A young woman who'd apparently broken into Ed's lockbox and taken a gun.

As Matt shut the door to the downstairs guest room where little Eli slept, he reconsidered his decision to stay in the same house as the young woman. The Millers had convinced him it would be safe because they'd called a counselor and off-duty cop to keep watch over the girl during the night. They couldn't move her from the house in the middle of the night, nor had they made the decision yet to do so.

Matt joined Jenna, Ed and Nancy, who had settled around the kitchen table to decompress. Nancy brewed tea and put out a tray of fresh fruit and banana bread.

"How about a moment of thanks that no one was hurt," Nancy suggested.

Matt bowed his head.

"Lord, thank you for watching over us tonight," Nancy began. "For protecting us from harm, and helping Emily find comfort in Jenna's kindness. Amen."

A unanimous *amen* filled the kitchen. Matt thought he heard Jenna whisper a soft response but couldn't be sure.

"Well that was more excitement than I'm used to." Nancy slid the plate of fruit and bread toward Jenna. "And we've had our share of challenges with the girls."

"Why did she discharge the weapon?" Ed asked.

"It was a warning shot," Jenna explained.

"Warning who?"

"The man she thought was after her."

Ed shook his head.

"Those nightmares can seem very, very real," Jenna defended.

Matt wondered what kind of new nightmares would plague Jenna thanks to tonight's violence.

"Jenna," he said, "how are you doin'?"

She tipped her chin as if considering her answer. "Good. I'm okay. A little cold from being outside in the snow, I guess." She turned to Nancy. "Thanks again for letting us stay here tonight."

"You may stay as long as necessary." Nancy warmed Jenna's tea.

Jenna wrapped her hands around the teacup. "What will happen to Emily?"

"We'll have a meeting and discuss the best option," Ed said. "Our mission is to provide a safe environment for young women in trouble. What Emily did tonight, stealing one of my weapons..." He hesitated. "It goes against the principles of our farm. I'm not sure she can remain here."

"That's so sad," Jenna said in a soft voice. "I mean, it's her abuser's fault she has nightmares."

"It depends on the counselors' evaluations," Nancy offered.

"Counselors, plural?" Jenna said.

"Behavioral counselor and chemical dependency counselor," Nancy said.

"Some girls have had their share of issues with drugs before coming to the farm," Ed explained. "We understand that, but they must be on the road to getting clean, and we have our boundaries. It's the best way to provide a safe environment."

"How long do they usually stay?" Jenna asked.

As Ed and Nancy discussed the inspiration behind their safe haven, and its rules, with Jenna, Matt worried that the details might be too painful for her, sparking violent memories of her past.

Yet she'd sounded sincere, even confident, a moment ago when she'd said she was okay.

He leaned back in his chair and took a calming breath. Only now did his pulse seem to slow to a normal rate.

After the gunshot earlier, Matt had quickly let himself in the house and found Ed and Nancy coming down the stairs in a panic.

At first Ed thought it was a neighbor warning off a bear, but then they discovered Emily was gone, and the firearm lockbox in the pantry had been broken into.

"They know the rules when they come here," Ed said. "Inappropriate behavior is not tolerated. And stealing one of my guns—"

"She was out of her mind and thought she needed to defend herself," Jenna said.

"Be that as it may, it's grand theft," Ed said.

"When she came out of her trauma, she kept apologizing and asking for your forgiveness. Isn't that what good Christians do? Forgive?"

"Jenna," Matt warned, questioning her tone.

"We do practice forgiveness, Jenna," Nancy interjected. "But we have to temper that with our goal of protecting our guests. If the counselors think her behavior is erratic to the point of being dangerous, we have to respect that evaluation and act accordingly."

"You can forgive someone and let them go," Matt said.

"How? How do you do that?" Jenna challenged.

"By realizing that all that anger and resentment you carry only serves to destroy you from the inside," Matt said, recalling his own anger with the driver who'd hit Sarah's car, causing it to slide into a tree, killing her upon impact.

Then again, if she hadn't been going twenty miles over the speed limit, she might still be alive. And she might still be alive if she and Matt hadn't argued, again, about his job being more important than their relationship. Maybe if he'd paid closer attention, maybe if...

No, he'd given up blaming himself and everyone else for her death.

"Forgiveness, well, it brings you out of the darkness," he said.

"Amen to that," Ed said.

Matt glanced at Jenna's puzzled look. He suspected he'd be interrogated about this conversation in the future, although he wasn't sure it was wise to share more details of his life, to cross even further over that line than he already had.

He was developing feelings for Jenna North. Time to put the brakes on before this thing between them spun out of control.

"We will certainly forgive Emily," Nancy said. "The bigger question is, will she be able to forgive herself?"

* * *

Nancy's words still haunted Jenna the next morning. *Will she be able to forgive herself?*

Jenna forced herself to stop thinking about self-forgiveness, frustrated by the resentment that particular thought conjured up. Instead, she focused on Eli. She'd thankfully awakened before the little boy, maybe because his sleep had been interrupted a few times last night, which caused him to sleep late.

She washed up and dressed in clothes Nancy set aside for her, chosen from the wardrobe they kept for guests. The older woman had explained that most of the time, the young women came with nothing other than the clothes they wore when rescued.

Jenna could relate.

She headed for the kitchen to make Eli's morning bottle. As she passed by the living room, she noticed Matt was gone from the couch, the blanket neatly folded and draped over the back. He said he'd sleep better on the sofa than in a bed, but she wondered if he was actually positioning himself as the first line of defense.

I will protect you. An appreciative smile tugged at the corner of her lips.

The smell of coffee drew her into the kitchen, where she poured herself a cup, then warmed Eli's formula. There was enough for two, maybe three more bottles. They'd have to make a run to the store soon. As the bottle warmed, she leaned against the counter and noticed a high chair at the table. It seemed the Millers were prepared for anything.

The back door opened. Nancy came inside and kicked her boots on the mat. "Good morning."

"Morning. The coffee's amazing."

"I'm glad you like it. Ed got the high chair out of storage."

"I noticed. Thanks."

Nancy hung her jacket on the coatrack and stepped out of her boots and into clogs. "Eggs and toast for breakfast?"

"I'm not much of a breakfast person."

"Pancakes it is." She winked.

"Where is Matthew?"

"He and Ed are out doing chores."

Jenna was afraid to ask, but she had to know. "And Emily?"

"We're still debating. I see I guessed right about your size." Nancy scanned Jenna's sweatpants, T-shirt and fleece.

"Thanks, it's very comfortable."

"When you and Matt go to the store today, you can pick up more clothes, and supplies for the baby. Is he still asleep?"

"Yes. I want to be ready," Jenna said, shaking the warmed bottle.

"Smart girl."

Jenna felt such comfort, such support from Nancy. It reminded her of the Guardians, how she'd felt safe every step of her journey. That gave her an idea.

"Nancy, if you decide that Emily is too much of a risk, I might have an alternative for her."

Nancy glanced up from mixing the pancake batter.

"I know of a group that helps women get away from violent situations. They might consider working with Emily."

"You have such a good heart, Jenna. So generous."

Warmth flushed Jenna's cheeks. She wasn't used to being praised.

The cry of a baby echoed through the house. "That's my cue," Jenna said.

"Bring him into the kitchen. My grandchildren loved my blueberry pancakes when they were his age."

"Sounds good."

By the time Jenna got to the bedroom, Eli was standing in the crib, gripping the top rail, tears streaming down his face.

"Hey, buddy, no need to cry." She noticed that he'd dropped his polar bear on the floor. "Look, it's Bubba." He rubbed it against his cheek and the cry turned into a whimper.

"Okay, hungry boy." Jenna offered the bottle, which he took with a firm one-handed grip. She carried him to the dresser that doubled as a changing table, complete with a soft pad and four-inch lip around the edges so he wouldn't roll off. Jenna absently started humming. Eli's eyes rounded with fascination at the sound.

It was strange, how she naturally changed his diaper, how she always seemed to know what would calm him. Yet it made sense, because she'd spent months preparing for her own child's arrival.

Thank you, Joey. Because of you, I'm able to take care of Eli.

The thought sparked warmth in her chest that melted a little of the cold, hard grief.

Once dressed, she carried Eli toward the kitchen, glancing upstairs and wondering how Emily was doing today. Jenna would call Patrice to inquire about the Guardians helping the young woman, but she'd have to tell them everything, including that Emily's trauma had resulted in a night terror that caused her to steal a gun.

"That might be a deal breaker," Jenna whispered to herself.

She and Eli entered the kitchen just as Matthew and Ed came in through the back door.

"Good morning," Jenna said, relieved to see him.

"Morning." Matthew took off his jacket and hung it on the rack.

"Any word from Marcus?" Jenna asked.

"No," Matthew answered.

"How'd the little dude sleep?" Ed reached out to squeeze Eli's foot.

Eli buried his face against Jenna's shoulder, still sucking on the bottle and clinging to his bear.

"Oh, he's playing shy, is he?" Nancy teased.

"He's certainly taken to you." Ed nodded at Jenna.

"Yeah, I guess he has," Jenna said, lightly kissing his head.

"Pancakes will be ready in a few minutes," Nancy said.

Jenna shifted Eli into the high chair and adjusted the tray in place. She glanced up and caught Matthew watching her.

"What, am I doing it wrong?" she asked.

"No, ma'am, quite the contrary."

She turned to Eli, wanting to avoid an awkward moment, another compliment that would make her blush bright pink.

"You two were out awhile," Nancy said to the men. "Didn't think picking stalls would take that long."

"Had some catching up to do," Ed said. "Although he couldn't explain why Jenna threw my gun into the snow last night."

Jenna shrugged. "Guns aren't my thing."

"Boo!" Eli dropped his polar bear. Matthew picked it up and put it back on his tray. Eli dropped it again.

"Ah, we're playing that game, are we?" Matthew said with a smile.

It all felt so surreal, sitting in this bright yellow kitchen with a little boy in a high chair, surrounded by such lovely people.

She enjoyed watching Matthew play with Eli, as if the federal agent hadn't a care in the world other than making the child giggle.

"I wonder if Tim and Miss Westbrook will stay for breakfast," Nancy said.

"Tim and Miss Westbrook?" Jenna said.

"The off-duty police officer and the counselor," Nancy said. "They're still upstairs."

"That reminds me, I want to call the people I mentioned last night, in case Emily can't stay here," Jenna said. "Could I use your phone?"

"Sure." Ed grabbed the cordless phone off the cradle and handed it to her.

"Can you watch Eli for a minute?" she asked Matt.

"Of course."

Jenna went into the living room to make the call. At this point she trusted the three people in the kitchen, but still felt protective of the Guardians.

"Hello?"

"Patrice, it's Jenna."

"I was hoping you'd call. How are you?"

"I'm good, at least for the time being."

"I'm so relieved you're okay."

"Thanks. I had great support last night." Jenna told Patrice about the Millers and their mission of helping women in trouble. She described Emily's violent reaction after being plagued by the nightmare.

"Makes sense," Patrice said. "She was reliving the horror."

"The thing is—" Jenna hesitated "—she stole a gun from the couple here, and they might not be able to let her stay, especially if they have more guests arriving in the next few days. I don't suppose…?"

"You want me to ask the Guardians if they can help?"

"Would you?"

"I'd be happy to."

"Thank you so much. I'll get the number of the farm and you can speak with Nancy. I—" Jenna hesitated "—I don't know where we're going next or what kind of danger awaits us."

"Do you want to come stay at my place?"

Jenna couldn't rely on the Guardians forever. She needed to take care of herself at some point. "Thanks for the offer, but I'm with an FBI agent who is committed to helping me."

"And you trust him?"

"I'm working on it."

"I have faith in you."

Jenna wished she had that kind of faith in herself.

"I need to get Nancy's phone number. Hang on." Jenna went back into the kitchen and asked the Millers for the number of their landline.

"Better yet, let me speak with her." Nancy motioned for Ed to take over pancake duty.

"I'll go see if Tim and Miss Westbrook are staying for breakfast." Ed made a quick escape.

"It's just pancakes," Nancy called out with a smile, then turned to Jenna. "He's afraid we'll be eating hockey pucks for breakfast."

"I'll take over." Matt stood and went to flip pancakes.

Jenna handed Nancy the phone and sat next to Eli to keep him entertained.

"Hi, this is Nancy." Nancy went into the living room, leaving Jenna and Matthew alone with the little boy.

"You can cook?" Jenna said.

Matt glanced over his shoulder. "Got to. I'm single and can't stand fast food."

"That's rare—I mean a bachelor not liking fast food."

"Don't get me wrong. I like an occasional pizza or a burger. I guess I'm kind of a health nut though. The cheap and greasy fast food can be a killer." He hesitated before flipping the pancakes. "Sorry."

He was apologizing for mentioning death by junk food, as anyone might in a normal conversation.

"You *will* be sorry if you don't get this guy a

pancake pretty soon," Jenna said to lighten the mood. "He's almost done with his milk."

"We'll hit the store this morning before we leave town," Matt said. "He probably needs more formula, and I could use some clothes."

"We're not staying, even for one more night, are we?"

"Do you like it here?"

"Yeah. It feels normal, maybe even…safe."

Matthew chuckled as he turned to her. "You're the only civilian I know who gets threatened by a crazed woman with a gun in the middle of the night, and that feels safe."

"You know what I mean. The other parts, the Millers, this." She motioned to him, then reached out and stroked Eli's arm.

"It does, doesn't it?" he said softly. "Feel normal."

She couldn't rip her gaze away from his intense blue eyes. Her heartbeat sped up. What was happening here?

"May I ask you something?" he said cautiously.

"Sure."

"Aren't you worried about your ex-husband coming after you?"

The mention of her abuser shattered the tender moment.

"No, the group that helped me escape did a good job of covering my tracks."

"But guys like that don't tend to give up."

"He's in jail," she said. "After he put me in the hospital, I decided to press charges. Besides, my friend made me learn how to shoot."

"Yet you threw my firearm into the snow at the truck stop and tossed Ed's gun last night."

"I know how to handle a gun, but I don't relish the thought of shooting someone."

A few moments of silence passed, then he said, "I hope you never have to."

There he was, that gentle man again, offering comfort and compassion.

It made her uneasy.

"Bah!" Eli tossed his bear and it slid across the kitchen table.

"Someone's getting restless," she said, thankful for the interruption. She didn't like talking about Anthony, or the deal she'd agreed to in order to extricate herself from his life.

Matt flipped the pancakes. "I'd better make another pot of coffee too."

"Can I help?"

"Nope, I'm good."

Yes, he certainly was, she mused as she watched this broad-shouldered man move around the kitchen with ease.

But this pleasant scenario wasn't real, and she didn't know Matthew well enough to conclude he was a good man.

As he went to work on the coffee, she took a long, deep breath and enjoyed the scene a moment longer: a kind man cooking breakfast for Jenna and a child. She closed her eyes briefly, and the sweet smells and comforting sounds of a loving kitchen filled her senses with peace.

The coffee maker ground the beans, shattering the moment with a memory she thought she'd buried years ago.

Anthony's irrational rage and hateful words.

Fresh coffee—what does it take to make a fresh pot of coffee?

He'd hurled the glass pot across the room. Jenna ducked. The pot crashed against the wall, shattering into pieces.

Get down on your knees and clean that up!

She turned toward the closet.

What are you doing!

I'm getting the broom.

Clean it up with your hands.

But, Anthony…

He came at her, eyes blazing fire—

"Jenna?"

She glanced at Matthew, who stood only a few inches away. He narrowed his eyes as if deciding what to say. He was an intuitive man, and he knew she'd just been someplace else.

That dark place.

"Two pancakes or three?" he said.

Good, he wasn't going to ask her to explain her sudden mood shift.

"Go ahead and put three on a plate and I'll share with Eli," she said.

"Sounds good." When he didn't immediately turn away, she refocused her attention on Eli.

The longer she and Matthew made eye contact, the more likely he'd ask questions about her past, and she'd eventually open up to him. Yet she didn't want to. Sharing too much information could be dangerous, on many levels.

Ed joined them in the kitchen. "You made fresh coffee. Thanks."

"So, a couple dozen pancakes?" Matt said.

"Yep, I think I convinced them to stay for breakfast."

"Is Emily still asleep?" Jenna asked.

"Just woke up. She kept apologizing, begging me to let her stay. Poor kid."

Nancy came into the kitchen and hung up the phone. "What a nice lady," she said to Jenna.

"Patrice is the best."

"I think Gloria's Guardians could be a good option if Emily doesn't stay here."

Jenna cringed slightly at the use of the group's official name in front of Matthew, but he seemed to be conversing with Ed about how to make the perfect pancake.

"Ma!" Eli shouted, tapping his fingers to his lips.

"What a silly fellow," Nancy said.

"That's sign language for eat." Jenna had seen Chloe communicate with her son using basic sign language.

"Sign language? Isn't that something," Nancy said. "How long are you two staying?"

"I figured we'd leave after breakfast," Matthew said.

"Better yet, let us take care of Eli while you shop for supplies. You certainly don't want a toddler underfoot while you're at the store."

Matthew slid a plate of pancakes in front of Jenna. "Are you comfortable with that?"

Putting her hands together in a hopeful pose, Nancy smiled at Jenna.

"The two of us would be less noticeable without Eli," Matt suggested.

"The little guy's safe here," Ed said. "And we don't have any guests coming for a couple of days."

"He'll take a midmorning nap while you're away," Nancy said. "That way he'll be refreshed for the next leg of your journey."

Jenna wasn't sure what to do. She'd promised Chloe she'd take care of Eli, and she'd done a good job so far. Could she risk leaving him at the farm for an hour or two?

"There is no wrong answer," Matthew said.

She glanced at Eli, who was savoring the pancakes he shoved into his mouth with his little hands. Who better to take care of him for a few hours than a grandmother who acted as a host for abused women?

The little boy might very well be on the run with Jenna and Matt for days, weeks even. Didn't he deserve a little normalcy?

Then she remembered Patrice's hope that someday Jenna would choose to make decisions from a place of love, not fear.

"We'll take him with us," Matt said.

"No." Jenna glanced into his blue eyes. "It's okay. He can stay with Nancy and Ed."

"Hallelujah," Nancy said, humming through the kitchen and pouring more batter onto the hot griddle.

Jenna smiled at little Eli, whose eyes widened with delight at biting into a juicy blueberry.

Matthew placed a gentle hand on Jenna's shoulder. Welcoming the gesture, she realized she was starting to feel comfort from his touch.

After breakfast they waited in the guest room for Emily, the counselor and the off-duty officer to leave. Matthew said the fewer people who knew that he, Jenna and Eli were at the Millers', the better.

Jenna settled herself on the floor to play with the little boy. Matthew joined them, pressing noise-making buttons on a fire truck, to Eli's delight. Once again, Jenna was lulled into the mirage of a happy family.

"Jenna?" Matthew said.

She looked at him.

"You okay?" he asked.

"Sure, why?"

"Your expression changed."

And he was way too intuitive. "I'm okay." She grabbed a foam ball. "Eli, look!"

Eli spun around and she tossed him the ball.

He caught it and toddled across the room. He tripped on a block and tumbled forward.

Jenna dove to catch him, but was a second too late. He hit his head on the window ledge and started to whimper. "Ow-ee."

She hugged him and grabbed his bear. "You're okay, little boy. I'll fix the ow-ee." She kissed his forehead.

"Bubba's gonna give you a kiss too." Matthew nuzzled the boy's cheek with the bear, and whimpers quickly turned into giggles.

"Good save," she said.

He winked at her.

The echo of voices drifted through the door. Jenna tipped her head and could hear Emily's voice. She was crying, begging for forgiveness.

Jenna sighed and hoped Gloria's Guardians could help the young woman.

Eli suddenly wound up and tossed the foam ball at Matthew's face.

"Oh, yeah?" Matthew said in a silly voice.

The little boy charged. Matthew caught him and gave him a big hug.

"You ever think about having children?" Jenna asked.

"Nah, not with my hours."

What a shame, because he was a natural with Eli.

Nancy tapped on the door and cracked it open. "Everyone's gone. How's the little guy doing?"

"Back and forth between high octane and wanting a nap," Matthew said, standing up.

"Why don't you two get going? Ed and I will take care of Eli's every need."

Half an hour later, Jenna and Matt were at the Super Store in town, picking out supplies. She felt so relieved that Eli hadn't put up a fuss when they'd left him behind. Of course it helped that Ed was playing Legos with the little boy, distracting him so she and Matthew could leave unnoticed. They decided to take Ed's truck as a precaution.

Jenna's goal was to purchase clothes, baby supplies and snacks. She wasn't stressed about Eli because she'd made the decision to leave him with the Millers from a place of love for the child, not fear of danger.

Once the cart was filled with baby items—formula, diapers, baby wipes, backup pacifiers and clothes—she found hair color and then went to the women's clothing section. She was especially excited to find the baby carrier Patrice had mentioned. It would allow Jenna to conveniently strap Eli to her body. Matthew stayed close, acting the role of supportive husband and doting dad.

"Blond, huh?" he said, analyzing the box of color while she sifted through a rack of shirts.

"What's wrong with blond?"

"Seems kind of harsh for such a pretty face."

She snapped her attention to him.

"Sorry, that just came out." He tossed the box into the cart and glanced at her. "You're blushing?"

"I've had three compliments today. A world record for me."

"You deserve more than three a day," he said with a slight smile.

She broke eye contact, unnerved by the tender moment. "You're trying to make me blush again."

"What's that about?" he said.

"I'm not used to getting compliments, so I blush." She furiously searched the rack. "It's embarrassing, but—"

Her words caught in her throat because he'd interlaced his fingers with hers. It was such an intimate connection. She glanced at his concerned expression.

"Come with me. Leave the cart," he said.

She followed his instruction, still processing the physical contact.

As he led her through the women's clothing section toward the back of the store, she studied the hard set to his jaw and his pursed lips.

"What's going on?" she said.

"I think they found us."

"*They* as in Billings's men?" She squeezed his hand for strength.

He squeezed back, but didn't look at her. Matthew led her through an employees-only door. Where was he taking her?

He pulled her into the stockroom, where rows of consumer goods were stacked high up to the ceiling.

"Matthew—"

"Shh." He guided her into a small alcove with boxes on either side of them. "I need you to trust me on this."

And he kissed her.

Chapter Six

"Hey, what are you…? Uh, disgusting," someone said behind them.

Matt had seen a teenager turn the corner up ahead, eyeing his phone. Knowing the kid would be able to identify him and Jenna, Matt did the only thing he could think of.

He kissed Jenna North.

Breaking the kiss, he whispered, "Sorry," against her ear.

Matt held on to her as he listened intently to the sounds in the warehouse, waiting until he was sure the teen had passed by and they were safe.

Then again, would the kid run off and tell security he saw two customers necking in the stockroom?

"What…what just happened?" she said.

"I saw a security guard leading a cop in our direction. We needed to disappear."

"But you kissed me."

"A teenager was about to spot us."

Poking his head around the corner, Matt saw the cop and security guard walking in the opposite direction. Matt needed to get Jenna out of here. He handed her the truck keys, but she put up her hands to refuse them.

"Jenna, you haven't changed your hair color. You'll be easily recognizable. Take Ed's truck. Get to the farm. If I'm not back in an hour, take off."

"What are you going to do?"

"Distract them so you can get away."

"I'm not leaving."

He looked into her green eyes. "You are, and you know why?"

She shook her head.

"Because Eli needs you. I can take care of myself. Now go." He motioned to the dock where they unloaded goods.

With a reluctant sigh, she glanced both ways and took off toward the exit. As she approached the door, she shot him a quick glance before disappearing into the sunshine.

Sudden regret knotted in his gut. What if this cop was dirty and there were men waiting for her outside? Matt started to follow her.

"Stop right there," a male voice ordered.

Matt slowly turned around.

The store security guard and police officer approached him.

"I was looking for the bathroom, sorry," Matt said.

"Yeah, right," the security guard, who appeared to be in his midtwenties, said. The cop was older, but not by much.

"Are you alone?" the police officer said.

"Yes, sir." Because he was. At this moment anyway.

"Let's go." The cop, whose badge read Richter, pulled cuffs off his belt. The hair pricked on the back of Matt's neck. Really? Officer Richter was cuffing Matt for trespassing in the stock area?

"He's gotta be a part of the crew," the guard said.

"Crew?" Matt asked.

"Save it," the guard said. "You're done stealing from us."

What had Matt walked into?

"Come on." Richter motioned to him.

Matt didn't resist, not wanting to make a scene, and offered his wrists. The cop snapped the cuffs in place and led him through the store to the public exit. Heat rushed to Matt's cheeks at the shameful march past young mothers who held their children close, and employees taking pictures with smartphones.

Great. Now his face would be plastered all over the internet, making him an easy target. Yep, it had been a good decision to separate from Jenna.

But was she safe?

Once outside, he glanced toward the spot where the truck had been parked. It was gone. He sighed with relief.

Then he scanned the lot and caught sight of it, the window down, Jenna watching as Matt was led to the cruiser. He shook his head slightly, warning her to keep her distance.

Officer Richter put Matt in the back seat and shut the door. He stood outside the car and called in on his shoulder radio. A good thing, since Matt could use a few minutes to strategize.

At first he'd thought this was related to the money-laundering case, but when the security guard accused Matt of stealing, he realized this was more likely a wrong-place, wrong-time situation. Talk about bad timing.

Didn't matter. He had to talk his way out of this and get back to Jenna.

He'd promised to protect her and Eli, and he would fulfill that promise.

He debated what and how much to tell Officer Richter. Should he admit he was FBI? Continue his role as Matthew the janitor? Maybe a little of both? If he told this police officer he was undercover, maybe he could enlist his help in fleeing the county.

Not likely. Billings would probably reach out to cops statewide, making up some story about the janitor and the child kidnapper, Jenna North.

It had been a wise move to send Jenna away. Matt strained to look out the window. The truck was nowhere in sight.

Leaning back against the seat, Matt planned out his next steps. He'd tell Richter that he was undercover FBI, but couldn't share specifics of his case.

The door opened and Officer Richter got behind the wheel of the cruiser.

"Officer, I need to tell you something," Matt started.

"No, you don't. You have the right to remain silent…"

Jenna paced the Millers' kitchen, anxiously twirling her silver ring. She wrestled with panic that taunted her thoughts.

More than two hours had passed, and still no word from Matt.

"Jenna, please relax," Nancy said, sitting at the kitchen table.

"I'm trying," Jenna said, unable to stop her anxious pace.

Eli was still napping, and the bottle was warming for when he awakened. Ed had gone back to the Super Store, and Jenna had given him her emergency cash to purchase the items she'd left in the cart.

"It was a misunderstanding," Nancy said. "They'll figure it out."

"We should have heard something by now." Jenna stopped and looked at Nancy. "He told me to leave if he wasn't back in an hour but… but I can't bring myself to abandon him."

"You care about Matt," the woman said in a knowing voice.

The memory of their kiss made Jenna's lips tingle all over again. It had been years since she'd let a man kiss her.

Years since she actually enjoyed kissing a man back.

That hadn't been a real kiss, she reminded herself. It was a maneuver to keep them out of danger.

"He's a good man. I can see why you've fallen for him," Nancy said.

Jenna felt the need to correct her. "It's not like that. He's helped me so much. I owe it to him not to leave him behind."

"You may stay here as long as you like. However, we do have new guests coming in forty-eight hours, which means more people will know your whereabouts."

"True," Jenna said.

"Matt explained your situation, how people are looking for you and that law enforcement from Cedar River are involved in something nefarious."

"He told you what happened to Eli's mother?"

"Yes." Nancy patted the table. "Please, sit with me."

Jenna collapsed in a kitchen chair. Nancy put her hands together and whispered something under her breath. For once, Jenna wished she could join her in prayer, wished she knew the right words to ask for help, to beg for Matthew's safety.

"Amen," Nancy whispered and smiled at Jenna. "Do you pray, Jenna?"

"No."

"Why not?"

Jenna shrugged. A few seconds passed.

"Why do you pray?" Jenna asked.

"Because surrendering my worries to God gives me such peace. After all, God does not want us to worry."

"How do you know that?"

"In Philippians it reads, 'Be careful for nothing; but in every thing by prayer and supplication with thanksgiving let your requests be made known unto God.'"

The woman's faith was so pure, so sincere. If only Jenna could feel the same way about God—but He'd abandoned her far too many times for Jenna to have faith.

"Why are you afraid to pray?" Nancy asked.

"He'll just ignore me again."

"Are you sure He's been ignoring you? Maybe you didn't see the blessing."

"I lost my baby because of an abusive husband," Jenna said flatly.

"Oh, honey, I'm sorry." Nancy leaned over and gave her a hug.

A tear trailed down Jenna's cheek.

No, she couldn't afford to cry. Tears meant weakness.

Jenna broke the embrace and stood. "I'd better pack. When Ed gets home with the supplies,

I had better leave. That's what Matthew would want me to do, to keep moving."

"How about I put together some food for you and Eli?" Nancy stood and went to gather supplies.

She didn't seem offended in the least that Jenna had brushed her off and shut down the conversation about God and prayer.

"That would be great, thanks," Jenna said. "I'll help."

Because she had to do something to keep busy until she left. The not knowing, the worrying about Matthew, was tearing her up inside.

Please, God…

She caught herself reaching out to the Lord and quickly pulled the thought back. Being around the Millers must be affecting her better judgment.

"Oh, here comes Ed," Nancy said, peering out the window. "And a police car. That's curious."

Jenna rushed to the window and spotted the Millers' truck, followed by a police car.

"I'll wait in Eli's room until you tell me it's safe." Jenna grabbed the bottle.

Nancy turned to her. "Oh, okay."

It must not have occurred to Nancy that the

police car could be here for Jenna, that somehow Billings's men had found her.

She rushed into the guest room, and shut and
locked the door. Heart racing, she scanned the
room for options. Didn't make sense to climb
out the window with Eli. She wouldn't get far
in the snow.

If he can't find you, he can't hurt you.

Jenna scooped Eli out of the crib. The little
boy fussed a little, but not much. She went into
the oversize closet and shut the door. Eli started
to squirm so she offered him the bottle.

She struggled to calm her frantic thoughts.
What if this was it? What if the police were
here to take Eli back to his father and arrest
Jenna for kidnapping? Jenna scolded herself for
not getting something in writing from Chloe
about her wishes that Jenna be Eli's guardian.
But Jenna hadn't sensed the danger was immediate, that she would, in fact, find herself Eli's
guardian within minutes of her conversation
with Chloe.

And here Jenna was, cornered again. Hiding. Terrified.

No, she counseled herself. Nancy and Ed
would surely protect her and Eli.

They'd do their best, sure, but they wouldn't break the law. They were good people.

She was alone. With danger hovering in the next room.

"It's locked," a muted male voice echoed from the next room.

They were here. They were going to break into the bedroom and find her.

Hugging Eli, she whispered, "I won't let them hurt you."

Seconds stretched by. Then minutes. It felt like forever.

Three soft taps vibrated against the closet door. She bit back a soft gasp.

"Jenna?"

The closet door opened, and Matthew's silhouette hovered above her.

"What are you guys doin' in there?" he asked. "Playing hide-and-seek?"

Eli kicked his feet with delight.

"I thought… I wasn't sure…" was all Jenna could get out.

"It's safe. You can come out."

She didn't move, still processing his words.

"Here, I'll take Eli," he said.

She clung tighter to the child.

It's safe.

She knew better. It was never safe.

Her body started trembling uncontrollably, and she wasn't sure why. It felt like her mind had shut down and the rest of her was in survival mode.

"You wanna know what happened after you left?" Matthew said, sitting on the floor beside the closet. "First, I was handcuffed and marched through the store like a criminal. I guess I can say I know how *that* feels now. Then the local cop starts to read me my rights, even though I'm trying to explain that I'm FBI. Figured that might earn me a get-out-of-jail-free card. He wasn't buying it. Apparently I fit the description of a guy they think is behind a theft ring at multiple retail stores. You know, tall, dark and handsome with a charming personality. What do you think? Does that pretty much describe me?"

Jenna glanced at him. Handsome? Yes, he was handsome.

He was also smiling. Smiling?

"Everything's...okay?" she said. He wouldn't be smiling if it weren't.

"It's all good."

"But...you were arrested?"

"Taken in for questioning. Eventually managed to convince the local police I'm FBI. It helped that Ed showed up to confirm my identity and that I've got history with Millers' farm. I explained that a case drew me to the Super Store and I was following someone when they found me in the back. Said I'm undercover and wanted to keep it that way, which is why I didn't reveal my identity to the security guard."

"They released you?"

"They did, and everything is A-okay."

They weren't coming to take Eli away.

They weren't going to lock Jenna up.

She took a breath. "I wasn't sure I'd ever see you again." It suddenly hit her how much she'd miss his company, his strength, maybe even… his faith.

"You know I'll always do my best to get to you," he said.

She nodded.

"I made you a promise, Jenna."

"Yes, you did."

"Come on out, sweetheart. It's all good, for now."

At first Matt didn't think he'd be able to coax her out of the closet. He recognized that look on her face. He'd seen it before, both on abused victims...

And on Jenna.

This remarkable woman, determined to protect her friend's child, still struggled with post-trauma issues.

Being thrown into this dangerous situation as Eli's guardian was definitely not helping. He wondered what would help.

She was out of the closet, but chose to stay in the bedroom, while Matt joined the others in the kitchen. He could hardly blame her, considering Officer Richter's presence. The fewer people who knew her whereabouts, the better.

It had been Ed's idea to invite the cop to the farm as a gesture of thanks for contacting Matt's supervisor to confirm his identity instead of locking Matt in a cell.

As Ed and Nancy chatted with Officer Richter about town happenings, Matt excused himself to call his boss. He stepped out onto the front porch.

"Pragge," he answered.

"It's Weller. Thank you for clearing things up with the local PD."

"You're welcome. You on your way back to Cedar River?"

"Not yet, sir. I won't leave Jenna and the child until I'm confident they're safe."

"I'll send an agent right away."

Something told Matt that she wouldn't be safe with just any agent.

"We tried that before at the hospital, and one of Billings's men showed up."

"What are you insinuating?"

"I don't believe in coincidences, not where criminals are concerned."

"They were probably listening to the police scanner. You said a trooper escorted you to the hospital?"

"Yes, sir."

"Then that's how they knew."

"I'm not convinced."

"We need you back at the community center."

"Sir, instinct tells me the Jenna North situation is related to the money-laundering case. Give me a few days to prove it. I'll call my boss at the center and say I need a few days off."

Silence, then: "You've got forty-eight hours."

Pragge ended the call. Matt heard the inference behind the order—if he didn't return to his post in forty-eight hours, his career with the FBI would be in serious jeopardy, if not immediately over.

He rolled his neck and called Mrs. Harris at the community center, leaving a message that he had an emergency and needed to take some personal time.

Two days. He had two days to figure this out.

He went back into the house and joined Ed, Nancy and Officer Richter in the kitchen.

"Want a warm–up, Matt?" Nancy started to get up from the kitchen table.

"I've got it, thanks." Matt refreshed his mug of coffee.

"Officer Richter joined our local police department six months ago from…?" Nancy glanced at the cop.

"Seattle," Richter answered.

"How are you liking it so far?" Ed asked.

"A lot more snow than I'm used to."

"Yes, but not as much rain," Ed offered.

"I don't mind the rain." Officer Richter turned to Matt. "How long have you been with the FBI?"

"Ten years."

"Your supervisor sounds like a tough guy."

"He's feeling a lot of pressure to close a case."

The cop finished his coffee and placed his mug in the sink. "Well, let me know if there's anything I can do to help." He handed Matt a business card. "Sorry about bringing you in."

"You were doing your job." Matt tucked the guy's card in his shirt pocket.

"Ed, Nancy, thanks for the coffee." With a polite nod, Officer Richter left.

"Such a nice young man," Nancy said.

Matt went to the window and watched him pull away. "I'd better pack up. Ed—" he turned "—what do I owe you for the supplies?"

"Nothing. Jenna gave me a bunch of cash. Here's the change."

Matt took the money. Old habits die hard, he thought. He assumed she kept a wad of cash handy in case she needed to make a quick escape.

"I wish you could stay a few days," Nancy said. "We love having Eli, and I think Jenna could use a little TLP."

"You mean TLC?" Matt said.

"No, I mean TLP. Tender loving prayer." Nancy winked.

"That she could, but it's better if we keep moving. You may like Officer Richter, but he might innocently mention my presence to a coworker and word could spread. I'm not sure who to trust."

"Even on the police force?" Ed said.

"Even on the force."

"Okay, well, I'll bring the shopping bags in from the truck." Ed grabbed his coat off the rack.

"And I'll organize them for you," Nancy offered.

"I can't thank you guys enough," Matt said.

Going back to the guest room, Matt hoped and prayed that Jenna was okay. A cold chill had rushed through him earlier when he'd opened the door to an empty room. The thought that she'd been taken…

But she hadn't been kidnapped. She was huddled in the closet, clutching the little boy in her arms. Matt fought the urge to kneel down and pull her into his arms, to hold her until she no longer trembled with fear.

He knew Jenna had to come out of her traumatic moment on her own, by her own will and strength. That was the best way for someone with an emotional wound like that to heal.

And that's what he wanted for the lovely Jenna North—he wanted her to heal and be at peace.

To feel safe.

The only way to accomplish that was to stay

with her and protect her, because he wouldn't abandon someone he cared about.

He...cared about her?

You're never here. Your job is more important than our relationship.

Sarah's words taunted him, reminding him how he'd failed, and how that failure led to her senseless death. He'd prayed to God to forgive him for not being there for Sarah, for not making her a priority. He wouldn't make that mistake again.

Jenna would not die because Matt was distracted by his job. Somehow he had to protect Jenna *and* satisfy his boss. Time to take the offense and determine a connection between the money-laundering case and Chloe McFadden's murder, because his gut was screaming that they were connected.

He tapped on the bedroom door. "It's Matt."

"Come in," she called.

He opened the door and hesitated, appreciating the sight before him. Jenna sat on the floor helping Eli make a tower of wooden blocks. Matt's heart warmed.

Would he ever come home to this sight? Would he be able to find balance in his life, to draw the boundary that would allow him to be a good agent and also have a family?

"Look what Eli made," she said.

The little boy grinned, a twinkle in his eye. What a resilient kid. With a firm grip on his white polar bear, he swung at the tower of blocks and they crashed to the floor.

He dove at Jenna and she caught him in her arms. "What a silly boy."

She tickled his ribs, and he giggled through the pacifier clutched between his teeth. Rocking the little boy with ease, she glanced at Matt.

Oh, she'd recovered all right. It seemed that she, too, was resilient.

"Is the police officer gone?" she asked.

"He is."

"I'm glad your supervisor vouched for you."

"He did, but I got an earful."

"About?"

"He's cranky that I'm not back at the community center sweeping floors."

"Oh, right." She hesitated. "Your crucial undercover assignment."

"Protecting you is just as crucial, Jenna. Come on, we'd better get going."

"Do I have time to change my hair color?"

"How long do you need?"

"Probably an hour."

"That'll work. Will give me time to do a little digging. Ed has offered to swap trucks temporarily."

"Sounds good. You think Nancy can watch Eli while I do my hair?"

"I think she'd be offended if you didn't ask. She's going to miss him when we leave."

Jenna nuzzled Eli's hair. "Hear that? Everyone loves you."

She was right. And Matt topped that list. Who wouldn't love a sweet little boy with an infectious giggle and full-cheeked grin?

Matt's phone vibrated and he glanced at the screen. "Blocked number," he said.

"Maybe it's Marcus."

He didn't miss the hope in her voice. "Hello?" Matt answered.

"Is Jenna there?"

"Who's calling?"

"Marcus, Chloe's cousin."

"Hang on." Matthew handed her the phone.

"Hello?… Yes, oh, thank you so much for calling back. Chloe gave me your contact information… I'd rather not say over the phone, but Chloe was confident that you could help us."

Matthew fisted his hand, not wanting to pass off Jenna and Eli to a stranger.

"What's the address?... Sure, text it to this number," she said into the phone. "I'm not sure, maybe a few hours. I must warn you, it's dangerous."

Then she actually smiled.

"Oh, that's good to know. Thanks." With a sigh, she handed Matt the phone.

"You look happy," he said.

"I can see why Chloe wanted me to find Marcus. He's a former Navy SEAL who works in private security. His cabin is a little over three hours away. He gave me the access code and said he'd meet us later."

"He's not there?"

"No, he's on his way back from a job. He'll arrive tonight. His neighbor plows the drive for him when he's out of town so he said we should be fine."

"I'll do a background check on Marcus, just to be safe."

"Hopefully by tomorrow you'll be able to hand me off and focus on your real job."

He nodded in response. He should be pleased with the development. Instead, a flash of dread ripped through him. Would he really be able to leave the fragile Jenna North in the hands of a stranger?

While Matt waited at the kitchen table for Jenna, he called his good friend Agent Bob Barnes at the Bureau to do the background check on Marcus. Matt trusted Bob probably even more than his own boss at this point.

"What's got Pragge all worked up?" Bob asked.

"I called an audible."

"And you need me to catch the pass?"

"Something like that. Can you do a background check on Marcus Garcia, former Navy SEAL?"

"Sure, no problem. What about your current assignment?"

"This is related to the money-laundering case."

"Then why is Pragge snapping everyone's heads off?"

"I haven't convinced him of the connection yet. I might need your help with that too."

"You're gonna owe me."

"All-you-can-eat pizza at Marietti's?" Matt offered.

"Deal. I'll get working on this."

"Thanks, man, appreciate it."

"You're welcome. Be careful."

Matt studied his phone, hoping he'd made the right decision, that he hadn't exposed himself and Jenna to more danger by involving Bob. But Matt trusted Bob, especially after everything he'd done to support Matt after Sarah's death.

Bob had listened to and challenged Matt about his self-blame.

You didn't put her in the car. You didn't speed through town during a snowstorm.

No, but their argument had caused Sarah to tear off, wanting to get away from Matt as quickly as possible.

"Hey," Jenna said.

Matt noticed her standing in the doorway, but didn't respond right away. His mind was stuck in the past.

"That bad, huh?" She fingered her blond hair.

"No, sorry. I was distracted. It looks good."

"Thanks, but I know it's kinda harsh."

"Not harsh. Different, but you could never look harsh."

A smile tugged at the corner of her lips, and she glanced at the floor. Pink crept up her cheeks.

She looked adorable.

That's when it hit Matt that handing her off to a Navy SEAL who didn't have an emotional connection to Jenna might be the best way to keep her safe, because if Matt didn't watch it, the line between protector and love interest might not only blur, but could disappear completely.

How was that possible? After Sarah's death he'd made himself a promise not to get emotionally involved until he took a less demanding role with the agency.

"You okay?" She studied him as if trying to read his mind.

"Sure, we're packed and ready to go."

Matthew seemed oddly quiet during the drive to Marcus's cabin. At first Jenna thought he might be concerned about the intense snow falling across the Montana countryside, but then she sensed it was something else. His silence worried her.

"Did you find out anything about the case? Or about Marcus?" she asked.

"Marcus is clean."

"Oh, that's a relief. What about the case?"

"Nothing new. I'm limited as to how much I can do remotely."

She wondered if he regretted leaving his post at the community center to protect Jenna and Eli.

"Well, it won't be for much longer," she said. "Once we find Marcus, you can get back to Cedar River."

He didn't answer, not even a nod or grunt.

Then she had another thought: maybe he didn't like the idea of abandoning her and Eli. Had he felt the same tug of intimacy toward her that she'd been feeling over the past twenty-four hours? She tried telling herself it was normal to feel so close to someone this quickly considering the circumstances. Patrice thought Jenna had been growing dependent on the attorney who took her case against Anthony, and she'd cautioned Jenna. But what she felt for the lawyer had been pure gratitude. She couldn't thank him enough for doing the work pro bono and extricating her from the abusive marriage.

The way she felt about Matthew seemed different, which didn't mean it was any more real than what she'd felt for her attorney. It was another form of gratitude, that's all.

Then why did his opinion of her blond hair matter so much?

Forget it, Jenna. This is not a real relationship.

In truth, she'd noticed Matthew the janitor months ago, noticed his kind demeanor, his natural way with kids when he told them to slow down as they raced through the community center.

"Where did you get that?"

His question startled her.

"I'm sorry?"

He nodded at the braided silver ring she twirled on her right hand. "You tend to play with your ring when you're thinking."

She eyed the piece of jewelry. "Patrice from Gloria's Guardians gave it to me."

He already knew the name of the group, so she didn't feel the need to keep it a secret any longer.

"The ring is a reminder that we're all connected, and they're always there for me, that God's always there," she said. "I wish I could believe that."

"Why can't you?"

She shook her head, feeling herself being pulled down that dark path.

"Look at the positive ways God has touched your life," Matthew said. "The women who helped you escape your abusive husband, and the fact you've been able to keep Eli safe. You've been through trauma in your marriage, but that trauma gave you strength to take care of little Eli."

"I suppose, but I just can't believe in God."

"You don't have to," he said. "God's always there, whether you believe in Him or not."

No, this was definitely not someone she could grow more attached to, not with his strength of faith. She glanced out the passenger window.

"I didn't mean to upset you," he said.

"You didn't." She turned to check on Eli, who slept peacefully in the back.

"He's blessed to have you in his life."

She snapped her attention to him. "I wouldn't say that."

"I would." He glanced at her.

Jenna's heartbeat sped up. She ripped her gaze from Matthew's assessing eyes and looked out the front window. In the distance she saw a small cabin, lit with a soft glow.

"That must be it," she said, thankful they were close.

"The lights are on. Maybe he beat us there."

"Actually, he said he'd turn the lights on remotely from his phone."

Matthew drove down the long, narrow driveway, somewhat plowed and bordered by a four-foot wall of snow on either side. "I'll leave the keys just in case."

"No," she said.

"Excuse me?"

"We're stronger together, Matt. Besides, it'll be safe. No one knows we're here except for Marcus."

"Perhaps, but I'm leaving the keys, for my peace of mind."

Matt continued around to the back of the property and parked next to three cars.

"He said he collected cars," she offered.

"Wait here."

He grabbed his gun from the glove box. Leaving the keys in the ignition, he got out of the truck and headed around to the front of the house.

When Matthew disappeared out of sight, Jenna turned her attention to Eli, who stirred behind her.

"Hey, little one. You awake?"

She climbed into the back seat and stroked his cheek, still thinking about Matthew's words, that Eli was blessed to have Jenna in his life.

Eli opened his eyes and kicked his feet, motioning to his mouth to indicate that he was hungry. She pulled a pack of fruit snacks out, something to keep him happy until they got inside. She wondered what was taking so long.

She glanced at the cabin. Through the falling snow she spotted Matthew stumbling around the corner motioning wildly.

Before she could comprehend what was happening, a man rushed Matthew from behind and tackled him.

Chapter Seven

They'd found her. How was that possible?

Jenna froze, unable to think, paralyzing fear shooting across her body to her fingertips.

She thought she'd conquered the fear after she'd left Anthony and relocated safely to Cedar River. If that were the case, she'd be taking the offensive right now instead of cowering in the back seat with a child who needed her protection.

Eli burst into wails, breaking the spell.

She climbed into the front seat and gripped the steering wheel with trembling hands.

"I can do this." She shoved the truck into gear and hit the gas. The back wheels spun, digging into the snow. The last thing she wanted was to get stuck.

She needed to calm down.

She didn't dare glance up again, didn't want the distraction. Matthew would tell her to put Eli first, to flee, escape.

Taking a deep breath, she touched the gas pedal, more gently this time. Anthony rarely let her drive, always criticizing her for not signaling properly or for riding the brake.

What, are you stupid?

"No, Anthony, I'm not stupid," she ground out.

Clenching her jaw, she grew even more determined and pulled away. When the wheels started to lose their grip she eased up on the gas.

The truck was moving, slowly, but it was moving. Once she felt the wheels grip the snow, she increased pressure on the accelerator, eyes locked on the main road in the distance. Snow started blowing sideways, the storm intensifying, making it a challenge to see. She flicked on the wipers.

A gunshot echoed across the property.

She shrieked, instinctively ducked and picked up speed.

She was done being afraid. Always on edge. She was a fighter.

Faster, she had to go faster.

Another gunshot rang out. The truck jerked left. The bullet must have hit her back tire.

She struggled to regain control. Gripped the wheel. How far could she drive with a flat tire?

Please, God, help me.

She'd do what was necessary to protect Eli, what she hadn't been able to do for Joey.

A third shot pierced the night air.

She jerked the wheel. Left, right. She had to get control.

The truck jettisoned forward into a snow-bank. The momentum snapped her forward, and her head banged against the steering wheel.

Stars flashed across her vision.

Matt pulled on the metal handcuffs binding his wrists, his arms wrapped around a wooden support beam. His attacker had gotten Matt in a choke hold, applied enough pressure to make Matt pass out, then dragged him in here.

The guy only got the advantage because Matt needed to warn Jenna about the danger—the assailant who'd jumped Matt inside the cabin.

All was eerily quiet outside. Jenna had to have gotten away, right? Or else the guy had found her and Eli, taken them...

He pulled violently on the cuffs, panic eating away at his insides. He almost lost it, and he cried out to God, begging for help.

No, she'd be okay. She had to be. He wouldn't accept the alternative. Although still traumatized by her past, Jenna was a strong woman determined to save the little boy's life.

Nothing would stop her.

Matt scanned the room for a way to free himself. Who was this guy anyway? He must be working for Billings, although why not send the two men who'd assaulted Matt at the truck stop?

Bigger question: How had Jenna and Matt been tracked to Marcus's place?

No one knew they were coming here except for Marcus, and his background check had come up clean.

Agent Bob Barnes confirmed that Marcus was a decorated former SEAL who'd gone into private security work.

A gunshot rang out in the distance.

Then the wail of a car horn.

"No." He pulled more vehemently on his cuffs, panic, rage and desperation rushing his body.

He had to get it together, had to calm down so he could think.

Minutes ticked by slowly, painfully, as his imagination sucked him into the dark place, a familiar place.

Unable to stop her, to save her.

Hearing how they'd had to cut her out of the crumpled car.

Her dead body.

Guilt sliced through him. His fault; it had been his fault. Just like whatever was happening to Jenna out there was also his fault.

He yanked on the cuffs, the metal scraping his skin, his wrists starting to bleed. Intellectually he knew this was not helping, but his panic was stronger than his intellect.

A passage in the Bible came to mind—*Casting all your care upon Him; for He careth for you.*

It was worth a try. Repeating the verse from the Book of Peter, Matt took a deep breath and closed his eyes, forgiving himself for allowing the current situation to get so out of control. Forgiving himself for losing his advantage…

For the fact that he might lose Jenna.

No, he wouldn't allow that thought to torture him.

Repeating the Bible verse over and over, he continued to scan the room for something to use on the handcuffs.

The cabin door opened.

His attacker entered the cabin, carrying a crying Eli in the car seat.

"Where's Jenna?" Matt demanded.

Without a word, the guy placed the car seat by the sofa and went back outside.

She had to still be alive.

He wasn't sure he could survive the alternative.

Eli started wailing and kicking his feet.

"Hey, Eli," Matt said.

His little arms punched the air. The boy wanted out of his car seat, probably needed a diaper change and he was no doubt hungry too.

"It'll be okay, buddy," he offered. Matt remembered how Jenna had sung to him in the truck. He softly sang a favorite country ballad, and the little boy's eyes widened at the sound of Matt's deep voice. What Eli really needed was his pacifier, his little white bear.

A hug from Jenna.

A few minutes later the door opened again, and the bearded guy stormed inside.

Carrying Jenna over his shoulder.

Matt automatically fisted his hands. "What happened?"

The assailant dropped Jenna on the sofa and went to look out the window. Even from here, Matt could tell the snowfall had turned into a blizzard.

"Is she okay?" Matt demanded. He couldn't

see her well enough to determine her injuries, but thought he saw a smudge of blood on her cheek. "Well, is she?"

"She's unconscious."

"But is she okay?"

"How would I know?" the assailant shouted and glared at Matt. "I'm not a doctor."

Upset by the guy's tone of voice, Eli burst into another round of wails.

The guy snapped his attention to the little boy. With narrowed eyes and a firm set to his lips, he took a step closer to Eli.

"I can calm him down," Matt offered.

The man took another step toward Eli.

"Try giving him the Binky," Matt said.

"I don't do kids."

"I practically raised my nephew. They call me the baby whisperer."

The guy glanced from Matt to Eli, considering.

"Look, you've got the gun," Matt said.

"That's right, I do." The assailant slowly turned and went to the sofa. Hovering over Jenna's unconscious body, he pressed the gun barrel against her head. "I would have no problem pulling the trigger on this one."

Matt fisted his hands. "I understand."

The guy trailed the tip of the gun against her hairline, as if caressing her, toying with her. Matt clenched his jaw so tight he thought it might snap.

Eli's sobs grew louder, more insistent.

"The baby?" Matt prompted.

Casting one last, sinister smile at Jenna, the man crossed the room. He pulled a small key out of his pocket and came up behind Matt, probably wanting to avoid a head butt or other aggressive move. Matt would never risk something like that until he was free of the cuffs.

The guy placed the metal key between Matt's fingers.

Then he stepped away, walking back to the sofa where he repositioned himself behind Jenna.

Matt unlocked the cuffs, stood and tossed them on the kitchen table. Rubbing his wrists, he went to Eli and kneeled. Inside his snowsuit he found the boy's pacifier hooked on a ribbon clipped to his overalls. "Here ya go, buddy." Matt popped it into Eli's mouth and unbuckled him.

"Leave him in the car seat," the guy ordered.

"Do you want him to stop crying or not?" Matt said.

The jerk raised an eyebrow and nodded at the gun aimed at Jenna.

"He won't stop crying unless I get him out of this wet diaper," Matt said.

The guy motioned toward the door where he'd dropped the diaper bag. Matt went to work by removing Eli's snowsuit and picking him up. "It's gonna be okay, buddy."

He grabbed the diaper bag on his way to the kitchen table, intensely aware of the gun pointed at Jenna's head.

The man made a phone call. "It's Veck. I need a pickup. My car's blocked. I'll text you the address... That's unacceptable." He glanced at Matt. "I've got them... No, I said ASAP... No guarantees." He hung up and texted something into his phone.

"What's this all about anyway?" Matt asked, unzipping the diaper bag and pulling out diapers and wipes. He'd continue to play the role of Matt the janitor and see how far that got him.

The bearded guy glanced briefly out the window.

"I never thought helping out a friend would be so dangerous," Matt said. "Any chance I'm gonna live through this?"

No answer. Matt lay Eli on the portable

changing pad and removed the boy's pants to get to work on the fresh diaper.

"I mean, what do you want from an innocent woman like Jenna?" Matt said.

"Innocent? She kidnapped a kid."

Good, at least Matt had gotten him talking. That was his goal, get him talking and make him see Matt, Jenna and Eli as human beings, not as an assignment.

"Eli's mother asked Jenna to protect him."

"This woman's unstable," the man said. "I've been hired to retrieve her and the child."

"Who hired you?"

"You ask a lotta questions."

Matt secured the new diaper in place. "Can you blame me? You choke me unconscious, handcuff me to a beam and now you're threatening to kill Jenna. All I did was help out a friend."

"This friend got you in a pile of trouble."

"Yeah, well, I'm guessing if you were going to kill us you would have done so by now."

"Don't test me."

Matt picked up the little boy and rocked from side to side to comfort him.

"Buh-buh," Eli said, with a whimper.

Matt spotted the white bear in his diaper bag.

"You want this?" He pulled it out and nuzzled it against the kid's cheek.

"He's quiet. Put him back in the car seat," the guy ordered.

"He'll just start wailing again." Matt rocked Eli and made his way across the cabin toward Jenna.

"Stay back." The guy aimed his gun at Matt and Eli.

Matt hesitated. "You seriously think I'm gonna pull a ninja move while holding this child? I want to check on Jenna."

"She's got a pulse."

Matt took a step closer and noticed redness forming below her eye and blood seeping from a cut above her hairline.

"You've seen her. Get back."

Matt did as ordered, considering his next move. With his thumb pressing against his fingertips, Eli tapped his mouth with a whimper. The little boy was hungry.

"Got you covered, big guy." Matt dug in the diaper bag and pulled out a multigrain bar, squeezable applesauce and crackers.

"Don't suppose you'd go get the cooler from the truck?" Matt asked the assailant.

The guy narrowed his eyes.

"Didn't think so." Matt put Eli down and opened the applesauce.

Thanks to the snacks, Eli wasn't fussing anymore. With wide eyes, he held the applesauce container and sucked it down.

"How much trouble did I get into by being a good friend?" Matt asked the guy.

The bearded man shook his head.

"That bad, huh?"

The guy shrugged.

"Can you at least tell me who's behind all this?"

"They need the kid. That's all I know."

But why? That's what Matt couldn't figure out.

"No, Joey, no," Jenna muttered, thrashing from side to side. "I can't... My baby," she groaned with an emotional intensity that ripped through Matt's chest.

"Joey...no!" She sat straight up, sobs racking her body.

"What's wrong with her?" the thug said.

Matt picked up Eli, who gripped the applesauce in one hand and his bear in the other. "Jenna, you had a nightmare," he said. "Open your eyes."

"My baby, he's gone... My baby," she cried,

rocking back and forth, while squeezing her head between her hands.

"Jenna, look at me." Matt kneeled beside her. He wasn't sure what was going on, but he had to shake her out of this devastating spin. "Sweetheart, open your eyes. Eli needs you."

"My baby?" she whispered.

"No, Eli, remember?" Matt encouraged.

With a half gasp, she looked at Eli, and her brows knit together in a confused frown.

"It's okay. We're all okay," Matt said.

She studied Eli as if she knew something was wrong, that he wasn't the child she'd cried out for, but couldn't make sense of who Eli was.

"Buh-buh." Eli reached out with his hand and tapped Jenna's nose with his bear.

"That's right, Eli, Bubba will make it better," Matt said.

Jenna blinked and a tear trailed down her cheek.

"It's okay," Matt said.

She shook her head and flopped back down on the sofa.

"That's it. Relax." He stroked her blond hair with one hand, while holding Eli with the other. A few minutes later her breathing slowed and she'd fallen back asleep.

Eli swung the bear at Jenna, but Matt caught it before it made contact. Rest was what she needed. The longer she slept, the longer she'd be at peace and not realize the severity of their situation.

He released Eli, who toddled across the cabin toward the kitchen. Matt followed him, baby-proofing along the way. His thoughts were absorbed with Jenna's desperate cry for Joey.

"What was that about?" the thug asked.

"Haven't a clue."

"Uh-huh. You called her *sweetheart*."

He couldn't help it; the endearment had slipped out. "So what's next?" Matt pressed.

"They're coming to get us." He shot a quick glance out the window at the intensifying snowstorm.

The weather would delay his associates' arrival, whoever they were, hopefully giving Matt time to figure out how to get the advantage over the assailant without putting Jenna and Eli at risk.

Yeah, and how was he going to do that? He suspected Jenna suffered from a concussion and that's what had caused her to confuse Eli with a child named Joey. She was so vulnerable, to both her past and the cruelty of the man standing behind her. Matt clenched his jaw against the anger eating him up inside.

Crazed emotions weren't going to save them from this mercenary. Matt had to push his worry aside and come up with a plan.

Casting all your care upon Him; for He careth for you.

A few hours later darkness blanketed the remote Montana countryside. The snowstorm had developed into a full-on blizzard.

The assailant seemed edgy, pacing from window to window. Of course he was anxious. This assignment wasn't going anywhere near as planned. He'd been hired to retrieve Jenna and the little boy, but instead was stuck in a cabin with an incoherent woman, an energetic toddler and Matt, an unknown who could potentially overpower him.

It probably didn't help that at this moment Eli was being incredibly cute, toddling from one piece of furniture to the next, burning off energy from eating applesauce, crackers and two multigrain bars for dinner. Even a hardened man like this mercenary wasn't immune to Eli's charm.

The guy kept checking his phone, firing off

text messages, probably demanding his associates plow through the storm to get to him ASAP.

Eli started fussing, flopping down on the floor and crying in between gasps of breath. It was obviously bedtime.

Matt changed Eli's diaper. "He's ready for bed."

The guy narrowed his eyes, as if trying to discern Matt's strategy.

"I'm going to put him down in the bedroom," Matt said.

"He can sleep here."

"With all these lights on?"

"Fine, put him to bed."

His tone actually sounded pleasant. Little Eli might have crept his way into the guy's heart.

"But don't do anything stupid." He pointed the gun at Jenna.

On the other hand...

"It might take me a few minutes." Matt gently picked up the fussy child. Eli whimpered and rubbed his eyes with a clenched fist.

Matt went into the bedroom and shut the door. His first instinct was to look for a way out, but he shoved that thought aside considering the reality of his situation.

Matt, Jenna and Eli were captives of a mercenary without a soul. Even if Matt fled the cabin, he'd never make it far in a blizzard, and he couldn't leave Jenna behind.

"Let's get you settled." He clicked off the overhead light and turned on a bedside lamp, submerging the room in semidarkness.

Not wanting to put Eli on the bed for fear he'd roll off, Matt shoved the mattress onto the floor. He pulled back the comforter and laid Eli down. The boy kicked his feet and cried out, not wanting to sleep, unwilling to miss the action.

Matt lay down beside Eli and rubbed the furry polar bear against the boy's nose. "What's Bubba doin'? Is he kissing you?"

The boy blinked teary eyes at Matt.

"Kiss, kiss, kiss," Matt whispered.

While trying to calm the little boy into sleep, another part of his mind drifted to Jenna.

She hadn't awakened since her nightmare about Joey a few hours ago. Matt hoped she didn't wake up while he was in here with Eli. He didn't know what Jenna would do if she thought something had happened to Eli, that someone had taken him.

Matt hummed to the little boy while his

brain fired off questions. How had the bearded guy known Jenna and Matt were on their way? Had they been wrong to trust Marcus? Or were they being tracked somehow?

This wasn't the time to figure out who'd had a role in this. He needed to soothe Eli to sleep and develop a plan for a safe escape.

That gave him an idea. Since Marcus was a former SEAL turned security professional, he would no doubt keep weapons in the cabin. Matt could use a firearm right about now.

Eli rolled onto his tummy, stuck his bottom up in the air and sucked intently on his pacifier. Matt stroked his back, whispering, "Good boy, such a good boy."

A few minutes later, Eli stopped fussing and Matt removed his hand. The boy didn't stir. He had drifted into a deep sleep.

Matt eased off the mattress and quietly searched the room for a weapon. With Eli in here, Matt might have a chance to rescue Jenna and take down the assailant in the living room.

A slim chance if he wanted to avoid Jenna getting shot in the process.

Opening the dresser drawers, he sifted through Marcus's clothes, but found nothing.

He moved on to the closet because that's

where Matt kept his lockbox for his gun. He glanced at Eli, still sound asleep. Matt searched the top shelf. Nothing. He kneeled and tapped on the closet floor searching for a secret compartment, but it was solid.

Where would Marcus keep his firearm?

Matt stood and scanned the room.

A trained soldier would want easy and quick access, and might not worry about locking it up because he didn't have children living with him.

Footsteps echoed from the next room.

Matt repositioned himself beside Eli.

The door cracked open, and light from the living area poured into the room.

"Shh," Matt said, stroking the boy's back.

The guy peeked at Eli. As if he thought Matt was going to abscond with the child out the window into a blizzard.

"Close the door," Matt said.

The man's eye twitched with frustration, but he closed the door.

Matt stood and continued to search for a gun. Checking the nightstand, he found a flashlight. That would come in handy.

He grabbed it and froze. Thought he heard something.

The roar of an engine outside.

Not good. The bearded guy's men were closing in.

Matt concentrated on finding a weapon. He dropped to the floor and searched beneath the bed, aiming the beam of light left, then right across the floor.

Nothing.

As the engine grew louder, Matt realized it sounded more like a snowmobile.

The engine stopped. They were just outside.

Matt lay flat on his back and pointed the flashlight beam up, beneath the bed.

"Bingo." In a holster attached to the underside of the metal frame was a firearm.

"Good man," he whispered, reaching for it. Just as he heard a scream.

"No! Let me go!" Jenna cried out.

Chapter Eight

Matt ripped the gun out of its holster and bolted across the bedroom. He hesitated. Charging in there with guns blazing wasn't going to help any of them. A squeak from Eli drew his attention to the sleeping child.

He had to be smart about this. Needed to know what he was dealing with before he took aggressive action.

Cracking the door open, he peered into the living room. Instead of multiple men storming the cabin, the bearded guy stood behind Jenna with a gun to her back. He was dragging her toward the front door.

"Tell them you're friends with the owner," the bearded guy ordered.

So these were not *his* men? Interesting.

"The owner?" Jenna seemed out of it, disoriented. She stumbled as she reached the door, bracing herself with an open palm against the sturdy wood.

"Don't mess up," the bearded guy growled.

"Where's Joey?" she asked.

"Who?"

"I mean Eli—where's Eli?" She snapped around to glare at the guy.

Pretty gutsy.

"Your friend's got him in the other room."

She started to look toward the bedroom, but the guy smacked the back of her head with an open palm.

"Hey!" she shouted.

Matt would certainly need to pray for self-control if he ever got this jerk alone.

"Everything okay in there?" a muffled voice called through the main door.

Matt gripped the gun. Watching, waiting. He was ready.

She opened the cabin door. "Yes?"

"Ma'am, I'm Officer Patterson with the county PD. Do you live here?"

"No, I'm… I'm visiting my friend, Marcus."

"Is everything okay? You look—" he paused "—upset."

"I… I was asleep."

"Oh, I'm sorry to have disturbed you."

"That's okay."

Matt hoped the cop would leave so he could take care of the bearded guy without putting the cop in danger.

"Ma'am, are you alone?"

"No, my friend Matt is here with me."

"May I meet him, please?"

Jenna glanced over her shoulder at the assailant.

Matt held his breath. Now what? If Matt came out of hiding, the bearded guy would shoot the cop and possibly Jenna.

The bearded guy eased his gun into the back of his jeans and opened the door wide. "Officer," he greeted the policeman.

"Matt…?"

"Tomlin."

Yet he'd identified himself as Veck when he'd called for backup.

"The storm's not letting up for at least forty-eight hours," the cop said. "I hope Marcus left a fully stocked pantry."

Something felt off about the conversation. Matt wondered if the cop was a rookie, unable to sense danger. He continued to stand there, making small talk.

Behind him, Matt heard the window slide

open. He shut the bedroom door and spun around, aiming his weapon at a man on the other side of the window. The guy pressed his forefinger to his lips, indicating they should be quiet. Matt didn't lower his weapon.

The man, midthirties with dark hair and eyes, climbed through the window and gazed down at the sleeping boy.

"That must be Eli," he whispered, and then looked at Matt. "I see you found my favorite piece. Under the bed frame on the right side?"

Matt lowered the weapon. "Marcus?"

He nodded, peeled back a rug and popped open a hidden door. He pulled out a duffel bag and slung it over his shoulder. "Officer Patterson's a friend. He's supposed to figure out how many guys broke into my place."

"You knew they broke in?"

"Got an alert on my phone. What are we looking at?"

"One guy, not afraid to kill."

"Neither am I."

"My priority is to protect the woman and child."

"Me too. When Patterson leaves, go back into the living room and protect the woman. Eli will be safe in here. I'll take care of the rest."

Marcus motioned for the gun. "My piece?"

Matt shook his head, still not a hundred per-cent sure this guy was solid.

"You can't take that into the living room," Marcus said.

Matt studied him but didn't give up the gun.

"You don't trust me. Fair enough," Marcus said. "Just know I'm really good at what I do." He climbed out the window and disappeared into the dark night.

A few minutes later, the vibration from the front door slamming indicated Officer Patterson had left. Matt placed the gun on top of a row of books just as the door to the bedroom opened.

Jenna stepped inside, but only partially. The thug was holding on to her arm. "Is Eli okay?" she asked.

"Yeah, he's sleeping." Matt went to her and squeezed her hand. "Everything's fine."

She still seemed out of it. The thug released her and motioned them to the sofa. Once there, Matt put his arm around her shoulder and pulled her close. She didn't fight him. The sound of a snowmobile echoed through the window.

"She's a smart girl," the bearded guy said. "She followed orders." He glanced out the window.

"I woke up and Eli wasn't here." Jenna looked into Matt's eyes. "You weren't here."

"I'm sorry," he said. "Eli needed to sleep. He's one tired little tiger."

"I should have been awake. I should have helped you."

"Rest is the best thing for a concussion. A wise person once told me that."

They shared an awkward smile, remembering when Jenna had given Matt that very advice after he'd been assaulted at the truck stop.

"What if he wakes up?" Jenna said, glancing over her shoulder at the bedroom door.

"He's out. Trust me."

She nodded and repositioned her head against his shoulder. He pulled her tighter against him, readying himself for whatever Marcus was planning.

The anxiety that pinged through Jenna like a pinball seemed to wane the longer she leaned against Matt—a good thing because she needed to find clarity, and she needed to get grounded again. Her head injury had messed up her thinking, like it had years ago after Anthony took out his rage on her.

When she'd awakened earlier she'd been

snagged by a memory: She was in the hospital crying out for a son she'd never know on this earth.

Anger bubbled up inside her. She would not let this vile bully hurt Eli. She started to sit up, but Matthew whispered, "Shh, it's going to be okay."

She studied his warm blue eyes, eyes that radiated hope and faith. How was he able to do that?

"How's your head?" he asked.

"It aches but I'm okay, I think."

The lights clicked off and they were suddenly plunged into darkness. Matt rolled them both onto the floor and shielded Jenna by wrapping his body around her.

"Get over here." The bearded guy scrambled across the cabin and tried to grab Jenna, but couldn't get past Matthew.

She heard Matthew grunt as the guy kicked him, but Matt wasn't letting go.

The cabin door slammed against the wall.

A gunshot rang out.

She yelped.

"It's okay," Matthew said against her ear.

Heart pounding with panic, she closed her eyes.

Tried to pray.

She couldn't remember any scripture, anything that could help calm her nerves.

"Casting all your care upon Him; for He careth for you," Matthew said, as if he sensed her need to reach out to God.

She repeated the phrase in her mind over and over during what felt like hours of a violent struggle.

Then, just as suddenly, silence blanketed the room.

"You guys okay?" a man asked.

The lights clicked on.

"Looks like you're just fine," the guy said with a touch of humor in his voice.

Matthew released Jenna and helped her sit up. They both leaned against the sofa.

A stranger stood beside the door, his boot resting on the bearded guy's back. The thug's wrists were bound and he grunted in protest.

"Jenna," Matthew said. "This is Marcus."

"Marcus, wow." She glanced around the room, noting the overturned chairs and broken lamp. "How did you…?"

He pointed to goggles on the top of his head. "Night vision." He glanced at the thug. "Didn't stand a chance."

Jenna cocked her head. She thought she heard…

Yep. Eli was crying.

"Go ahead," Matt said.

That's when she realized he was holding her hand. It felt natural and comforting.

It felt good.

"Thanks," she said, but didn't want to let go.

He released her hand. "Hope I didn't crush you."

"You didn't." In truth, she'd felt safer than she had in a long time. Thanks to a man's protection. She never thought she'd feel that way. Ever.

"Want me to check on him?" Matthew offered, probably wondering about her hesitation.

"No, I'm good." She glanced at Marcus. "Thanks for the save."

"Sure. So what's going on with my cousin Chloe?"

Jenna's safe feeling was ripped out from under her. "She…"

"I'll explain everything," Matthew said. "Go to Eli."

"Thanks." She didn't want to relive the memory, the fear.

Fear. She needed to seriously deal with that emotion so it wouldn't consume her every thought, especially if she was about to comfort a child.

She opened the bedroom door and went to Eli. She touched his lips with the Binky, which had fallen out of his mouth. He latched on to it, but still whimpered.

She wasn't sure what the official pacifier rules were regarding at what age a child should relinquish it, but she figured he deserved every comfort she could offer considering the circumstances.

"Bubba, my bubba," she said, making up a song. "I love my baby bubba." She stroked his cheek with the stuffed animal. He rolled onto his side and grabbed the bear. Jenna continued to sing, and Eli kept sucking on his pacifier. His eyelids drifted closed.

The gunshot must have awakened him. Poor child. She hoped he didn't have nightmares from everything that was happening.

For half a second she wondered if she was doing the right thing, or if she should take Eli back to his father.

Gary is a monster, Chloe had said.

Jenna had experienced her share of those, yet couldn't remember ever experiencing kindness from a peaceful, compassionate man.

Until now.

Until Matthew.

As she sang to Eli, she wondered what would happen next. The bearded guy's associates were still on their way, which made Jenna, Matthew and Eli easy targets. They should flee the cabin and take refuge elsewhere. How long could they keep running, and how would they escape with a snowstorm barreling down on the countryside?

Panic threatened to take hold. Then she remembered Matthew's words: *Casting all your care upon Him…*

Yes, that's what she'd do. She'd surrender her worry to God.

As she stroked the little boy's hairline, she continued to whisper sweet words.

"Precious little boy, you are so very loved."

For the briefest of moments, she thought she felt a flicker of love from God touch her heart. *…for He careth for you.*

She considered the last few hours, how she'd survived a car accident and being held hostage. How Marcus showed up in time to help them, and the incredible peace she'd found in Matthew's arms.

Was God looking out for her? Had her subconscious prayers, in fact, been answered?

With a sigh and a squeak, Eli rolled onto his

tummy, his butt up in the air, clutching the white bear against his cheek. She covered him with the blanket and stroked the back of his head, humming softly.

Thank you, God, for protecting this beautiful child.

As the minutes passed, she was distracted by the sound of low male voices drifting from the other room. She took a deep breath, finding strength to deal with Marcus's grief when she rejoined them. Could God help with that as well? Could He help her be there for Marcus without the man's grief pulling Jenna down into the darkness?

That's when it hit her that all these years since she'd left Anthony, she'd been running from darkness and grief, from any and all conflict. Yet, along with joy, these were a part of the human experience. She admitted she hadn't truly dealt with the darkness haunting her—she hadn't dealt fully with her violent past, which meant she hadn't healed and couldn't move on.

The past would haunt her indefinitely. As long as she allowed it to.

In essence, she was letting Anthony control not only her present, but also her future.

That thought made her angry, but in a good way. It wasn't a victim-like anger, it was a warrior-type outrage, the kind that builds strength from within, inspires a person to stand up for herself and not back down from a fight.

To not back down from fear.

Convinced Eli had drifted off into a sound sleep, Jenna slid off the mattress. She made a makeshift wall around the edge of the bed with pillows and blankets. Standing up, she hovered beside the little boy and felt a surge of strength pour through her.

Strength, determination and courage.

She quietly crossed the room, hesitated at the door and took a deep breath. "Please, God, help me be strong."

For Eli, for Marcus and for herself.

She stepped into the living room and gently shut the door behind her. Matthew was sitting at the kitchen table. The bearded thug and Marcus were gone.

"Officer Patterson took him into custody," Matthew said, in answer to her unspoken question.

"And Marcus?"

"Helping escort the guy to Patterson's patrol car. It's parked on the main road."

"Do we need to leave?"

"Not right away. Marcus and I checked the

assailant's text messages. His men were delayed by weather. We sent a response text from our bearded friend claiming that he was able to get his car out after all and he's on his way. That'll buy us some time."

"His car?"

"Apparently you blocked it when you banked the truck."

"Oh, right. I'm not sure how much damage I did to Ed's truck. Sorry."

"Come sit down." Matthew motioned to her. "Coffee's brewing, or tea if you'd prefer."

"I'll get some in a minute." She crossed the room and placed her hand on Matthew's shoulder. "Thank you, again, for everything."

She wondered if he sensed that her gratitude went far deeper than saving her and Eli's lives, that he'd been able to do something she didn't think possible—offer her peace.

"That sounds ominous," Matthew said.

She searched his blue eyes. "What do you mean?"

"It sounds like you're saying goodbye."

"No, that's not what I meant."

But they both knew the goal had been to find Marcus, who would take over protecting Jenna and Eli.

"How's Eli?" Matthew changed the subject.

"Good, asleep." She shifted onto a chair next to him. "He's such a trooper."

"That he is. And you?"

She absently touched her forehead where she felt a bruise forming. "I have a little bit of a headache, but my vision's okay."

"That's not what I meant. Who's Joey?"

"Joey." She hesitated. "Joey was my unborn son. He died after Anthony shoved me down the stairs."

Matthew touched her hand. "I am so sorry, Jenna."

She nodded.

"Anthony went to jail for homicide?" he asked.

"No, aggravated domestic battery."

"But you lost your child."

"I needed to extricate myself from his abuse as quickly as possible and wanted to avoid a public trial. He wouldn't plead guilty to homicide, but agreed to plead guilty to domestic battery. He spends three years in jail in exchange for a quick divorce. I wish the pain had been quick as well, but it will always linger."

He squeezed her hand in a compassionate gesture. But she didn't want this to turn into a pity party. "Did you tell Marcus about Chloe?"

"Yes. He blames himself for not taking her more seriously."

"What do you mean?"

"She sent him an email last week stating she wanted to flee with Eli."

"And he ignored her?" she said, unable to keep the judgment from her voice.

"According to Marcus, Chloe tended to be dramatic at times." He glanced at Jenna. "Did you find that to be true?"

"I suppose a little, but that doesn't negate her feelings."

"Agreed. Yet if someone constantly sounds the alarm, after a while people start to hear nothing but white noise." He pursed his lips.

"Why do I sense you're speaking from personal experience?"

Matthew shrugged. "I think the coffee's ready. Or did you want tea?"

"Tea would be great."

He went to the hot water kettle and she watched him scoop instant coffee into two mugs, put a teabag in a third and pour hot water into all three. He rejoined her at the table and slid the tea in front of her.

"Thanks." She wrapped her fingers around the mug. "So, we were talking about overly dramatic people who cry wolf. Does that have anything to do with—" she hesitated "—Sarah?"

He snapped his gaze to meet hers, but she didn't see anger there or even irritation. Sadness dulled his blue eyes instead.

"I'm sorry. It's none of my business." She dipped her teabag in and out of the mug a few times.

"How did you know about Sarah?"

"When you were injured at the truck stop, you said her name. You apologized to her."

He stared into his coffee. "She was my almost fiancée."

"Almost?"

"The night I'd planned to propose, she got in a car accident and died."

"Oh, Matthew." She reached over and touched his hand wrapped around the coffee mug.

"At the time, I blamed myself," he said.

"What? Why?"

"The night I proposed, we got in a fight and she tore off in a crazy state. She wasn't paying attention to the road, was driving too fast for the conditions and got hit by a truck."

"Why would you blame yourself?"

"I should have been more considerate of her

feelings, I guess. Instead, I thought she was being selfish and overreacting."

"To what?"

"My job, how dangerous and demanding it is. When I worked an undercover assignment, I could go months without seeing her and she'd worry herself into a state. She knew when we started dating what she was signing on for, and I think she liked it, being able to say she was dating an FBI agent. I never pretended to be a nine-to-five kind of guy." He glanced up at Jenna. "Sorry. I don't know why I'm telling you all this."

"I'm glad you are." She squeezed his hand, encouraging him to continue.

"Anyway, I thought a marriage proposal might help ease her fears, but instead she lost it. Started shouting about two people making a marriage, not one, that she'd be raising our children on her own, that she'd have to give up her career as a physical therapist. I thought I was doing the right thing by proposing…" His voice trailed off.

"Of course you were. You loved her."

He glanced at Jenna with regret in his eyes. "I should have gone after her that night."

"You couldn't have prevented the accident."

"No, but I could have stopped her from leaving in such a crazed state."

"We all have regrets about what might have happened if we'd made a different choice."

He nodded and sipped his coffee.

"May I ask, why didn't you stop her? I don't mean that to sound judgmental."

He shook his head. "I spent a year and a half asking myself that same question, praying on it, praying for forgiveness."

"Did you get it?"

"Yes, but I had to face an ugly truth. I was actually relieved she wanted to break up. And then…well, I had to admit that we weren't meant to be together, but I couldn't bring myself to break up because she needed me, she needed someone with integrity, someone to take care of her. She'd been emotionally damaged by her father and other men in her life. I didn't know that until we were together for a couple of months. She was good at hiding her emotional scars with humor."

Jenna wondered if that's why Matthew had assigned himself as her protector, because he had a driving need to protect women.

"Do you still blame yourself for her accident?" Jenna asked.

"Actually, no." He sat back in his chair. "I've learned you can't control other people's choices, but you should pay close attention to what's going on, you know, be present."

"That's what I was doing with Chloe when she came to see me."

"You're a good friend," Matthew offered.

"Maybe."

Matthew cocked his head in question.

"A better friend would have been able to save her life," she said.

"In those circumstances you would have been overpowered. There's nothing you could have done."

Jenna shrugged. A few seconds of silence stretched between them. It wasn't uncomfortable silence, but contemplative.

"What happens next?" she asked. "Will you be heading back to the community center?"

"You're that anxious to get rid of me, huh?" He winked.

On the contrary, she dreaded the moment he left her and Eli, even though she was confident in Marcus's ability to protect them.

"I assumed once we found Marcus that you'd go back to your normal, undercover life," she said. "That sounded weird, didn't it?"

That charming half smile tugged at his lips. "Let's confer with Marcus before we make our next move. He knows the area and the local law enforcement, and he's obviously pretty good with strategy."

Marcus reentered the cabin, tapping his boots on the rug by the door. "The guy's name is Brian Veck. Mean anything to either of you?"

"No," Matthew said.

Jenna shook her head.

"Patterson will run him through the database to see if anything pops." Marcus shucked his jacket and hung it on the coatrack. "He's charging Veck with breaking and entering, kidnapping, assault and attempted murder."

"Attempted murder?" Jenna echoed.

"Yeah, he tried to kill me—oh, wait, you didn't see it because the lights were out." Marcus smiled.

"Your coffee's on the counter," Matthew said.

"Thanks." Marcus grabbed the mug and leaned against the kitchen counter. "I still can't believe what happened to Chloe."

"I'm so sorry, Marcus," Jenna said.

"What did she get herself into?"

"I think it's related to a money-laundering case I'm working on," Matthew offered.

"She left me a voice mail about wanting to leave Gary, but I was running a protective detail for a family overseas and had to stay focused. I emailed her that I'd get in touch when I returned to the States." He shook his head. "I can protect complete strangers, but can't even take care of my own family."

"No one could have known her life was in danger," Jenna said. "I certainly didn't."

"Why Chloe?" Marcus glanced at Jenna, and she had to steel herself against his painful expression.

"I think her husband was involved in the money laundering somehow," Matthew said.

"Okay, but why kill *her*?" Marcus pressed.

"She probably knew too much. Either she heard something or saw something she shouldn't have," Matthew said.

"She was certainly scared when she came to see me," Jenna said.

"And now it sounds like your life is in danger." Marcus nodded at Jenna. "But what do they want with Eli?"

"Gary obviously wants his son back," Jenna said.

"Not happening, not if he's in any way responsible for my cousin's death." Marcus turned to Matthew. "You're going after Gary, right?"

"That's why I was undercover at the foundation's office, to determine who was involved and find evidence to support our case."

"Then you need to get back there and put the guy away. I'll protect Jenna and Eli."

Matthew glanced at Jenna and she nodded her approval of the plan, even though her heart panged with the anticipated loss of a good friend.

A friend? Really, Jenna?

"Is that what you want?" Matthew asked her.

No, of course not.

"Yes," she said. "If it will put an end to the threat against Eli."

Matthew ripped his gaze from Jenna and addressed Marcus. "I figure we've got until tomorrow morning before they come looking for Veck."

"I'll keep watch tonight. I'm jet-lagged anyway, so night is my daytime. You two get some sleep."

"I'll get the portable playpen from the truck for Eli, and Jenna can take the bed." Matthew crossed the room and put on his coat.

It was almost like he needed to get away from

Jenna, to put distance between them. He hesitated before opening the door, as if he wanted to say something to her. Instead, he left and shut the door behind him.

The next morning Jenna did her best to be strong as she played with Eli, even though her heart was breaking.

Matthew had left without saying a final goodbye. Once he'd clicked into agent mode, he apparently couldn't be distracted by feelings that had grown between him and Jenna.

Or maybe she was kidding herself and the feelings were one-sided.

No, they'd obviously grown close or else he wouldn't have opened up so completely about Sarah's death. He'd claimed that he had forgiven himself for the accident, but Jenna wasn't so sure.

For one thing, she was puzzled by the idea of self-forgiveness.

Marcus entered the cabin. "Looks like a good day ahead. Sun's shining. Main road's clear. I'm able to track Veck's main contact through his phone. They're a solid six hours away." He went to the kitchen. "I've got surveillance set up around the property so we'll know if anyone's coming."

"That's great," she said, continuing to play blocks with Eli.

"Once we got the truck out of the snowbank, and changed the tire, it started up just fine. There was a little damage to the fender, but nothing serious. That was a good move, to block the drive so the thug couldn't get out."

"It wasn't intentional."

"Matt was sorry he missed you this morning. He hopes to get back to Cedar River by midday."

"Good, that's good." Except *good* didn't describe how she felt at this very moment.

"It's normal, ya know."

She glanced at him. "What's that?"

"To develop a connection to someone who's protecting you."

"How did you…?"

"It's my business, remember? Protecting people."

"So I'll stop missing him after a while?"

"Sure, no doubt."

His response didn't sound convincing.

"How's my little cousin doing?" Marcus grabbed Eli and held him up like he was flying. Eli giggled and kicked his feet. Marcus put the boy down and tugged on his overalls. "Very stylish, dude."

Eli giggled, turned and ran back to the coffee table to play with his blocks.

"What's the plan?" she asked.

"My buddy has a place near the Idaho border. I'll take you there and we'll wait it out until we hear back from Matt."

"I hope we're not interfering with your work schedule."

"No problem. I got it covered."

He grabbed his phone and eyed the screen. "That's not good."

Jenna sat up.

He grabbed a pair of binoculars off a bookshelf and looked through the front window. "Whoa, you've gotta go."

"Me, what about you?"

He calmly picked up Eli's snowsuit and Jenna's jacket. "Get the diaper bag."

"Who's here?"

He pinned her with steely dark eyes. "If you want to survive, you'll need to follow my orders."

She nodded and went into the bedroom to get the baby's diaper bag. Although tempted to look out the window to see what was happening, she knew time was critical and that her best option was to follow Marcus's orders.

When she reentered the living room, she noticed wooden boards were pulled up, exposing a hole in the floor by the fireplace.

"That's my safe room," he said, by way of explanation. "It opens to a tunnel that leads to the shed out back. Take Eli to the shed and wait until someone comes to get you. I'd suggest you use the snowmobile back there, but that'd be impossible to manage with a kid."

"Wait, a safe room? With a tunnel?"

"The shed's not heated, but you'll be okay in your snow gear. I'll text Patterson to retrieve you, okay?"

"But who's out there?"

"Looks like the Feds, but I can't know for sure. Go on," he said calmly.

"But Marcus—"

"Chloe chose you to protect Eli because you're strong, Jenna. You can do this."

With a nod, she climbed down the stairs to the safe room and he handed her Eli. Then he tossed their snow gear down and pointed. "Switch is on the left."

She felt around and flicked it on. A soft glow illuminated a room full of supplies, including weapons, food and water.

"Follow the tunnel to the shed," Marcus repeated.

She glanced nervously toward the dark opening leading into the tunnel.

"Flashlight is by the entrance, see it?"

She nodded, but couldn't speak past the fear tightening her throat.

"Oh, and Jenna—"

Pounding echoed from the front door.

"Go, go." He shut the trap door.

She stared at it for a few seconds, gathering her thoughts...and her courage.

Please, God, give me courage.

With a sudden rush of purpose, she got Eli dressed in his snow jacket. She put on her own jacket and scarf, keeping a close eye on him as she fumbled around the small room.

"Let's go, buddy," she said.

She strapped Eli in the baby carrier, positioning him against her chest. "Ready for an adventure?" she said brightly, because she knew children sensed your emotions, your fear, and would react accordingly.

"Buh-buh," he said. She grabbed the white bear out of the diaper bag and handed it to him. The little boy snatched it and giggled, burying his face into the soft fur.

She aimed the flashlight into the tunnel. "I can do this."

The ground was covered with wooden planks that served as a floor, and the walls were braced with beams. A quick flash of it collapsing made Jenna hesitate for a moment.

With a determined breath, she stepped into the dark passageway, hearing Marcus's words echo in her mind—*Chloe chose you to protect Eli because you're strong, Jenna.*

"I am strong."

As she forged ahead, she heard pounding from above, then the sound of men shouting, someone giving loud orders, and more pounding. She blocked out the distraction, determined to reach her goal: getting to safety and waiting for Marcus's friend, Officer Patterson, to come get her.

In the meantime, she'd keep Eli happy and distracted in the shed. She pushed aside the thought that the men would come looking for her there.

"Isn't this something, Eli?"

His eyes widened and he looked around. Fueled by determination, and love for this innocent child, Jenna focused on the ladder in the distance.

She picked up her pace, ignoring the walls that felt like they were closing in, the darkness barreling down on her from behind.

Approaching the end of the tunnel, she set the flashlight on the ground, pointing it upward. The beam illuminated a door up above.

"Here we go, buddy." She ascended the ladder, hoping the door would easily open. She didn't want to think about being stuck down here.

She tapped on the door. "Help Jenna, buddy."

Eli reached out and tapped as well.

"One, two, three…"

She pushed it open with ease, and relief poured through her. She climbed up into the shed and took Eli out of the carrier. Shucking the diaper and her messenger bags, she scanned the shed for anything immediately dangerous to Eli. Because the supplies were locked in tall metal cabinets, it seemed pretty safe.

There was one window, facing the cabin,

which had probably been designed for Marcus to keep an eye on what was happening if he ever needed to escape and hide out in here. A few minutes later, she noticed two dark SUVs driving away from the property toward the main road.

Driving away? Which meant…they'd taken Marcus?

Eli hugged her leg and let out a squeal. He was bored, or tired, or a little of both. It was about time for his midday nap. She put him back in the carrier, facing her.

"It's okay, baby boy. Everything's okay."

If only Matthew were here.

No, she had to learn to take care of herself and Eli without Matthew's help.

She rocked Eli from one side of the eight-by-eight shed to the other. He squealed and kicked his feet. She kept moving, humming, and he finally quieted down. She looked at his sweet face and realized he'd fallen asleep from the movement.

"We'll be okay," she whispered, stroking the back of his head.

She thought she heard a soft tap at the door. Officer Patterson had certainly arrived quickly.

She opened the door…

To the angry expression of Chloe's husband, Gary.

"What are you—?"

"I'll take my child now," he demanded.

Chapter Nine

No matter how hard Matt tried to convince himself that leaving Jenna behind was the right thing to do, he still felt like he'd made a colossal mistake.

Intellectually it made sense for him to return to his undercover assignment, to continue to expose the money laundering. That would essentially make Jenna safe again.

From Marcus's performance last night, Matt could tell the guy was equipped to handle any situation. Having confirmed Marcus's background with Bob Barnes yesterday made it easier for Matt to leave Jenna behind.

Not easy, but manageable. It was the best choice, especially given the circumstances and Bob's comment about Pragge threatening to dismiss agents who couldn't follow orders.

Matt's phone rang and he recognized Bob's

number. He hit the speaker button. "Tell Pragge I'll be back at the foundation office tonight."

"Matt, it's about Marcus Garcia."

Matt gripped the wheel. "What about him?"

"There's a warrant out for his arrest."

"For what?"

"Assault and battery."

"I thought you said his background was clean."

"It was."

Matt slowed down and yanked the wheel left, doing a U-turn in the middle of the highway. "Why didn't you tell me this yesterday?"

"The warrant was issued this morning."

"When did this assault supposedly happen?" Matt asked.

"Last night."

"Impossible. He was with us."

Matt sped up, trying to control his panic, his frustration that he'd left Jenna when she needed him most.

"Who issued the warrant?" Matt asked.

"Cedar River PD."

"Chief Billings?"

"You got it."

Which meant they'd found a connection between Chloe and her cousin Marcus, and were closing in…

On Marcus and the cabin.

On Jenna and Eli.

"Is Jenna North okay?" Bob said.

"She will be."

"You're going back, aren't you?"

"Yep."

"What do you want me to tell Pragge?"

"Tell him I'll check in later."

Matt ended the call and hightailed it back to the cabin. He hadn't been driving all that fast when he'd left, a part of him not in any rush to return to his assignment.

Admit it, Matt, you didn't want to abandon Jenna.

He'd left the cabin half an hour ago, so if he doubled his speed he'd make it back in fifteen minutes.

"Hang in there, Jenna," he said, thankful that the plows had done good work overnight to clear the highway of snow.

With a bulletin out on Marcus, the authorities, local and national, would be on the lookout for him. That included Marcus's friend, Officer Patterson.

No one could be trusted.

Chief Billings no doubt figured with Marcus out of the way, Jenna would have no one to turn to.

How did they even find Marcus? It seemed like he stayed off the grid pretty well, and Matt was sure a guy like that would disable the GPS on his phone so as not to be tracked.

Then again, if they went through Chloe's phone and checked her email, they'd see she'd reached out to her cousin. Maybe they couldn't find him, but they knew he lived in Montana, and what better way to enlist the help of state-wide police than to release a false bulletin?

Even if Officer Patterson remained loyal to Marcus, there were surely other officers who knew about the former Navy SEAL living in the area. People tended to know each other quite well in remote areas like this, sometimes their lives depending on being able to rely on neighbors.

He turned onto the long drive leading to the cabin. He didn't see any squad cars out front. Relaxing his fingers on the steering wheel, he took a deep breath. He'd make it back in time. They hadn't been discovered. Yet he still had to get to Marcus and let him know about the danger, danger that had put Jenna and Eli in the crosshairs as well.

He parked and rushed to the cabin. Knocked. No one answered. "Marcus!"

With a closed fist, he pounded on the door.

He darted left and looked through the window.

Marcus's chair that he'd used to keep watch was tipped over, a table lamp was on the floor and the rug was bunched in a corner.

"No," Matt ground out.

He went around and checked all the windows, trying to find a way in. The bedroom window was unlocked and he climbed inside.

The first thing he saw was the portable crib. They wouldn't have intentionally left this crucial piece of equipment behind. Which meant Jenna and Eli had been taken?

Or perhaps they'd fled the scene in a hurry, and the overturned furniture was the result of frustrated thugs who'd lost them again.

"Jenna, where are you?"

He went through the cabin looking for indications that they'd safely escaped. Then he heard it. Shouting.

It was coming from outside.

Matt pulled out his gun, left the cabin and made his way around back.

"We're not going with you!" Jenna cried out.

He spotted her being pulled through the snow by Gary McFadden. Eli, strapped into his carrier against her body, half squealed and half cried.

"We've got to get out of here!" Gary shouted.

"Think about your son!" she cried.

He spun around and got in her face. "That's right, he's my son! Mine!" He pointed at his own chest to make his point.

That's when Matt realized Gary gripped a gun in his hand.

"Let's go!" Gary yanked on her arm.

Where was he taking her? Didn't matter. Matt had to do something, and quick. He put away his gun, not wanting to escalate the situation, and trudged through the snow.

"Gary McFadden!" he called out, putting his hands up in a gesture of surrender.

The guy spun around and pointed the gun at Matt. Jenna looked surprised, and very relieved, to see Matt.

"Let Jenna go," Matt said.

"What are you doing here?"

"I'm FBI."

"You're a janitor," Gary scoffed.

"I'm undercover, and Jenna is under my protection, as is your son."

"I can protect my own son!" he shouted, as if trying to convince himself.

Eli burst into high-pitched wails. Still clutching the gun, Gary glanced at him. He released Jenna's arm and reached out to his son.

Jenna turned slightly in a protective stance.

"I'm supposed to protect him," Gary said in an oddly soft voice. "And Chloe."

Matt and Jenna shared a look. The man had gone from enraged to remorseful in less than two seconds.

"Gary, what's going on?" Jenna asked.

"I'm a dead man walking."

"What do you mean?" Jenna asked.

"You're right, Jenna. I'm a danger to my child." Gary touched the back of his son's head. "Please, don't let them hurt my boy."

"I get that you're scared," Matt said. "Let us help you."

Shaking his head, Gary said, "It's too late. I should have never gotten involved."

"It's the Guerro drug cartel, isn't it?"

Gary snapped his attention to Matt.

"Work with us. Help us shut them down," Matt said.

"No, I have to finish this. Make things right." He pressed a kiss on top of Eli's head. "You'll be okay, buddy. As long as you have your Bubba, you'll be okay."

"You can't keep running." Matt took a few steps closer.

"Stop." Gary pulled out the gun.

Jenna squinted and protected the child with her arms.

"I'd never hurt my boy." Gary glanced from Jenna to Matt and back to Jenna.

He must have realized his actions belied his proclamation because he lowered the weapon.

"Why are they after Eli?" Matt asked.

"Leverage. I want out. There is no getting out. And now I've put Eli's life in danger." With a defeated expression, Gary took a step back, then another.

That's when Matt noticed a snowmobile fifty yards away.

"You're right, Jenna. It's dangerous to be anywhere near me. I'm so sorry, Eli." Gary turned and trudged toward the snowmobile.

"Gary!" Matt shouted, and started after him.

"Forget about me! Love my son!" He climbed onto the snowmobile, started it up and sped away before Matt could get to him.

Matt went to Jenna and hugged her, with the little boy between them.

"I can't believe you came back," she said against his shoulder. "What happened?"

"I found out there was a warrant on Marcus."

"I thought he was one of the good guys."

He broke the hug. "He is. The warrant was issued by Billings, who claims Marcus assaulted someone last night."

"But he was with us last night."

"Exactly. Let's go before we get more company." He started to lead her to the cabin.

"Wait, our stuff is in the shed."

They went back to the shed and grabbed the diaper and messenger bags. As they headed for the cabin, he was careful to help Jenna manage the snow. Although Marcus had shoveled a path early this morning, snow drifts covered part of the walkway now.

"What were you doing back here?" he asked.

"When the men in the SUVs came to get us, Marcus had me take a tunnel leading to the shed. He said he'd notify Officer Patterson to come to my aid."

"Considering the warrant, I'm not sure we can trust even him at this point. A tunnel, huh?"

"Yep, and a good thing, or I'd be wherever Marcus is right now."

"But you're not, you're okay."

"Are we?" she said. "They keep coming and we keep running. I'm not sure we'll ever be truly okay."

He wondered if she was talking about this particular situation, or if she was referring to her past.

"We've got more to work with now," Matt said. "Confirmation that Gary was involved with the money laundering will get my people on board with my plan."

"Which is?"

He glanced down into her brilliant green eyes. "To keep you and Eli safe."

"You're not going back to Cedar River?"

"No, ma'am."

"How can you work your case if you're not there?"

"Let me worry about that. For now, let's get someplace safe."

"I've heard that before." She snapped her attention to him. "Sorry, that wasn't meant as a criticism of your abilities."

"Maybe it should be."

"Matthew—"

"Hey, I think we know each other well enough that you can call me Matt."

"Matt, don't blame yourself for what just happened."

"I shouldn't have left you." They approached the cabin and he hesitated. "It won't happen again."

They packed the portable crib and supplies in Ed's truck and headed north toward the Canadian border. Jenna wasn't sure where they'd end up, and she didn't care much because at this moment she felt safe.

Thanks to Matthew.

Rather than judge herself for her growing dependence on him, she relaxed into the feeling. She'd learned from Patrice that stress and fear take a horrible toll on one's body, and that to fully heal, Jenna needed to embrace peace whenever possible.

Right now, with Matthew behind the wheel of the truck, and Eli asleep in the back seat, she felt a peaceful calm warm her body.

She sighed and found herself thanking God.

Matthew's faith must be wearing off on her.

"I'm going to stop at an ATM," he said.

"Won't they track your location?"

"They will, but from there we'll double back and go southwest, toward Idaho."

"What's in Idaho?"

"A cluster of cabins I heard about from a

buddy of mine. We'll stay there until I can get backup."

"You mean, you're going to enlist the help of your counterparts at the FBI?"

"Yes."

Her peaceful moment was suddenly shattered. "Do you think that's a good idea?"

"We can't do this alone, Jenna. It's okay to ask for help. I thought you'd appreciate that more than anyone."

He was referring to her support from Gloria's Guardians. "Maybe I have a better idea."

"I'm listening."

"I'll call Patrice and see if we can stay with her for a while."

"That would be putting her in danger."

"She's a tough lady, and no one knows about the group, or my connection to it. We'd be safe there."

"At this point I'd rather not involve civilians."

"I understand, but these women are used to dealing with dangerous situations."

"Are you willing to risk exposing their service?"

She considered his comment.

"Let's go with my plan for now, okay?" he said.

She nodded. "What about Marcus?"

"I'll call my buddy at work and see if he can track down what happened to him."

"I hope he's okay."

"He's resourceful. I'm sure he's fine."

When they stopped at the ATM, she watched Matthew shield his face from the camera with the brim of his baseball cap.

He got back in the truck and they headed southwest. His phone rang on the dash cradle, a blocked number.

"Could be work," he said. He pressed the speaker button. "Weller."

"Matt? It's Chief Billings."

Jenna held her breath.

"Yes, Chief?" Matt said in a calm voice.

"Hope you don't mind me calling. I got your number from Kyle Armstrong."

"No problem. What can I do for you?"

Jenna glanced into the back seat at Eli, who had fallen asleep.

"I've got a few more questions about the break-in at the community center and was hoping to catch up with you today."

"Today's not good for me. How about tomorrow?"

A pregnant pause was followed by, "How about nine a.m.?"

"Sounds good."

"Officer Armstrong speaks very highly of you."

Matt glanced at the phone with a worried frown. "Thank you, sir."

"He's working on the break-in, tracking leads and looking for the man who assaulted you. Let's hope Officer Armstrong is as able to defend himself as you were."

"I'm sure he is, sir," Matthew said in a low voice. "Goodbye."

He hit the off button and smacked the palm of his hand against the steering wheel. "Unbelievable."

"What?" Jenna questioned.

"That was Billings's not-so-subtle threat that Kyle's life is in danger because of our friendship."

"Wait, no, he wouldn't hurt one of his own men," she said. "Would he?"

Matt shot her a look.

"What are you going to do?" she asked.

"I've gotta warn Kyle." He reached for the phone and hesitated. "How do I even explain this? I mean, I've been lying to him this whole time."

"It's your job as an undercover agent."

With a nod, he made the call.

"Hey, Matt," Kyle answered. "Missed you at coffee this morning."

"Yeah, sorry."

"You okay?"

"I need to talk to you about something important."

"Hang on. Yeah, Chief?"

Matt gripped the steering wheel.

"Sure thing. Okay, Matt, I'm back."

"I need you to listen to me very carefully."

"O-kay," he said with a half chuckle.

"You trust me, right?"

"Sure."

"Is Billings standing close by?"

"Yeah, why?"

Matt glanced at Jenna and shook his head. Jenna guessed he wouldn't share the information if there was a chance Billings could read Kyle's reaction.

"I'd better let you get back to work," Matt said, defeated.

"Not so fast. What's up?"

Matthew seemed to consider his options for a few seconds, and then he said, "I need you to do me a favor."

"Okay, as long as it's not hauling cement

blocks to Hunter's farm again. My shoulders still ache from that favor," he joked.

"Kyle, I need you to read Jeremiah chapter twelve verse six. New Living Translation. Can you do that for me?"

"Odd request, but okay."

"Just between you and me. Don't even mention it to your chief."

"No problem. I doubt he'd be interested," he said.

"Thanks. And...be safe." Matt ended the call.

"Jeremiah chapter twelve verse six?" Jenna questioned.

"It's about your family, your brothers, turning against you."

By nightfall they'd reached their destination, the Lazy Shade Resort. Actually, it wasn't much of a resort, but more like a cluster of rustic cabins.

Matt booked a two-room cabin, complete with kitchenette, and paid for two nights with cash. He wasn't sure it was prudent to stay much longer than a couple of days.

It was a remote location and should be safe enough to give him time over the next forty-eight hours to work the case, to draw more connections between the cartel, Gary and Chief Billings.

The man who had threatened Matt's friend.

Matt rolled his neck, struggling to push his anger and worry aside. He had to have confidence that his friend would read and understand the message in the scripture.

He picked up supplies from the general store on the resort grounds, and went back to the cabin. He knocked four times and the door cracked open to Jenna's lovely face, her wide green eyes looking up at him.

She swung the door open and he spotted Eli leaning against the coffee table, playing with his stuffed bear and a plastic car.

"He seems pretty happy." Matt entered the cabin.

"I just gave him a bottle. I probably shouldn't be giving him bottles at this point, but it calms him down."

Matt cast one last glance outside and shut the door behind him.

"Hungry?" he asked, heading toward the kitchenette.

"Always hungry," she said.

The rental unit had an open living space with a separate bedroom, similar to Marcus's cabin.

"I bought canned beef stew, canned yams and pretzels."

"Hang on, I thought you were a health food guy."

"The store had a limited selection. Fresh fruit isn't delivered until the morning. Trust me, you didn't want me to bring home the wilted greens or overripe bananas."

She smiled, and he was lost for a second, lost in the fantasy of having a life with this woman.

For real. Not pretend, like this was.

Snap out of it, Weller.

"What else have you got there?" She peeked into the bag.

"Canned chicken à la king, in case you don't like beef."

"What's this?" She pulled a box of pancake mix out of the grocery bag.

"Breakfast."

"Why not dinner?" she said.

"Why not dinner," he repeated.

Eli squealed and ran around the coffee table, once, twice, three times.

They both smiled at his enthusiasm, then Jenna's smile faded.

"What?" Matt asked.

She shook her head.

"Jenna?"

"I feel guilty."

"About what?"

"That I feel happy right now."

"You deserve to feel happy."

"Not when Eli's mother is dead, his father will surely be dead soon, your friend Kyle is in danger and who knows what happened to Marcus."

He pulled her into a hug. "We don't know what the next few days will bring. Enjoying the peaceful moments will help us stay strong during the challenges ahead."

She looked up at him. "How did you become this person?"

"I'm not sure I understand the question."

"You don't freak out about stuff. You're so wise and so...grounded. I've never known a man like you."

"I'm not perfect, Jenna."

"I know," she whispered.

The way she looked up into his eyes...

He leaned forward and kissed her, the connection shooting sparks of energy through his body. This felt so incredible, so normal and right.

Alarm bells went off in his head.

This growing personal connection to Jenna would put her in more danger. It would definitely distract him from doing his job—protecting her and Eli.

He broke the kiss and stepped back. "I shouldn't have done that. I'm sorry."

Disappointment shuttered her eyes.

"That was inappropriate," he added. "Emotional involvement between us will throw me off my game."

"No worries. I was probably giving off signals or something."

"Don't take responsibility for my actions."

Her eyes widened as if he'd insulted her, and then she quickly turned to Eli.

"What are you doing, little man?" She went to him, using the child to derail the conversation.

The kiss. The intense connection growing between them, a connection he suspected had developed in part because of the danger hounding them.

But these feelings, the kiss, none of it was real.

Really, Weller? You sticking with that story?

She pulled a toy out of Eli's bag, and Matt turned on the TV with the remote. Any sounds were preferable to awkward silence. He'd crossed the line.

The little boy burst into giggles. Eli's joy reminded Matt of what he'd been missing: a wife, a family.

Sarah had been right when she said being married to Matt meant raising children as a single parent. He couldn't expect any woman to agree to those terms because, well, no one could love Matt enough to live under that kind of pressure.

He glanced over his shoulder into the parking lot. The same five vehicles that had been parked when he and Jenna arrived were still there. No new cars had pulled in.

Redirecting his attention to the television, he surfed a few channels until he found the news.

And there, filling the screen, was Jenna's face.

He took a few steps closer to the TV.

"We're standing outside of the Cedar River Police Department, where the chief just finished a news conference about a missing child, Eli McFadden..."

Clutching a building block in her hand, Jenna snapped her head around to look at the television. As the reporter continued, Jenna's face drained of color.

"If seen, the Cedar River Police request you call the one eight hundred number at the bottom of your screen. The suspect, Jenna North, is not considered dangerous, but the child has a medical condition and needs to be returned to his family immediately. Back to you, Amy."

"A medical condition?" Jenna glanced at Matt. "Chloe never said anything about a medical condition."

"That type of alert creates a sense of urgency to motivate witnesses to call the police."

"Even more people will be looking for us now."

As if on cue, someone pounded on the cabin door, and Matt drew his weapon.

Chapter Ten

Jenna instinctively grabbed Eli. Matthew motioned for her to take the little boy into the bedroom, out of sight.

They both knew the reality of this situation: they were trapped in the cabin with no escape route.

She snatched Eli's diaper bag and rushed into the bedroom.

This was it, the end. Her brain spun with panic. It had to be the authorities coming to take Eli away from her, arrest Jenna for kidnapping and give the child back to his father.

No, that wouldn't happen, because Gary was on the run. So where would this precious little boy end up?

She shut the bedroom door. Eli squirmed against her, wanting to get down and play. She glanced at the closet. Her first instinct was to hide…

"No more hiding," she said softly.

Instead, she put Eli down on the floor with a few toys, and she searched the room for a weapon, something with which to defend herself and Eli.

As she went through the closet, she decided she could use a wire hanger to poke someone in the eye. It would inflict more pain than was necessary, but it would serve the purpose, giving her time to get away.

Could she overpower a thug sent to retrieve her and Eli? If not…

She prayed that Matthew would stop the guy from getting into the bedroom. If he couldn't, Jenna would be ready.

As she untwisted the hanger, she wondered how on earth Billings's men kept finding them. Tracking them to Marcus's cabin made sense because he was Chloe's cousin, but how had they found out about this remote spot? Jenna was using a burner phone, and Matt had disabled his GPS. Maybe Chief Billings had tracked them from the recent phone call using triangulation? No, she'd watched too much TV. A small police department like Cedar River wouldn't have access to such technology, would they?

Eli entertained himself by opening and closing the nightstand drawer, putting his bear inside, then taking him out. Jenna uncoiled two more hangers and folded them together to create a four-pronged weapon. She clutched the hangers in her right hand and pressed her ear to the door, but the wood was too thick to hear much. On one hand, she was relieved she couldn't hear what was going on because that meant no one could hear Eli's squeals of delight each time he'd find Bubba in the nightstand drawer.

On the other hand, her adrenaline pumped with the anticipation of the bedroom door crashing open and a violent encounter between her and one of Chief Billings's men taking place. She stood behind the door.

Waited.

Inhaled slow, deep breaths.

Casting all your care—

A tap on the window made her yelp. She spun around and spotted Marcus waving from the other side of the glass. Rushing across the room, she slid the window open.

"Marcus, how did you—?"

"Later. Hand me the kid."

She hesitated.

"Don't second-guess yourself now, Jenna.

The local police are on the other side of the bedroom door questioning Matt, and they're coming in here next to search for you and Eli."

Trust your gut. Patrice had taught her that. Well, Jenna's gut told her Marcus was one of the good guys.

She tossed her weapon on the bed and grabbed Eli and his bear.

Marcus reached out and she passed Eli through the window. "Bring his bag. Don't leave anything of his behind."

She stuffed Eli's things into the bag and dropped both hers and Eli's bags out the window. She climbed out and landed on the soft snow.

"Close the window," Marcus whispered.

She slid it down, aware of the blue and red lights flashing across the parking lot. Marcus motioned her away from the small cabin.

Jenna couldn't worry about what would happen next.

About what was happening to Matt.

He'd want her to concentrate on keeping herself and the little boy safe.

Marcus led her down a shoveled walkway past four cabins to a clearing at the north end of the property. He opened the back door of an insipid dark sedan and placed Eli into the back seat of the car. Jenna climbed in beside the little boy.

"You don't have a car seat," she said.

"I'm hoping we don't have to go anywhere."

He shut the door behind her. She entertained Eli by offering him a toy truck. Marcus slid behind the wheel and shut the door.

"How did you find us?" she asked.

Marcus glanced over his shoulder. "Planted a tracking device on the kid's overalls. Tried to tell you back at the cabin, but didn't have a chance."

"What happened with the men who took you into custody?"

"I told them you left yesterday. I said if they released me, I'd help them track you down."

She snapped her attention to him.

"It's called being a double agent," Marcus said. "I convinced them I'm an innocent bystander who could care less about my cousin Chloe or Eli. It wasn't hard to believe. Because my work is so all-consuming, I didn't have much contact with my extended family." He handed her a blanket from the front seat.

"Thanks." She tried draping it around Eli's

shoulders, but he would have none of it. "Who took you into custody?"

"Said they were federal agents, but I'm not convinced. Their IDs didn't look real, and once they figured out I could be bought, they let me go—well, with a tracker on my phone. They didn't think I'd notice. Idiots."

"So they followed you?"

"Nah, I tucked the phone beneath the front seat of an eighteen wheeler headed south. Anyway, picked up my spare vehicle from a storage facility outside of town and followed you guys here. I heard on the scanner that local authorities were checking out all cabins, resorts, you name it, in Bonner County. I figured once they questioned Matt, they'd move on to the next cabin, and when they're done questioning everyone on-site, they'll check it off the list and head west. After they're gone, the resort will actually be the safest place to hide out for a few days."

"Safe would be nice for a change." Jenna glanced in the direction of their cabin, but couldn't see anything. "Don't you worry that they'll come ask you what you're doing sitting here?"

"They've already asked. Said I'd been driv-

ing for twelve hours and needed to catch some
sleep. They bought it. They're looking for a
couple and a little boy, not a single guy who
hasn't shaved in a week."

She wheeled one of Eli's toy trucks across
the leather seat. "By the way, Gary found me
in the shed."

"What? How?"

"I have no idea. You think he's tracking Eli
like you tracked him?"

"I should check the kid's stuff. Hand me his
bag."

She passed it to him. "Gary seemed scared.
He said he wanted out. That's why they're after
Eli, for leverage against him."

"What did that lug nut get himself into this
time?" he muttered.

"This time?"

"I did a background check on the guy before
Chloe married him. Gary likes to push the en-
velope. He built his business by breaking into
secure IT systems and exposing their vulner-
abilities. Maybe he broke into one system too
many."

"Or maybe he's involved with the cartel."

"What cartel?"

"Matt thinks there's a connection between

Chief Billings and the Guerro drug cartel suspected of laundering money through the foundation."

"Does he have proof?"

"Not yet."

"Too bad. That would put a quick end to all this." He rolled Eli's clothes up one piece at a time and repacked them in the bag. "It's clean."

"How did you track us?"

"Top right button on his overall strap."

Jenna looked closely and saw a small dark disc.

"Cops are headed this way," Marcus said. "Stay down."

Jenna coaxed Eli onto the floor and draped the blanket over herself and Eli. "We're in a fort, Eli," she whispered. The floodlights from the parking lot gave off enough light to illuminate the blanket fort. Eli reached out with a dimpled finger, poked at the blanket and giggled.

Time seemed to drag by as she struggled to keep Eli entertained so he wouldn't cry out for something, such as a bottle, which she didn't have handy.

You can do it, Jenna. You're a natural at this.

She dug into his bag for a new and exciting

toy to entertain him. "What's this?" She pulled out a clear wand with sparkling stars that glittered as they slid from one end to the other. The little boy's eyes lit up.

She steeled herself for the tap on the window from police, demanding to check Marcus's car again.

Casting all your care upon Him; for He careth for you.

At least she knew God cared for Eli, an innocent child.

She used a visualization technique her counselor had taught her after she'd left Anthony. She pictured taking her anxiety and fear and forming it into a snowball, then hurling it toward a tree, where it exploded into pieces. She much preferred the freedom of release to the bondage of anxiety.

As she pointed the star wand up toward the top of their fort, she noticed her trembling hand.

Apparently her visualization didn't totally ease the trepidation in her body.

"Look at those beautiful stars, Eli," she said softly. "Blue and green and red."

Eli grabbed the wand out of her hand and waved it left, then right. As he swung it over his head, he hit the blanket and she suspected they'd lose their cover if she didn't act quickly.

"Eli, look at this." She pulled a pink plastic pig out of his bag and made a soft oinking noise.

Eli giggled and mimicked her. She couldn't help but smile.

She fully embraced this moment, even with danger looming close, and surrendered her worry to God.

"We're clear," Marcus said from the front seat.

Jenna threw back the blanket. "They're gone?"

"They're pulling out of the lot." He slid a device out from beneath the driver's seat and clicked it on. "Let's listen in on the scanner."

"Base, we've cleared the Lazy Shade Resort, over," a voice announced.

"Where to next, over?"

"South to Coeur d'Alene, over."

"Ten-four."

Marcus glanced at Jenna. "Let's get back to the cabin. We'll leave the car here in case we need to make another escape out the bedroom window." He winked.

"Eli's going to wear a cape, like Superman, aren't you, Eli?" She packed up his toys and wrapped the blanket around him. "Ready."

Marcus got out and opened the door for her.

She noticed he'd brought the scanner with him so they could continue to monitor police activity. Even though he said police had left the premises, she still found herself peeking between cabins to scan the parking lot for cops.

They made it back to the cabin and reentered the same way they'd left, through the window. The minute she put Eli down on the floor, he ran back to the nightstand to continue his game of hide-and-seek with Bubba the bear.

The boy was remarkable. If only Jenna could be as unflappable as Eli.

As she headed for the door to the living area, Marcus stepped in front of her.

"Let me go first," he said.

He slipped his gun out of a holster at his belt and cracked open the door. She watched as his eyes darted left and right.

She instinctively went to stand near Eli.

Marcus pushed the door wide, stepped into the living area...

And froze, raising his hands.

The county police officer had asked pointed questions, which Matt answered directly. Then the cop said he needed to search the cabin. Matt held his breath when he pushed open the bedroom door, trying to figure out how to explain Jenna and Eli's presence.

When the cop turned, thanked Matt and left, Matt bolted into the bedroom.

They were gone. Vanished. He rushed to the closet.

Empty.

He looked out the window. No sign of them.

Matt tried coming up with an explanation. She wouldn't have taken Eli away.

Not willingly, at least.

He shoved the window open. Boot prints were visible in the snow. As well as a second set of prints, and both led away from the cabin.

They'd taken her and the child. Matt had failed to protect them.

Panic coursing through his body, he rushed into the living room and grabbed his jacket to go in search of Jenna and Eli.

Then he heard a thump in the next room. Matt stalked silently across the cabin, positioning himself beside the bedroom door.

It creaked open, and a pistol pointed through the doorway into the cabin.

"Drop the gun," Matt said.

The intruder did as ordered and stepped into the living area.

Marcus.

Didn't matter. Matt couldn't trust anyone.

"Take it easy," Marcus said.

"Drop the pack."

Marcus squatted and let it drop off his shoulders.

"Matt—"

"Where are Jenna and Eli?" Matthew said.

"We're here," Jenna said, stepping up to the doorway.

He couldn't look at her, not when he needed every ounce of attention to be on Marcus.

"Eli and I are fine," Jenna said. "Marcus kept us safe. What are you—?"

"Go sit at the kitchen table," he ordered Marcus.

The former Navy SEAL did as ordered.

"Jenna, tie Marcus's hands behind his back. There's duct tape in my bag."

"But Matt—"

"Do it."

She hesitated, and then followed Matt's order. The little boy toddled behind her. Noticing the barrel of his gun pointed across the room, Matt felt remorse about Eli witnessing Matt's aggressive stance.

But he had no choice. He needed to keep Jenna safe.

He wasn't going to lose her again.

Jenna led Eli to the sofa and handed him his bear. "Bubba wants to play."

Matt didn't take his eyes off Marcus, who directed his gaze to the floor.

Jenna went to Marcus and tied his hands behind his back. "Sorry," she said softly.

"It's fine. Matt's doing his job."

Standing, she planted her hands on her hips and squared off with Matt. "I don't get it. He's on our side."

"Don't be naive, Jenna. He led the authorities here."

It was the only explanation as to how they'd been found so easily.

"I didn't, Matt, honest," Marcus said.

Jenna wandered closer to Matt. "Then why would he protect me and little Eli?"

"It probably earns him a bigger payout in the end."

"He's Chloe's cousin. Eli's cousin," Jenna argued.

"Then how did the police know to check this resort for us?"

"It was a random check," Marcus argued.

"Because you knew we were here." Matt leaned against the wall and lowered his gun. "How did you know our location?"

"He put a tracker on Eli's overalls," Jenna said.

"Making sure you don't lose your payday, huh, Marcus?"

"There is no amount of money worth Eli's life," the man argued.

"Save it. I found out your bank account has a little over a hundred-dollar balance, and you've got a balloon payment due on your cabin next month."

Marcus didn't say anything at first. Matt supposed that was because it was hard to argue with the truth.

"I've got an explanation if you're willing to listen," Marcus said.

Matt nodded, not that he'd believe the man's lies.

"I keep most of my money offshore to protect my clients' identities," Marcus explained. "I can log in on my phone and show you my accounts. I've got over three hundred thousand in my Cayman account."

"You have an answer for everything, don't you?" Matt said.

"Plus, the job I recently completed is going to deposit ten grand into my US bank account."

Matt heard the man's words, but his explanation didn't ease the distrust in his heart.

"What can I do to convince you I'm on your side?"

"I believe him," Jenna said.

Matt glanced at her innocent and trusting expression. How could she be so naive after everything that had happened to them?

"Marcus said they let him go because he agreed to be a double agent," she said.

Matt snapped his attention to Marcus.

"He's pretending to work for them so he can help us protect Eli," Jenna continued.

"You're too trusting," he ground out, adrenaline still pulsing through his body.

"If he'd wanted to turn me over to Billings, he would have taken us away."

"But he didn't, and now they know where we are. We're easy targets," Matt said.

"Matt—" Marcus began.

"I'm not talking to you," Matt interrupted him.

"Marcus said we'd be safe here because police checked the premises and didn't find us, so there's no reason for them to come back,"

Jenna said. "We listened to the scanner. They're headed south."

Matt couldn't take his eyes off Marcus, trying to logically assess the situation. What Jenna was saying made sense. Marcus could have left with Jenna and Eli.

But he hadn't. He'd brought them back inside.

To Matt.

Because being here, in a cabin that had been checked and cleared, was the safest place for them to hide.

It dawned on him that Jenna was being the grounded one, while Matt orbited in crazy world.

Because he cared so much about Jenna. Were his feelings making him paranoid and distrustful when he didn't need to be?

"May I speak?" Marcus asked.

Matt nodded.

"I'll admit I agreed to be their spy to find you guys and expose your location. I could have done that just now, but I didn't. Matt, I'd never do anything that would put Eli in jeopardy. You've gotta believe me."

Silence permeated the room as Matt studied

the man tied to a chair. Eli ran up to Jenna and raised his arms.

"What's your story, little man?" she said, picking him up.

Protect them. You have to protect them.

"We need to pack up and get out of here," Matt said.

"That's a bad move—"

"Quiet," Matt interrupted Marcus.

"Matthew?" Jenna said tentatively.

He glanced at her as she bounced little Eli in her arms.

"Why not listen to the scanner to see if it's safe to leave?" She went to Marcus's bag, pulled out a scanner and walked it over to Matt.

He holstered his weapon and clicked it on.

For the next few minutes they listened to the activity of local law enforcement. Cops were spread out everywhere. Of course they were, because a child's life was at stake—a child with a phantom medical condition.

Leaving the resort and fleeing on any surrounding roads would be risky.

And extremely dangerous.

As Matt fought to find clarity, he struggled against the panic that had blinded him when he'd opened the bedroom door and they were gone.

"My gut tells me staying here is the best choice," Jenna said.

Her gut told her. This woman who'd been abused by her former husband, chased by thugs for the past few days and survived more than one dangerous situation was relying on instinct. She was able to trust her gut, while Matt's was a tangled mess.

Thinking critically, as an agent without a personal agenda, Matt catalogued the facts in his mind—Marcus's background check had come up clean. Marcus could have turned Jenna over to Billings's men—twice now—but he hadn't.

Jenna and Eli were safe. They were here, right in front of him.

Because Marcus had protected them.

"You can leave me tied up if you want," Marcus said. "I'm okay with that."

Matt glanced from Jenna to Marcus and back to Jenna. They both looked at him like he was a little insane, maybe a lot insane, and with good reason. Matt's perspective had been blown apart.

He was falling in love with Jenna North, which put both Jenna and Eli at risk.

"Look," Marcus began. "Chloe didn't have an easy childhood. My aunt and uncle were mean drunks. I saw what was going on, but I was just a kid. Chloe suffered her share of abuse and I couldn't protect her. I'd really like to help protect her son."

It was a reasonable request, an honorable request, from a man who loved his family.

Matt started to come down from his adrenaline rush and realized his paranoia stemmed from the feeling that someone close to them was feeding information to the other side, setting up Matt, Eli and Jenna to be snared like animals in a trap.

As he studied Marcus, the sounds of a playful little boy drifted across the cabin. A boy who was happy and safe.

Jenna touched Matt's arm. He couldn't look at her. He'd just lost his concentration, his professionalism. This time it didn't threaten anything, didn't put them at risk.

But next time?

Bottom line—the thought of losing Jenna had destroyed his ability to think clearly.

You're in big trouble, Weller.

When she squeezed his arm, he glanced into her caring green eyes.

"What do you think?" she asked.

Voices echoed from the scanner and it was obvious that the county officers were heading away from the Lazy Shade Resort, in both directions. Assuming the thugs who'd been after Jenna, Matt and Eli were also listening to the scanner, and using that information to decide where to look next, Matt decided that staying put was a safe choice, at least for now.

He also admitted he was overreacting in regards to Marcus, whose background check had portrayed him as a dedicated soldier who'd earned a medal for valor in combat. What more did Matt want?

He crossed the cabin, pulled out his knife and cut Marcus's hands free. "Sorry."

"No problem. I appreciate how much you care about Eli."

More like how much Matt cared about Jenna. Not good. He had to...

What? Stop caring about her? That ship had sailed and wasn't coming back to port. Instead, he had to make a responsible decision: find a replacement guardian, someone who'd have the necessary perspective to protect Jenna, not put her at greater risk.

Jenna studied him with an odd expression, as if she were trying to read his thoughts. Matt turned to the counter to make coffee.

"I'm not sure what the plan is, but I've got a tablet in my bag if that'll help," Marcus said.

"Getting Gary to testify against the cartel would be the biggest help," Matt said.

"That weasel?" Marcus went to retrieve his tablet. "Not likely."

"What do you mean?" Matt asked, scooping grounds into the coffee maker.

"I did surveillance on Gary before Chloe married him." Marcus sat at the kitchen table with his tablet.

Jenna continued to play with Eli, but her eyes were on Matt.

"As I told Jenna," Marcus started, "Gary would hack into IT systems to prove his talent as a tech specialist. The companies he broke into were either so grateful that they hired him as a consultant, or in some cases they threatened to take legal action."

Matt turned to Marcus. "Were charges ever brought against him? Because we never found any."

"Nope. He only exposed his identity to companies that had something to lose."

"I don't understand."

"Companies that were involved in questionable activity, maybe even criminal activity. Basically Gary would breach their system, they'd threaten to bring charges and he'd threaten to expose them. Then they'd back off."

"That's a good way to make enemies," Matt said.

"You're thinking this may not be related to the cartel's money laundering?"

"Perhaps, except that Gary's exact words were, *There is no getting out*," Matt said. "That sounds like the cartel."

"Although he didn't come out and admit it," Jenna offered.

"Maybe he didn't want to incriminate himself?" Marcus suggested.

"It would help to have access to Gary's emails," Matt said.

"I know a guy—"

"We need to keep this legal," Matt interrupted Marcus. "I'll contact my IT guy at the agency."

"Marcus, did you tell Chloe about Gary hacking into secure systems?" Jenna asked.

"She didn't want to hear it. She was so in love, kept saying how her life was finally working out and she'd found a kind man to take care of her, someone who was the opposite of her dad. She was angry with me for trying to ruin her happily-ever-after and, well, we didn't talk much after that."

"She was in love with the idea of love and security," Jenna said softly.

Matt sensed she was speaking from experience.

"Some would say Gary was pretty harmless, just manipulative for a buck," Marcus added.

Jenna handed Eli a toy. "Not so harmless if his work put his family at risk."

"True," Marcus agreed.

Matt joined Marcus at the table, careful to avoid Jenna's scrutiny. How was he going to do this? How was he going to leave her and Eli in someone else's care and not share his reasons for the decision? Because he knew if he told her of his plan, she'd push back.

He sensed she was feeling it too, this pull between them.

"You okay?" she said with a questioning frown.

She knew something was up, and somehow

he had to distract her from figuring out his next move.

"I'll be better once we put an end to this thing."

They spent the next day going through online files, even Jenna's work files, to see if the flow of money was going through her foundation fund. She certainly hoped not. The thought of somehow being a party to the cartel's money laundering sent a shudder down her spine. Is that why the big donations had come in? Because they were being funneled from the cartel?

While she took care of Eli, either Matt or Marcus would keep an eye out the window, as the other took the lead on digging into the case via the tablet.

Jenna stretched out on the bed beside Eli for his afternoon nap. As she lay there, humming the little boy to sleep, Matthew's words taunted her:

I'll be better once we put an end to this thing.

So would Jenna, although she admitted she didn't want her time with Matt to come to an end. How dysfunctional was that? He was just doing his job, that's all.

Yet last night he'd seemed irrational about

Marcus being a threat. She wasn't sure she'd be able to talk him out of his dark place. Ironic that she'd been the grounded one in that situation.

Ironic and refreshing. Jenna was learning to cope with dire situations more quickly than ever before. She no longer felt the need to run every time things got hard.

With a sigh, she studied the ceiling and pictured an easier life where she and Matt went for pizza, took Eli sledding, or even…attended church.

Wow, where had that thought come from?

She remembered him talking about how God had touched her life, how He brought the women of Gloria's Guardians to her, how she'd developed strength through tragedy.

Matt's words had resonated deep within Jenna. Somehow this man had peeled away the resentment encapsulating her heart, the anger she clung to against a God who never seemed to listen.

Yet hadn't He? After everything she'd been through these past few days, Eli was safe. And Jenna was still safe too, even with a police bulletin out on her.

She silently thanked God.

As night darkened the cabin, Eli awoke in an irritable mood. She completely understood since she wasn't one to wake up with a grin on her face most mornings either. She changed him, gave him his bear and went into the living room, where Marcus sat at the kitchen table, studying his tablet, and Matthew kept watch out the window.

"How'd you sleep?" Marcus asked.

Matthew glanced at Jenna and offered a strained smile, but didn't say anything.

"Eli slept pretty well, didn't you, little dude?" she said. He rubbed his cheek with his bear and leaned against her shoulder.

"Wish I could say we've made progress," Marcus said. "But even the FBI tech can't crack Gary's code and back doors to his files."

"So we're no better off than we were a few hours ago," Jenna said, heading into the kitchen.

"Jenna?" Matthew said.

She turned to him.

"We'll figure it out."

A sudden crash sounded from the bedroom.

"Stay here," Matt ordered, drawing his firearm.

He rushed across the cabin and disappeared

into the bedroom just as something hurled through the living room window, shattering the glass.

"Close your eyes!" Marcus shouted.

Chapter Eleven

Clutching Eli, Jenna dropped to the floor and shielded his face. Taking purposeful deep breaths, she was able to calm her racing heart and focus on protecting the little boy.

The front door slammed open with a crash.

"Get on the ground!" a man shouted.

The police? No, but they'd already been here, Marcus said—

Another crash was followed by a grunt.

Something was flashing behind her eyelids, probably a flash bomb, which is why Marcus had yelled to keep her eyes closed.

Suddenly a firm hand gripped her arm.

"Let him go!" a man shouted.

She clenched her jaw, knowing what was coming next and not caring. Nothing would make her release Eli.

Something smacked her in the head. She saw stars. But still wouldn't let go.

The child wailed into her ear.

"She won't let go of the kid!"

"Kill him!"

Kill Eli?

The man jerked back and released her. She guessed Marcus had come to her aid.

Clicking into protective mode, she opened the cabinet door beneath the sink and did a hand search for something she could use against her attacker. Then she got an even better idea. With a swipe of her hand, she cleared everything out from under the sink.

Against his protests, she slid Eli into the cabinet and shut the door. Again, without opening her eyes, she felt around for a bottle of something she'd taken out of the cabinet. She opened one and sniffed. A pine-scented disinfectant. Perfect.

She turned her back to the struggle going on behind her and pretended to still be holding Eli.

Men's grunts echoed across the cabin.

The flashing stopped.

"Bedroom clear!" a man shouted.

The bedroom? Where Matt had gone to check out the sound of a breaking window?

"Get 'em!" the other guy shouted, but it sounded like he was still tangling with Marcus.

She waited. Took a deep breath.

Tuned in to her highly sensitized instincts honed from years of anticipating when Anthony was coming for her.

She sensed the assailant was getting close.

And the next moment he pinched her arm and yanked her back.

In one fluid movement, she spun around and jerked the open bottle of disinfectant upward, making sure to keep her eyes closed in case of backsplash.

The guy cried out. His gun went off, causing her ears to ring.

"I can't see!" the man shouted and stumbled back against the kitchen table.

Behind her, Eli screamed from his safe hiding spot.

"Stupid cow!" the other guy said.

He was no longer fighting with Marcus. No, he was headed her way.

Deep breath, deep breath.

She curled into herself, clutching the bottle.

Cracked her eyes open.

He grabbed her and she jerked the bottle upward, but he yanked it out of her hand. She scrambled to get away and he grabbed her hair.

She screamed. Someone dove at the man...

Matthew.

He flung the attacker across the kitchen table. The gun flew out of his hands and slid across the floor. Eli pushed against the doors beneath the sink.

Jenna slammed her foot against the cabinet to keep Eli safe, and splayed her hands across the vinyl floor to grab the gun. Could she really shoot someone? Yes, if it meant saving her life.

Eli's life.

Matthew's life.

Her fingers wrapped around cold steel. With a firm grip on the gun, she scooted back to her protective position against the cabinet where Eli's muted cries echoed.

Casting all your care on Him…

She aimed the gun, ready to shoot.

Marcus lay unconscious a few feet away. The thug she'd nailed with the disinfectant had disappeared, probably into the bathroom to wash out his eyes.

Matthew and the other attacker punched and kicked, stumbling back toward the kitchen. That's when she spotted the blood on Matthew's shirt.

They hit the floor and rolled, getting dangerously close to slamming into Jenna. She held her position.

Should she do it now? Shoot the attacker?

What if she missed and shot Matthew by accident?

They rolled again. Knocked over a chair. The attacker pinned Matthew, pummeling his fist into the bullet wound. Matthew cried out and rolled away. The attacker turned to Jenna.

She pulled the trigger.

The guy stumbled backward, just for a second. Then he lunged and ripped the gun out of her hand before she could fire again. He'd obviously been wearing a protective vest.

He pulled her to her feet.

She stomped on the top of his foot and jerked her fingers up to poke him in the eyes.

He caught her wrist. His wicked eyes glowed with delight. He grabbed her neck with his firm hand.

She kicked, swung her arms.

Just as stars flitted across her vision, a chair smashed against the side of the guy's head and he released her.

Matthew. He was up again, fighting to save her life.

Jenna skirted away just as Eli flung open the

cabinet and tumbled onto the floor. She grabbed the little boy and held him close. Rocking him back and forth, she whispered, "It's okay, sweet boy. It's okay." Even though she knew it wasn't.

Please, God, help us.

"Matt, stop!" Marcus shouted.

Jenna opened her eyes and spotted Matthew, swinging a chair leg at the attacker over and over again, a wild expression pinching his forehead. She almost didn't recognize him.

"Matt!" Marcus tried grabbing the wooden weapon out of his hands, but Matt yanked it away. "Stop! You're going to kill him!"

Hooked by fury, he was being pulled further into the darkness.

Because the man he was beating senseless had tried to strangle Jenna to death.

She stood and cupped Eli's head against her shoulder. Stepping closer to the violent scene, she said firmly, "Matthew."

He hesitated and looked at her with empty blue eyes.

"It's okay. You can stop now. We're all okay."

He blinked, as if his brain had gone offline, shut down. He glanced at the guy on the floor.

"He's neutralized," Marcus confirmed.

"What about the other guy?" she asked.

A car door slammed outside and an engine turned over.

"He probably didn't want any of this." Marcus nodded at the unconscious man on the floor. "Hate to state the obvious, but we've got to get outta here."

Matthew didn't move at first, still staring at the beaten man.

"You guys take my car," Marcus said. "I'll drive your truck in case they're looking for it."

"What about Matthew's gunshot wound?" Jenna said.

"I'm fine." He stood, wavered slightly and avoided eye contact. "Let's move."

Matthew wasn't fine, and Jenna had to do something to help him. He'd sacrificed himself so many times for her.

As she cast a quick glance at her semiconscious passenger, guilt taunted her. He'd wanted to go to the authorities from day one, to follow proper channels, but her posttrauma issues made her suspicious, especially of law enforcement, and even of Matthew. And now this man couldn't get proper medical attention because they needed to keep moving.

After a few hours in the car, Eli started squirming and she decided to pick up food. A little sustenance would help her think clearly and map out their next steps.

Catching her reflection in the rearview, she realized she looked different from her former self.

Nor did she feel like the old Jenna, the weak Jenna who cowered from bullies. A flash of the scene in the cabin replayed in her mind: flinging disinfectant, kicking the man's leg...shooting him in the chest.

She was stronger now, more confident. Even with police and cartel thugs looking for her and Eli, she wasn't afraid.

She was determined.

Just as Matthew had been determined to save her life ever since the night he'd found her fleeing the community center. They'd grown close as they escaped danger, danger that almost drove him to commit murder on her behalf. She'd never forget the lost look in his eyes as he hovered over the attacker, gripping the chair leg. He would have continued hitting him, but somehow she'd pierced his adrenaline trance and had gotten through to him. His expression of rage eased into confusion and then...remorse.

In Jenna's opinion, he had nothing to be

sorry about. Jenna would have done the same thing, if she'd had the physical strength, to save Matt's life.

That's what you did for the people you loved.

Love? Was that even realistic considering how they'd met?

She couldn't think about that now. Her biggest concern had to be keeping the three of them safe.

Staying under the speed limit so as not to draw unwanted attention from authorities, she mentally prioritized her goals: keep Eli safe. And don't let Matthew die.

She glanced at her passenger yet again. Matt was still semiconscious. He couldn't offer suggestions or advice about what to do next.

She was on her own and in charge of protecting the two people she cared about most in this world. She could do this and she knew how, only Matthew probably wouldn't approve.

A few minutes later she pulled off the expressway to get food. And make the call.

"What…why are we stopped?" he asked, blinking his eyes open.

"I'm picking up food. May I borrow your phone?"

He nodded and handed it to her.

"Can you stay here and protect Eli?" she said.

"Yeah," he replied groggily. "Sure."

"I'll leave the keys in case you need to get out of here quick."

"I'm not going anywhere without you."

"Eli's safety comes first, remember?"

He nodded.

Eli's safety. The sweet boy had been exposed to way too much violence. He kicked his little feet and reached for Jenna.

"Hang on, buddy," she said. She went into the back seat and made sure he had his pacifier and bear. "Be right back."

A new kind of strength surged through her. She was the protector now, and she would succeed.

She tucked her hair into a knit cap and crossed the parking lot. A plan had clearly formed in her mind. She hesitated outside the restaurant and made her first call.

"Hello?" Patrice answered.

"It's Jenna."

"Oh, my friend, I've been worried about you."

"I need a favor. It's a big ask, so don't feel bad about saying no."

"Go on."

"Do you have anyone staying with you?"

"Not at present, no."

"Not Emily?"

"The Millers decided to give her another chance."

Jenna smiled to herself. "Good, that's good."

"How can I help?"

"My friend's little boy is still in danger. He needs a safe place to stay while I sort things out."

"Of course he's welcome here."

"It could be dangerous. Bad men are after him."

"All the more reason for the Guardians to protect him. How far away are you?"

"I'm guessing about four hours. I have to make a stop first."

"Want me to meet you halfway?"

"No, but let's not meet at your place. I don't want to expose the network."

"How about Remington's Pancake House?"

"Too public. There's the old gray barn historic site just outside of Post Falls. You know it?"

"No, but I'll plug it into my GPS and find it."

"I'll text you when I'm half an hour out."

"Sounds good."

With renewed hope, Jenna went into the restaurant and stepped up to the counter to order food.

"May I help you?" a teenager behind the counter asked.

"Sure, I'll have three burgers with fries and a chocolate shake."

"Everything on the burgers?"

"Ketchup and mustard only. Hey, have you seen a man with three little kids in Broncos gear?"

"Um…"

"You can't miss him. He's super tall."

"No, sorry."

"Okay, thanks."

"Three burgers and large fries," the cashier repeated.

"Oh, and two orders of chicken tenders." Jenna sighed. "I'd be in big trouble if I forget the tenders. With honey and ranch sauce."

"Sounds good."

Jenna paid and stepped aside for the next customer. Ordering a lot of food and asking about a man with three children gave the illusion she was with a group, not just one man and a child.

She mentally repeated her goals once more: *keep Eli safe*. Check. She would place him safely and anonymously with Patrice.

Don't let Matthew die. There was only one way to accomplish that goal.

A few minutes later, she collected two bags of food and headed for the car. She glanced through the back window, and her breath caught. She didn't see Matthew in the passenger seat. Jogging across the lot, she looked through the driver's side window.

Matthew lay unconscious on the front seat. She flung open the back door and placed the food beside Eli, then handed him a French fry to nibble on. He squealed and sucked on the fry.

She opened the front door. "Matthew?" She felt for a pulse. Weak, but steady.

Propping him up against the passenger door, she climbed into the car. Upon closer inspection, she saw that blood had soaked through the dressing Marcus had applied to Matthew's gunshot wound.

"You're gonna be okay," she whispered and pulled out of the parking lot.

"Jenna," Matt said on a gasp, opening his eyes.

Surrounded by pale-colored walls, he fought the confusion pickling his brain.

"Matt."

He turned to the source of the sound and was looking at his friend, Officer Kyle Armstrong.

"Kyle?" he croaked, his voice weak. Matt shifted, and pain seared down his arm to his fingertips. Right, he'd taken a bullet in the shoulder at the cabin.

"We're here in an official capacity."

"Where's Jenna?" Matt asked.

"That's what you're going to tell us." Chief Billings stepped into view. Matt realized his uninjured arm was cuffed to the bed.

"You're under arrest for kidnapping," Billings said.

"Kidnapping?"

"We thought Jenna North kidnapped the child, but it's obvious you kidnapped both the woman and child and held them hostage. What for, money?" Billings said. "What did Gary Mc-Fadden promise you? And where can we find him?"

"I don't know."

"Not good enough," Billings said. "There's a warrant out on Gary McFadden for embezzlement. He's been diverting funds from the Broadlake Foundation into offshore accounts. We suspect his wife is going to meet up with her husband in another country."

Matt clenched his jaw. They both knew Gary's wife was dead, and the killer was standing here spewing lies.

"You must have found out about their little side business and decided the best way to get some of that money was to kidnap the child," Billings continued.

Matt didn't argue or explain himself. There was no sense losing energy by fighting well-crafted lies.

"But for the McFaddens to leave their little boy behind?" Billings said. "In the care of an unstable woman like Jenna North? How cruel. It wouldn't surprise me if both the woman and child came to a tragic end."

Matt fisted his cuffed hand.

"What was your role in this?" Kyle questioned. "Were you Jenna North's bodyguard? Hired to protect the child until he could be reunited with his parents?"

"Lawyer," Matt said.

Billings's eye twitched. Kyle shook his head in disappointment.

Billings stepped around to the other side of the bed and analyzed Matt's dressing. "I was shot once. In the thigh. Hurt like a red-hot poker searing into my skin."

Matt glared at Billings, waiting.

"I wonder if it hurts as bad in the shoulder as it did in the leg?" He reached out.

"Chief," Kyle said, eyeing his phone. "A witness spotted the vehicle heading east on I-90."

Billings didn't shift away, his fingers mere inches from Matt's wound.

"Chief, we should be there to help bring her in," Kyle prompted.

She? Jenna? They'd located her?

"Leave him cuffed to the bed," Billings said.

"Yes, sir."

Billings retreated and started for the door.

"Jeremiah, huh?" Leaning closer to Matt with a closed fist against the bed for support, Kyle said, "You're no longer my family."

Shame coursed through Matt, then panic. His friend hadn't understood the meaning of the scripture reference. He didn't know Billings was a threat, and Kyle's life was in danger because of his friendship with Matt.

Kyle quickly turned and marched out.

Billings cracked a victorious smile. "We'll be back."

They disappeared into the hallway.

With a sigh of frustration, Matt fought the helplessness coursing through him. He shifted slightly. And felt something cool beside his cuffed wrist.

The key to the cuffs.

Adrenaline kept Jenna's mind sharp. She was only twenty minutes away from the barn and had texted Patrice that she was close.

She hadn't wanted to involve Patrice, but she was out of options. She surely wasn't going to turn herself and Eli in to the police, not with the lies being broadcast about her. Eli would end up in Child Protective Services with strangers who could very well have connections to the cartel.

The boy's father had said they were after Eli for leverage against Gary, and Jenna would make sure they wouldn't get anywhere near the child.

Jenna had taken charge.

She'd left Matthew at the hospital without his gun because she remembered him saying before that it would alarm staff. So she locked it in the glove box. Eli would stay with Patrice, and Jenna was driving Marcus's car that no one could trace back to her.

She'd found Agent Barnes's number from Matthew's cell phone and left the agent a message about where she'd taken Matthew for medical care. She said she would turn herself in to authorities once she'd found a safe place for little Eli.

It was time to stop running.

She'd never give up Eli's location, not until the case was resolved and she knew the child was safe. That goal would no doubt result in her being arrested, tried and convicted for any number of federal crimes.

She didn't care. All that mattered was Eli's safety.

Jenna finally felt like the person Chloe had hoped she was: a woman who wouldn't back down or be intimidated.

A friend who wouldn't let anything happen to Chloe's child.

Eli squawked from the back seat.

"What's up? You lose your Bubba? We're almost there, baby boy," Jenna said.

She turned right onto the dark drive leading to the abandoned farmhouse. As she got closer, she looked for Patrice's car. She'd probably parked out of view in case a local patrolman cruised by on his or her shift.

A light blinked from inside the barn. Jenna sighed with relief. Patrice was there, waiting.

All would be well.

She parked in back, beside Patrice's SUV, and grabbed Eli out of his car seat. Handing him the white bear, she headed for the barn.

"You ready to meet my friend? You're going to like her." Jenna kissed his forehead and stepped inside the barn. "Patrice?"

A flashlight clicked on, blinding her. "She's dead."

Chapter Twelve

Matt uncuffed himself and went to the closet, half expecting his clothes to be missing. Instead, he found a plastic bag with jeans and a clean shirt.

"Thanks, Kyle," he whispered and got dressed.

As he was slipping on his boots, a nurse entered the room. "What are you doing out of bed?"

"Had to use the washroom."

"You had to get dressed to do that?" With a raised eyebrow, she said, "Do I need to call security?"

"I'm FBI, working undercover."

"Sure you are."

He sighed. "Ma'am, I don't know how to convince you, but my case has gone south and I'm afraid a young woman and a child might be killed if I don't get to them."

The middle-aged nurse studied Matt. He held her gaze, hoping she'd read truth in his eyes.

"I'll be back in thirty minutes to check your vitals," she said.

She was giving him notice. He had half an hour to get as far away as he could.

There was only one choice to be made: he needed the resources of the FBI. Even if he wasn't sure whom he could trust, he had to start somewhere.

He had to find Jenna.

Searching his pockets, he realized his phone was missing. He vaguely remembered Jenna asking to borrow it, which meant he could have work track her location. He hoped. He prayed.

Keeping his head down, he exited the hospital without incident and walked north, toward a convenience store lit up in the distance. He had to call in, report to his supervisor and ask Bob for help in tracking Jenna.

A car pulled up beside him and the passenger window rolled down.

"Get in," Bob said from behind the wheel.

"How did you—?"

"Jenna North called me."

"You have her in custody?"

"Not yet."

"We've gotta find her, they're—"

"You really want to have this conversation out here?" Bob said.

Matt got into the car. They pulled away, quiet for a few minutes.

"The Guerro case is blown," Bob said. "All the money's gone, and someone with major tech skills went in and made it look like Jenna North disappeared with the funds."

"Gary," Matt muttered. "No, that makes no sense. He said the cartel was after him, that he'd developed the scheme and wanted out."

"Maybe he found his own way out by pinning it on Jenna. Pragge is out of his mind that the case is in shambles."

"Does he know you're here?"

"Are you kidding? I don't want to lose my job, and you're his least favorite person right now."

"We need to find Jenna," Matt said.

"How do you suggest we do that?" Bob asked.

"She has my phone. Let's get someone at work to ping it for us."

But twenty minutes later, they were unable to get a location on Matt's phone. Had she ditched it because she didn't want to be tracked?

Jenna was out there, alone, with no one to turn to.

"Patrice," he said.

"Who?"

"A woman who helped Jenna before when she escaped her abusive husband."

Matt contacted Nancy Miller and asked for Patrice's phone number. From there, Matt took a chance that Patrice still used a landline.

She did, and they were able to ascertain Patrice's address.

Going to Patrice made the most sense, since Jenna had been abandoned by Marcus and had given up on Matt's ability to protect her.

Regret tore through him. Exposing Patrice could jeopardize the Guardians, something Jenna was adamant she didn't want to do.

"I need a favor," Matt said to Bob.

"Another one?" Bob teased.

"Don't share Patrice's location with anyone else."

"Why, what's she into?"

"Helping people."

"Sounds noble. I wouldn't want to mess with that."

"Thanks."

A few hours later they pulled up in front of the house. The living room was lit up and the porch light glowed, as if to welcome visitors.

They approached the house and hesitated.

The front door was ajar.

Bob withdrew his firearm. When he realized Matt didn't have his gun, Bob pulled a second one from an ankle holster and offered it to him. He motioned that he was going around to the back of the house. Matt nodded and, gun in hand, toed the front door open.

The living room had been tossed, as if someone had been looking for something. Furniture was tipped over, a ceramic lamp lay in pieces on the floor and cabinet drawers were pulled out, papers strewn across the rug. He checked each room carefully, making it to the back of the house. As he stepped out on the back porch, Bob came around and joined him.

"It's clear," Matt said.

"Clear out here too." He holstered his gun and peeked into the back window. "What happened?"

Matt shook his head, unable to speak, to find words to state the obvious: They'd found and taken Patrice, Jenna and Eli.

He was too late.

He'd failed to protect them.

Why, Jenna, why did you leave me at the hospital?

Because she'd seen his violent side and knew he was capable of beating a man to death. A traumatized and gentle woman like Jenna North couldn't be around that kind of darkness.

"What do we do now?" Bob asked.

"Find Jenna."

"Over my dead body," a woman said behind Matt.

Bob reached for his weapon.

"Don't even," the woman threatened. "Let me see your hands."

"Ma'am, we're FBI agents," Bob said.

"I fell for that once already. Drop your weapons!"

This had to be...

"Patrice?" Matt said, placing his gun on the ground and turning to her.

The middle-aged woman aimed a shotgun at his chest. Her lip was bloody and a bruise was forming on her cheek.

"What happened?" he asked.

"I survived my fall over the cliff, no thanks to your friends."

"What friends?"

"Two guys who claimed to be cops. Cops don't threaten innocent people, and they surely don't hit 'em."

"I'm sorry that they hurt you."

"Hurt me? They threatened to kill me unless I told them where Jenna was. Well, I escaped and slid down the ravine where they couldn't find me."

"You're a strong woman. An inspiration to Jenna."

"Go on, get outta here." She motioned with her shotgun.

He had to convince her he was one of the good guys. "I can prove I'm here to help Jenna."

"One…two…" she counted.

Matt put his hand up to prevent Bob from withdrawing his gun in self-defense.

He nodded at Patrice. "Jenna and I spent a lot of time together. We grew very close. She told me about her ex-husband, and how Gloria's Guardians came to her rescue. She was able to protect a little boy this week thanks to you."

"Three…four—"

"Wait." Matt extended a calming hand. "Her ring, her silver braided ring. You gave it to her as a reminder that you and the Guardians are always there for her, that God's always there. Please, you've got to help me find her."

She lowered the weapon. "You're really him?"
Matt nodded.

"And we're really federal agents," Bob snapped.

"Do you know where she is?" Matt asked Patrice.

"I know where she was going. If they took my car, they do too."

Jenna turned to flee the barn. And was immediately blocked by a tall, broad-shouldered man.

"Nah-uh," he said.

She clung tighter to Eli and looked into the eyes of a killer, the husky, broad-shouldered guy who'd been with Chief Billings the night of Chloe's death.

It was over.

No, I will not accept that.

"Where's Patrice?" she said sharply to the thug.

"I told you, dead," a voice said behind her.

She spun around and a lantern clicked on, illuminating the other side of the barn and…

Chief Billings.

As he sauntered toward her, Jenna's pulse pounded into her throat.

"You're a real pain, ya know that?" Billings said.

"What did you expect me to do? Turn this innocent child over to a killer?"

"Me?" He stopped mere inches from her. "A killer? No, I'm the Cedar River police chief, who found the suspect that embezzled money from the Broadlake Foundation and then kidnapped a child because she'd lost her own."

Jenna held her breath. How could he know about Joey?

"I'll take the child." Billings reached out for Eli.

Jenna turned away from him.

"You can't take him where you're going," Billings said.

"You'll never be able to prove any of this in a court of law."

"I won't have to."

"Hello, Anna."

She gasped. It was Anthony's voice.

Her former husband stepped out of the shadows and offered a menacing smile. "I've missed you."

Her first instinct was to cower. Her second instinct was to fight.

"Shouldn't you still be in jail?" she snapped.

"Early release for good behavior." He winked.

"More like you paid somebody off."

"My, my, you've developed quite the attitude," Anthony said. "I can fix that."

She'd like to see him try.

"I'm sure the loving couple would like some time alone," Billings said and reached for Eli.

Once again she turned away.

"You're being ridiculous," Billings said. "I'd never hurt a kid."

"Then why do you want him?"

"To draw Gary out of hiding. He's made a mess of things."

"You mean the cartel?"

Billings's eyes flared. "Anthony, I'm relying on you to make this disappear."

The tall thug grabbed her shoulders and yanked her back against his chest. Eli wailed.

"Look at that, she and the child have bonded," Anthony said.

She held on as long as she could, but Billings was too strong. He ripped Eli out of her arms.

Then Anthony laughed.

Eli cried, reaching out for her.

Rage consumed her, followed by something even stronger.

Protect Eli.

In a blind fury, she kneed the tall guy in the crotch, ripped the gun out of his hand and smacked it against the side of his head. He stumbled backward. She spun around just as Anthony was about to grab her.

With a quick motion, she broke his nose with the gun, and he cried out in pain.

She aimed the weapon at Billings…who was pointing his gun at Eli. "Put it down."

Now what? If she relinquished her weapon, she was dead. If she didn't, Eli was dead.

She put out her free hand in surrender. And spotted Anthony charging in her direction. "I'm gonna kill you!"

She aimed the gun and fired. He fell to the ground, gripping his shoulder.

"*You* will never hurt *me* again," she said.

She glanced at Billings, who seemed surprised that she'd actually shot Anthony.

"Add attempted murder to the charges," Billings said.

"Let him go!" Gary cried.

Billings spun around and fired a shot into the darkness.

Eli screamed and kicked, making it impossible for Billings to get off a straight shot. He put Eli down and the boy toddled off. Jenna dove to grab him.

Gary rushed Billings.

A shot rang out. Then another.

Jenna backed up toward the exit.

"Get back here!" Anthony shouted, coming after her.

She aimed the gun…

But before she could squeeze the trigger, another shot rang out.

Anthony collapsed mere inches from her. She stared at him, unable to move.

"You're okay," Matthew said. He placed firm hands on her shoulders. She stood there, staring down the barrel of her gun at Anthony's motionless body.

Matthew reached around and slid the gun out of her hand. "Let it go."

She did, but she couldn't look away. Matthew kneeled to check Anthony's pulse. He glanced at Jenna and shook his head.

Her former husband was dead.

Matthew stood and pulled Jenna against his chest. He held her tight, with Eli between them, stroking her hair.

"You're under arrest!" a voice shouted behind her.

Patrice touched Jenna's arm and offered a nod.

"You're okay?" Jenna asked, happy to see her friend.

"I'm tough, remember?"

Only then did Jenna see Eli's father, Gary, motionless on the ground, and a second agent cuffing Chief Billings.

"You have the right to remain silent…" the agent said to Billings.

"Eli… Eli," Gary croaked.

Matthew extended his arm, as if offering to take Eli to his father.

"I can do it," Jenna said. Matthew and Patrice escorted Jenna over to Gary. "Can you cover up his wound?" she asked Matthew.

He took off his jacket and draped it over Gary's stomach, where he'd been hit.

"Ambulance is on the way," the other agent said.

Holding Eli, Jenna kneeled beside the little boy's father.

"Eli." Gary smiled and reached out to touch Eli's cheek. Eli turned away.

"He's scared," Jenna said. "Lots of loud noises, right, buddy?"

"Did you set up Jenna to take the fall for the money laundering?" Matthew asked.

"What?" Jenna said.

"Did that before, when I...planned to run with Eli." He looked at his son. "I thought I could keep him safe. I thought..."

"You can still keep him safe," Matthew said. "Give us something to shut down the cartel."

"This is your chance to be a hero for your son," Jenna added.

Gary nodded, a tear trailing down the side of his face. "There's a flash drive in his bear. It has everything, recordings, accounts."

Matthew glanced at the bear Eli clutched in his hand.

Gary's eyes misted over, and he looked at Eli. "I'm so sorry. I love you, tiger."

Eli pressed his cheek against Jenna's shoulder.

"Eli, your papa has an ow-ee," Jenna said. "He needs a kiss."

"Ow-ee." Eli touched his head where he'd bumped into the window frame at the Millers' farm.

"Can you give him a kiss to make it better?" Jenna encouraged.

Eli whipped his head around and looked at his dad. Jenna put Eli down. He leaned forward and kissed Gary on the nose.

"What a good boy," Jenna said.

Eli turned to Jenna and hugged her.

"Feels...much better," Gary said, before his eyelids fluttered closed.

Chapter Thirteen

"They were after Eli to control his father?" Patrice asked, as they sat in a conference room at the FBI field office.

"Looks that way." Jenna offered Eli a sippy cup with water, but he was more interested in playing with his wooden trains.

Jenna, Eli and Patrice had been taken to a field office to make their statements. Matthew rode with them, but said little.

Unfortunately Gary hadn't survived.

"And Anthony… I still can't believe he got early release and found you," Patrice said.

"He'd hired someone to break into my attorney's office and found my address, a PO box in Cedar River. From there, he hired a private detective, who eventually tracked me down. Anthony had him go through my apartment." Jenna shuddered. "I remembered thinking things were out of place, but figured it was posttrauma paranoia."

"You thought it was over with Anthony."

"The PI kept me under surveillance and became familiar with my routine. Somehow he got access to my messenger bag and put a tracking device inside so he'd always know where I was." She hesitated. "So Anthony would always know."

"How long had this been going on?"

"A couple of months."

"What was Anthony waiting for?"

"He only got out a few weeks ago. My guess is he enjoyed the hunt, planning what he'd do to me in retaliation for sending him to jail. We had all kinds of criminals tracking us. Just when we thought we were safe at the Lazy Shade Resort, Anthony sent thugs to kidnap me. When that didn't work, and knowing that I was wanted for kidnapping Eli, Anthony contacted Billings. They probably had a great time planning my demise."

"Someone should have notified you that Anthony had been released."

"For all I know there's a letter waiting for me in the PO box, but I only check it periodically. I honestly thought he was done with me."

"The man was a bully."

"I'm sorry you got caught up in all this. I never should have called you."

"Yes you should have. As I said many times when you stayed with me, we can't face our challenges alone, nor should we have to."

"But the Guardians... Have I put them in jeopardy?"

"No. Your friend Matthew gave me his word he wouldn't expose our network. Who knows, maybe someday the FBI will need our help."

"I love your attitude."

Patrice glanced at Eli. "And you love that little boy, don't you?"

Jenna nodded, smiling at Eli as he made a choo-choo sound.

"And Agent Weller?" Patrice said.

"He loves Eli too."

"I meant, how do you feel about Agent Weller?"

Jenna snapped her gaze to Patrice. "I know, these feelings are inappropriate," Jenna said.

"I didn't say that."

"You were about to. I get it. Only—" She hesitated. "He's the first man who has ever made me feel safe."

"That says a lot, considering what you've been through this past week."

"I guess."

"What is it?"

"I'm not sure he feels the same way." *Even though he's held me, comforted me...kissed me.*

"Well, the way he asked me to help him find you sounded more like the plea of a man in love than that of an FBI agent."

The door opened, and Matthew nodded at Patrice. "They're ready to take your statement."

Patrice patted Jenna on the hand and left.

"How's the little guy doin'?" Matthew asked, sitting at the conference table beside Jenna.

"He's great."

Silence permeated the room. There was so much to say, but how to say it?

"What will happen to Eli?" she asked.

"Marcus is on the way."

Jenna nodded, fighting back the grief at having to say goodbye to the adorable child.

Would she have to say goodbye to Matthew as well?

"What a crazy week," she said. "Is your case solid against the cartel?"

"Yes, ma'am. Everything's on the flash drive, just as Gary said."

"Why didn't he turn it over to the authorities earlier?"

"He wanted to avoid making enemies with

the cartel. He hoped to control the situation and stop having to move money around for them. The cartel hired Billings to keep an eye on Gary. I suspect Billings has been corrupt since his days as a border patrol agent."

"Yikes."

"Gary wanted out. The cartel refused. Gary figured he'd use blackmail, like he did with corporations, but the cartel decided to go after his family. At the end of the day you'd do anything to protect your family."

"So true."

Another awkward silence.

"I'm glad your ex-husband will never hurt you again," Matthew said.

"Thank you."

He glanced at her with regret in his eyes. "I'm sorry."

"For what?"

"For failing you, for not being there when you needed me most."

"But you *were* there for us at the barn, and you saved us so many times before that."

"Jenna—"

"Hear me out, Matt. Facing off against Billings and my ex-husband on my own wouldn't have been my first choice, yet it gave me such strength, strength I never knew I had."

He shook his head and glanced down at the floor. "You never should have left me behind."

"You mean at the hospital?"

"I understand why you did it—"

"Because you were bleeding to death."

"Because you no longer felt safe around me."

"Whoa, you're going to have to explain that one."

Eli ran up to her with a blue train. "Choo-choo!"

Without taking her eyes off Matt, she joined Eli on the floor and started playing trains with him. "Matt?" she prompted.

"The guy in the rental cabin—you saw me almost beat him to death."

"Because he tried to kill me," she stated. "Go on."

"You saw what I'm capable of."

"Didn't you see what I am capable of? Anthony's bloody nose and bloody shoulder? That was me. I may not have fired the bullet that killed him, but I shot him to protect Eli. That's what we do for the people we love."

Whoops.

He looked up, pinning her with intense blue eyes.

"I love Eli, don't you?" she fumbled, correcting herself.

His gaze drifted to the little boy, then back to Jenna.

He was about to say something when someone tapped on the door and it cracked open. A man introduced himself to Jenna as Supervisory Special Agent Steve Pragge. "Glad to see you and the little guy are okay, ma'am."

"Thanks to Agent Weller," she said, to drive her point home.

Matt was no longer looking at her.

"He kept us safe," Jenna added, concerned about how she'd craft her argument to Matt once they were alone. She couldn't make him admit he was in love with her, nor should she have to.

"Bubba," Eli said.

Jenna grabbed a replacement white bear and handed it to him. He frowned and turned back to his train.

"Weller certainly went off book on this one," his boss said. "Defied a direct order to drop you off and go back to his post."

She wondered if Matt's job would be in jeopardy because he'd decided to protect her and Eli.

"But his instincts to stay with you helped us build this case," Pragge said. "That's what makes a good agent, putting the job first."

Ah, the job—the perfect excuse for Matt to distance himself from Jenna and deny his feelings. He'd held her in his arms and made her feel safe, even loved. He'd probably argue those were the actions of a man just doing his job. Hogwash.

"The flash drive outlines everything," Pragge continued. "It's an indisputable link from the cartel to the money-laundering scheme to Billings. We've got Billings on video killing Chloe McFadden. He'd wiped the building's feed, but apparently Gary had set up his own cameras to keep track of things at the foundation. Billings is turning state's evidence in exchange for negotiating his prison location. As a cop, he wouldn't survive long in the general population."

"Well, I can make myself available to testify if you need me," Jenna offered.

"I appreciate that." Glancing at his phone, Pragge said, "I've gotta take this."

He left Jenna and Matthew alone. Tension stretched between them.

"You sure you'd be up to testifying if they need you to?" Matthew asked.

"Matthew, I'm a strong woman and I'll do what's right by my friend."

"I know you're strong, Jenna. I'm just doing my job by—"

"Really, Matt?" She stood and squared off with him. "So your question has nothing to do with your feelings for me?"

He glanced down at the industrial carpeting. "I'm sorry if I led you to believe—"

"Stop, okay? Stop using your job as an excuse so you won't have to admit the truth." She didn't know where this bold woman had come from, but she liked her, and it felt amazing to articulate her truth in such a raw and vulnerable way. "Hey, look at me."

When he did, she thought she might lose her nerve. His expression was guarded, his eyes shuttered.

"You can say the danger of the past week drove us into each other's arms, but it's more than that and you know it," she said. "God knows it."

"There's no room in my life for a relationship."

"Why not?"

"If Sarah's death proved anything, it's that I'm not good husband material."

"Sarah made a choice. She chose to drive recklessly. Now it's your turn to choose. Are you going to embrace love or run away from it?" Jenna picked up Eli. "We're going to the fountain for a drink."

She was unable to stand there one minute longer arguing with him about what was so obvious to Jenna. As she reached the door, she hesitated. Maybe if he wouldn't listen to her, he'd listen to God.

"Isn't there a quote in the Bible about truth, about it setting you free?" she said. "I think you should find that scripture."

She left the conference room and approached the fountain, knowing it would entertain Eli to slurp up the cold water. Besides, she needed to get away from Matt and his denial. For the first time in her life, she knew the truth in her heart—Matt loved her just as she loved him.

"Hey, Jenna." Marcus approached her, alongside special agent Pragge.

She took a deep breath and forced a smile.

The time had come for her to say goodbye, not only to the man she loved, but to the little boy she loved as well.

"Hi, Marcus," she said with forced charm. "I'm so glad you're okay."

"You as well." He reached out for Eli, but the little guy clung to Jenna.

"Eli, you remember Marcus?" she encouraged.

Be strong, Jenna, stronger than you've ever been in your life.

"Bubba." Eli rubbed his eyes.

"I think he forgot something." Matt joined them in the hallway, carrying the white bear. He offered it to Eli, but the child knew it wasn't his real bear, which had been confiscated for evidence.

Eli started to whimper.

"It's okay, buddy," she said, stroking his back.

"Or this?" Matt offered the Binky.

She took it and placed it in Eli's mouth. Eli sucked and leaned his head against her shoulder.

"You're gonna have fun with your cousin Marcus, little one," she said.

Please, God, help me do this without upsetting Eli.

She gripped him under the arms and peeled him off her, pain arcing through her chest. She smiled and kissed his cheek. "Love you, buddy."

As she handed him to Marcus, Eli whimpered against his pacifier.

"He likes multigrain bars and apples for breakfast. Scrambled eggs would be good too. But no more bottles at mealtime."

Marcus took the whimpering child.

Jenna turned and walked away. "Big boys use sippy cups."

She purposefully walked down the hall to the ladies' bathroom, rushed up to the mirror and took a deep breath. The tears broke free, and for the first time she was okay with that, accepting herself and even forgiving herself for crying. She finally understood that crying was not a sign of weakness, as Anthony had claimed, but a cleansing of emotions.

And she had plenty of those.

It took a good month before things settled down and Matt could return to Cedar River. He wanted to meet with Kyle, who'd temporarily taken over as police chief. Matt owed his friend an explanation and an apology.

"I wish I could have told you what was going on," Matt said to Kyle as they sat in the Bean & Brew Coffee Shop on Main Street. "Sorry about that."

"Hey, I get it. You were doing your job." Kyle sipped his coffee. "Where are you off to next? Another undercover assignment?"

"They've offered me a Supervisory Special Agent position."

"That's great news. Congratulations." He reached out to shake Matt's hand.

Matt stared into his mug.

"That is great news, right?" Kyle withdrew his hand.

A month ago a promotion like this would have been Matt's ultimate goal, his brass ring. Today, well, today he felt like there had to be more to life than a demanding, all-consuming career.

Perhaps a life with a special, loving woman and even children?

The memory of Jenna's smile flashed across his mind—her smile and Eli's giggle.

"Have you seen her yet?" Kyle asked.

Matt snapped his attention to his friend. "Who?"

"Jenna North."

"No, why would I… Wait, you mean she came back here?"

Kyle nodded.

Matt wouldn't know her whereabouts because he'd intentionally avoided anything relating to Jenna, wanting to put it all behind him. He'd even tried to avoid thinking about her, although on most days he'd failed miserably.

"The little boy is with her," Kyle added.

"Eli? I thought Marcus was his guardian."

"Marcus came into the station and introduced himself. Nice guy. I got the feeling he can't be a full-time parent because of his business, so he and Jenna have an arrangement."

"What kind of arrangement?" Matt growled.

Kyle chuckled. "It's not like that. They're both committed to doing what's best for the boy. Marcus bought property half an hour outside of town, and I'm guessing he bought the bungalow Jenna's living in as well. It's down the block from me, Garth and Willie."

"She moved into a cop neighborhood?"

"Yep. The town has really rallied around her to offer support."

"That's great."

"It's one of the reasons I love this place. You kinda liked it too when you lived here, didn't you?"

"I did. I liked it a lot." It was the one time Matt had felt like he truly belonged and was accepted for who he was, not for his level of performance.

"So, you're here, she's here…why not stop by?"

"It's complicated."

"No, it really isn't. You care about her, she cares about you—"

"Why do you say that? Did she say something?"

"No, and I won't pass her a note from you in class either. Come on, Matt, it's obvious."

"What's obvious is she needs a devoted man with integrity who makes her feel safe and is good with kids."

"Not that you are even close to fitting that description," Kyle teased. "My turn to share scripture. John chapter eight verse thirty-two."

"You're the second person to mention that particular scripture to me."

"Yeah, well." Kyle leaned back in his chair. "It's a good one, my friend."

There was nothing more beautiful than a sleeping child, Jenna thought as she stood over Eli's crib. He made a sweet little squeaking sound as he exhaled, clutching his new Bubba tighter.

She was glad he'd finally embraced the new stuffed animal with as much vigor as he'd had for the original.

Eli somehow had been able to leave the past behind and move on. He didn't cry too much for his parents, but then, she and friends in town had kept him fairly occupied.

Friends. She thought she'd only had one good friend, Chloe, but had been proven wrong this past month. Ladies from Bible study stopped by to help her unpack and offer parenting advice. The police officers in the neighborhood came by to make sure she felt safe and to share their cell numbers. One of the officer's wives brought dinner and, knowing her husband was working the 3 to 11 p.m. shift, Jenna invited her to stay. The other officer's wife took Eli for a few hours twice a week for a playdate with her toddler. The third police officer in the neighborhood was Kyle Armstrong, who wasn't married and was Matthew's friend.

Matthew.

She shook off the memory of a lovely kiss and sneaked quietly out of Eli's room. Shutting the door, she scanned the living room littered with toy trucks, trains and even a small playpen filled with plastic balls. The people of Cedar River had been incredibly supportive and didn't blame Jenna for the community center being shut down due to the investigation.

Jenna had been out of a job for only a few days when Marcus showed up with Eli. Marcus pleaded with Jenna to help him raise the little boy. She thought she was dreaming at first. She could hardly believe Eli was really there, reaching for her.

Marcus said parenting seemed to come so naturally to Jenna and she'd proven she could protect the child. They drew up guardianship paperwork, and Marcus encouraged Jenna to consider officially adopting Eli.

She didn't hesitate to contact an attorney and get things started.

Marcus offered financial support for Jenna and the child, but then they got word that Gary's will left everything to Eli in the form of a trust, and Jenna was the trustee. He'd revised the will only days before his own death. They'd have to wait for the case to be solved first, to make sure none of the money he'd left Eli was the result of criminal activity, but so far it looked like a separate account with legitimate money would be available, according to Agent Pragge.

She'd been in touch with either him or Agent Barnes, but not Matthew. It was as if he had no interest in what happened to Jenna.

Shaking off the thought, she kneeled on the living room floor and picked up blocks. Although exhausted from taking care of Eli, loving this little boy also energized her.

There was a soft tap at the front door. Marcus had insisted she get a video surveillance app on her phone that allowed her to see who was there.

Pulling the phone out of her pocket, she clicked on the app. And gasped at the sight of Matthew's handsome face filling her screen.

She sprung up from the floor and automatically ran her hands through her hair, wishing she'd put on blush or mascara today, but there hadn't been time.

"He's probably here on business," she muttered. That had to be it.

She took a deep breath. Opened the door.

He offered her a bouquet of daisies.

"Wow, thank you, Matthew. They're beautiful."

"I brought some stuff for the little guy too." He nodded at a shopping bag beside him on the porch.

"Come in," she said. "Is this about the case?"

"No, everything's good there."

Which meant…

Excitement fluttered in her belly. She led him toward the kitchen in the back of the house.

"Nice house," he said.

"Thanks. It's perfect for Eli and me. No stairs for me to worry about, and nice soft carpeting in case he takes a tumble." She pulled a water pitcher down from the cabinet to use as a vase.

"Looks like they've done some good updates. I noticed new windows. That should keep the house warm in the winter."

"It has so far." She filled the pitcher with water.

"I suppose you've got an energy efficient furnace?"

"Is that why you're here? To discuss my heating and cooling system?" she teased, turning to him.

"Sorry, no. I just…" He sighed and held her gaze. "John chapter eight verse thirty-two."

"What?"

"'Then you will know the truth, and the truth will set you free.' That's the scripture you were referring to."

"Oh."

"You're right, it did set me free once I admitted it to myself."

"Admitted…?"

"I always thought the job was my first priority, that I wouldn't give it up for anyone. The truth is, I hadn't found the woman I wanted to give it up for."

She was speechless at first, and then said, "Wait, you're leaving the FBI?"

"Maybe, I don't know. It depends."

"On what?"

"On you."

"I don't understand."

"Sure you do." He smiled. "I've missed you."

Her heart burst, and she went into his arms. As they clung to each other in the small kitchen, she thanked God for showing Matthew the way back to her.

Jenna leaned back and looked up into his smiling face. "What does this all mean, Matt?"

"It means I love you and we'll figure out the rest as we go."

"I have never felt so blessed in my life," she said.

He brushed a soft kiss against her lips. "Amen to that."

★ ★ ★ ★ ★

Colorado Mountain Kidnapping
Cate Nolan

MILLS & BOON

Cate Nolan lives in New York City, but she escapes to the ocean any chance she gets. Once school is done for the day, Cate loves to leave her real life behind and play with the characters in her imagination. She's got that suspense-writer gene that sees danger and a story in everyday occurrences. Cate particularly loves to write stories of faith enabling ordinary people to overcome extraordinary danger. You can find her at www.catenolanauthor.com.

Visit the Author Profile page
at millsandboon.com.au.

But they that wait upon the Lord shall renew their strength; they shall mount up with wings as eagles; they shall run, and not be weary; and they shall walk, and not faint.

—*Isaiah* 40:31

DEDICATION

For my daughters, Nora and Aislinn. You are my world. Thank you for all your love and support as I worked on this book.

And for Fenway, my faithful muse who crossed the rainbow bridge while I was writing it. I love to imagine you running along the beach with Daddy.

And finally, to those who gave all in service of their country, and for those who bear the scars.

Chapter One

Isabelle Weaver was fighting fatigue as she snuggled on the sofa with her five-year-old daughter Mia. Snow drifted softly past the window of her friend Jess's cozy cabin shrouding her view of the mountains. Isabelle yawned. After an exhausting day of entertaining two children while her friend had some appointments, Isabelle deeply appreciated the early evening calm. Jess's baby was finally sleeping peacefully in her crib in the bedroom, and Mia was drawing pictures of snowmen. Isabelle sipped her tea and sighed contentedly. Colorado in January was an entirely new experience for her. She pulled her heavy sweater closer around her shoulders and was just contemplating lighting a fire to ward off the chill when her ringtone abruptly shattered the silence.

Isabelle grabbed for her phone, trying to answer before the baby woke. Seeing her friend's name on the display, she spoke quietly. "Jess, where are you? I was getting worried—"

Jess cut her off almost at once. "Take the girls. Get out of the house—immediately."

"What? Is this a joke? What's going on?" But Isabelle sensed the answer even before Jess replied. Her friend sounded out of breath, terror threaded through her voice.

"No joke. Go."

"Where are you? Let me call for help."

For a moment, Isabelle heard nothing but Jess's raspy breath. "Isa, go. It's life or death. If—"

A gunshot exploded in the distance. Isabelle froze. Had she heard that through the phone or from outside?

"Jess?"

"If I don't make it back, protect Laura. The lawyer in Breckenridge has guardianship papers." Jess's voice lowered to a choked whisper. "Make sure she knows I love her."

"Jess—"

"Isa, go now!"

A squeal of tires and another gunshot sounded in Isabelle's ear before the phone went dead.

"Mama, is Aunt Jess coming home now?"

Before she could even think how to answer her daughter's question, Isabelle heard car wheels crunching on the gravel driveway. Though a part of her brain wanted to hope it was Jess, her gut said otherwise.

Mia jumped up. "Aunt Jess." She ran for the door.

"Mia, no!"

Isabelle launched herself off the sofa, managing to grasp her daughter's arm just before she reached the door. She put a finger to her lips and slid along the wall to the window so she could peer out from behind the heavy winter drapes.

Just as she'd feared, it was not Jess's car.

Doors opened on both sides and two men emerged.

With guns.

"Mia, come with me right now." Her harsh whisper must have conveyed the seriousness because her daughter didn't protest. Isabelle's heart broke as she took in Mia's frightened expression. She crouched down beside her. "Aunt Jess asked us to take Laura and go out the back. We have to be very quiet, so we don't wake Laura."

Mia's face brightened and Isabelle knew she'd concluded that this was a game. Maybe it would be best to let her think that.

"But, Mama—"

Fists pounded the door.

Isabelle didn't hesitate. As she grabbed their jackets off the hook, Mia reached for hers. "I can do it, Mama."

Isabelle put her finger to her lips as a reminder. Mia nodded and grinned. Isabelle guided her into the bedroom. She took a moment to stuff her phone into her jeans' pocket before crossing to the window. "I'll help you climb out and then hand Laura to you. Wait for me. I'll be right behind you."

Isabelle's heart was thumping as she struggled with a sash that felt like it had been painted shut. Rising panic fueled her efforts as she took a deep breath and put everything she had into a mighty shove. The sash went sailing up. *Please, Lord, don't let the men have heard that.*

Heart in her throat, Isabelle stuck her head out to make sure she wasn't delivering her daughter into danger. There was no sign of the men, so he turned and gave Mia a kiss before whispering, "Remember, we have to be very quiet. We don't want to wake Laura."

Mia smiled impishly and held her finger over her lips before she scrambled over the ledge and dropped to the snowy ground.

Isabelle pulled her own coat on, then turned to scoop the sleeping baby from the crib. She swaddled the blankets around her, creating a sling she then used to lower her into Mia's arms.

Please, Lord, let Laura stay asleep. A crying baby would give them away in a heartbeat.

Once Mia had the baby securely in her arms, Isabelle glanced back. She scanned the room as she tried to focus her scrambled thoughts.

The banging on the door sounded like they'd break through any minute. It underscored the panic ringing through her body. She needed her purse and her car keys, but they were on the kitchen counter. There was no time to go back for them. *Life or death*, she reminded herself as she climbed over the ledge. Her fingers were still gripping the sill when she heard something crash against the front door.

Isabelle dropped to the ground and took Laura from Mia. "We have to run as fast as we can to the tree house, okay?"

Mia nodded and took off across the snow-covered yard. Isabelle ran closely behind her, making a beeline for the trees. Terror dogged her steps. Her breaths came in heavy gasps as the baby weighed down her arms and she struggled to keep herself between Mia and the line of sight of anyone in the house.

She needed to call for help, but she didn't dare stop. If she could reach the tree line, she'd have time to call the sheriff. Another loud crash sounded from the house, followed by angry voices. Isabelle's heart sank.

"Mama, who is that?"

The tremor in Mia's voice escalated the fear coursing through Isabelle's body. "Ignore them, baby. We have to keep running."

They reached the tree line and Isabelle bent over, gasping for breath. The baby whimpered, and Isabelle wanted to moan in unison. Instead, she wrapped the blanket more securely and tucked Laura into a football hold.

Only then did she dare a look back, at which point she nearly collapsed in despair. Their footsteps shone like an arrow across the snow, pointing in the direction they'd traveled.

Isabelle's limbs felt paralyzed, and she had to fight through the terror that was numbing her brain. What should she do? How could she protect these children?

She was mere feet from the tree house, but that wouldn't be a refuge now that the men could see where she'd gone. She needed to keep running. But first she had to call for help—now, before the men followed her trail.

Isabelle reached into her pocket for her phone, hoping to at least have time to get through to a 9-1-1 operator, but her hand came up empty.

Her phone must have fallen from her pocket as she'd climbed out the window.

Despair snowballed, colder than this Colorado winter. Shouts from the house made it clear she couldn't go back. One man stood at the window gesturing and shouting to another who had just rounded the corner.

A shot rang out behind her. Bark splintered off a tree and sliced across her shoulder. Isabelle's terror ratcheted up. How could she possibly protect Mia and Laura with men shooting at them?

Isabelle squeezed her eyes shut. *Dear Lord, help us.* Another shot cracked the air and Isabelle felt the impact as it shattered a branch above her head, dumping snow down on them.

Mia whimpered. "Mommy, I'm scared. I don't like this game."

Isabelle's heart cracked. In a perfect world, she could take the time to comfort her daughter, but then, in a perfect world, no one would be shooting at them. Keeping the girls alive took priority for now. She hardened her resolve as she wrapped her free arm around Mia's shoulders and guided her behind a tree. "We have to pray to Jesus to help us, sweetie," she whispered. "Remember the prayer I taught you? 'Jesus, I trust in you.' Just keep saying it over and over."

As Mia repeated the prayer, Isabelle quickly studied their surroundings. There was less snow cover in the woods. Maybe she could find a path that wouldn't show their footsteps so clearly.

She grasped Mia's hand and started off at an angle opposite to where she'd been headed. She tried to step on the leaves and pine needles as much as possible. Praying that the motion would keep Laura calm, she and Mia quickly made their way from one cluster of trees to another.

When she felt like she couldn't take another step because of the stitch in her side, she stopped to listen. She could hear the voices still, but they sounded far off. Had the gunmen lost their track?

The thought no sooner crossed her mind than she heard another shot fired in the air, but it didn't hit anything near her and the children. Hoping they were just trying to flush her out, Isabelle trudged on. There was a break in the woods up ahead, and she could just make out a fence, one of those stockade types that looked like it was meant to keep the world out. If only she could find a way behind it. She leaned down and whispered to Mia, "See that fence? We're going to go there and try to get inside."

Mia's eyes widened with fear. Isabelle's heart ached. She'd do anything to replace that fear with the laughter and joy she usually saw. And she would. As soon as they were safe.

Mia tugged on her arm, keeping her from moving forward.

"Come, sweetie. We have to go behind the fence."

"No." Mia dug her heels in. "The scary man lives there."

Isabelle cast a glance over her shoulder. "What scary man?"

Mia wrapped her arms around Isabelle's leg as she replied. "I heard Aunt Jess tell you he's like the billy goats. They're scary."

Another time, she would have laughed, but now Mia's words gave her pause. When Jess had said her neighbor was reclusive and gruff, Isabelle had assumed he was just someone who cherished his privacy. Could Jess have meant something worse?

Close by—too close—a branch cracked and footsteps crunched through the frozen undergrowth. Isabelle's heart sank as she heard the man call to his partner. Their path had been discovered.

If her choice was an unfriendly neighbor or men with guns, the answer was obvious. She didn't care how gruff he was if he would only let them shelter behind his fence until she could call for help.

"Mia, we don't have a choice right now. Run!"

Isabelle shifted Laura in her arms, urged Mia forward, and made a dash for the fence. *Please God, let someone be home*—even if he wasn't nice.

They ran through the snow, looking for a gate, but there was no break in the long fence. Isabelle was ready to collapse in exhaustion by the time they rounded the corner. A groan escaped her lips as she saw nothing but another lengthy wood wall ahead. She paused for a breath, taking solace in the knowledge that the men in pursuit hadn't broken through into the clearing yet.

"I can't run any more, Mama."

"Just a little bit more, baby. We're almost

there." They had to be. Somewhere along this fence there had to be a gate, didn't there?

"Come on, let's race." Grateful that Mia responded to the challenge, Isabelle summoned her energy and dashed down the length of the paneled line.

"Mia, wait," she called in a loud whisper as her daughter raced around the corner.

"I found the gate, Mama."

Relief turned Isabelle's knees to water as she struggled the remaining distance.

She scanned the metal gate frames, looking for a bell, but there was nothing. Given how her day was going, that fit perfectly. A hermit probably wouldn't have a bell.

Isabelle raised her fist to knock on the gate just as one of the men rounded the far corner.

She briefly considered running, but there was no way they could continue to outrun him. Terror coursed through her as she saw the other gunman turn the far corner.

With gunmen closing in from both sides, they were out of options.

She quickly pulled Mia into the alcove formed by the frame. Raising her fist, she pounded with all her might. "Help us, please," she screamed. "Open the gate!"

★ ★ ★

Adam Dalton's head jerked up at sounds from outside. He'd been reading by the fire, his service dog, Chance, resting at his feet when his lights dimmed and a musical chime sounded. Though he'd designed his security system specifically to avoid triggering his PTSD, that particular sequence alerted him to danger. Adrenaline surged through his body and Chance's head lifted as the dog went on full alert.

Adam rested his hand on the Golden Retriever's head, allowing the contact to calm his own racing heart while he opened his tablet and scanned the security app.

Three sides showed nothing, but the view on the fourth side made his breath catch. Someone was pounding on his gate. He zoomed in to see the image more clearly. A woman and a child. He focused his attention and raised the volume until he could make out a faint call for help.

He pressed the button on the intercom. "Do you need something?"

"Let us in, please! Before they kill us."

Sooner than Adam could respond, the sound of gunshots exploded through his speakers.

His heart started to race again and black spots danced in front of his eyes.

Chance leaned into his leg. Adam settled back and ran his hand over the dog's head. The softness of the fur centered him.

He turned to the camera. More gunshots sounded and the woman's pleas were more desperate now.

Although every instinct screamed *hide*, he couldn't ignore her. He took a deep breath and pressed a button. The gate swung inward and he called through the intercom, "Come in."

Caught off balance, the woman fell forward, twisting her body as she hit the ground. She rolled sideways and he caught a glimpse of a bundle wrapped in a blanket. Was she holding a baby?

Shouts and more gunfire drew his attention away from her. He pressed another button and watched anxiously, praying the gates would close in time.

One man managed to angle the tip of his gun just in time to fire a shot before the gate clicked into place locking the men outside. The shot went off to her right, just missing the small child. He had to get down there and help them.

"Chance, come." Adam took the elevator

to the ground floor. While it descended, he put a call in to the sheriff, asking his friend to send backup. By the time Adam managed to get to the front door and fling it open, the child and the woman carrying the baby were making their way up the path. He stepped out onto the porch.

It went against his every introverted inclination to invite strangers into his mountain home, but they stood before him, a huddled trio in desperate need of help. The baby was crying, the child looked terrified, and the woman appeared on the verge of collapse. An inner chivalric instinct he'd thought long dead surfaced.

"Come inside. You'll be safe here."

As they stepped up onto the porch, the woman raised shell-shocked eyes. Her expression resonated deep within him. He recognized that state of disbelief where a part of your brain knew you'd experienced something traumatic, but for the most part, you had not begun to process anything beyond the terror.

He ushered them inside and shut the door firmly behind him.

The woman's whole body sagged in relief. "Thank you for letting us in. I don't know what we would have done—"

Another shot sounded from outside, followed by the sound of shattering glass.

She flinched and glanced wildly around. "We have to call the sheriff."

"I already called. He's on his way. In the meantime, you're safe here. They may shoot out a window, but they can't get in."

"You're sure?"

He held up his tablet. "I can monitor from here. See." He held out the device so she could eye the four screens. One of them showed the men pacing outside the fence. "There is no way for them to get over the wall."

She still looked doubtful, but there was nothing more he could do to reassure her until the sheriff arrived. What should he do with them until then? It had been too long since he'd allowed anyone other than his mother and sister inside these walls. He had no idea how to play host.

Adam quietly took in a calming breath and relaxed. He could use his military training and focus on their immediate needs. If he thought of this as a rescue mission rather than as having guests in his home, he could function. The woman was shivering, so the first thing was to warm them up.

"Let's go into the parlor. I'll build a fire so you can dry off."

She came reluctantly, her gaze glancing off the high ceilings and shrouded corridors. Seeing his home through her eyes, he suspected she was wondering if she was heading deeper into danger. He wanted to assure her, but his social skills were too rusty. Words failed him. He hadn't even managed to introduce himself.

He opened the door into a formal room he rarely used. The fireplace was kept ready, though, so he quickly lit the fire and pulled the sofa closer so they could feel the heat. He stood back, letting her unwrap the baby and settle the child beside her.

Next, he needed to gather intel. "Can you tell me what happened? If I update the sheriff, he can send out an alert for the gunmen, so they don't escape. Who are they?"

The woman closed her eyes and drew in a ragged breath. She was still struggling to calm herself. "I don't know."

"It was supposed to be a game, but the bad men chased us with their guns."

Adam glanced over at the child who was peering out from beside the woman. He wanted to pursue the point, but he sensed a need to distract the girl before the woman would speak.

He knelt to be at eye level with the child. "My name is Adam. My dog is good at defeating bad men. Would you like to meet him?" At her shy nod, he signaled Chance. "This is Chance. He's a working dog, so he waited for a command from me, but he's friendly."

The child scooted to the edge of the sofa and held her fingers out for the dog to sniff.

"Would you like to sit and pet him?"

She beamed at him. "May I, Mama?"

How could anyone resist that sweet, imploring look?

Mama didn't. She nodded and Adam was rewarded by a slight easing of the strain on her face. Once he had gotten the child set up on the floor beside Chance, he turned his attention back to the woman.

"Tell me what happened."

She shivered involuntarily. He grabbed a fleece blanket from a pile at the end of the sofa and helped her drape it around her shoulders.

"Thank you." She cradled the baby and huddled into the blanket. "I don't know what to tell the sheriff. I was babysitting for my friend. This is her daughter, Laura. That's Mia—my daughter." The woman nodded toward the older child gently petting Chance.

"She called and told me to take the children and get out of the house. We climbed out the back window as those men broke in through the front door. They started shooting at us. We ran and they chased us through the woods. I saw your gate and started banging." She got the words out in one breath and then shuddered and sank deeper into the blanket.

"Where is your friend?"

Her face fell and he immediately feared the worst.

When she spoke, her soft voice sounded confused, uncertain. "I don't know." She cast a glance at the child and spoke in a low voice. "When she called… I heard gunshots… I don't know."

A tear slid down her face and again Adam was overwhelmed by uncertainty. She was a stranger and a woman, and he had no idea how to comfort her. "I'll call the sheriff again." He glanced down at the child with the dog. "I'll step out into the hallway so she can't hear, but I won't leave you."

"Thank you, Adam."

He'd started for the door but turned back. "I didn't ask your name."

"Isabelle Weaver."

"I'd say pleased to meet you, Isabelle, but under the circumstances…" His voice faded off as she smiled.

Her entire face lit up, the worry fading momentarily, and his heartbeat sped up again. This time Chance didn't help.

He closed the door behind him, but just before it clicked into place, he heard the child's voice.

"He doesn't seem like the billy goat, Mama. He's a nice man."

Warmth spread through his chest. He had no idea what the billy goat reference meant, but it had been a long time since anyone had called him nice.

But nice didn't keep people alive.

Chapter Two

By the time she'd finished recounting the story to Sheriff Nate Brant, all Isabelle wanted to do was to crawl into bed and sleep for a year—an impossible wish with two children to care for and a target on her back.

"I'm sorry we have to impose on you even longer," she apologized as Adam returned from seeing the sheriff out.

He waved off her concern. "Nate was right to have you wait. Let him secure the scene while you stay here, out of danger." Isabelle winced at hearing Jess's house referred to as a crime scene. She'd been trying to stay strong, but just that wording was enough to pierce the numbness and send tears rushing to her eyes.

"Is there anything I can get for you?"

She started to decline, but Mia's head popped up from where she still snuggled with Chance. "I'm hungry, Mama."

"Let me see what I can find to help with that. Chance, stay."

Adam headed off into the dark hallway. When he returned, the delicious aroma reminded Isabelle of how long it had been since they'd eaten.

He set down a tray with soup, crusty bread, and a plate of chicken fingers that made Mia squeal in delight. Isabelle sampled the soup and her taste buds shared Mia's enthusiasm.

"Mmm, this is delicious. You made it?"

He looked up sheepishly. "I heated it. My mother and sister worry about me starving if left to my own devices, so they stock the freezer."

She glanced at the plate of chicken fingers but didn't say anything.

Adam laughed. "Those are all me."

He quickly sobered. "Nate called while I was in the kitchen. He'll be back soon to pick you up. He needs you to look over the house, see if anything is missing."

Other than Jess.

"A bit of good news, though. I checked my security footage. It picked up some pretty clear images of the men—"

The baby wailed, interrupting Adam, and she looked up at him in desperation. "She must be hungry. I don't suppose your mother stocked you with baby food too."

He frowned and shook his head. "No, but I could probably mash some carrots."

For some reason, the image of this tall, rugged man mashing carrots for a baby undid the composure Isabelle had managed to cling to until now. She rose and began to pace the room as the realization of her responsibility for baby Laura settled on her shoulders. Tears pooled in her eyes as she cuddled the infant. *Oh, Jess. What is happening?*

By the time they'd finished eating and feeding Laura, Sheriff Brant arrived to escort her to the crime scene. "We should leave the children here with Adam," he suggested.

"No." Realizing how rude her response had sounded, Isabelle apologized. "I'm sorry. I just—"

Adam stayed her apology with a raised hand. "I understand. You need the children where you can see them. I'll come with you and keep them in the car."

His gentle tone and kind expression nearly undid her again. "Thank you."

They went out and settled the children into a car seat and booster the sheriff pulled from his trunk. At the last minute, Adam ducked back inside. He came out bearing a heavy jacket. "It will be too big, but it's warmer than yours."

Isabelle gratefully accepted the coat and snuggled in its warmth as she climbed into the back seat and instinctively slumped down. Nate had come and gone with no sign of the gunmen, but a wave of anxiety left her feeling vulnerable as they exited the safety of Adam's compound.

The drive down to Jess's house was much faster than her flight through the woods had been. Too fast. Isabelle chewed on her lip to stop herself from begging him to turn around. It would take more strength than she had left to enter that house. She offered a silent plea. *Lord, give me strength.*

The driveway was blocked off with crime scene tape, so Nate pulled up in front of the house. He turned to Isabelle. "We should leave the children here. I can have a deputy stay with them." He glanced at the man beside him. "Or maybe Adam can babysit."

Isabelle's nerves were too on edge to consider leaving the children with a man who was a veritable stranger.

"You can trust him, Ms. Weaver," Nate murmured before adding in a teasing voice, "I'm sure he could handle a baby."

The sheriff's words and tone reassured her. His gentle ribbing tone resonated with the feel of an old friendship. She sent Adam an apologetic smile. "Do you mind?"

"No, go. Do what you need to. Nate's right. A crime scene is no place for children."

Except these children had lived through the crime.

"Thank you. I'll take the baby, though. She's starting to fret, and you've already gone above and beyond today."

The sheriff led the way across the lawn. "I'm avoiding the drive since you said they parked there."

Isabelle stepped over a small mound of snow and stopped to adjust the blanket around Laura. She tugged Adam's coat around her shoulders before starting toward the house again. He had been so generous to them. The thought of his kindness fueled her courage.

As they approached the door, she hesitated again, fussing at the blanket, at the way the folds were twisted.

"Ms. Weaver? It won't be any easier five minutes from now," Nate urged softly.

"Isabelle, please. And I know." She also knew why she was stalling. Walking through that door was tantamount to admitting that Jess was involved in something extremely dangerous.

Stalling wasn't going to change that.

Nate's hand touched her elbow gently. "I'm here with you. The sooner we go in, the faster we can get on with finding your friend."

Isabelle pressed her lips to the baby's soft fluff of hair. "We'll find your mama," she promised and then shoved her shoulders back, lifted her head and faced the sheriff. "Okay. Let's do this."

Despite her resolve, her footsteps faltered as she stepped through the doorway. Nate had said the house had been tossed, but that word hadn't prepared her for the chaos.

Her eyes watered as she took in the scene. Memories of Christmas morning flooded her mind. A week ago, she and Mia had spent the night so the girls could share Laura's first Christmas morning. Now the tree had been destroyed, flipped on its side, and ornaments littered the ground. What had they hoped to find by doing that? It just seemed malicious, and that ratcheted her fears.

She turned her gaze to the kitchen where she and Jess had teamed up with Mia to make

Christmas pancakes. Just hours ago, she'd stood at that same stove warming Laura's bottle. Her purse and car keys still sat on the counter, but absolutely everything else was chaos. She pushed back the horror of the scene and tried to study the room.

"Someone was angry." It seemed such an understatement, but Nate had asked for her impressions.

"Why do you say that?"

"Because there's the obvious evidence of a search—the drawers pulled open, the sofa slit, the closet door ajar and the contents strewn around." She shuddered thinking that the men who had done this were the same ones who had chased her into the woods. If Adam hadn't let them in… Tremors started and her whole body began to shake violently.

"Isabelle, I'm here. You're safe."

The feel of the sheriff's hand on her shoulder tethered her, and slowly the tremors subsided. She shook off the thoughts and circled the room, focusing on what lay before her.

"They were looking for something, but there's more, a second layer of violence that scares me on a deeper level. Because who destroys a Christmas tree when they're looking for people? Who rips stockings from the mantel?"

Nate nodded. "Very perceptive. But you have no idea what they were looking for?"

"Besides us? No."

She ran Jess's words through her head again. "When Jess called, she told me to get out of the house. She didn't indicate there was anything here I should take besides her daughter."

The sheriff came to stand beside her so they could take in the room from the same perspective. "I want you to think outside the box for a minute. Could Jess have done this? Could she have been with the men?"

The idea filled Isabelle with such hope that, for the first time, she realized how terrified she was that her friend had not survived.

"No, this wouldn't have been Jess looking for anything. She wouldn't have had to toss her own house. She'd have known what she'd wanted."

"Unless she wanted it to look like she didn't know."

Isabelle stopped her visual search of the room and turned to face the sheriff. "What are you implying?"

He held up his hands in surrender at her accusatory tone. "I wasn't implying anything."

"But you're thinking something."

"You're a mind reader?"

"I'm a mother. I know when someone is being evasive."

He gave a chuckle. "Okay. Well, I'm keeping an open mind, but based on what you've told me and the evidence at this crime scene—and the lack of it—there are several possibilities."

"And they are?"

"I'm holding them close to my vest at the moment, so I can keep that open mind."

Isabelle had to respect his investigative process, but that didn't stop her from forming her own conclusions.

"This is what I'm thinking. One." She ticked the number off on her finger. "The men came back here and searched the house—which they could have done quickly because it isn't very big. They were angry that the children and I got away and took it out here.

"Or two." She ticked another finger. "They had Jess with them and were trying to get her to deliver something. When she didn't, they destroyed her home."

He nodded, and her heart sank. She really didn't want it to be true. Because that didn't bode well for Jess.

"Or, three. They left, and Jess came back on her own before you got here."

The sheriff shrugged. "All three are possible, but I'm not jumping at anything until the crime scene team is done and I see what they've got."

Isabelle had to accept that. "If we're done, may I go look for my phone?"

"Sorry, no. But I'll ask the deputies to keep an eye out."

She understood. They couldn't have her tramping through a crime scene. "Am I allowed to take baby supplies?"

"I'd prefer we not disturb anything. With all this mess, anything we change could alter the evidence. When we catch these guys, and we will, I don't want anything interfering with their prosecution."

Isabelle nodded. "Got it. I have some supplies for her at my house." She sighed as fatigue washed over her. "May I go home now?"

"I'll have to find someone to drive you."

"It's okay. Besides Mia's booster seat, I have another seat for Laura in my car. It's parked out front."

"With all the tires slashed."

Isabelle closed her eyes and sagged against the wall.

"I'm sorry, Isabelle. Damaging your car must make it feel more personal."

She heaved a sigh. "It became personal when they started shooting at me."

Once Isabelle had gone into the house, Adam had let Chance settle on the back seat. As he glanced at his dog tucked against Mia. Adam wondered for the umpteenth time how he'd managed to get himself caught up in this. To be fair, they'd come to his gate, and it would have taken a man with a far colder heart than his to turn away a woman and children in such desperate straits. He couldn't live with the guilt if they came to harm. After his years in Afghanistan, too many deaths already weighed on his conscience.

But knowing it was the right thing to do wasn't the same as being comfortable. Truthfully, this was the most human interaction he'd had in five years. Pretty much the only real interaction he'd had with anyone other than his mother and sister. And Nate. He and the sheriff had served three tours together, and Nate was possibly the only living person who truly understood what Adam had endured. Sometimes he wondered if he would even have survived were it not for Nate's persistent friendship.

The sound of the front door closing interrupted his musings, and Adam looked up to see Isabelle and Nate walking down the path. His heart went out to the woman trudging over the snowy lawn. There was another answer for why he'd had to help. Regardless of the personal cost, how could he turn his back on someone who was so bravely coping with this difficult situation?

She snuggled the baby close, but there was a new weariness to her and she looked even more frail than she had earlier. Nate walked beside her with his phone to his ear. Adam could tell from his posture and facial expression that it was not good news. The sheriff disconnected the call as they approached the car, and from the set of his jaw, Adam got an uneasy sense that his involvement wasn't over. "Back to the floor, Chance."

Nate held the back door open to help Isabelle into the vehicle. He came around, got in the driver's side, and turned to Adam, his expression sober.

"There's been a bad accident up on the ridge. I need to head up to the site, but I can't leave this crime scene unattended. If I leave the deputy here, will you take Isabelle home?"

Isabelle spoke up before Adam could reply. "Again, I'm sorry to be so much trouble. Apparently, they slashed my tires, but I can wait here for someone to come back. You've already done far more for us than necessary. I couldn't possibly ask you to help again."

"It would be better for Adam to take you."

Adam read the subtext in Nate's blunt statement. Whatever he'd seen inside had made the sheriff wary of Isabelle leaving on her own. Questions rose in his mind. Did his friend think Isabelle was at risk? Or did he suspect her?

The sheriff cleared his throat. "I'm sorry, Isabelle. Until we know who they are and what they want, we really don't know how safe you are anywhere."

And just like that, Adam found himself agreeing to help. There was something about this woman that slipped beneath his wall of reserve and undid his reclusive instincts. He turned in his seat to reassure her. "You didn't ask. Nate did. And he's right. You've had a rough day. Let me take you home."

All the fight seemed to leave her at his offer. Emotion flitted across her face. Relief welled in her eyes. She bowed her head for a moment before lifting her head to him and nodding. "Thank you."

The sheriff made quick work of retrieving Mia's booster and the spare car seat from Isabelle's car before he drove them back to Adam's house. After leaving the seats on the ground by the open garage, and promising to update them when he knew anything, Nate took off.

Adam watched the taillights disappear down the lane as Nate's words echoed in his brain. *We really don't know how safe you are anywhere.* Panic clawed at his throat. He was now solely responsible for safeguarding a frightened woman and two innocent children. He should never have accepted responsibility. He should have volunteered to stay at the crime scene and let the deputy take them home. He wasn't enough to protect them, he—

The solid bulk of Chance leaning into his legs cut off the panicked thoughts before they could overwhelm him. Adam ruffled his hand through the dog's fur. He took a deep breath and cleared his throat. "Let me just get these seats in the car and we can head to your house."

Isabelle angled her head and offered a tentative smile. "Have you installed one of these recently? The directions are ridiculously complicated, but I've done it enough times that it's second nature. Why don't you take the baby while I set up the car seats?" Isabelle held Laura toward him.

Left with no choice, Adam accepted the baby, who started to squawk as he shifted her awkwardly, trying to find a good hold. Isabelle laughed and, for a moment, his heart stilled at the unexpectedly joyful sound.

"She's not a bomb," Isabelle joked then looked thoughtful as Laura continued to cry. "Did you ever play football?"

Adam nodded.

"There's something called a football hold. Babies love it. Just cradle her the way you would a football while running for a touchdown."

Adam shifted the baby as directed, and her cries instantly turned to happy gurgles. Amazed, he rocked her gently while Isabelle installed the car seat and got Mia perched in her booster seat.

Once everyone was settled and Isabelle's address was programmed into his GPS, Adam started the car down the driveway. The soft snow from earlier had turned to sleet, and he wanted to get her home quickly. "Do you have supplies for the baby at your house, or should we stop somewhere?"

"I have enough to get through the night." A heavy silence hung in the air for a few minutes before Isabelle spoke again, her voice low, presumably to keep her daughter from hearing.

"About what Nate said…"

Adam heard the tremor in her voice and wished there was something he could say to set her fears to rest.

"Do you think he's serious? I mean not serious but…right? About the danger."

Adam debated how to answer. He could give her the truth—that Nate would not have said anything without a reasonably strong belief he was right. Or he could play it more gently and say the sheriff was just taking precautions. But if he downplayed it and something happened to her or the girls, then it would be on him.

He shrugged. "I don't know, Isabelle. I can only say I've never known Nate to be an alarmist. If he thinks your safety is at risk, we should be careful."

Adam heard her swallow. A quick sideways glance showed her fighting back tears. Adam wanted to reach across and take her hand, comfort her. But what comfort did he have to offer really? Except… "We should pray."

Isabelle looked surprised at his response.

He shrugged. "It's what I do when I don't know what else to do. I remind myself that God is in control." The words sounded so simple spilling from his lips. They gave no indication of the hard-fought battle it had taken him to get to this place of trust in God. An ongoing battle, like so much of his recovery.

"Mama taught me to say 'Jesus, I trust in you.'"

Adam smiled into his rearview mirror. "That's an excellent prayer, Mia."

Isabelle nodded, so he focused his gaze on the road that was icing over and whispered the words he could hear Isabelle praying with her daughter. "Jesus, I trust in you."

The words settled a calmness over the car that lasted until he made the turn onto Isabelle's street.

"Which house is yours?"

She didn't answer right away. "Isabelle?"

"The one with a car in the driveway." The tremor was back in her voice, alerting him.

"Not your second car?" He realized in that moment that he knew nothing about her. Did she have a husband who was waiting for her? The thought bothered him more than it should.

"Not mine."

Adam slowed as they pulled closer.

"Adam, wait. That's the car the men were driving."

"The gunmen?"

She could barely get the words out. "I think. Yes. It's the same make and color as the car that was at Jess's house."

"Okay, don't panic." The command was as much for himself as it was for her. "They won't know my car. Just don't look over that way as we drive by. We'll just keep driving down the street."

"It's a dead end."

Adam blew out a breath. This just got better and better. "How many other houses are there?"

"Five and a cul-de-sac."

He thought for a minute. "Here's the plan. You slide down in the seat, so they don't see you. I'm going to drive down the road and circle back. If anyone is watching, hopefully they'll think I dropped you off back there."

"Or you could really drop me off. There's a path through the woods. It comes out the other side."

"No. If you had a cell phone, I'd consider it, but it's too dangerous to separate with no way to communicate. Is the path wide enough to drive down?"

"It's barely wide enough for a stroller."

Scratch that idea. If he'd had the truck, he might try it, but not with the SUV.

Adam glanced over at the house as he drove by. He could see lights on and silhouettes of men moving around inside. "Take my phone and call the sheriff. Tell him about the car and that there are two men inside." Her soft whimper made his heart ache, but she dutifully took the phone and made the call as he circled around the cul-de-sac and headed back.

"There's someone on the stoop now, so stay down. I'll let you know when we're past. Hopefully, they'll just think I made a wrong turn."

The first bullet slamming against his windshield put paid to that notion.

"New plan. Hang on!"

Chapter Three

Adam sped to the corner and made a sharp right. Isabelle held her breath as the car skidded on the icy road. She wanted to beg him to slow down, but men firing bullets was an even more deadly threat than the icy roads. She glanced at the children in the back seat and whispered another prayer. *Lord, please help us.*

"Talk to me, Isabelle. I don't want to get trapped in another dead end. What do I need to know about these streets?"

Isabelle pushed back at the terror that was threatening to overwhelm her. She knew this neighborhood. She just had to think clearly to figure it out. "These streets are all dead ends, but take the next one down, right after this curve. There's a house at the end with a drive-way that goes through to the next block."

"That will do." Adam flew around the curve then slammed on the brake as he headed into the hard turn. The car fishtailed again, but he quickly corrected and raced down the dark street.

Isabelle clung to the safety handle and continued to pray. They were traveling far faster than she'd like on a residential street with lights few and far between. "Could we pull into a driveway, turn off the lights and wait?"

"Too late," Adam muttered as a pair of headlights swung around the corner behind him, eliminating that option.

She fought against the fear threatening to paralyze her. "The road curves up ahead. The house with the driveway is the last one on the left. If we can get far enough ahead, they might not see us. The driveway is long and goes behind the house. Usually there are no cars outside, but sometimes they park near the garage. The garage opens on both sides, but there's also a paved area beside it. If you drive around it, you'll come out the other side and onto the street."

Adam didn't ease up on the gas until he swung into the driveway.

Isabelle gave a soft cry of disbelief as the car's headlights lit up the driveway—and the solid wall of snow that blocked their path. "Oh no!"

Her gaze flew from the blocked drive to Adam's face. His expression was grim, his jaw set. Guilt for involving him flooded her. "I'm sorry."

"Don't worry. I have a plan."

He had a plan? How could he have come up with something so quickly. Her brain had barely had time to register the danger, but he was already swinging the car in a circle. He pulled all the way to the end of the drive, against a huge snow drift.

"Maybe they won't see us?"

He chuffed a sound somewhere between a chuckle and a grunt. "Maybe. But I'm not banking on it." He lowered his voice, but the tone was urgent. "I need you to open the glove compartment and hand me the gun."

Gun. Shivers raced through Isabelle. What did he have in mind?

"Isabelle. Now."

The urgency in his voice jolted her out of her shock. Her trembling fingers fumbled with the latch, but finally she got it open and reached in for the handgun. Her brain couldn't wrap itself around the idea that she was in a car with the children, with men after them, and she was holding a gun. She passed it to Adam with lightning speed and turned, hoping to see the children asleep. Mia stared back, her eyes wide with terror, and Isabelle's heart cracked a little more.

Adam rolled his window down and a chill wind blew through the car. Laura started to whimper. "Do I have time to climb back there with them?"

"No. I need you to get down below window level, but stay belted in."

Tremors shook her body, a combination of fear and the cold. Why hadn't she ridden back there? She should be there to protect her babies. "Mia, stay as low as you can."

A squeal of tires alerted her that the other vehicle had caught up. *Please, God, let Adam's plan, whatever it is, work.* She huddled in her seat, watching him as she repeated her prayer in a litany. He was so still. She could feel the icy tension radiating off him, but he sat calmly, gun resting on the window frame, waiting.

Laura's whimpers rose to a cry and Isabelle prayed she couldn't be heard over the sound of the engine. "Shh, baby, it will be all right."

The next few moments passed in a blur of sound and motion, gunshots, tires squealing, metal scraping. And then Adam was gunning the engine and she felt the car take flight. Mia screamed, Laura's wails rose to a crescendo, but Adam remained calm. "You can sit up now, but keep your seat belt tight."

"What?" Still in a state of shock, Isabelle listened to him speak to her daughter. His voice was gentle, but it had a detached quality to it that sent chills down her spine. She glanced at his white-knuckled grip on the wheel, and suspicions grew.

"Mia, I'm sorry if that scared you. Everything is fine now. I only shot out their tire so they can't chase us anymore."

"Thank you, Mr. Adam."

Isabelle's heart swelled, overwhelmed with gratitude for this man who not only protected them, but who took the time to reassure an anxious child. As she turned to thank him, she could see the tension still etched in his neck and shoulders, the jaw so firmly set it looked frozen in place. Dread overcame her already shattered nerves. She knew that look. She knew the signs of a man gripped in memories of war. A new kind of fear settled over her, one that twisted a knot in her stomach—and had nothing to do with the men who'd been chasing them.

★ ★ ★

Adam entered the living room, taking in the sight of Mia asleep, snuggled against Chance. She seemed so peaceful. Unlike Isabelle, who was pacing the room with a fretful Laura on her shoulder.

"Any updates?" she asked as he knelt to add a log to the fire.

"I spoke with Nate. He didn't have anything to report except it seems the accident may have been a decoy to draw him away from the crime scene."

Isabelle gave a little shiver, making Adam wish he'd had better news. She continued to pace with the baby for a few minutes before perching on the edge of the sofa.

"Did he describe the car?"

"No. Why?"

"I've been worried the accident involved Jess."

At least he could reassure her on that score. "No, I asked. Nate said the plates were not registered to her."

Isabelle released a soft sigh and settled back into the sofa. "I've been so worried. I didn't even properly thank you for all of this." She gestured to the remains of the meal he'd laid

out. "And for stopping for diapers and formula."
She smiled softly. "And crayons. You won Mia
as a friend for life with those."

She closed her eyes for a moment, taking a
deep breath before she opened them to smile solemnly at him. "You were our hero today, Adam.
I can't thank you enough."

Uncomfortable with the praise, Adam shrugged
and tried to brush it off. "Crayons and diapers do
not a hero make."

"Maybe not, but it was clever of you to suggest she draw what scared her."

He avoided the questioning look in her eyes,
the one that wanted to ask how he knew about
art therapy. "Why don't you try to get some
rest? We don't know what tomorrow will bring,
and you must be exhausted."

A shiver ran through her. "I've tried. But every
time I close my eyes, I relive it. If you hadn't let
us in, I don't know—"

"Breathe, Isabelle."

She did as directed, taking several gulping
breaths before she managed to smooth them
into a regular pattern. "Will you talk to me?
About other things. Happy things. Tell me
about your life here."

A chuckle rolled through his chest. Happiness

and his life did not exactly go hand in hand. But he understood her need to talk, to fill the silence and turn off the brain.

"There's not much to say about my life. I create adaptive technology."

Isabelle shifted the baby so that Laura was cradled in her arms. "What does that mean?"

Adam laughed. "It's a fancy name for an age-old job. I tinker with things, try to find ways to make them accessible to people with different needs."

"Like these lights?"

Adam was impressed. "What did you notice?"

"There's something different about them. A softness, a tint. They don't feel as overwhelming."

"Very perceptive. My mother gets migraines. This diffused and tinted lighting is less offensive." His mother wasn't the only one who benefitted from the lights, but he had no plan to discuss his brain injury or PTSD with a woman he'd just met, no matter the circumstances.

"That's so clever of you. Did you always… what did you call it? Tinker?"

"My father had a workshop. He was always playing around with designs. I guess I came by it naturally." And relied on it for survival after his injury.

"Tell me about some of your other designs."

Adam spoke softly, hoping the gentle rhythm of his voice would lull her to sleep. Within minutes, he was rewarded as her eyes drifted closed and her head lolled back against the sofa.

At least one of them could relax.

He rose and gently eased Laura from Isabelle's arms. The baby nestled sweetly against his chest as he stood there, trying to absorb the tranquility of the scene. If one didn't know the background, and what had brought Isabelle and the girls to his door, it would be easy to believe this was a quiet family evening.

Something caught in his throat at the thought. *Careful there, Adam*, he admonished himself. It would be too easy to let down his guard and start wanting things he couldn't have, because this was just the sort of idyllic family life he'd once dreamed of having—before war had stolen all his hope.

Frustrated and angry with himself for falling prey to false illusions, Adam settled Laura into a bed of blankets and strode to the window overlooking his yard. He forced himself to take the deep breaths he'd just recommended to Isabelle. What he really needed, though, was to be outside in the woods, with the wind in his face, breathing the fresh pine scent of the trees, feeling the musty earth beneath his feet. Nature had given him the closest thing possible to a cure for his brain injury and PTSD. It had pulled him in and centered him, but tonight, the forest didn't offer the haven he'd come to rely on.

Below him, bright lights from the wall gave the illusion of safety and adequate security, but he knew from harsh experience that deadly dangers could lurk in the impenetrable dark beyond that perimeter.

As he revisited the day, and all the ways it could have gone worse, the spotlights flashed in his eyes, triggering his brain. Darkness began to close in, forming a tunnel as the light grew fainter and smaller. His body tensed as he peered down the tunnel. He couldn't see the enemy, but he knew they were out there. Ready. Waiting.

His chest tightened, his breaths coming in short uneven gasps. He couldn't control the rush of adrenaline, the need to lash out at a force he couldn't see.

A weight pressed insistently against his leg.

He tried to shove it away and his hand settled in soft fur. Even then, he tried to push back, but the furry creature was insistent, head butting him and knocking him slightly off balance. That motion interrupted the panic and, as he threaded his hands through Chance's soft fur, the darkness slowly began to recede. Lights glimmered softly in his field of vision.

He took several deep inhales and felt his chest ease, his heart rate become more regulated. He closed his eyes and offered a prayer of gratitude. *You are my strength, Lord. Yours is the glory. Yours is the power.* He ruffled Chance's fur, more lightly this time. "Thanks to you too, buddy."

Isabelle woke feeling stiff and disoriented. She blinked, looking around the room. When she saw Mia asleep by the fire, everything came rushing back at her. Jess's call. The escape through the woods. Adam letting them in. The crime scene and car chase. Talking with Adam.

She must have fallen asleep, like Mia had.

Realizing it was Chance easing away from Mia that had woken her, she turned her head to see where he'd gone. Her breath caught in her throat at the sight of Adam in the grip of a panic attack. *No. No. No.* Fear and regret washed over her. Fear because she knew this too well. Her husband had suffered PTSD. She'd lived with the fallout from it—his savage temper, his flashbacks, the way he'd court danger rather than accept help. She'd been on the verge of leaving him for her daughter's sake when he'd been killed in that last risky mission.

Now she and Mia were dependent on another man who suffered the same way. And that brought on regret, because suddenly everything that had puzzled her made sense—his rusty manners, the isolation of his life, his very home. It didn't take superpowers to understand he'd basically built himself a sanctuary inside a stockade fence.

And she'd invaded it.

Guilt swamped her. She'd sought refuge from him, brought danger into his life again, and unknowingly triggered these attacks. She hadn't been mistaken in the car. He'd fought off an attack then by going into warrior mode. Just like her husband had.

But Adam had Chance. Even as she watched, she could see the dog break the cycle. The tension in Adam's posture relaxed. And that eased something in her heart. Adam was not Daniel.

He'd been nothing but kind to her and deserved kindness in return.

She might have invaded his world and brought danger to his sanctuary, but she had also been trained to help someone with PTSD.

She rose and started walking slowly toward him, speaking softly as she approached. "Thank you, Adam, for everything you did for us today." She paused when she was an arm's length away, knowing not to invade his personal space without invitation. "I'm sorry we brought this into your life. You didn't ask for it, but you opened your home to us and provided safety. You protected two innocent children and a terrified woman. I'm so grateful to you for not turning us away. Instead—"

"How did you know?"

Isabelle hesitated only a minute. "That you're a protector? It was evident in every action you took today. You put your own well-being at risk for us—to protect us."

As she kept talking, she noticed his grip on Chance loosen. His shoulders relaxed. He stood silently for a moment. "You recognized what just happened. How did you know?"

She didn't pretend to misunderstand. "My

husband completed four tours in Afghanistan. Each one aggravated his PTSD a little more."

"And?"

Her head dropped. "He didn't come home from the fifth deployment."

"I'm sorry."

She cleared her throat. "Thank you."

He turned back to look out the window. "When?"

"Three years ago."

"Mia?"

"She was very young, and he was gone most of the time. And when he was there—well, he was never really there."

Silence fell between them and Isabelle searched for some normal conversation to fill it. "Thank you again for thinking to get the crayons for her. She loves to draw."

He chuckled. "I noticed."

Isabelle glanced at the drawings scattered across the coffee table.

"I meant what I said. You've been amazing to us. So welcoming when I know this must be hard for you."

He shrugged and continued to stare out into the yard.

She could see his reflection in the window

and noted the tension building again. Had she said something wrong?

Suddenly, he backed away from the window and turned to face her.

"They've breached the perimeter."

She looked at him in disbelief. "That sounds like a line from a bad movie."

"I'm serious. We have to leave—now."

"I thought you said your security was excellent."

"It is. And they've breached it. Which means they're not your average criminals and we have to get out of here fast. Gather whatever you can grab in two minutes."

While Isabelle picked up the baby, Adam lifted a sleepy Mia. "No need to wake up, sleepyhead, we're just going for a ride."

"Mama?"

"She's right here with Laura."

Mia glanced over, smiled at her mother, and snuggled back into Adam's arms. "And Chance?"

"Leading the way."

Isabelle watched Adam reach down to grab the crayons and pad of paper, and her heart melted despite her fear. She snatched up the diaper bag and followed him through the doorway.

"We'll take the elevator down."

Isabelle heard the tension in his voice despite his matter-of-fact tone. When the elevator opened, she realized they were on an entirely different level from where they'd entered earlier. There was no time for questions as Adam led her to a Range Rover. She should have been surprised to see he'd transferred the car seats earlier, but she was learning not to be surprised by how prepared he was.

They rapidly settled the girls into their seats. Isabelle wanted to stay in the back with them but remembered Adam needing her help earlier. She kissed each girl on the forehead and then reluctantly closed the door and climbed into the front seat.

As soon as she was belted in, Adam powered the engine on and pressed a button that opened a door in the back wall. "This driveway takes us out a different way. It will buy us some time."

Isabelle watched him in confused wonder. The man who, minutes earlier, had been in the grip of a panic attack was now a warrior, laser-focused on keeping them alive. Despite her regret for bringing triggers into his life, she breathed a prayer of thanks to the Lord for directing her to Adam's home.

They sped down a narrow side drive and

stopped when they reached the intersection where it met the main road. Adam checked both directions before turning right.

"We're not heading into town?"

"No. Presumably that's what they will expect."

Isabelle shuddered in fear at the idea of these unknown criminals out there anticipating her next move. It seemed second nature to Adam, and she wasn't certain if that reassured or frightened her more.

They drove in silence for only a few minutes before headlights lit up the road from behind, illuminating a heavy truck bearing down on them.

"Brace yourself," Adam muttered as the truck bumped them from behind. A popping sound and whoosh was all the warning they had before something flew by the car and exploded, filling the road ahead with dense red smoke.

Isabelle could barely breathe through her terror as she turned to check on the children. "Adam, what is that?"

"A smoke grenade."

The danger of her earlier flight through the woods paled compared to this new terror.

Adam sped up, putting distance between

them and the truck, but the wall of red smoke rapidly expanded, covering the entire road. Isabelle couldn't see a thing as Adam drove through the crimson cloud. Then she felt the car jolt as he suddenly swerved off the road.

Pine tree branches smacked against the windshield.

Isabelle screamed and covered her eyes as the forest closed in around them.

Chapter Four

Isabelle's scream echoed through the vehicle as the SUV careened through the dark forest like a runaway train, taking out branches as it continued down the mountain. How had it come to this? Who were these men and why did they want to kill her?

"Isabelle, it's okay." Adam's voice broke through her terrified thoughts.

Nothing is okay, she wanted to cry. *Someone is trying to kill me and these babies, and I have no idea why.*

His voice persisted. "See that safety hold in the roof? Grab on to it. The ride will be rough, but we're not crashing."

"You're sure?" Peering at him through her clasped fingers, she could see his profile outlined by the light from the dash and thought she saw the hint of a smile despite the grim circumstances.

"I am."

"But the girls—"

"Will be fine. Their car seats are secure."

Isabelle turned to check for herself. Mia's eyes were wide and Laura was whining, but they looked physically fine.

"Let me guess. You have a plan?"

He did laugh at that. But he never took his eyes off the road. "I do."

Road. She let the word register. They were now back on an actual road, not plunging off the side of a cliff. Now that she could breathe, Isabelle took a moment to study the snow-packed dirt illuminated by his low-beam headlights. Calling it a road might be generous. It was more a rough worn track lined by towering pine trees. "What is this?"

"An old logging trail. It runs parallel to the road—more or less. But hang on tight. It wasn't built for full-size cars."

Isabelle was grateful for the warning as the SUV seemed to suddenly plunge again. The screech died in her throat this time, but she didn't let go of her grip.

Despite Adam's calm words, the sight outside her windows was terrifying. His choice of vehicle made sense now. They seemed to be driving straight into a forest, and no ordinary car would have been able to push through the branches that hung low over them and scratched the roof. It was like being in a carwash when those big rollers came at you. Maybe she could ease Mia's fear by describing it that way.

She glanced over her shoulder, ready to re-assure her daughter, but the sight that met her eyes stole her words. Mia was leaning over from her booster seat, trying to comfort Laura. The soft sound of her daughter singing a lullaby flooded Isabelle with love and pride. In all honesty, she was a little in awe of her own daughter and her fierce love for Jess's little girl.

"She's just like you."

Adam's gentle words surprised her. "Apparently, she's braver than I am. I didn't hear her screaming." Now that they had escaped the imminent threat to their lives, shame at her reaction flooded her.

"Isabelle, cut yourself some slack. It's been a very long day. You have nothing to be embarrassed about. I think you've been amazing."

A flush of another kind suffused her. "I've only done what I had to." She hesitated a moment then lowered her voice. "I'm so sorry I dragged you into this. I shouldn't have—"

"Shouldn't have what? Banged on my gate

to save the children's lives? Shouldn't have run from men trying to kill you? Isabelle, you have done absolutely everything right today. You've been as brave as any soldier I ever fought with."

"Until I screamed like a baby."

He laughed again, and the sound of it warmed her heart.

"Thank you, Adam. You've been pretty amazing yourself."

"There you go. We're a good team. We just—"

His words were cut off by the sound of rapid fire from above. Bullets hammered the door of the SUV. The driver's-side window was hit and spider-webbed. "Get down"

Adam killed the headlights and threw a cloth over the dashboard. They were instantly enveloped in a darkness so deep that Isabelle couldn't see an inch in front of her. "Mia?" Panic washed over her at the thought of the babies being hit by that barrage.

"I'm okay, Mama."

"Adam?"

"Fine. Remember how I told you the road ran parallel to us?"

Isabelle squeaked out a yes.

"That's the bad news. Apparently, they know it too. But there is good news. They can shoot from up there, but they can't get down here unless they go get a smaller vehicle and follow."

"They can't climb down?"

"No, it's a sheer drop-off from the road. They could come in on foot, but we have too much of a head start."

Adam had slowed the Rover to a crawl. How could he even see where he was going? "What do we do now if we can't use the lights to see the way?"

He let out a deep sigh. "I'm going to need your help."

Isabelle closed her eyes and prayed. "Okay. What do I have to do?"

"I want you to open your door a crack—just enough that you can see the edge of the road. I'll keep driving, but you have to make sure I stay on the road. I would do it from my side, but my door's jammed—the bullets must've hit the locking mechanism."

"I can do that. But won't they hear the engine?"

"It has a special insulation that makes it more like a soft purr, but we're not going to stay in it much longer anyway. Mia?"

"Yes, Mr. Adam."

"I loved listening to your singing, but with the door open we have to be very quiet now, okay?"

"Okay."

Adam's voice had dropped to a whisper. Heavy silence fell over the SUV, silence that pulsed with tension and the absence of a sweet lullaby. Isabelle rubbed her eyes, praying that she would wake up and find this nightmare was over.

"Why do you think they stopped shooting?"

"I don't know."

That didn't reassure her. "Is it too much to hope they got tired and went home?"

He chuckled softly. "We can hope...but let's keep moving. Whenever you're ready."

Isabelle eased the door open and was immediately hit by a shower of ice pellets. She shrugged them off, just grateful they weren't bullets. Following Adam's lead, she whispered, "We're about a foot from the edge."

The SUV eased forward. "Let me know if I get closer than six inches."

Muscles strained against the tension in Isabelle's arms as she tried to hold the door open against the impact of icy-coated tree branches. The wind was picking up, whistling through the gap hauntingly. Isabelle shivered but kept her gaze glued to the snow-dirt mix as she clung to the door with all her might. "So far, so good. Totally straight."

Inch by inch, the Range Rover crept along in the dark with only the occasional hint of moonlight through the trees to guide them.

"Oh, you're getting too close." Isabelle's eyes were glazing over and she'd nearly missed the way the SUV was drifting toward the roadside. She couldn't see beyond the dirt ridge, but she was pretty sure she didn't want to know how sharply it dropped off.

Adam adjusted, and they were headed straight again. Time slowed into a monotonous crawl along the edge of the trees. The snow had ended, and moonlight peeped from beneath the clearing clouds.

"We're here," Adam finally whispered.

Isabelle peered into the darkness but, despite the moonlight, she couldn't see anything other than trees behind more trees. "Where is here?"

"Well, this is stop one. We ditch the car here."

Isabelle didn't even want to ask what came next. Ditching the car sounded too much like it involved walking, and she was beyond exhausted. "We can't stay here for the night?"

"Not unless you want to freeze to death."

Before she could breathe a word of assent, Adam turned the wheel sharply.

"Adam, you're off the path."

"I know."

What was he doing? She pulled the door closed and sank into her seat, raising her arms protectively as the SUV drove straight into a wall of trees before coming to a stop in a clearing.

"Wait here," he murmured. "I need to camouflage the car. Then I'll come back for you. It's only a short hike to the cabin."

Isabelle simply nodded. Exhaustion kept her silent as Adam walked away from the SUV.

Adam knew he was pushing Isabelle and the children beyond their physical limits, but he had no choice if they wanted to live. While he layered the SUV in pine branches and scattered leaves and snow, his brain calculated the best way to transition to his cabin. He wove the last set of branches in place, satisfied his camouflage would hide their trail—at least for the night.

He opened the driver's-side door and stuck his head in. "Stay here for a few minutes. I just want to scout and make sure we've left them far behind." What he didn't tell her was that if they hadn't lost the men, they were in deeper trouble than he wanted to consider. His hiking cabin would give them shelter, but it had no defense capability.

Adam crept back along the trail, sticking to the tree line and pausing every few steps to listen. The forest was full of the sound of branches crackling as the wind put pressure on the snow-laden boughs. He stood. Silent. Eyes closed. Making himself insignificant... almost invisible—a technique he'd first learned in the army and perfected in his forest therapy classes—until he felt one with the natural world around him. He could hear an owl hoot in the distance, but it was a calm and normal sound, not alarmed by an intruder. No other animals gave any indication of disturbance. High above, on the roadway, he could hear the regular passing of traffic, but deep within the woods, peace reigned. Slowly exhaling his relief, he opened his eyes and headed back to his SUV.

Isabelle had fallen asleep in the front seat and the girls were both asleep in the back. Peace reigned in here, as well, and after the day they'd been through, he hated to wake them. But he had no choice. The temperature was sinking fast and running the engine for heat would defeat the point of camouflage.

Adam eased into his seat and leaned toward her. "Isabelle," he whispered.

She woke in a flash, reflexively raising her arms in a defensive move. "Isabelle, it's me, Adam. It's all clear. We can head to the cabin." He kept his voice low, his arms resting limply in his lap, so she wouldn't feel threatened as she came fully alert.

She blinked, confusion evident on her face. Adam fought the urge to comfort her. Something about Isabelle called to his protective instincts. In her sleepy state, she looked so vulnerable. He dragged his thoughts back to the task at hand: getting them to the cabin safely, keeping them alive.

"I was going to carry Mia piggyback and hold Laura, but Mia's sleepy and I don't want her to fall. If I carry her, can you manage the baby?"

Isabelle nodded and a resolute expression settled on her face. "I will."

"Okay, it should only take us about twenty minutes to get there."

Her eyes widened, but that was the only sign of distress she showed.

"Is it safe to get out now?"

"Yes. I tracked back far enough to be sure they haven't followed."

He noted the wary relief on her face, his words seemingly having given her a new energy. She opened Mia's side of the car and climbed in beside her daughter. Adam knew he should afford her some privacy, but he couldn't force himself to avert his eyes. There was something in her gentle touch, the soft whisper of her voice waking Mia, that inspired him.

"Mr. Adam is going to carry you on a new adventure. Are you ready?"

The soft-spoken words drifted to him. He could barely make out Mia's sleepy response, but Isabelle backed out of the vehicle and guided the little girl to him.

"Hey, sleepyhead," he teased. "Ready to find the enchanted cabin in the forest?" He was rewarded with a gleam of excitement in her eyes.

While he got a blanket to wrap around Mia, Isabelle lifted Laura from her car seat and snuggled the baby deep within her coat. Adam grabbed the diaper bag and they headed deeper into the forest.

Moonlight filtered gently through the clouds. He stepped up beside Isabelle. "There is no sign of the men, but humans aren't the only dangers in this forest. Walk carefully, stay on the snow as much as possible, and try not to make a sound."

Her wide-eyed look of terror drove a knife through his heart. He reached for her arm. "Trust me. Do as I say and we'll be fine."

Chapter Five

Isabelle yawned, stretched, and looked around the small room where she'd slept with the girls. Last night she'd been nearly comatose by the time they'd dragged themselves inside, so she hadn't taken time to observe more than the beds. She glanced over at the two sleeping children. It hadn't taken much to get them settled in. Once the novelty of being in a cabin in the woods had worn off, Mia had curled up beside Chance and immediately fallen into a deep sleep. Sometime during the night, the dog had slipped away, but Mia still slept. Laura had fretted a bit, but a change of diaper and a bottle had settled her too. Isabelle had crashed not long after. It was both a testament to her trust in Adam and a sign of the depth of her exhaustion—mental and physical—that she'd slept so soundly.

The aroma of fresh coffee pulled her from

the cozy nest of blankets. She shivered as she stood, so she pulled another blanket over Mia and grabbed one to wrap around herself. Still tired, she stumbled out of the bedroom in search of Adam.

As she studied the dwelling through drowsy eyes, Isabelle could see that the cabin had a simple, rustic layout. The room where she'd slept with the girls was more of an alcove curtained off from the larger living area. There was also a small kitchenette and a bathroom. Beyond the living room, the outside deck was covered in at least two feet of snow, indicating that no one had used it in a long while. The sun was just rising, casting light through branches that sparkled and shimmered with their icy coating.

Adam stood in the far corner, talking into his phone, Chance at his feet. Isabelle could only make out scraps of the conversation, but it was enough to confirm he was speaking with Nate. A different sort of chill shivered through her. Was there any news?

Adam stared out the window, so deep in conversation that she assumed he hadn't heard her, but she was wrong. As she moved to the counter and poured a mug of coffee from the steaming pot, his voice dropped so she could no longer hear.

What information was he exchanging with Nate that he didn't want her to know? Fear for Jess suddenly warred with concern for their own safety. Isabelle knew she'd had little choice, but she had willingly placed their lives in the hands of a man she knew next to nothing about.

She sipped the coffee and tried to force a semblance of calm to her anxious thoughts. Adam had proved nothing if not that he was selfless and responsible. She had nothing to fear from him…right?

A memory of his panic attack flashed before her eyes, followed quickly by a surge of guilt.

He suffered PTSD, and had apparently lived as a hermit, yet he'd been willing to risk his own mental health for their safety. Thinking of how gentle and funny he'd been with Mia made her want to know more about him. What reservoirs of strength did he carry that allowed him to submerge his own needs in favor of protecting and comforting a frightened child?

She owed him at least a measure of trust.

Isabelle stared out the kitchenette window as she waited for him to finish the call. Fresh snow had fallen overnight, covering their footprints up to the cabin. It was as if they'd never come this way at all. She pulled the blanket closer and cradled the warm coffee mug between her hands as her mind considered how easy it would be to erase their entire existence. As easily as gentle snow erased their footprints.

"Whatever you're thinking, it isn't that bad."

Isabelle started at the sound of Adam's voice close beside her. Thank goodness she had him to protect them, because she was obviously not good at staying alert.

"I'm thinking a blueberry muffin would go great with this coffee." She turned and pasted a smile on her face. "Not that I'm not grateful for the coffee," she amended quickly.

"I can offer a granola bar."

Her smile turned genuine. "Perfect."

He opened a cupboard and pulled out a box. "Your choice. Chocolate chip, chocolate almond or double chocolate chip?"

"Someone likes chocolate."

"It's a universal favorite, so I keep them stocked."

All the questions she had been too tired to think of last night rushed to her mind as she bit into the bar. "What is this place?"

"It's a long story. Short version is, I like to

hike and it's good to have a safe place to spend the night if necessary."

Isabelle wanted to know more about that long story, but it was clearly something he wasn't ready to share.

"We need to talk."

The abrupt change and Adam's sudden matter-of-fact tenor unnerved her. Instantly gone was the gentle man who had teased Mia. This was the soldier again, the man she could picture commanding a team. "Is there news?"

"Not yet. Are the children still asleep?"

Isabelle's nerves frayed even more. "They were when I got up. I imagine they'll be out for a while given how late it was when we got here."

"Let's go sit by the window so we don't wake them."

The bite of granola stuck in her throat. She liked friendly Adam much better.

There was a sofa across from the windows and a chair set catty-cornered. Adam stood by the chair and indicated she should sit on the sofa. She sat, pulling her blanket closer and wishing the soft cushions would envelop her.

"Adam, you're scaring me. What's going on?"

He took a sip of his own coffee then set it

aside before answering. "We don't know what's going on. That's the problem. Nate has heard nothing. There's been no ransom, no sign of an abandoned car, no witnesses to a struggle. If not for the call you received, it would appear Jess simply vanished into thin air."

Isabelle set her coffee down before her trembling hands could drop the mug. She sank deeper into the cushions and hugged her arms to her chest.

"I need you to tell me everything you know about her."

The gruff tone of his voice startled her. Suddenly, she started to shake as she remembered Nate's questions. "You think she's involved in something bad."

Adam gave her a direct look. "She's definitely involved in something bad. The question is—was it voluntary or not?"

A tear ran down Isabelle's cheek, quickly followed by another. She could not believe this nightmare. As if on cue, Laura began to cry. "I have to get her before she wakes Mia."

Adam stood. "I'll get her while you fix a bottle. Then we'll talk."

Isabelle stumbled into the kitchen area and fumbled with the diaper bag. Tears were streaming in earnest now, and she could barely see what she was doing. Swiping the wetness away with the edge of her sleeve, she took the bottle, measured the scoops of formula, and opened a bottle of water to mix it. She shook the baby bottle and wiped up the mess she'd made with her unsteady hands. When she turned back, Adam had Laura on the sofa, cooing to her as he changed her diaper. Isabelle's head spun as Adam morphed back into their caregiver.

She brought the bottle to the sofa. Adam handed over Laura without a word, then went to grab the coffee pot. After topping off both of their mugs, he sat down across from her again. Isabelle couldn't bring herself to meet his gaze, but she felt its heat.

When he spoke, his voice was gentler. "Isabelle, I don't have to tell you how serious this situation is."

She nodded. "Yeah, I think I've got that."

"In order to figure out what happened, we need to know more about Jess, about her life, her background. You're the only one who can help with that. I want you to tell me everything you know about her."

Isabelle gazed down at the sweet baby guzzling her bottle, and her heart broke. "I want to help. Truly, I do. But I don't know where to start."

Adam leaned forward, elbows on his knees,

and steepled his fingers. "How long have you known her?"

"A year. Maybe less" She paused to do the mental calculation. The two of them had formed a bond so quickly that it shocked her to realize it had been a much shorter time. "About ten months."

That seemed to surprise him.

"It feels like so much longer," she added weakly.

"How did you meet?"

"Mia and I lived in Oklahoma. My husband was stationed there. After he died, I was grief-stricken." She bowed her head, not wanting him to see the wave of emotion she was sure was visible on her face thinking of that awful time.

"You met Jess in Oklahoma?"

"No." Isabelle shook her head and forced herself to focus on the task. "Once Daniel was gone, I had no place there anymore. People were kind, but I felt uncomfortable, like I was a reminder of the worst that could happen." Her voice faltered.

"So, you came here? What made you choose Colorado?"

She smiled sadly, gave a half laugh. "It wasn't

so much that I chose Colorado as my car chose for me. It sounds like such a cliché. My car broke down, I fell in love with the town, and I stayed."

She fidgeted with the blanket Laura was wrapped in. Adam waited patiently.

"That would be the simple answer. The deeper one is that I was in a really bad place emotionally. My husband was dead, and I was lost. I didn't know how to move forward beyond the day-to-day care of my daughter. I wasn't functioning as the mother Mia needed. I knew it wasn't fair to her for me to live in the past. She had a future, even if I didn't, and I needed to help her embrace it. So, I decided to make a fresh start. I had no idea where to go, but I decided to consider it an adventure. We'd drive until we found someplace that felt like home." She paused for a moment, looking for the right words to continue.

"Danny would have laughed at me because I was always such a planner—every minute of our lives, our future planned out and tracked on spreadsheets." She shrugged helplessly. "That obviously didn't work, so I decided to place my trust in God and my faithful car." She laughed. "I still trust God."

* * *

Adam sucked in a breath at the simple faith of her declaration. She was trying to make him laugh, but instead she'd revealed so much of herself to him. He hated doing this, making her revisit such a traumatic time in her life, but they needed something to go on, some information to help figure out what had happened to Jess and who was after Isabelle and the children. He deliberately ignored the uncomfortable twinge he'd felt hearing her talk about her dead husband, and pushed on. "Then what happened?"

"That's when I met Jess. I had the car towed to a service station and was looking for some place to wait. Jess was helping out in the gardens at the church when I wandered in to pray. Mia started chatting with her, telling her all about our car woes, and, before I knew it, Jess had offered me a room in the parish guesthouse and—"

"Wait, the parish has a guesthouse?" Adam had lived on the outskirts of this town for years, but it was a sign of his reclusive life that he had no idea what she was talking about.

Isabelle smiled and his heart lit up in response. "It's called Samaritan Home—you know, after the parable. It's a place where anyone down on their luck can find welcome for however long they need it. Jess said she'd stayed there when she first got to town, so she could recommend it."

Adam promised himself he'd find out more about Samaritan Home from Nate, but right now he focused on what Isabelle had said about Jess. "So, she was new to town also? When did she arrive?"

Isabelle's face fell. "Sorry, I don't know. I think I didn't realize at first that she hadn't been there long. She seemed so at home in that garden—almost like she'd grown up there. She knew the pastor well. I didn't really think about it at the time. I guess I imagined her coming here as a child. It was only later, when she made a comment in passing, that I realized she had only come to town recently. Ironically, we had very similar situations—though her car hadn't broken down. But that's what Jess is like. She seemed like she'd been here forever because she makes friends easily wherever she goes. People love her."

Her voice cracked, but Adam forced himself to deepen the probe. He had too many questions to stop because this was upsetting her.

Their safety had to be his priority. "What about Laura's father?"

"I don't know. I didn't ask."

Adam was incredulous. "Why not?"

Isabelle got defensive. "Because it isn't my business to ask people to divulge their darkest secrets to strangers they've just met."

He acknowledged that. "But later, when you came to be friends, she didn't say anything then?"

"No." She shrugged. "We were too busy with our current lives to talk about the past. Though..."

"Yes?"

"You asked if I noticed anything."

He waited.

"Sometimes when I'd come upon her sitting with Laura, she would be staring out into the forest as if she was thinking of something that made her very sad." Isabelle cuddled Laura a little closer.

"But you don't know what it was? You didn't ask?"

"I did once, but she denied there was anything wrong, said she had dust in her eyes. I took that as a request not to pry."

Adam's frustration grew. There had to be

something here he could use. "Let's go back over yesterday morning. Tell me again what happened."

Isabelle sighed and shifted the baby. "Jess called and said she had a sudden appointment in the morning, and could I possibly come watch Laura. Of course, I said yes. That's what we did for each other. If I'd asked, she'd have done the same. We were two single mothers who had become close friends and we relied on each other for everything."

"She never mentioned family?"

Isabelle bit down on her lip. "Only to say she didn't have any. It was when we were trying to decide what to do about Christmas. She said she had no family, so she and Laura were on their own. That's when we decided to spend it together."

"When did she ask you to become Laura's guardian?"

Isabelle thought back. "About two weeks ago."

She stood to burp Laura and began pacing the room with the baby on her shoulder. "I wondered what made her ask. She said she felt vulnerable as a single parent. Who would care for Laura if something happened to her? Who could she rely on?"

"Did she indicate she had some reason for worrying?"

"No. I assumed it had something to do with our conversations about family, about feeling vulnerable as single parents. We'd talked a lot about that over Christmas."

Adam stared out the window, pondering what she'd said. It all made sense in a way. He understood that if Jess was keeping life-threatening secrets, she wouldn't have wanted anyone to know. She provided for her daughter's safety, which was her main concern. Except, there was one thing she apparently hadn't considered. She hadn't factored in that whoever was a threat to her, was also a threat to Laura and, by extension, to Isabelle and Mia.

Adam's ringing phone interrupted his thoughts.

"Yes, Nate?"

As he talked, he surreptitiously watched Isabelle. She was upset, which was understandable. He'd asked some deeply personal questions. And yet, despite all his questioning, he had no more answers than he'd begun with. In fact, he only had more questions, the biggest one of all being whether to trust Isabelle's answers. He believed one hundred percent that she sincerely cared for Laura and was terrified of the men chasing them. What he couldn't ascertain was if she was being truthful with her responses about Jess. She was definitely terrified for her friend. But could she also be covering for her?

Chapter Six

"We need to pack up and move out."

Isabelle stopped midstride. She'd been pacing the room with Laura as she'd tried to process all the questions Adam had posed. She was still reeling, not so much from his questions, though, as from the realization they'd forced on her—how little she really knew her friend. She'd thought of them as so close, sharing everything, but Jess had obviously been keeping secrets.

"Isabelle?"

She shook herself. "Sorry. What did you say?"

"That we have to leave. The tires on my SUV are shredded, so Nate is going to meet us out by the road. It will be a hike, though. Maybe half an hour, so we need to get going."

Her body and mind screamed in rebellion at the idea of another hike through the woods. Every muscle ached from all the running yesterday. It didn't matter. Reminding herself that these men were trying to keep her alive, and not wanting to show him any weakness, Isabelle just nodded. "I'll wake Mia."

While Mia ate a granola bar and drank water, Isabelle packed up the few belongings she'd brought. Within twenty minutes, they were ready to go.

Something was different, though. She couldn't put a finger on it precisely, but the tension that had arisen between them this morning lingered in the air. Of course, Adam was still kind with Mia, walking with her perched on his shoulders. Isabelle could hear them whispering, and she could see Adam's arm extend as he pointed to things in the forest. Isabelle smiled. Mia would be eating up the attention. Isabelle was struck again by how different her life and Mia's might have been if Daniel had been open to treatment like Adam clearly was.

As she trudged along behind Adam and Mia, with only the monotony of her own thoughts for company, Isabelle searched her memory. What did she know of Jess's past? It was hard not to wish she'd dug deeper, thought to question, but the truth was she hadn't asked any questions because she hadn't wanted Jess asking them of her in return.

Isabelle buried the troubling thoughts. They weren't relevant. It wasn't her past that Adam was questioning. Her failed marriage was no concern of his, because it had no bearing on his need to keep them safe. She hadn't shared any of those details with Jess either. Which left her wondering… What details about her past had Jess deliberately not shared? Who was Laura's father? Did he have anything to do with the current threat?

Pressure on Isabelle's leg startled her. She glanced down to see Chance nuzzling her thigh. He looked up at her almost as if he sensed her sadness. Was it possible? She bent down to ruffle his golden fur.

As she straightened, Chance ran ahead to Mia and Adam and tugged on Adam's pant leg. Adam turned to look back. Isabelle laughed. "I think he's telling you to wait up for the slowpoke."

Adam slowed and waited for her to catch up. "We're almost to the edge of the road, but I want to stay within the tree line until Nate gets here."

"You think we're still being followed?"

"I don't want to take any chances. There was no one following us in the woods, but…" He shrugged.

It was only then Isabelle realized that, while Adam may have been chatting with Mia, his eagle-eyed attention had been on their surroundings. And Chance had also been working. Together they'd been engaged in constant surveillance. All while she'd been lost in thoughts of the past. It was time to clear her head and focus on staying alive.

"Where is Nate taking us?"

"He said to the station. I think he wants to go over some things with you."

More questions. Isabelle's brain ached.

She heard the sound of an approaching car just as Adam's phone buzzed. She started toward the road, but he put an arm out to hold her back.

"Yes?… Got it."

He closed the phone. "Deeper into the forest—fast." He was guiding her behind the trees even as he gave the command.

"I take it that car is not Nate."

"No. Nate said he realized he was being tailed so he pulled over. The car passed him and headed our way."

"How was he being tailed?"

"Anyone can pick up a tail. Nate's an experienced army ranger and sheriff. If he thinks he was being tailed, A—they're good and B—he's right. But because he's experienced, he knew how to lose them before he got to us."

Adam lowered Mia to the ground and had them duck behind a thick cluster of trees. "Chance, stay. Protect."

"Where are you going?" Isabelle couldn't help the panic that infused her voice.

"I just want to get closer to the road to get details on the car. I won't be visible to them, and I'll be right back."

Isabelle peered through the branches. True to his word, Adam melted into the forest thanks to the camouflage pattern of his coat. She was grateful for the dark brown coat he'd given her too. If nothing else, she could pass as a tree trunk.

The silly thought prompted a slightly hysterical giggle. She tried to swallow it, but Mia heard. "What's so funny, Mommy?"

Isabelle crouched beside her daughter and whispered into her ear, "We look like part of the trees. Let's hope no birds decide to make a nest in our hair." Mia's reaction simultaneously warmed and broke her heart. Her little girl laughed, but she did it in a whisper.

Isabelle's heart stuttered. *Oh, Jess. What have you gotten us involved with?*

Adam stood within the tree line, waiting. He hadn't wanted to divulge to Isabelle how concerned he was by the persistent tracking. He needed time to talk to Nate alone, get a sense of what his buddy was thinking.

He stilled as the car that Nate had described came into view. If he hadn't been suspicious from Nate's description, the slow speed would have given it away. As beautiful as this forest was to him, there was nothing to make the average driver proceed so slowly unless he was searching for something.

And that something was Isabelle and the girls.

Thinking ahead to assess all possible outcomes was part of his training and, right now, he knew one thing. They needed a better plan. Waiting for Nate and then taking the time to get everyone settled into his car was too risky. Who knew when the driver might decide to circle back? He sent a text to Nate, telling him to wait where he was. He'd get Isabelle and the girls and meet him there.

Adam was headed back through the trees when the first sharp pain sliced through his head. His breath caught as his vision blurred. He slumped against the nearest tree trunk and closed his eyes.

Burying his head in his hands, he tried to massage away the stabbing pain. He was used to headaches. They were an annoying constant reminder of his brain injury. They'd gotten slightly better when Chance had come into his life.

Despite the pain, he smiled thinking of his buddy. Everything was better with Chance around.

The fact that this headache was so strong was an indication of the toll these events were taking on him. Like being back in action, muscle memory had his body responding to the threat with heightened senses. His body was on high alert. He massaged his temples again, but it didn't stop the pounding pain. What he really needed was an ice pack, his bed, and a darkened room. With none of those available to him, Adam knew he had only one option. He usually avoided relying on medication because he didn't want to spend his life hooked on pain pills. But there were times it was unavoidable, and this was one. He needed to be able to concentrate. Surrendering to the need, he dug into his backpack for the pill and swallowed it with a swig of water from a canteen at his hip. He pushed away from the tree and took some deep breaths, waiting for the meds to kick in and the pain to subside.

The sound of an approaching car pulled him out of himself. It was the same car, on its way back. Had the driver seen something? Had Isabelle or the girls moved?

Swiftly but silently, his heart pounding in tune with his head, he darted through the forest, breathing a sigh of relief only when he came to the clearing and found them hidden where he'd left them. Crouching down beside Isabelle, he uttered a prayer of gratitude before whispering directions.

"We have to go back into the forest and work our way around to Nate."

The look on her face told him she understood even as she asked, "He's looking for us?"

Adam nodded. "We can't risk going out to the road. I told Nate where to meet us. It's a parking lot hunters use, but since it's not in season, we're okay."

"How far?"

Adam saw the fatigue in her eyes even though she tried to make the question casual. "About ten minutes, give or take."

Isabelle nodded.

"Why don't we switch off? Mia can walk with you, and I'll take Laura." He didn't want to admit that carrying Mia on his shoulders was a problem, but the medication sometimes threw his balance off and he didn't want to risk falling with her perched up high.

Isabelle nodded. She handed the baby over and took Mia by the hand. They set off through the forest on a path at a diagonal to the road. True to his estimate, it took only ten minutes despite their flagging energy.

Once Nate had Isabelle and the girls settled into the car, he turned to Adam. "You okay?"

"Yeah, just a headache."

Nate looked at him with knowing eyes. "How bad?"

"I'll live."

"Need me to take them into protective custody?"

"Not yet."

Nate stood with his arms folded across his chest but nodded. His friend knew better than to try to talk him out of this. "What's the plan?"

"I was going to take them to the station, go over things, but this tail makes me think we need a change of plans."

A sense of unease churned in Adam's gut. "You think there's a leak?"

"Don't know." Nate shrugged. "Since I don't, it seems best we go somewhere else. What about Claire's?"

Adam was surprised by the suggestion. His sister Claire ran a dog training center just on the other side of town. "I don't know. I don't want to bring danger down on Claire and the dogs."

"Just until I can find a safe house—and figure out what's going on."

"Let me check with Claire."

"Already did. She's waiting for us."

Adam eyed his friend with raised eyebrows.

"What? She's happy to help. Says she knows both Jess and Isabelle from church."

That was something new to ponder. Adam climbed into the sheriff's vehicle, wondering if his sister could possibly shed any light on the situation with Jess.

"Where are we going?"

Adam recognized the blend of fear and tension in Isabelle's voice and reminded himself how difficult it must be for her to have lost total control of any aspect of her life. He understood that feeling all too well. "We're headed to my sister's ranch. I think Mia will enjoy it," he added.

"Isabelle, I have some good news," Nate interjected as they came to a stop at a light. "My deputy found something of yours." He reached to hand her a bag with her phone.

"Oh, thank you. Where was it?"

"In the bushes under the window."

"That makes sense. I guess it slipped from my pocket when I was climbing out the window. Please tell him thank you for me."

"Will do. When we get to Claire's, I'd like to see the texts Jess sent you."

"Okay. There's a new one here now."

"What?" Nate whipped his head around. "What does it say?"

"The tree holds all the answers."

Adam frowned. "What does that mean?"

Isabelle shrugged. "I have no clue, but it means she's alive, right?"

Nate swung the car down a long driveway. The sound of barking dogs was the first indication they'd arrived. Adam smiled despite his residual headache when he saw Mia's eyes light up.

"My sister runs a dog rescue. This is where Chance came from." He was gratified to see the tension ease from Isabelle's face as she watched her daughter's excitement. As dangerous as the circumstances were, Isabelle had to also be concerned about the long-term effects all this may have on her daughter. Claire and her dogs would be a welcome distraction. But as they got out of the car, and Chance bounded alongside Mia to meet Claire, he reminded himself that he couldn't afford to be distracted. The girls' lives depended on him.

Claire came out to greet them and, after being nearly toppled by an enthusiastic Chance, she warmly welcomed Isabelle and Mia. She then turned and threw herself into his arms. Her hug was fierce, and when she drew back, Adam saw the sheen in her eyes.

"It's good to have you here."

Embarrassed, knowing her heart was in the right place, but that her assessment of the situation was overly optimistic, Adam quickly shifted the tone. "Thank you for being willing to take us in."

Claire was, by nature, alert to nuances in body language and expression. Adam knew it was one of the qualities that made her so good with dogs. In this case, it let her quickly pick up on his subtext. She turned her attention back to her guests.

"Why don't you come in and let me get you settled? I've got soup warming because you must be cold and starved." She spoke to Mia, "I hope you like grilled cheese."

Lunch was followed by a tour of the facilities while Claire explained how she took in rescue dogs and trained them for a variety of tasks. Some became therapy animals like Chance, but others went on for additional training to work with police or fire canine units.

Adam appreciated all his sister was doing to help her guests feel at home, but he needed time and access to a computer. When Isabelle suggested she put the girls down for a nap, Adam seized the opportunity to go work in Claire's office. He wanted to see what he could find out about Jess's background.

Half an hour later, frustration growing, he sat back in the chair and ran his hands through his already tousled hair. Feeling eyes on him, he turned to see Isabelle standing in the doorway with mugs of steaming coffee. "Claire needed to attend to the dogs, but she thought you might appreciate some fuel for your brain."

His sister also seemed to think she was a matchmaker. As Adam accepted the coffee, he made a mental note to set Claire straight. "Thanks. Maybe it will clear my head."

"How's your headache?"

He stopped with the mug at his lips and stared at her over the rim. "What did Claire say?"

"Nothing. I recognized the signs. Daniel used to get headaches too."

Something in the way her face held stiff as she responded prompted him to ask, "How did he cope with them?"

She dropped her gaze and he could no longer see the expression in her eyes. She shrugged. "Different ways. Sometimes he—"

Almost simultaneously, a cacophony of barking erupted from the kennels and a heart-stopping scream emanated from down the hall.

Isabelle dropped the mug of coffee, oblivious to the splatter of hot liquid and the shattering cup as she whirled and raced through the doorway, Adam right on her heels. Chance bounded past them both and tore into the room where Isabelle had left the girls to rest.

"He took Laura!"

Mia's words reached him, pushing Adam to run faster. By the time he made the doorway,

Chance had a grip on the pant leg of a man climbing through the window, Laura in his arms. Adam dashed across the room, yanked the man back by his coat, and snatched Laura from his arms. He handed the baby over to Isabelle while Chance kept his grip on the man's pant leg. "Take the girls and go call Nate. Chance and I have him."

"Think again," the man growled. With a quick jerk, he grabbed the standing lamp and swung it at Chance. Instinctively, Adam threw himself between his dog and the attacker, taking the brunt of the impact. The man took advantage, yanking his pants free and catapulting through the open window in one smooth move.

Adam glanced at Isabelle standing frozen in the doorway. "In the kitchen, there's a phone with a direct line to the kennels. Call Claire. Tell her to let the dogs loose. Then call Nate." Without waiting for a response, he launched himself through the window with Chance following on his heels.

Chapter Seven

Adam landed in the snow. He rolled and bounced back up to his feet and took off after the would-be abductor. The man had a head start, and was properly outfitted for the weather, but Adam was not about to let the lack of a coat or shoes hinder him from pursuing this man who had attempted to kidnap an innocent baby. Capturing him would give them their first real break in this case.

That thought gave Adam an extra spurt of energy, but without shoes, his socked feet kept slipping in the snow. He was losing ground. Then the sound of an engine caught his ear. There was a road running behind the ranch, so the engine raised a concern. Did this guy have an accomplice waiting for him? Knowing he needed to run faster, Adam paused long enough to pull off his thick socks before launching himself forward again. He had to catch the man before he reached the road.

Adam gained ground as the man made for the tree line. He abruptly turned to the right seconds before gunshots from the woods peppered the ground around Adam. With an accomplice confirmed, Adam began zigzagging to avoid the gunman's aim, but he was losing precious ground in the process.

His hopes were sinking fast. There was no way he could reach the man in time. But with his adversary mere steps from the road and freedom, Adam felt a sudden change in the air and realized Claire had unleashed the pack of dogs. A wild flurry of animals flew across the lawn. Adam recognized three that she was training for K-9 suspect apprehension. As Claire called commands, they raced past Adam, surrounding the man and forcing him away from the road. They formed a circle around him, snarling and holding him captive as surely as any handcuffs could have done.

The sound of the car receded and Adam chuckled. It seemed there was no honor among kidnappers. This man had been left to take the fall all on his own.

Claire strolled up beside him, holding out a

pair of boots and a leash. Once Adam's feet were protected, she commanded the dogs to sit and signaled to Adam that he could enter the circle.

He smiled as he accepted the leash to secure the prisoner. "Nice work, sis."

Adam turned to the man, who stood in stony silence, still warily eyeing the dogs. "Who are you? What do you want with Isabelle and the children?"

The man glared back at him but maintained his silence.

"Have it your way." He turned back to Claire. "Maybe the dogs would like to encourage him to walk around the front of the house?"

At Claire's command, the dogs fell in around them. With the canine escorts nudging, they forced the man back across the lawn to the house, arriving just as Nate's vehicle pulled up.

Nate stepped out and stood, hands on hips, chuckling. "Isabelle said you needed help, but I guess she was wrong."

"Claire and her dogs get full credit. You should have her train one for you." Adam noticed a blush sneak up his sister's face as Nate hung his head and shuffled his feet. Adam was struck by the suspicion he'd missed something. Was there more than friendship between his sister and his friend? His speculations were interrupted when another official-looking car pulled up behind the sheriff's.

Nate took custody of the alleged kidnapper and read him his rights while Adam focused on the woman who emerged from the car.

"Who is she?"

Nate stared straight ahead as he held the rear car door open for the now-handcuffed captive. His voice was barely audible. "She's the intake caseworker for child welfare."

Adam's heart sank. "She's not here to take Laura, is she? Did you call her? Why'd you do that? Isabelle will be crushed."

Nate shrugged, but Adam heard the strain in his voice as he replied. "She was with me when the call came in. Asked about the case and then insisted she had to come see to the safety of the baby."

Adam stared after the somber woman who was now following Claire up the path. He forced his emotions under control. "You can't let her take Laura, Nate. This attempted abduction changes everything." The thought crystalized even as he said the words. "They're not after Isabelle. They want Laura. I'm sure of it." He paused. "I just don't know why."

"I might have the answer to that, but let me

take this guy in first and see what I can get out of him. I'll be back later."

Adam didn't like to be left hanging, especially with the caseworker here, but he could follow up with Nate later. It was more important that he get inside and support Isabelle right now. He had to make the caseworker see reason. He couldn't let her take Laura into her care because, if he was right, that would be a deadly mistake.

This attempted abduction had just proved that Laura was the one who needed his protection most.

Isabelle paced the room with Laura on her shoulder as she spoke with the woman. What was her name? Isabelle searched her memory but couldn't remember. Her brain had ceased to function the minute the woman had introduced herself as the caseworker here to take custody of Jess's daughter. Alice? Yes, that was it. She'd said her name was Alice Grant, but to Isabelle she was just another person who was a threat to Laura. Isabelle walked to the window and shifted Laura to the other shoulder, trying to buy some time. Where were Adam and Nate? She needed their support.

"Ms. Weaver, without proof that you have

legal custody, I am required to remove the child…for her own safety."

Shivers raced through Isabelle's body and she hugged Laura closer, as if by the sheer force of her love she could change the outcome. "I showed you the text from Jess."

"I'm sorry. That's not enough, given the circumstances."

"I told you. There are guardianship papers. Jess appointed me to be Laura's guardian."

"I need to see the papers."

Panicked, Isabelle tried to remember what Jess had said. With her lawyer, right? She glanced at her phone to check the time and her heart sank as she noticed the date. Sunday. It was highly unlikely she could reach the lawyer on a Sunday.

She knew this woman was trying to do the right thing, but taking Laura from the only family she had left was not it. Frantic, she tried to think. "I can call the lawyer in the morning. He'll have the papers…" Her voice trailed off as the caseworker shook her head.

"Please understand, Ms. Weaver. I am not trying to be difficult. It is my responsibility to see to the child's safety."

"I love her like my own daughter. I will

keep her safe." Isabelle was desperate now. "She knows me. She feels safe with me. Her mother is my very best friend. I would do anything to keep her from harm."

"But you can't promise that, can you? Someone who is after you just tried to abduct her. If you truly love her, you will agree that me taking her is the only correct choice."

Terror seized Isabelle at the caseworker's words and her thoughts flew to Mia. Praise the Lord, Claire had left with a whispered promise to take Mia to the kennels. Did Alice know about Mia? Because, based on her comments, the next logical step would mean the caseworker would be taking her daughter, as well, for her safety of course. She couldn't let that happen. She couldn't lose Mia or Laura.

But then Alice's words echoed again in her heart. *If you truly love her...* A tear slid down her cheek, plopping on Laura's head. The baby looked up, started. As Isabelle stared into her precious face, so much like a mini-Jess, confusion overcame her. She wanted what was best for this child, but how could she possibly know what that was?

"Why do you think she will be safer with you?"

"Ms. Weaver, I was with the sheriff when he

got your call. This child's life was just in danger because of the men after you! You can't properly protect her."

"You're wrong."

Adam's voice rang out so strong and clear that Isabelle latched onto it with actual physical relief. She cuddled Laura to her chest as Adam strode across the room toward the caseworker.

"Former army ranger Adam Dalton." He extended his hand and waited. Isabelle bit back a smile. Her own personal knight in shining army fatigues to the rescue. Not that he was actually in uniform, but despite his jeans and heavy sweater, he carried himself in a way that bespoke his former rank. The presence of her gallant rescuer sent a flood of relief through Isabelle's body.

Alice accepted his handshake but challenged his words. "How can you say I'm wrong? This baby was almost kidnapped."

Isabelle hugged Laura even closer as she protested. "But Adam rescued her. He risked his own life to save her."

She could tell from Alice's raised brows that her argument was futile.

Adam moved to stand beside Isabelle and rested a hand on her arm to steady her. He took a moment to look deeply into her eyes, and her body began to calm.

He stroked Laura's head; his touch so gentle, Isabelle felt it like a balm to her soul.

He turned back to the caseworker. "You're wrong about Isabelle being the target. The real target is this baby."

Isabelle gasped. Her legs went weak and she sank into a chair as calm deserted her.

Adam cleared his throat and continued. "Nate took the prisoner in for interrogation, but he will confirm this truth. If you take this baby, you are not only putting her life in jeopardy, but you will be putting an innocent foster family in the path of ruthless criminals."

Isabelle started to shake. What was Adam talking about?

"Nate and I will arrange a safe house for Isabelle…and the baby." Adam paused to allow his words to sink in. "I know you'll need more details, but we cannot release them at this point. I'm asking you to trust our judgment as professionals who are used to assessing risks."

Alice was obviously as shocked by Adam's words as she was, but as Isabelle watched, she could see that the caseworker seemed to at least be considering them. For the first time, Isabelle felt like maybe she could breathe again.

"I'll need to confirm with Sheriff Brant." Alice looked at Isabelle. "And I'll need to see those papers."

Isabelle nodded. "I'll contact the lawyer."

Alice stepped into the side room to make her call. When she returned, she cast them an odd look and spoke briskly. "Nate confirmed your concerns." She faced Isabelle. "Based on the sheriff's information, I will leave her with you temporarily, but I will need a copy of the papers the attorney will file with the court to make it permanent. You'll need a criminal background check and…"

Her voice droned on, but Isabelle's brain drowned out the words. She couldn't think about permanent now. Permanent meant not finding Jess. Permanent meant her friend was dead. She wasn't ready to accept permanent yet.

Adam nudged her side and Isabelle jolted. Alice was still speaking.

"These are highly unusual circumstances. Our goal is always to see to the child's best interests. Nate has convinced me you and Adam are the best we can do for Laura. For tonight." She gave a pointed stare. "If anything changes, you will notify me immediately."

Isabelle nodded her assent. Alice seemed to

soften. She reached out and stroked a hand over Laura's tiny fist.

"I can tell you truly love her." She smiled sadly. "I hope Nate can find her mother."

Isabelle sniffled and the tears slipped down her cheeks. Something they could agree on.

After Alice left, Isabelle collapsed onto the sofa.

"Adam, what were you talking about? What do you mean Laura is the target?"

"Think about it. That man in custody, he didn't come after you or Mia. He tried to snatch Laura. He was halfway out the window with her when Chance latched onto him."

Isabelle held Laura closer, as if that could somehow remove the threat, but she mulled over Adam's words. "I hate it, but that makes sense. If they were after Jess, then Laura would be next." She looked up at him, knowing it was wrong to drag him deeper into her problems but not knowing where else to turn. "What are we going to do? How can we keep her safe?"

"Let's take it one step at a time. For tonight, Nate is going to send a deputy out to watch the house. Between that, Claire's dogs, Chance, and all of us on alert, she will be safe. In the morning, we'll see what the lawyer says. Maybe he knows Jess's true story."

"Okay." She was talking more to herself. Trying to absorb it all. "Okay. We can do that."

But suddenly everything collapsed in on her and she began trembling.

Adam sat beside her on the sofa and, wrapping his arm around her shoulders, drew her into the shelter of his embrace. The warmth. The safety. His strength. Her emotions were on overdrive. Tears brimmed in her eyes, spilling over and running down her face. She choked back the sobs that threatened to break loose. Adam held her close and soothed her, all the time talking to her in soft words, telling her how lucky Laura was to have her, how brave she was. What a wonderful mother she was to both girls.

Isabelle's head jerked up at that. "Where's Mia?"

Adam smiled and opened his phone to show her a picture of Mia surrounded by puppies. "While Alice was talking to Nate, I texted Claire and asked her to keep Mia down there."

"Thank you." The sobs built in her throat again. "I was so scared Alice was going to take Laura, and then when she started talking about the danger, I was afraid she would take Mia too." Isabelle took a deep breath and forced herself to relax, tried to smile. "And then you came in and saved the day."

Adam laughed softly and the sound eased her tension.

"I didn't even thank you for before, for rescuing her." She looked up at Adam, knowing admiration was shining in her eyes, but not even trying to hide it. "I don't even have words to make you understand what it means to me. You've been amazing with everything you've done for us, but the way you dove through that window and took off after the kidnapper…" She paused and blinked, still in awe of his quick action. "You risked your life for Laura, for a little girl you've known less than forty-eight hours."

Their faces were so close as Adam bent over Laura and tickled her little toes that Isabelle could feel his indrawn breath, the sudden burst of tension, and just as quickly, she felt his exhale. Isabelle looked up as Adam looked down, and a long moment passed between them. He winked at her. "Anything for my football baby."

Chapter Eight

The sound of sleet hitting the windows woke Isabelle, but she refused to open her eyes. It would take a month of uninterrupted sleep to recover from the past two days. And it wasn't over yet. This morning she had a meeting scheduled with Jess's lawyer. Once she'd found the email last night, she'd contacted the lawyer. The fact that he had responded so quickly on a Sunday evening had both alarmed and relieved her. Maybe he knew something. Maybe she could at last get some answers, something to help them understand what this was all about.

The horror of the previous night came washing over her. She had come so close to losing Laura. And Mia! Her daughter had been so brave but, as a mother, it was terrifying to think of her child challenging a kidnapper. Isabelle rolled over, ready to snuggle with her precious girl before facing what promised to be another long and dangerous day.

Her arm met empty air as she rolled to her side. Where was Mia? Panic surged and she bolted upright, her gaze searching room.

Laura was still asleep in the crib. That meant everything was okay, right? Adam had decided Laura was the target, not Isabelle, not Mia. So, if Laura was still safe…

Isabelle's panicked thoughts raced ahead as she pulled on a heavy robe and started for the door. She caught herself. No, she couldn't leave Laura alone. She gently lifted the infant, cradling her as she hurried into the hall, calling for her daughter.

The sound of Adam's voice drew her toward the kitchen. She burst through the doorway with Laura, her gaze raking the room. "Where's Mia?"

Adam intercepted her before she got far. "She's fine, Isabelle. She's having breakfast and coloring."

Isabelle peered around him, needing to see for herself. Sure enough, Mia was sitting at the table with a stack of drawings beside her.

She exhaled slowly and suddenly her legs couldn't hold her. Adam caught her by the elbow and steadied her. "She's fine," he repeated softly. "She woke up early and was hungry."

Isabelle tried to focus on breathing before approaching Mia. The last thing she wanted to do was to frighten her daughter. When she felt steady, she looked up at Adam, intending to thank him, but the intensity of his gaze made her wobble again. She sucked in a breath, nodded, and pulled away to go to her daughter.

"Good morning, sweetie." She leaned over to kiss the top of Mia's head, and the sweet scent of rose shampoo filled her head, centering her. "What are you drawing?"

Mia squirmed around in her chair and grinned up at her. "Hi, Mama. Mr. Adam remembered to bring my crayons. He said I should draw what scared me. See?"

Isabelle glanced at the pictures—a child's view of the man climbing out the window with a baby and the dog tugging on his pants. There were talk bubbles and bright colors and a hero in a cape.

"It's not so scary now," Mia told her solemnly.

Isabelle glanced up, but Adam was busy at the stove. She shook her head, thanking God again for bringing this generous man into their lives. "Mr. Adam had a very good idea. What else did you draw?"

Mia held up a pile of papers. Most had a little girl and a dog. "You like drawing Chance, don't you?"

Mia beamed with pride. "He's Mr. Adam's special dog. I love him."

Isabelle's heart melted.

Adam pushed away from the stove. "Who's ready for pancakes?"

Mia's hand shot up. "I am!"

"Remember, we can't share these with Chance."

Mia nodded. "Chocolate is bad for dogs."

Isabelle stopped flipping through the drawings and looked at Adam, who was advancing with a plate stacked high with pancakes—chocolate-chip pancakes.

The color drained from her face and she suddenly felt light-headed.

"Isabelle, are you okay?"

The look of concern on Mia's face matched Adam's voice.

Isabelle pulled herself together and forced a smile to her face. "Yes, I just have to go change Laura's diaper." She turned and fled down the hallway.

Back in the relative safety of her room, Isabelle laid Laura back in the crib. With shaking hands, she reached for a clean diaper, but her fingers were trembling too badly to get the package open. Laura was going to start wailing any minute, and she didn't want Adam or Mia coming to investigate. She ran into the bathroom, thrust her hands under cold water, and then splashed more on her face until she felt her heartrate begin to slow. She leaned on the vanity and stared at her reflection as she forced herself to take deep steady breaths.

When the force of the blood rushing in her ears eased, she could hear the murmur of voices from down the hall, Mia's high-pitched giggle in response to the low rumble of Adam's voice.

She closed her eyes, took a breath. In for three, hold for four, out for five. Repeat. And repeat. Slowly, her body eased.

Mia was safe. She was with Adam, a man risking his life to save her. A man who made her pancakes. A man who faced his post-traumatic stress rather than drinking his way through it. Adam was not Daniel. Mia was not in danger—from him.

She turned into the bedroom and on steadier legs walked back to Laura. She leaned over the makeshift crib and tickled her tummy until

Laura gurgled happy sounds. Once she had the clean diaper in place, she lifted the infant and cuddled her to her chest. "Sweet baby, I'm going to make sure you are safe until we find your mama. No one is going to take you away from me." She started humming a tune that had always soothed Mia. "Hush little baby," she crooned as she gently rocked the baby.

A sound in the hall caught her attention and she looked up to find Adam standing in the doorway with a mug of coffee and a plate of toast. "I thought you might need something before we left for the lawyer's office. Laura's bottle is warming."

What had she ever done to deserve this wonderful man? She sighed softly as she raised her eyes to his face. "Thank you."

He smiled. A gentle smile that reached her soul. "You're very welcome."

"Claire was kind enough to offer me some clean clothes, so I'll dress while the bottle is warming. We should be able to leave soon. Where's Mia?"

A chagrined expression covered his face. "She's with Claire, getting cleaned up. I might have made a mistake with the pancakes. There was syrup everywhere."

Isabelle laughed. "She loves her pancakes and syrup."

He hesitated. "Then I didn't do something wrong feeding her?"

A part of Isabelle wanted to tell him, to trust him, to spill the whole sordid story...but this wasn't the time.

"You did the absolute perfect thing."

He studied her but obviously saw something that decided him against asking anything more. "Enjoy the coffee."

Isabelle sank onto the bed and, as she sipped from the mug, she tried with all her might to forget the last time she'd seen Daniel. The morning Mia had last had chocolate-chip pancakes with her father—right before his reckless drinking almost killed her.

The drive into Breckenridge was tense, sleet making travel hazardous, but it was the prospect of the upcoming meeting that most had their nerves on edge. Even the children were restless in their car seats. Mia would almost certainly have preferred to stay with Claire and the dogs, but after the kidnapping attempt yesterday, Isabelle was not letting either girl out of her sight, and Adam couldn't blame her.

He glanced at her in the seat beside him. Her fingers were tightly clasped in her lap, and he wondered again what had triggered her reaction this morning. Her anxiety at waking up and not finding Mia was understandable, but she'd calmed down and been fine until he'd served breakfast. What had set her off? He'd thought for a moment that she was going to explain when he'd brought her coffee, but she'd clammed up and focused on this trip instead. Adam knew he was the last person to talk about not sharing your deepest thoughts, your fears, but if Isabelle was keeping secrets that could impact this case, he needed to know.

The sun was breaking through the clouds as Adam parked in the lot behind the office building. They walked around to the front so Mia could shake her sillies out. Adam watched Isabelle dancing and singing with the girls on the wet grass, and his heart gave a funny lurch that was followed by a burst of determination. Isabelle was such a generous and loving person, taking in Laura without a second thought, even knowing the risk. He renewed his vow to do whatever it took to return her life to normal. She deserved nothing less than his best, regardless of any personal cost.

The security guard in the lobby waved them through with barely a glance. Lax security set Adam on edge, and he went on full alert as they entered the elevator. Isabelle glanced at him, and he saw that she'd made the same observation.

The elevator chimed their arrival. The doors opened and he took note of the elegant office space as they stepped out into the empty reception area. The elevator doors shut behind them and silence closed in. An eerie silence that had his instincts telegraphing warnings. Shouldn't a law firm, even a small one, be bustling at this time of the morning? Granted the lawyer had given Isabelle a rushed appointment, before office hours, but shouldn't someone have been there to greet them?

"Wait here," Adam whispered so only Isabelle could hear. "Something feels off." His gaze raked the reception area. "Better yet, take them into that ladies' room. Stay there until I come get you."

Isabelle nodded her assent. "Mia, sweetie, come with me while Adam checks us in, okay?" She winked. "I want to change Laura's diaper before we meet the lawyer. Wouldn't want to

stink up his fancy office." Mia giggled and followed her mother.

"Wait." He held a finger to his lips and
opened the door to the ladies' room. "Anyone
in here?" he asked softly. When there was no
reply, he stepped inside and quickly scanned the
room. He came back out and nodded to Isabelle. Then he winked at Mia. "No one to be
offended by stinky diapers."

Once Isabelle and the girls were hidden away,
Adam eased himself through the open glass
doors that led from reception to the inner offices. There was no sound from within. No
tapping fingers on keyboards, no sounds of a
printer and, most telling of all, no voices.

Every army ranger instinct was on alert. Yes,
it was early, but the open door meant there
should be some sign of life. A whiff of freshly
brewed coffee scented the air as Adam warily
headed down the hallway. But before he could
exhale in relief, a different smell, one he recognized from far too many battlefields, stole
his breath. He was torn between the need to
investigate and an urgency to get Isabelle and
the girls away.

Reassuring himself that they were safe in the
bathroom, Adam crept forward. A shaft of light

shone from the office at the end of the hall, so he headed that way, peeking into every open door he passed. There was no sign of life anywhere, but no sign of any disturbance either.

The coppery tang grew stronger as he neared the end of the hall.

Adam flattened himself against the wall and held still, listening intently for any sound to indicate trouble. He drove all fear for Isabelle from his mind and focused on sensing any other physical presence.

When he felt nothing, he pulled his gun and swung into the doorway.

"Drop your weapons—"

The sight that met his eyes severed his words. A man, presumably the lawyer they were to meet, lay on the floor, blood pooling around his inert body. Again, the urgent need to get Isabelle away overwhelmed Adam. But this man held clues. If there was a chance he was still alive…

Careful not to disturb any evidence, Adam gingerly stepped toward the man. A door slammed in the distance and he froze. His instinct was to give chase, but those still here needed him more. He knelt and checked for a pulse but felt nothing. He called 9-1-1 to summon help, said a quick prayer for the man, and sent a quick text telling Isabelle to stay.

His years of army training and battlefield experience kicked in as he searched for the source of the blood loss. Based on where the blood continued to pool, he gently lifted the lawyer, for he no longer had any doubt that's who this man was. A gaping hole under his left shoulder blade gave the answer. On the off chance the man was still alive, Adam ripped off his own jacket and sweater. Bunching the sweater as firmly as he could, he wrapped the arms of his jacket around the man, pulling them tight to try to hold the sweater in place. And then he prayed again as he went to wait for the police.

Police and medical technicians soon swarmed the building, and Adam had to stay to answer questions. Relief filled him when he got a text from Isabelle telling him the security guard was going to bring her to a café in the lobby to keep Mia from viewing the crime scene.

He didn't like the idea of being separated from them, but he understood Isabelle's need to protect her daughter from seeing the violence. Mia had already been exposed to far too much for a child of her age.

* * *

The elevator door closed behind them. Mia glanced at the security guard and then looked up at Isabelle.

"Mama, where's Adam? Why isn't he with us?"

"He had to stay with the police. They need his help with something."

Mia tugged at her sleeve until Isabelle met her gaze again. "Did something bad happen?"

Isabelle sighed heavily. She set the baby carrier down and wrapped both arms around Mia. "I'm afraid so, baby." She squeezed tight. "But Adam will take care of it. He'll take care of us."

Isabelle could feel the tremors in Mia's body. Her daughter was going to need so much help to get over these experiences once they were safe. And they would be safe. She surprised herself to realize how very much she believed that. She hadn't known Adam more than a few days, but her faith in him hadn't wavered.

Faith. That brought her up short. She should be praying, not relying on Adam, not placing her faith in a man. She was ashamed to realize she hadn't yet said a prayer for the lawyer who'd been injured, maybe dead, nor had she thought to pray to God for guidance.

I'm sorry, Lord. You above all know Your plan for us. Please help me to know what to do. Please help me to know how to deal with Adam.

The elevator dinged their arrival, and she mentally whispered one last prayer as they stepped from the elevator into the building's empty lobby. *Please protect the girls.*

Police had sealed off the building entry, and Isabelle could see a crowd gathered on the sidewalk outside. She turned to the security guard. "I am not taking these children out into that crowd. Is there somewhere else we can go?"

The security guard stopped to check with the police officer standing watch. "There's a small indoor café and atrium on the ground level. It's been sealed off from outside, but the officer said we can wait there," she reported.

Isabelle nodded her agreement. Hopefully, the café was open. She could use some coffee and maybe a muffin would distract Mia, although the idea that a muffin could distract from what had occurred upstairs was absurd.

The café was quiet but open for service, so Isabelle got food and drinks and then settled them at a table in the far corner. She sipped her coffee and watched Mia feed bits of blueberry muffin to a giggling Laura, while the security guard went over by the windows to make some calls. Isabelle's thoughts kept drifting to what was going on upstairs and the inescapable conclusion that she had brought this on the lawyer with her phone call. Guilt weighed heavily.

"Mama, can we take Laura to look at the flowers?"

Isabelle refocused on Mia. "Hmm?"

Mia pointed at the small fountain in the middle of the room. It was surrounded by pots of poinsettias obviously left over from a Christmas display.

Isabelle didn't like the idea of being out in the open. She'd prefer to stay huddled in their corner. But how much longer would Adam be upstairs?

"It's okay if you don't want to, Mama."

Isabelle wanted to cry at the nervous resignation in her daughter's voice. She couldn't pretend to Mia that everything was okay and then tell her she couldn't even look at flowers around a fountain. Isabelle scanned the nearly empty café. Aside from the workers, who must have been there before the police descended, there was only a line in the courtyard outside as people slowly snaked to the pickup window for their morning coffee. Nothing appeared threatening.

"Do you want to see the pretty flowers, sweetie?" Isabelle cooed as she unstrapped Laura from the baby carrier and shifted her to her hip.

Laura gurgled happily, which made Mia laugh. Isabelle's heart lifted at the joyous sound, and she uttered a prayer of thanksgiving for the resiliency of children.

They walked over to the cascading fountain and Isabelle let the tranquil setting filter through her. The cheerful splash of the water eased her tension, and Mia's sweet voice combining with Laura's bubbly sounds made her smile. Mia had a way of communicating with Laura that she and Jess had never understood.

She snapped a quick photo of the happy girls, hoping to one day be able to share it with Jess. Knowing Adam was probably stressed about being apart from them, she shared the photo with him and sent an accompanying message to reassure him they were safe.

To reassure herself, she searched out the security guard. The woman had moved to the coffee counter and, as Isabelle watched, she grabbed two paper cups and headed for the courtyard exit. She opened the door just enough to hand the cup through to a man standing outside.

After closing the door, the guard turned and

walked back to their table. As she sat down, Isabelle realized she'd left all their belongings unattended while she'd let Mia play. Foolish, foolish, she reprimanded herself. But, really, the only things of value were the two precious girls, and they were right with her.

"Mia, I think we need to take Laura back for a bottle."

As they made their way across to the alcove, Isabelle noticed the guard had pulled her chair slightly away from the table, as if she didn't want to crowd them. It was a kind gesture, or maybe she just hadn't planned on doing duty for a woman and kids and wanted some privacy.

Isabelle took a long sip of her coffee as she dug in her bag for Laura's bottle. She pulled out the trusty pad and box of crayons and handed them to Mia. "Why don't you draw the fountain and the pretty flowers?"

Mia's face lit up. "I can add it to my collection."

"What collection?" Isabelle asked absently as she reached for her coffee again. She hoped Adam wouldn't be much longer because she was suddenly so tired.

"The one I'm making for Aunt Jess so I can show her what we did while she was gone."

Isabelle's heart stuttered and her eyes brightened in hope. She needed some of her daughter's optimism right now. She had to believe that Jess was alive and would be back.

She opened her phone to check if Adam had replied, but there was nothing. She sipped the coffee again as Laura drained her bottle, but tremors in her hands sent a frisson of concern down her arm. She set the bottle down and tried to shift Laura to her shoulder to burp her, but her arms suddenly felt too heavy to lift the baby. Her brain was getting foggy. Something was seriously wrong.

She turned to ask the security guard for help, but something in the way the woman was sitting, surreptitiously observing her, jangled warning bells in Isabelle's cloudy brain. She reached for the coffee again, but her hand stilled. Had someone put something in her coffee? She'd felt fine until they'd come back here and sipped it.

There was something shifting at the edge of her thoughts. A memory she couldn't quite grasp. A sense of something important.

Adam. She needed to send a message to Adam.

She reached for her phone, but it fell off the

table into her lap. She called to the security guard for help, but the woman just sat there, a smug look on her face. Panic seized Isabelle. With supreme effort, she forced her finger to steady so she could hit the microphone text icon. "I need help. Been drugged. Security guard won't help—"

The phone clattered to the tile floor as a hand wrenched her arm. Her last image as consciousness faded was of the security guard reaching for Laura.

Chapter Nine

Adam paced the foyer, waiting for a police update. His phone dinged and he glanced down. A photo of the two girls made him smile, but a second text came through just as he was about to respond.

I need help. Been drugged. Security guard won't—

The nagging unease that had been roiling in his gut burst into full-fledged terror. Adam immediately tried to call, but Isabelle's phone rang through to voice mail. He scanned the room, looking for the security guard who had let them in. He was being questioned by police, so Adam dashed across the room and interrupted.

"The other guard—the one who took the woman and children down to the café—who is she?"

The guard glanced at the officer then shrugged. "Never saw her before. She showed up this morning. Said the regular guard had called out and the agency sent her as a replacement."

Adam's heart started to race. Light danced around the periphery of his eyes and his chest began to tighten. He recognized the signs of an impending attack but fought the rising panic. Isabelle needed him—functioning and able to rescue her. Chance was with Claire, so he had to fight this on his own. He had to. Three lives were at risk.

Just that thought made his chest constrict more and his breathing became labored. He closed his eyes and leaned forward. Resting his hands on his knees, he tried to imagine Chance beside him, bumping his leg, interrupting the panic cycle. He pushed back at the paralyzing thoughts, trying to use the techniques he'd learned. He couldn't surrender to a panic attack when Isabelle's life depended on him. He took a deep breath and forced out the question. "Where's the café?"

"Ground floor. Back side."

"What's this all about?" the cop asked.

Adam turned to the officer and showed him

the message. "Call for backup. Is there anyone downstairs? Radio them to get into the café. I think the people who killed the lawyer are trying to kidnap this woman and her children."

The officer got right on the radio but Adam couldn't wait. He pressed the elevator button, but nothing happened.

The security guard called to him. "Take the freight elevator. Back there." He pointed down the hall. "It will exit just behind the café."

Adam ran around to the freight entrance. He hit the call button and watched the display as the elevator ascended, ticking the numbers off in his head at the excruciatingly slow progress, knowing that each passing moment gave the kidnapper time to get away with Laura. A guttural cry locked in his throat at the thought of losing the little girl. Why had he let them out of his sight?

Please, God, let me get to them in time.

The elevator finally reached him. He didn't even wait for the doors to fully open before he slipped through the gap and punched the buttons to close the door and take him down. Like a caged beast, he paced the confines of the small moving room, wanting to pound on something, to do anything to take back his decisions of the last hour that had put Isabelle in danger.

No! Adam brought himself up short. He had to stop this. Rage was no more help than his panic had been. Isabelle and the children needed him to think like the trained warrior he was.

He knew how to do this. He knew how to prepare for a mission. Forcing himself to blank his mind, he exhaled slowly, forcibly expelling the oxygen from his lungs as he focused on tactical breathing until his emotions were locked away and his thoughts were strategic.

When the heavy elevator finally clanged to a halt, Adam was ready. He flattened his body against the side wall and waited for the door to open. He eased forward so he could see around the opening. Continuing to breathe slowly, he focused his attention on the noises coming from the café. As he listened intently, trying to isolate the sounds, he heard a voice he recognized. Mia's cries pierced his heart. His every instinct screamed at him to run to her.

Instead, he forced the pain aside and stealthily made his way down the corridor. He peered through the café door and saw chaos. Discarding his careful plans, he charged through the door. Isabelle was on the ground, surrounded by cops, and Mia was bawling about the baby. He wanted to rush to comfort her, but he saw her pointing to a door at the back of the room. Without a moment's hesitation, Adam pivoted and bolted across the floor toward what looked to be the café kitchen.

He pushed through the door and, with a glance, took in the stunned staff members. "A woman came through here with a baby. Which way did she go?"

A worker pointed a trembling finger to the hallway, but there was no one in sight.

Darkness started to crowd Adam's brain as he scanned the empty hallway. He pushed back, impatient with himself. Which way could she have gone?

"She went the wrong way, into the store-room."

Adam acknowledged the whispered comment with a nod. "All of you, vacate. Go into the café," he clarified.

As they quickly followed his command, he hurried along the corridor and eased through the doorway into the storeroom. He saw nothing, but he could hear the muffled sound of Laura crying.

Crouching, he made his way toward the

sound, taking care to stay hidden behind the stacks of boxes. When he reached the end of the row, he carefully shifted a box until he could see the security guard. She looked cornered, as if she'd just realized she had gone the wrong way and was trapped.

If Laura wasn't involved, he would have charged her, but he had to try to deescalate. He stepped in front of her. "Give me the baby."

He'd startled her, and she tried to back away. She stumbled into a stack of boxes and, as she fell, Laura flew into the air. Adam dove, catching the baby in his arms and rolling his body to take the brunt of the fall with his shoulder, holding Laura safely above the ground.

The woman scrambled to her feet and ran out the way he'd come in.

Adam hated letting her get away, but he had his precious little football gal and that was what mattered. A sense of calm washed over him. She wasn't Chance, but Laura's warmth and sweet smile of recognition pushed back the darkness every bit as well as his therapy dog would have.

Tucking Laura under his arm, he headed back to the café. Mia broke away from the officer and ran to him, tears streaming down her face. "Mr. Adam. You saved her."

Adam bent to his knee and caught the little girl into his arms, holding her tightly as she rained kisses across Laura's face.

Adam searched over her shoulder to where he could see the cops with Isabelle. His heart plummeted as he realized she was still on the floor. He eased back from Mia. "I need to check on your mama."

"She's sleeping,"

Adam glanced down at Mia. "Is that what the policeman said?"

She nodded.

He stood, shifted Laura to his shoulder and grasped Mia's hand. He was not letting either of them out of his sight despite his compelling desire to check on Isabelle. "Okay, let's see if they woke her up yet."

Mia gazed up at him. "Maybe she's like Sleeping Beauty. She needs you to kiss her."

"Huh?" Adam swallowed hard.

"Like in the story. The prince kisses Sleeping Beauty and she wakes up."

Adam chuckled, trying to force humor through the sudden tightness in his throat.

"I thought I was a billy goat?"

Mia covered her mouth with both hands and

glanced up at him with a deer-in-the-head-lights look.

He smiled and gave her another hug. "I think I hear your mama's voice. I guess she woke up without me."

Isabelle stared with flickering vision into a sea of blurred, concerned faces and all she could think was that she was going to be sick. Who were all these people? Where was she? Squeezing her eyes shut, she tried to dig through the fog and remember. A nagging fear that she was forgetting something vital heightened the nausea. Panic pushed through the murkiness as memories of a hand snatching Laura filtered into her brain in a mosaic of confusion and anguish. She tried to raise her head to find the girls, but the world swam and a gentle hand on her shoulder kept her from sitting up.

"No," she protested. "I have to get up. I have to find my daughters." Even through the haze, she recognized the importance of what she'd acknowledged. In her heart, in every way that mattered, Laura was hers and she needed to save her.

"It's okay, Isabelle. I have them. The girls are safe."

Chills ran along Isabelle's spine and down her arms as Adam's reassuring voice penetrated her fog. Adam had her girls. Adam. Her heart filled to bursting with gratitude for this man who only days ago hadn't existed in her world.

She tried to push up again, wanting to thank him, needing to see the girls, but a wave of dizziness set her back. What had happened to her? What was wrong with this body she could no longer control?

The gentle hand was easing her down again. "Ma'am, please don't get up. We need to check you out. Get you to the hospital."

"No, my babies. I need to see Mia and Laura."

And then, suddenly, Adam was squatting beside her, one arm holding Laura in the football hold she'd taught him and the other wrapped around Mia. "We're right here, Isabelle. I have both girls safe. I won't let anything happen to them."

Isabelle let Adam's voice wash over her and tension eased from her body. She still felt awful and sick, but Adam's voice brought a measure of peace. Whatever had happened, the girls were safe with him.

She put up a futile resistance when the paramedic insisted she go to the hospital. She might have been able to stand her ground against him, but Adam's gentle plea that she do it to reassure Mia forced her surrender. She hated that Mia was witnessing this. If conceding that she needed medical evaluation could ease the fear on her daughter's face, that's what she would do. But with one caveat.

"You'll come?" she asked Adam.

"I will. I'm going to call Claire to meet us at the hospital, and then I will be right behind the ambulance."

When she woke, it was to an overwhelming sensation of dim lighting and a woman she presumed to be a nurse was sitting at a computer cart and typing on a keyboard.

"Ah, there you are. She's waking up, Doctor," the woman murmured.

An elderly gentleman approached her bed, speaking softly to her. "How are you feeling, Ms. Weaver?"

Isabelle blinked and considered how to answer. "Better than before, but I still feel like I got caught in a stampede."

He nodded sympathetically. "Can you tell me what happened?"

Isabelle didn't know exactly. She squeezed her eyes shut and tried to work her way back through the confusion. "The security guard. I think she put something in my coffee. I started to feel sick, and I asked her for help, but she took the baby." Panic swirled at the remembered terror. "Laura! Where is Laura?"

The nurse stroked her hand. "Don't you go worrying about those precious girls. That fine man of yours is taking quite good care of them."

Isabelle thought to argue, to tell the nurse that Adam wasn't her man, but she was too tired to fight what she wished were true. Adam was a fine man. And handsome too. She smiled, and when the nurse smiled back, Isabelle knew she was reinforcing the wrong impression. Sudden sadness swamped her. Adam wasn't hers and he never could be. A tear slipped down her cheek.

She brushed it away and lifted her gaze to the doctor. "Do you know what she gave me?"

He nodded. "We're waiting on final toxicology, but my guess is she gave you Rohypnol. You've heard of roofies?"

Isabelle nodded, relieved to realize she didn't feel quite so dizzy anymore. "How long before it wears off?"

"It's starting to. The paramedics reported that your coffee was knocked to the ground and there was a sizeable puddle. Presumably, you didn't ingest a full dose. We'll know more when the tox results arrive. Until then, you should just rest. Doctor's orders."

"Doctor's orders," Isabelle mumbled as she drifted back to sleep.

"When is Mama going to wake up?"

The dulcet tones of her daughter's voice drew Isabelle from slumber once more. Her eyelids fluttered, fighting back as she tried to open her eyes. She wanted to be awake, wanted to see her girls.

"I think Mama needs a Mia hug," Isabelle whispered.

"Mama!"

The sheer joy in her daughter's voice blew away the last vestiges of drowsiness. Isabelle raised herself on one stiff arm, wincing at the sudden shaft of pain. She must have bruised her elbow when she'd fallen. "Where's my best girl?"

Mia tried to climb her way onto the bed, but the guardrail made it difficult. Adam swooped her up in his arms and set her gently beside Isabelle. As her baby girl nestled into her side, Isabelle fought back tears. Nothing had ever felt as good as holding her daughter. For a moment, she closed her eyes and let herself simply be, breathing in the familiar scent of her daughter.

But even as she cherished the moment, her brain tormented her with questions.

Why was this happening and what would be next?

Chapter Ten

Adam glanced at his phone. He had a message from Nate, asking him to call. He excused himself. "I need to take this outside." He nodded to the security guard and strode to the window at the end of the hallway as he placed the call.

"Hey, Nate. What's up?"

"Anyone with you?"

"Negative. I'm at the end of the hallway. Why?"

"Fingerprint results are in."

"And?"

"They're not what I expected. I won't lie. It doesn't look good for Isabelle."

Something twisted deep within Adam's gut. "What aren't you telling me?"

"Nothing. I'm not jumping to conclusions until I interview her and see her reaction." He paused. "But, Adam, be careful. Isabelle may have been hoodwinked by her friend…or you and I have been played for fools."

Adam glanced back at Isabelle's room and a pain stabbed in the general vicinity of his heart. He forced a lid on his emotions and focused on the conversation.

"Are you coming to the hospital?"

"No. I want to do this in private. I spoke to the doctor. He's willing to release her. I'll arrange an escort."

"Where are we going?"

"Back to Claire's temporarily while we figure this out. If we need a safe house, we'll take it from there."

Adam disconnected the call. He had to get back to the room and prepare everyone to leave, but first he had to rein his emotions into control. For a long moment, he just stood staring out at the snowcapped mountains in the distance. He was trained to evaluate and not leap to conclusions. He needed to keep that same sense of open-mindedness now.

Given everything that had happened, the most reasonable conclusion was that Isabelle was an innocent victim. If Nate had evidence to the contrary, Adam would reevaluate. But even if she wasn't, his role had not changed. He was there to protect the innocent. The verdict might be out on Isabelle, but the children were blameless and deserving of his care—however temporary.

He fought off the thought of how the girls had wormed their way into his heart. His arm felt empty now when he wasn't bearing the weight of his precious little football.

Adam steeled his emotions and headed down the hallway to Isabelle's room. When he entered, Isabelle was preoccupied with the nurse giving her release instructions. She smiled up at him, seeming genuinely glad to see him. His heart gave a little lurch.

"They're letting me go home." Her face fell. "Well, not home, but wherever."

Despite his best instincts, Adam answered reassuringly. "Nate is sending an escort. They'll know where we're going."

She nodded in acquiescence, but he could see it was costing her. He shoved his own emotions away and reverted to warrior mode. His only task right now was to get them safely back to Claire's.

Nate buzzed Adam when the car was outside. He turned to Isabelle. "Time to go."

Her face was pale, and Adam realized that

as happy as she was to be set free, she was apprehensive of leaving the safety of the hospital.

"It's okay," he promised. "Nate has you covered."

She nodded, and he fought the tug her brave expression had on his heart.

"We'll do this in stages. Claire and I will take the girls down. Once they're secure, I'll come back for you. The officer will remain on guard outside the door."

Once again, she nodded, though he noted she was careful not to move her head too quickly. "Still dizzy?"

"Some. The doctor said it was normal and will take a while to wear off."

"Okay. Rest here. I'll be right back."

He left without a backward glance and headed to the playroom where Claire had been entertaining the girls.

Mia saw him first and came running over. "Mr. Adam, I want to go home."

He crouched beside her. "How about we take a car ride back to Claire's and see Chance?"

"Will Mama come?" The thread of anxiety in her voice coiled inside him.

"She will," he reassured her. "She's feeling much better now."

He filled Claire in on the plan, and they all headed downstairs. Alert for anything even mildly threatening, Adam escorted them through the lobby to a side entrance. A dark SUV was waiting.

Adam rapped on the roof to get the driver's attention. The deputy popped the locks and came around to stand guard as Adam quickly settled the children inside. Once he'd gotten the girls harnessed into car seats, with Claire between them, he turned to the man. "Wait here. I'll be back with Isabelle."

The officer nodded his understanding, and Adam was just starting to close the door when alarms shattered the peaceful twilight and lights flashed in rhythm with the blaring sound.

Isabelle! Adam's first instinct was to send the driver on his way and head back inside to rescue her, but a flashback to the attack at the house changed his mind. If Laura was the true target, this was a distraction. He had to get the girls to safety.

He opened the passenger door and jumped in beside the surprised driver. "They won't be expecting me to come with you." He swiveled so he could see his sister. "Claire, where are you parked?"

"It was sleeting when I got here, so I opted to pay for indoor parking."

"Perfect." He turned to the deputy. "I want you to drive around to the ER entrance. Claire and I will take the children and head back inside. You drive around a few times and then head back to the station. Radio ahead to Nate so he can send other cars. Hopefully, whoever triggered this will follow you and we can lay a trap."

"Nate will have my head if I leave you," the deputy argued. "It's too risky."

Adam reconsidered his plan. It was hard to think with the blaring sirens. The noise and lights were triggering a panic attack, and he knew he could only hold it off for so long with all the sensory overload.

He pulled out his phone and quickly placed a call to Nate. Putting him on speaker, Adam explained the situation and then listened while the sheriff corroborated his plan. The deputy was clearly unhappy, and Adam made a mental note to discuss it with Nate later. For now, he had to escape.

They pulled up under the awning for the ER entrance and Adam reversed his earlier procedure, unharnessing the girls. He handed Laura to Claire and turned for Mia, who stared at him wide-eyed. He wanted to take the time to comfort her, but that would have to come later. For now, he could only whisper a reassurance.

People streamed out of the hospital as the alarms continued to screech. Pulling Claire to the side, Adam edged their way around the crowd and headed inside. He squeezed his eyes against the blinding lights and tried to focus his attention on the people in his care. If he focused hard enough, he could turn the sirens into white noise in his mind.

"Adam." Claire tugged on his arm. "The parking garage is the other way."

"We're not going there."

"But you said—"

"Trust me. I have a plan."

He thought he heard her mutter, "Of course, you do," but there would be time for sibling payback later. Now he needed a vacant office. That proved easy to find. With everyone evacuating, the administrative offices were all empty. He walked down the corridor, looking for a room with windows. At the end of the hall, the conference room stood empty and dark. Heavy shades had been pulled across a wall of windows. Perfect.

Glancing over his shoulder to make sure no one had followed them, he ushered Claire into the room and closed the door behind them. He quickly scanned the area for the safest hiding spot. There was a bathroom at the rear of the room, conveniently adjacent to the windows. He lowered his voice as he spoke to Claire. "Lock yourself and the girls in there. I'm going for Isabelle."

She looked back at him and he could see the consternation in her eyes.

"Will you be okay?" Before he could answer, she glanced at Mia then continued in a soft voice, "You know what I mean."

He knew exactly what she meant. Before he'd turned himself into a recluse, Claire had witnessed the devastating impact of his PTSD too many times to count. He wouldn't lie to her.

"I'm fighting it the best I can. It will be better once we're away from the here."

Locking Claire and the girls in the bathroom left him with an uncomfortable memory of doing the same in the lawyer's office. Vowing that this time he would rescue them before any more danger came their way, he set off in search of Isabelle.

★ ★ ★

Blaring sirens and flashing lights com-pounded the nausea and dizziness that still plagued Isabelle, but they were nothing com-pared to her fear for Adam and her girls. She wanted to run after him, but the security guard had warned her to stay locked in the room. It was her safest option. She couldn't argue that, but it wasn't her own safety she was con-cerned about. Only a deep sense of knowing that Adam would come back for her kept her sheltering in place. He didn't need her compli-cating things.

The wait was interminable. Alarms contin-ued to blare and she heard anxious voices as people evacuated the building. Second-guesses crowded her mind. Where were Adam and the girls? She needed to be with them. She should never have acquiesced to his plan. Worry plagued her. What had triggered the alarm? Was there a fire? Should she evacuate? Was she risking her life staying, or was it possible the people after her were behind this? Her anxiety had reached fever pitch by the time her phone dinged.

Isabelle almost collapsed in relief when she saw Adam's message.

I'm coming for you. Be ready.

Those six words settled her nerves momentarily, but it wasn't long before her thoughts were back in overdrive. If he was coming, where were the girls? Were they safe?

Isabelle began pacing the room. She chided herself for doubting Adam. He had been nothing but reliable. But as the alarms continued, another fear overtook her. What were all these lights and alarms doing to Adam? How was he coping? She'd learned enough from Daniel to know that sensory overload was a dangerous trigger. He should have taken the girls and left. He should have—

A quick rap on the door interrupted her thoughts.

"Isabelle, open up. It's me."

On legs weak with relief, Isabelle stumbled to the door and flipped the safety latch. She'd never been so relieved as at the sight of Adam standing in her doorway. He pushed past her and closed the door.

"What's happening? Where are the girls?"

Adam gently grasped her arms to steady her. "They are safe with Claire. We're going to go get them as soon as I explain my plan."

Isabelle nodded and took a deep slow breath, trying to calm herself. "What's happening? Is it real…or is it them again?"

"I'm fairly confident it's them. The alarms began just as I was loading the girls into the car."

"Did you send them off?" Panic rose again at the thought of the girls being separated from her in a time of danger.

"No. I remembered how they set off the dogs in the kennel as a decoy while they went after Laura, so I hid the girls in the building instead. Nate's going to meet us."

"Okay." She offered him a wobbly smile. "I knew I could trust you to protect them."

A shadow flickered across Adam's face, but Isabelle didn't have time to root out the cause. Adam was heading to the door. He turned abruptly and she almost walked into him.

"Are you okay to do this? It might be too strenuous since you're still recovering."

"I'm a bit shaky, but I'll do whatever we need to do."

Adam's smile of approval gave her a needed adrenaline rush. He opened the door cautiously and scanned the hallway before leading her out. The fact that there was no sign of anyone coming for her indicated either this was a false alarm and really a hospital problem…or he'd been right about them going after Laura.

Adam took her hand and tugged her along behind him. He stopped at the corner and peered around to make sure no one was in the corridor. Once he was certain the way was clear, he pointed to the stairwell and told her to run.

"What about you?" She wasn't leaving him behind.

"Two steps behind you."

The sound of heavy footsteps running down the hall they'd just exited gave Isabelle a burst of energy. She and Adam shoved through the door into the stairwell and flattened themselves against the wall. Before long, they could hear men talking. Isabelle listened carefully, trying to catch what they were saying. The voices were too muffled to make out the words, but the angry, impatient tone was warning enough. These weren't hospital workers. She held her breath, half expecting them to burst through the doorway, and only released it slowly when the voices receded.

Adam grinned at her. "Let's go before they decide to come back," he breathed. At her nod, he took her arm and led her down the stairs. The steep concrete staircase exacerbated Isabelle's dizziness, making her extra grateful for Adam's support. As they finally approached the exit, he signaled her to wait while he eased open the door.

"No sign of anyone," he assured her. "I think all the action is in the front of the hospital." He pulled out his phone and texted Nate. After a minute, he glanced up at her. "Nate was waiting around the side so as to not draw attention. He'll pull around now. We need to be fast, and once we're in the car, I need you to crouch on the floor."

His thumb grazed her cheek as he gazed at her. "Are you up to that?"

Flutters of awareness confused Isabelle. She was relying on Adam to protect them. He wasn't supposed to make her have feelings she'd thought had died years ago. She forced herself to nod and speak. "You know I'll do whatever I need to for my girls."

His face broadened into a deep smile and he concurred. "I do. You've been absolutely amazing."

Her cheeks flushed at the compliment and Isabelle lowered her head. She wanted to tease him, say something to diffuse the sudden tension, but she was at a loss for words and could only manage a whisper. "Thank you."

The sound of Nate's car arriving saved her from any more conversation. She stood silently while Adam verified it was his friend. Once confirmed, he opened the car door so it was flush with the hospital exit. Keeping her head low, Isabelle dashed the short distance and crawled into the back of the vehicle. Adam climbed in behind her and closed the door.

"Did anyone see us?" he asked.

"Not that I saw," Nate replied. "Where's Claire?"

"Locked in a bathroom off the administrative offices."

Nate drove around to the front of the hospital and pulled up beside the police chief's car. "Wait here," he directed them. He was gone about five minutes before he returned with good news. "The building is secure. Adam, you can go get Claire and the girls. Isabelle, I think you should stay with me."

Isabelle wanted to protest, to tell him that she wanted to be the one to rescue her girls, but something in Nate's voice warned her not to argue. Adam headed into the building, and

Isabelle uneasily observed Nate as they waited for Adam's return. Gone was the friendly man she knew from church. Tension radiated off him, and it set her nerves on edge. Something had changed and she had no idea what it was.

Chapter Eleven

Adam wanted to call it a successful day as the cars entered the drive to Claire's ranch. They'd survived the attack and had arrived safely, but his body still radiated tension knowing the most difficult part lay ahead.

Nate pulled his vehicle up to the house entrance. Adam and Claire, who had driven back in her car, went around to the garage. They parked the car and started up the path. Adam paused before they reached the house. Turning to his sister, he spoke in a low voice. "I know you need to see to the dogs, and I hate to ask more of you, but can you take Mia with you?"

Claire chuckled. "You really think Isabelle is letting Mia out of her sight?"

Adam closed his eyes a moment and breathed in deeply before letting his shoulders relax on a long exhale. "She won't have much choice. Nate needs to talk to her." He glanced over his shoulder to be sure they were alone. "Trust me, Mia shouldn't be within hearing distance."

Concern etched Claire's features, and she obviously had questions, but she simply bobbed her head in agreement. "Mia's wonderful with the dogs. It won't be a bother."

They reached the house just as Nate finished helping Isabelle and the girls from his car. "Hey, Mia," Claire called. "Want to come help me feed the dogs? I had a friend check on them, but I'm thinking they could use some love."

Mia turned her eager face to her mother. "Please, Mama."

Isabelle opened her mouth, and Adam was sure it was to veto the suggestion, but Nate stepped up beside her and spoke softly. Isabelle's expression grew grave. She gave a quick nod to Nate and then turned back to Claire and Mia. Only because he was watching so carefully did Adam pick up on her nervous tension.

"Go ahead, sweetie. I'm going to take Laura in for a bottle. But stay with Ms. Claire. Do whatever she tells you."

Mia took Claire's hand and skipped off to the kennels while Adam unlocked the front door. Chance was waiting as they entered. He bypassed Nate and Isabelle and leaned into Adam.

Immediately, Adam felt his body lighten. He knelt and buried his face in the dog's soft fur. "I missed you, buddy." Chance burrowed hard against him. Adam laughed. "I guess you missed me too."

Isabelle set the diaper bag down on the sofa and faced Nate. "I need to make a bottle for Laura. I don't want to keep you waiting, but we stand a better chance of speaking uninterrupted if she has eaten."

"You seem to know her very well."

Isabelle didn't pick up on the edge that Adam recognized in Nate's words. She rifled through the bag in search of powdered formula and a bottle. When she found what she wanted, she looked up and shrugged. "I guess I do. Jess and I are both single moms. We were lucky we had each other to rely on."

"You were very close?"

"Like sisters," Isabelle replied sadly. "We chose each other to be family because we had no one." She turned on her heel and headed into the kitchen.

Adam followed. He opened the back door to let Chance out, then walked over to the counter. "I'll make coffee while you get the bottle ready." Thinking of her recent experience, he reconsidered. "Or would you prefer tea?"

She smiled tentatively. "Thanks. It's going to be a while before I can look at coffee the same."

Nate came into the kitchen and sat at the big farm table. Adam brought the coffee and Isabelle's tea over and settled down, facing the window. Claire's kitchen overlooked a vast nature preserve and, though he would have preferred to be hiking in it, just looking at the snow-covered pine trees soothed his soul. He sipped his coffee and waited for Isabelle.

Five minutes later, when she was still fussing at the counter, Adam knew she was stalling. Was it just nerves, postponing what she feared was bad news, or was she hiding something? Nate sat patiently, but Adam wanted to know the info his friend had withheld.

"Isabelle."

She looked at him, her expression as frightened as a cornered animal's. Adam pushed back his chair and went over to her. "There's no use postponing this." He angled his head toward the table. "Nate has results he needs to talk to you about."

She looked at him, fear in her eyes, and his chest tightened. "You know what it is?"

Was he overreacting? Or did the idea that he knew seem to trouble her more?

"I don't know it all, and we won't until we talk to you."

Her head lowered in resignation, Isabelle walked to the table and sat with Laura on her lap. She reached for the bottle before realizing she'd left it on the counter.

Adam picked it up and set it on the table. "Would you prefer me to feed her?" he asked gently.

She clutched the baby close to her chest, almost as if she could ward off bad news. "No." She shook her head. "I'll do it."

She lowered her head and appeared to be whispering a prayer. Adam took his seat, facing her. After a minute, she looked up at Nate. "I'm ready."

Nate rested his palms on the table and leaned forward. "Isabelle, there's not any easy way to say this—"

"You found her body?"

"What?" Nate blinked. "No."

"Is that what you've been thinking?" Adam asked gently.

She nodded. "What else was I to think?"

Nate rubbed his eyes. "Not that."

Isabelle seemed to calm visibly at that news. "Then what is it?"

Nate caught her gaze and held it. "We got the fingerprint analysis back."

"Okay. Did it tell you who the men were?"

Nate shook his head.

Isabelle rolled her eyes. "Then what's the point of all this, if it didn't tell you anything—"

Nate broke in. "I didn't say it didn't tell us anything."

"Nate, please stop dancing around it. Just tell me what you found."

"We took fingerprints from Jess's house and more from the lawyer's office. We looked for a match but found only one. Presumably Jess's."

Isabelle mulled it over for a minute. "I guess that makes sense if she was in the lawyer's office to sign papers."

Nate nodded. "It would, except for one thing. The name they matched to was not Jess's."

Isabelle shook her head in confusion. "You've lost me."

"The fingerprints we took as elimination prints were from all the places in her home Jess might have touched. The kitchen, Laura's room, her bathroom. Those prints matched the ones found on a file and chair in the lawyer's office." Nate waited to see if she was following before he continued. "They matched, but not to Jess. The fingerprints belong to a woman named Julia."

"That's not possible."

Nate turned over a paper that he'd placed on the table. "Is this Jess?"

Isabelle leaned forward, studied it, and then looked up at him. "You know it is. You've seen her at church with me every week."

Nate sighed deeply. "Isabelle, this woman's name is Julia. Her husband was a highly respected engineer for a military weaponry company. He was working on a top-secret project two years ago when he suddenly went missing. His wife, Julia, was considered a suspect in his disappearance. Three months after he disappeared, she went missing too. No one had any idea where she went until we got this fingerprint match."

Adam had been closely watching the exchange, noting Isabelle's stricken expression. Her hands were trembling as she set the bottle back on the table. He rose quickly and walked around to take Laura. She looked up at him in panic. "No, you can't have her."

Adam crouched beside her, putting a supporting arm beneath Laura. "I don't want you to drop the baby. Let me hold her while you explain to Nate."

She looked up at him, eyes wide, then turned to face Nate. "Explain? You think I knew this?" Her gaze swung wildly to Adam. "You too? You think I'm a part of this…" She gasped for breath and her body convulsed. "How could you, of all people, think that after everything we've gone through? They drugged me to get this baby. How could—" She pushed back the chair and, clasping Laura to her chest, bolted from the room.

Adam wanted to follow Isabelle, to reassure her that he had not thought any such thing, but the reality was, he hadn't been sure. Despite her reaction, he still wasn't. He looked at Nate. The expression on his friend's face was bland, but Adam knew that beneath the quiet façade, Nate's brain was seething with the same questions, debating what to make of Isabelle's responses.

"I'm going to make some calls, see if I can find out more about this case." Nate paused and cleared his throat. "Can you reach out to your buddies, see if anyone has heard anything?"

Adam dropped his eyes as his chest tightened and apprehension darkened the edges of his vision. Reaching out to old comrades would be worse than tearing a bandage off a wound. It was more akin to ripping out the stitches that were holding him together.

Once he'd settled here in Colorado, he'd isolated himself from pretty much anyone in his military life, with the exception of Nate. When Adam had been drowning in a sea of undiagnosed symptoms, Nate had thrown him a lifeline, introducing him to the wilds of Colorado, to the healing power of nature. That meant Nate knew exactly what he was asking and thought it important enough to risk.

Adam walked over to the bay window and rested his palms against the cold glass as his mind sought solace from the forest. But his brain couldn't rest. He thought of Isabelle in the next room, the brave friend who was fiercely protecting a baby. The woman who, against his best instincts, had wormed her way into his life and maybe even his heart. To know the truth, for her, he would break his silence. "I'll make some calls."

Isabelle didn't know where to turn. The world was collapsing on her and she couldn't think straight. Jess wasn't Jess? Who was Julia? Had everything about this past year been a lie?

She sagged onto the bed. There had to be some explanation, some way to make sense of all of it. But she was so tired. Her brain was still dulled from the effects of the drugging and she couldn't even figure out how to begin to process this news. All she wanted to do was to go to sleep and wake up to find it had all been a bad dream.

Laura started to squirm in her arms, and Isabelle knew she was sensing the tension. She held her close. "Don't you worry, my darling," she murmured as she gently stroked Laura's back. "I'm here for you. I won't let anyone hurt you."

But even as she made the promise, she knew it was impossible to keep. She had no way to do it on her own, and the two men who were her only help now doubted her.

It was too overwhelming. She'd coped with so much these past few years—Daniel's erratic behavior, his death, her despair, and her efforts to be a better mother to Mia. Just when it seemed she was going to make it as a single mother, this avalanche hit. It was too much. She couldn't do it alone.

You're not alone, her heart whispered. *God is always with you.*

She closed her eyes and tried to feel the truth in that, tried to find the words to pray. It was wrong to rely on her own strength. God had been good to her and He would continue to be if she remained faithful. But she was so very tired.

Isabelle laid Laura down on the bed and curled up beside her. She closed her eyes, intending to pray, but she could feel herself drifting off. Maybe just for a few minutes she would rest.

"Mama."

Isabelle fought her way through a cloud of sleep, drawn by the joyful sound of her daughter's voice. The sound of baby gurgles sang to her heart and she listened to Mia whispering to Laura as she played piggy toes with the baby's foot. Isabelle opened her eyes, intent on cherishing this precious moment of the three of them at peace together because she knew it wouldn't last.

Once Mia saw she was awake, she bounced up to grab a paper from the table. "Look, Mama. I made you a picture."

Isabelle took the drawing and smiled. Yet another tree. This was not Mia's norm. "You're getting really good at drawing trees, sweetie." She ran her finger along the smooth crayoned shape. "Is there a reason you're drawing so many?"

Mia's eyes welled up and her fingers rose to graze her necklace. Isabelle's heart cracked. "You're drawing them for Aunt Jess?" The name came out automatically before her brain caught up. But if she was confused, she certainly couldn't tell Mia she had the wrong name. Not now. Until she knew something for sure, her friend would remain Jess.

Mia hung her head and nodded. "It makes me feel close to her."

Isabelle wrapped her arms around her little girl, pulling her near. "It's okay to feel sad. I miss her too." She brushed her hand over the golden charm, remembering Jess giving the necklace to Mia. She'd had a matching one made for Laura. "Sisters of the heart," she'd said. Isabelle's heart tightened with the memory. They'd been so happy, widows both of them, yes, but grateful for each other and the precious children God had entrusted to them.

And now those children were solely her responsibility.

Isabelle gazed down at the tree drawing. She

recalled telling Adam the story of how she and Jess had met, but the shortened version had left out so much—of their friendship, of the fragile bond of trust that had grown unbreakable. Until now.

Isabelle longed for those peace-filled days she and Mia had spent with Jess at Samaritan Home. She sighed softly, thinking of how Jess had shared her creative streak with Mia, how she had cultivated the little girl's love of art.

A memory surfaced of four-year-old Mia waving a paintbrush and splattering them all in green as Jess tried to include her in the painting of the mural. They'd joked that there had been more green paint on Mia than on the tree. Cleanup had…

Goose bumps rose along Isabelle's arm, multiplying until she was shivering with the force of the memory. The tree. Of course.

The tree holds all the answers.

That was the clue Jess had left and now, finally, she knew which tree Jess meant. It wasn't the Christmas tree, the one the men had tossed in their search for something. It was the tree she and Jess, with Mia's questionable help, had painted as part of a mural at Samaritan Home.

She had to tell Adam! Isabelle leapt from

the bed, then had to stop and steady herself. These waves of dizziness that came with sudden movement might continue for a while, according to the doctor—a side effect of having been drugged. She shrugged the feeling off. She could tolerate a bout of dizziness if it meant she got some answers.

Answers.

The word drew her up short as she thought of Nate's revelation about Jess and the fingerprints. Did she really want those answers? Did she want the fragile memory of her friendship with Jess to be crushed beneath the weight of more revelations?

The pause gave other questions time to surface. How would Adam react to this news? The last time she'd spoken to him, she'd accused him of doubting her. Wouldn't this news only reinforce those doubts? Would he think she had been hiding this information until she'd had no choice but to reveal it?

Laura's happy gurgles broke through her devastating thoughts and brought her clarity. Whatever the truth was, she needed to know it, because this baby deserved a future and a mother. It didn't matter what Adam and Nate thought of her, she needed their help to solve the mystery of Jess's disappearance. If Samaritan Home held clues, then she needed to find them.

Adam set his phone aside. He'd left messages with as many of his former army buddies as he still had numbers for. Hopefully, between his unofficial inquiries and Nate's official ones, someone would know something. He was about to start researching Jess—he caught himself, Julia, and her husband, when he felt a presence behind him. He glanced up to see Isabelle standing in the doorway, looking hesitant. She had Laura in her arms and was holding Mia's hand. His heart gave a lurch at the portrait they portrayed—a small forlorn family.

Wanting to do something to cheer them up, he forced a smile. "I hope you liked Mia's drawing."

Isabelle nodded, but she seemed distracted, troubled. Unsurprising really.

"Is Claire in the house?"

"She's in the kitchen. Mia was giving her drawing lessons, but she was going to start lunch."

"I'm going to bring the girls there and get a bottle for Laura. Then can we talk?"

"I'll wait here."

The trio left as quietly as they'd entered. Adam resumed his internet search while he awaited her return. He found several news stories about the disappearances written at the time, but nothing much in the way of follow-ups. Had interest waned? Or had the stories been squashed?

He heard Isabelle walking back down the hall, but made no effort to hide what was on his screen. She didn't appear to notice immediately.

"I will apologize to Claire when I can do it without Mia hearing, but I'm sorry. You two should not have to be caring for my daughter."

Her stilted, formal tone worried Adam. The news about Jess, his doubts, and her despair had cost them the easy camaraderie that had made the past few days manageable despite the stress. Seeking to regain that balance, he made a peace offering. "You've been through a tough time. It's okay that you needed to sleep. Claire doesn't mind."

"But the children are my responsi—"

He knew the moment her gaze landed on his screen.

"Is that about Jess?" She blinked. "I'm sorry. I can't think of her by any other name."

"This is about her husband, Robert. I've been

trying to find any information that might help us figure out what it's all about."

"Have you? Found anything, I mean. About him or what he was doing?"

"Not yet." He decided against telling her of his phone inquiries.

"About the drawings Mia has been doing."

Adam blinked at the quick change in topic. "Yes."

"They gave me a clue."

She stopped, seemed hesitant, almost as if waiting for his approval to continue.

"Mia's drawing of a tree gave you a clue?"

She nodded. "Remember that odd message on my phone? 'The tree holds all the answers'?"

At his quick nod, she continued. "And remember I told you about Jess giving us a place to stay at Samaritan Home? What I didn't mention, because honestly it just didn't seem important, was that while we were staying there, Jess, Mia and I painted a mural on the community room wall."

Her gaze fell away and she fleetingly closed her eyes. "Mia has been drawing that tree over and over as a way to stay close to her aunt. When she showed me the most recent one this afternoon, I was thinking...wondering how I could have been so wrong about Jess. I was re-membering that day of us painting and suddenly it all made sense."

She hesitated a moment. "I know it looks bad, like I might have been hiding this all along. And I understand why you might think I knew." She leveled her gaze to meet his. "I promise you, I didn't. This is as much a shock to me as it is to you. More so really. Jess was my best friend and my support through a really dif-ficult time in my life when I didn't know what I was doing or how to survive. To suddenly find out that none of that was real?"

She shuddered but continued. "I can't think about that now. I have two girls to protect from men who want something I don't understand." She pointed at the drawing. "This tree might hold the clue. But I'll understand if you're done with this. I'll find a way to do it on my own."

The words could have sounded pathetic, but her delivery was so strong, so intent, that Adam found himself believing her. Because he wanted to or because she was telling the truth? He didn't know. But he had to help. "Can we go there?"

"Yes. I can call the pastor and ask him to let me in. But what about the girls? I don't want to bring Mia back there, but leaving them here hasn't been safe."

"I'll arrange protection with Nate and Claire."

He could see the doubt creep into her face at the mention of Nate's name. "Isabelle, neither Nate nor I wanted to believe you were involved, but—"

"I get it. Neither of you knows me well enough to be sure I'm not. The thing is, I know I'm not, and I have someone after me, so I have to do something about it. At the moment, checking out the tree in the mural is the best lead I have."

Chapter Twelve

Tears welled in Isabelle's eyes as Adam pulled Claire's truck into the parking lot behind Samaritan Home. He seemed to sense her mood and gave her time.

She climbed out of the car and just stood and stared at the building. There was so much emotion tied up in this building—recovering from Daniel's death, building a friendship and a new life with Jess and Laura.

She started to tremble.

Adam came up beside her and rested his arm around her shoulder. She wanted to lean into him, but at the same time, she was mortified. Explaining her reaction would mean baring too much of the wrecked person she had been.

"I'm sorry. It's just…hard."

He squeezed her shoulder in acknowledgment, but she knew he didn't understand the half of it. He'd think it was about what had happened with Jess, and that was a huge part of it. But it was so much more, and all of that was also tied up in Jess.

All the memories, how fragile she'd been, still reeling from Daniel's death and her inability to cope. She'd known she wasn't being a good mother to Mia. She'd been barely able to function as an adult, so lost in despair over the loss of her husband, so wrapped in grief that she hadn't been able to save him. How many nights had she tormented herself with guilt? She'd been on a dark road, unable to see her way clear, but she'd been trying to find a new life to share with Mia, determined to do better by her daughter. Jess had thrown her a lifeline.

No matter what the truth was, she would always be grateful for that. She would always owe Jess.

Something settled in her at that. She needed to be here, to search this place as repayment to Jess for her new life. It was the very least she could do.

"Let's go inside. The pastor said he had a meeting across town but would leave the door open for us."

Walking through the doorway and into the huge rec room was like stepping back in time, but Isabelle pushed forward. She had a task to accomplish, and she needed to do it as quickly as possible.

"The community room is up on the second floor." She confidently led the way through a maze of rooms and up a wide staircase that had seen better days. Several of the sagging steps creaked when she stepped on them. Had the building always been this decrepit, or had it just fallen into disrepair since she'd last been there?

She walked ahead of Adam down the hall and stopped in the arched doorway to just take a moment and absorb the sight.

Adam gave a low whistle. "You and Jess did this?"

"Mostly Jess, with Mia's help. My talents don't run to art."

The far wall was divided into two huge plate-glass windows with a long stretch of wall between them. On that wall, Jess had painted an enormous weeping willow tree. Isabelle smiled, remembering how she and Mia had watched it take shape. Mia had been absolutely enthralled.

Even now, almost a year later, the mural was so vivid that the tree seemed three-dimensional.

Dazed, Isabelle walked over to the wall and ran her fingers lightly over the painted surface.

Memories crowded in. Jess feathering the brush to create the leaf patterns. Mia joyfully splattering paint. Isabelle had mostly been responsible for cleaning up the mess.

Adam came up beside her. "Where do we start? Do you have any idea where she might have put something?"

Snapping herself out of the memories, Isabelle focused her attention on their mission. She shook her head in answer to Adam. "Jess certainly didn't do anything while we were working on it. Maybe she came back later when she had something to hide."

"In that case, we should be looking for a loose board or a hole." Adam knelt and felt around the roots of the tree. He pressed on the boards, seeking any sign something had been removed and replaced.

Isabelle tapped on the wall, hoping to hear a hollow sound. Was it possible that within this wall there was something of worth? Something that would explain this dangerous mess they were in?

Her tapping resulted in nothing. The sounds were all solid, but as she examined the tree closely, that sense of three-dimensionality nagged at her. In her recollection, the mural had been a flat surface. But there was no sign of construction, no indication this painting was anything other than what they had created. Doubt assailed her and she began to worry this had just been a fool's errand.

"Claire keeps a toolbox in the truck. I'm going to run down and see what's there. Will it be a problem if we have to pry off some boards?"

Isabelle shrugged. "I don't think so." She ran a finger along the window ledge and it came away covered in dust. It had clearly been a while since this room had been used.

Adam left, and Isabelle walked back to the tree. "Talk to me, Jess. What did you do here? Where are your secrets?"

She stroked her finger lovingly over the whimsical designs—the owl sitting on his branch, the delicate shading of the leaves, a rainbow of birds. Those had been Mia's request. They were so lifelike you could almost hear them warbling.

It was all so realistic, down to the knothole in the trunk.

A shiver ran down Isabelle's spine.

That knothole was new; it had not been part of the original design she and Jess had created.

Isabelle leaned in and studied the tree. Jess was so talented, Isabelle felt like she could feel the rasp of the bark as she touched the nooks and crannies. She grazed her knuckle along the seam in the wall that ran behind the tree limb. It was definitely raised, part of the design that gave the tree the dimension that had been nagging at her.

She tapped lightly on the knothole. The gnarled branches with their lacy leaves nearly hid the bright bluebird that sat perched in front of it, his beak pointing toward the hole, almost as if it were looking inside.

The bird seemed to call to Isabelle. She continued to trace the outline until she reached the dark hole at the center. Her finger did scrape along a rough edge then, right before it disappeared into the darkness.

Isabelle gasped and fell back, almost afraid to look. Gathering her courage, she leaned forward again to examine the knothole more closely. It wasn't a painting. It really was a hole carved into the tree. She took out her phone and used the flashlight to try to see inside. The light appeared to bounce off something reflective. Excitement skittered along her spine as she angled herself to see better, but the hole was too small to get her head into. She stepped back again, wanting a wider perspective before she thrust her hand into darkness.

Isabelle heard the creak of a stair tread. "Adam," she called, "I think I found something."

There was no reply and unease shivered through her. Thinking quickly, she made her way to the closet in the corner and opened it, pretending to look up on the shelf. If there was someone besides them in this house, she couldn't let them know what she'd found.

She listened carefully, but all was silent.

Maybe she was wrong. No one was there.

It was probably just her nerves.

She pulled out her phone and called Adam. "I think I found something. Do you have a good flashlight?"

"In the truck. I'll bring it in."

"Were you just back in the house?"

"No, why?"

"I thought I heard something."

"I'll look around, but there are no other cars here."

Despite his reassurances and her own eagerness to see what was in the hole, Isabelle waited by the closet until she heard Adam's footsteps and his voice calling out to her. "It's only me."

He walked into the room loaded with an ax, a hammer, chisel, pry bar, some loose rope, and an industrial-size flashlight. He set the items on the floor before handing her the flashlight.

Isabelle's eyes widened at the sight of the ax.

"I'm hoping not to need it, but we'll see. What did you find?"

She led him to the tree and took his hand, placing it on the bark. She told herself the flush of excitement was just anticipation of what they would find.

"See this bird? See where it's pointing?"

Adam ran his hand along the wall, following the bird's line of sight right until his hand disappeared into the wall.

"Whoa."

"I tried to use the flashlight on my phone, but I couldn't see far enough into it."

"Let's use the one I brought. See if you can angle it from above my head, so I can see."

Isabelle stood behind him and shone the light over Adam's shoulder as he tried to peer inside. When he couldn't see, he thrust his arm into the hole.

"There's something down there, but I can't reach it." He readjusted himself and leaned his whole body into the wall, reaching down as far as he could. "My fingers are scraping the top of something metal, but I can't get a grip on it."

"Jess must have had some way of getting it in there."

"She probably just dropped it in. I think we're going to have to open the wall."

Isabelle hesitated only a minute. "It could be a matter of life or death. Pastor Frank will understand."

Isabelle watched as Adam tapped along the wall below the knothole. The tapping rang hollow most of the way down, but a foot off the floor, the sound turned to more of a solid thump.

It was all Isabelle could do not to grab the claw and rip open the wall herself. What would they find inside? Jess's text had implied there would be answers.

Adam made a small hole then handed the chisel to Isabelle to hold as he used the pry bar to pull back the plasterboard.

"I've got it." He reached into the opening, pulled out a long silver cylinder, and handed it over to her. He stuck his hand back in the wall.

"I'll take that, thank you."

Startled by the voice, Isabelle turned around and found herself staring down the barrel of a gun.

She hadn't imagined it before. There *had* been someone in the building—someone who was waiting for them to find this clue. She couldn't give him the canister, not when it probably held all the answers to Jess and her secret life.

Adam rose to his feet behind her. Just feeling his strength at her back gave Isabelle courage. She slung the handle of the cylinder over her shoulder. "Why should I give it to you?"

The man laughed and waved the gun in her face. "This reason enough?"

Her bones turned to liquid. Mia and Laura's faces flashed before her eyes. Who would raise her babies if he killed her? But then she thought of Jess.

"Pretty convincing," she murmured, taking a step forward. She reached to take the strap from her shoulder and in one smooth movement, swung it forward with the full force of her body. She aimed the canister at his head but continued into the swing and brought the chisel down on the hand that was holding the gun, sending it flying. She'd hit him on the wrist and blood poured from the wound, but he charged at her. She turned and ran, but he quickly caught her and ripped the cylinder away.

From the corner of her eye, she saw Adam retrieve the gun. He called out. "Let her go. Now!"

The man didn't loosen his grip. Adam fired. His impeccable aim sent a bullet through the man's knee.

With a howl, the man dropped to the ground.

Isabelle stepped up to him. "I'll just take that back now." She snatched the cylinder. He tried to lunge at her again, but his leg gave out.

Adam quickly tackled him and pulled his hands behind his back. "Hand me that rope."

Isabelle brought it and Adam quickly hog-tied the gunman.

"Who are you working for?"

The man was obviously in pain, but the look that settled over his face was a mix of fear and determination. He reminded Isabelle of the man they'd apprehended in the kidnapping attempt. He wasn't saying anything.

Adam shrugged. "Have it your way." He pulled out his phone and called Nate. There was no answer, so he called dispatch instead. When he finished, the man laughed crudely. "They'll never get here in time."

Adam ignored him. He picked up the ax and swung it into the wall, then stretched in and pulled out a backpack. He reached for Isabelle's hand. "We shouldn't wait around."

Adam didn't let it show, but the man's words troubled him. He sounded too confident. He and Isabelle started down the stairs, but the sound of cars arriving stopped him. "That's too soon to be cops. Is there another way out of here?"

Isabelle's face had drained of color and she was leaning against the wall. She nodded weakly. "I need a minute."

"I don't think we have one."

"Okay." She blinked, gathered her strength and pushed away from the wall. "We need to go up. There's a back staircase, but we can only get to it from the top floor."

"Can you do it?"

She faced him calmly. "I have no choice. Follow me."

Adam let her lead, but he stayed close behind, ready to catch her if she fell. He'd underestimated her, though. Isabelle's resolve was as strong as any soldier's he'd ever served with. She may have looked on the verge of collapse minutes ago, but she charged up the stairs as if she'd trained for it her whole life.

They were halfway up the last flight when the front door slammed open. Footsteps pounded in the foyer and angry voices rang out. Adam wished he'd taken the time to gag the man they'd tied up when he heard him calling out to his buddies. He could hear the men charging up the stairs and knew they were running out of time.

Isabelle had reached the landing and she signaled to him to follow her. Ignoring the open door straight ahead, she stealthily led him down the hallway and through a maze of rooms. Adam could hear shouts from below as they started up the staircase. It sounded like there were at least four pursuers, so they would fan out and search the rooms quickly.

Isabelle didn't seem fazed. She opened a door, cringing at the squeak, and guided him through. Once she'd closed it, she whispered, "Do you want to escape or try to trap them?"

Adam almost laughed. She was amazing—so bold and confident.

"I want to trap them, but we're outnumbered and I'm sure they're heavily armed. We need to get back to the girls."

He didn't want to say anything to alarm her, but the fact that they'd been so easily tracked worried him.

* * *

Isabelle hadn't been on these stairs in over a year. The last time had been when she'd played hide-and-seek with Mia. She had to think of this escape the same way—and ignore the deadly consequences of losing.

She pulled out a piece of rope she'd stuffed in her pocket and tied the door handle shut. It wouldn't stop the men, but it might buy some time. She quickly led Adam down the stairs. Because this house had been used for a variety of purposes over the years, most of the old features had been left intact. She'd been told the top floor had once been servants' quarters, which was why the staircase exited in the basement kitchen. These days that kitchen was only used for parish events. Hopefully, no one would think to look for them there.

Above her, she could hear doors slamming as the men searched. Part of her wanted to crawl into one of the closets and just hole up, but survival instincts ran strong when she thought of the beloved children waiting back at Claire's.

When they reached the basement, she stopped and explained the layout. The door ahead lead into the open cafeteria-style room. At the far end of the hall was a small industrial-style kitchen. The door from there led into the parking lot where they'd left the truck.

"The danger is that there is no way to know if anyone is on the other side until we open the door. But if the room is empty, it will be easy for us to get to the parking lot."

Adam nodded. "They haven't broken through upstairs yet, so let's just stand and listen for a minute."

Adam put his ear to the door, carefully listening for any sound. "I think we're clear—"

Pounding on the door above interrupted him.

"I wonder how long the rope will hold them back."

A resounding crash of the door hitting the wall answered that. Footsteps thumped down the stairs. Isabelle looked to Adam. "I guess we're taking a chance on the cafeteria."

"Let me go first. You wait behind the door. If it seems clear, I'll go right and you go left. We'll meet across the room."

Isabelle agreed. She waited for him to reach for the door and then stepped behind it. He turned the knob and jumped to the side as she took it from him, pulling the door wide. She held her breath, waiting to see his reaction.

"All clear," he breathed as he ducked into the

doorway and ran the perimeter of the room, hugging the wall.

With the sound of the men growing closer, Isabelle didn't waste any time. She ducked around the door and started to the left. Spying a rack of chairs, she pulled it in front of the door, hoping to buy time again. Once it was wedged in place, she took off toward the kitchen, where Adam was waiting for her. The kitchen door had a window, so she pulled back the curtain to check the parking lot. Her heart sank.

Adam was looking over her shoulder, so she felt the moment he noticed. All the tires on Claire's truck had been slashed.

Isabelle's spirits sank. Behind her, she could hear the shouts of the men in pursuit. Ahead lay a parking lot with the disabled truck. They were trapped.

Chapter Thirteen

"Come on." Adam opened the kitchen door, grasped Isabelle's hand, and dashed for the truck.

"What are you doing?" Isabelle asked as he opened the passenger side and helped her in. He ran around to the driver's side and climbed in before answering.

"We're sitting ducks if we wait here."

"But the tires."

"Won't be the first time I've driven on rims." Adam gripped the steering wheel and glanced over at her. "Make sure you're buckled in and hang tight. It's going to be bumpy." The church was on the outskirts of town, so he took a sharp right out of the parking lot and headed for the sheriff's station. He eyed sparks shooting out from the wheel rims and could only pray nothing ignited before he could get to help. But that wasn't the most frightening sight in his rearview mirror. A large SUV, with the advantage of four intact wheels, was bearing down on them. Adam pressed down on the accelerator and the truck shuddered. The wheel in the back was dragging and it was all he could do to keep them on the road.

"Call Dispatch. Tell them we're headed in town, but have a tail. Ask them to send extra backup."

Before Isabelle could make the call, a wail of sirens pierced the air with ear-shattering relief. Adam waved the lead car on and pulled to the side of the road as the second car whipped past.

Behind him, Adam could see the vehicle tailing him swing in a wide circle and take off in the opposite direction, a sheriff's SUV in pursuit. Relief poured through him. Driving this truck had felt like being back in combat. He fought the encroaching memories, trying to hang on to his focus and keep the attack at bay.

Beside him, Isabelle was trembling. Pushing his own torments aside, he reached for her hand. "It's okay. We're safe now."

She swallowed and nodded quickly. "I know. I'll be fine in a minute. But I need to get back to the girls. Make sure they're okay too."

Adam pulled out his phone to see if he'd gotten any response from Nate yet. Nothing. He didn't think the sheriff had been in either of the vehicles that had passed them, so he called again. This time Nate picked up.

"Almost there," Nate said. "I sent the other cars after them, but I'll come for you."

Just as promised, Adam saw the familiar sheriff's vehicle make the turn five hundred yards ahead. He waved Nate down. The sheriff hopped out and rushed to Isabelle's side of the truck. "You guys all right?"

Isabelle rolled the window down. "We're fine now that you're here."

"What happened?"

Isabelle started to speak, but Adam interrupted her. "Where are Claire and the girls?"

"Under guard back at the house, where you left them."

Adam inhaled deeply and let it out in a rush in an attempt to draw in some energy. "Why didn't you answer when I called?"

"I was interviewing a prisoner."

Adam just nodded and let his head fall forward.

"What can you tell me? Who should my deputies be looking for?"

Isabelle answered. "They must have tailed us

from Claire's. I thought I heard a sound while Adam was outside getting tools to break open the walls, but Adam didn't hear or see anything, so I figured it was just nerves. It wasn't. Apparently, the man was waiting to see what we found before trying to take it from us."

Adam lifted his head and laughed at that. The adrenaline rush was finally fading and laughter felt like welcome relief. He grinned at Nate. "You don't ever want to cross her. She swung a tube at his head and then gouged his hand with a chisel."

Nate ignored him and got right to the point "So, you found something? What?"

"We don't know yet. There was this cylinder the man tried to steal, and then there was a knapsack Adam grabbed at the last minute. We haven't had time to open either one yet."

"Can you give us a ride?" Adam asked. "We can look at everything once we get there."

"Sure thing. Let me just radio ahead to my deputies."

Isabelle climbed into the back of Nate's car, leaving Adam to sit beside his friend. Once Nate had called in an update, they headed to Claire's. They'd been driving for about fifteen minutes with Nate filling him in on his renewed frustration at the silence of their prisoner. "Someone is holding something over him, or he's scared, because he's not talking."

"Hopefully, we'll find something in Jess's papers to give us a clue."

"Does the nickname Silver Wolf mean anything to either of you?" Isabelle's voice sounded intrigued.

Adam swung his head around to her. "Why?" He could see that she had opened the backpack and was going through the contents. Annoyance tugged at him. He had no authority to tell Isabelle she couldn't look through her friend's belongings, but instinctively he'd wanted to be observing when she did.

She held up a brown notebook that looked like a soft-covered journal. "Apparently, Jess had been keeping notes on her investigation in this journal. His name is mentioned on one of the last pages, from about a week before she vanished."

"The name doesn't ring a bell to me," Adam answered. "Nate?"

Nate's mouth was drawn in a tight line and his expression was grim. "I've heard the name. What does she say about him?"

"She seems to think he's behind her husband's disappearance."

"I thought she was blamed for that." Adam knew his phrasing was a mistake as he observed Isabelle. Her brows drew together and her eyes took on a combative glint.

"What happened to innocent until proven guilty?"

Her tone challenged him more than even the words did, and Adam knew he was treading in dangerous territory. "Let me rephrase. If she is looking at someone else to blame, it would appear she was not behind her husband's disappearance, but is there anything in that notebook to indicate she had information about it? Knew he was planning to disappear?"

The tension that had held Isabelle like a coiled spring eased and her shoulders dropped. "No. Her first notes seem to be fearful, then angry at him—like she had discovered something. I'll have to read more closely. I was just scanning for anything that would jump out at me. This name did."

"Why don't you message some of our ranger buddies and see if they have any intel?" Nate suggested. "If this somehow involved the military, some of them might be more in touch than either of us still is."

Adam opened his phone and composed a message to the same former members of his unit that he'd contacted earlier. When he was done, he looked back at Isabelle. She still had her head bent over the notebook, but he noticed her rubbing her forehead.

"Dizzy?"

She looked up, her forehead drawn tight. He could see the fatigue radiating off her. She nodded and then winced at the movement. "Yeah, I've never been good at reading in the car under the best of circumstances."

"Set it aside," he said softly. "There will be time to look when we get back to Claire's. Why don't you close your eyes and rest until we get there?"

Her glance revealed her disquiet. "Because it feels like I'm wasting precious time that might cost Jess her life."

Adam startled himself with the strength of his reaction to her words, the yearning to comfort her. He'd long since resigned himself to the life of a bachelor. He had nothing to offer Isabelle—and even an offer of comfort was likely unwelcomed when coming from him. It had been only hours ago that he'd effectively accused her of criminal activity.

Adam sighed inwardly and faced forward. Isabelle was quite capable of surviving without him.

Nate's radio crackled, interrupting his musings.

"We lost them, boss."

Adam didn't recognize the voice, but it was clearly one of the deputies.

"Where did you lose them?"

"Out by Five Corners." The man's voice sounded baffled for a moment. "We were hanging tight on their tail and they just vanished— like some spaceship just spirited them away."

Adam watched Nate roll his eyes. "Well then, retrace your steps and find that portal."

Adam laughed out loud as Nate closed the connection. Nate shook his head. "My sci-fi rookie. He's got good instincts, though, so I ignore the woo-woo stuff. Let me check with the other car."

Adam stared out the window as Nate connected with his other deputy. When that driver also reported losing them in the blink of an eye, Adam's spidey senses started tingling. He checked his phone and was surprised to see it lit with responses. He scrolled down and the news got worse with each one.

"Uh-oh."

"What?" There was a thread of fear in Isabelle's voice, and he had the passing thought that this time it was justified. He glanced at Nate before answering.

"Quite a few of my buddies recognized the name. I have to call for more details, but it's clear. Silver Wolf is bad news. Really bad news."

Isabelle tried to continue reading, but the winding mountain road was making her dizzy and she was being distracted by the bits of conversation she could overhear. When Adam finally disconnected the call, he angled himself so she could see his face as he spoke.

"I'm not going to underplay this. The news is bad."

He looked at Nate. "Silver Wolf is an alias for Alexander Michael James III."

Nate made a groaning sound that twisted Isabelle's gut. "Who is he?"

"Short version, he's former military. He was dishonorably discharged for his rogue behavior. Last my friend knew, he'd headed up a band of ruthless mercenaries. That's when he picked up the name Silver Wolf."

Isabelle's blood went cold but she forced herself to speak calmly. "Why does he want Laura?"

Adam hesitated before answering. "I don't know yet. At a guess, I'd say it has something to do with her father's disappearance. Hopefully, we'll find out more when we get into the stuff Jess hid." He turned to Nate. "That explains why the men we've captured won't talk. We need to find a safe house pronto."

Nate's phone started to ring. "It's Claire. Can you get it? The road up ahead washed out in the storm and repairs aren't finished. I need to focus on driving."

Before Adam could answer, a gunshot ricocheted off the hood of the patrol car, quickly followed by a barrage of shots that showered down around them.

"Isabelle, get below window level," Nate ordered.

"What about you and Adam?"

There was a moment of silence as the two men locked eyes. A chill ran through Isabelle. She was seeing them transform into warrior mode.

"We've been through this before," Adam

finally admitted, his rough voice confirming her suspicions.

"We recently upgraded the vehicles," Nate interjected. "This one has the latest protection, but I'll be less distracted if I know you are out of the line of fire."

His attempt at reassurance fell flat. Isabelle wanted to protest that they wouldn't even be in this situation were it not for her, but she knew that would carry little weight. These men were born protectors. It was in their blood, and they were highly trained. Trying to argue would only distract them. She could help most by staying out of their way. And praying.

Nate got on the radio to call for backup while Adam scanned the mountainside, trying to locate their adversary. He tossed her his phone. "Text Claire. Tell her we're in a spot of trouble but to stay secure and we'll be there as soon as possible."

Isabelle could barely hold the phone with her trembling hands, but she forced her fingers to type out the message. She couldn't help herself from adding *I'm sorry* at the end. This was all her fault.

Well, no, it was Jess's fault. But actually, the blame was all on the mercenary, on Silver Wolf.

The phone pinged and Isabelle read Claire's reply. "She has both girls and is barricaded in the surgery at the kennel."

Isabelle offered prayers for Claire, the children and the dogs.

Please, Lord, keep Claire and the children safe and don't let any of Claire's rescues be harmed in this fight.

Nate's tense voice broke through her prayer. "What do you see up ahead?"

Adam pointed. "See that glint? I think they're up there."

"Notice how no other cars have come by in the opposite direction? I'm guessing they've barricaded the road up ahead. They're not letting us through alive."

Adam agreed, and Isabelle's heart skipped a beat at his calm revelation. How could they speak of this so matter-of-factly? They were on a strip of highway that cut through the mountains. One side was dense forest. The other dropped off sharply into a deep ravine. There was no way out but forward through this trap.

"They made a tactical error revealing too soon, though," Adam murmured.

"Agreed. That overlook up ahead—360 and reverse?" Nate suggested.

"Can you go in full speed and still pull out in time?"

"No, but I can make it look like I'm going to."

Isabelle swallowed her gasp. She'd driven this road often enough to know exactly which overlook Nate was referring to. The road gradually sloped up before curving and heading back down the mountain. At the curve there was a dramatic overlook. She'd always wanted to stop and take in the view over the valley, but she'd never had the courage to get out of the car with Mia in such a precarious location. And now Nate was going to risk a life-or-death maneuver in that very narrow spot.

Dear Lord, help us. She bowed her head to pray, murmuring the prayers of her childhood because she couldn't come up with words on her own. She was beyond coherent thought because, if she allowed herself to think, she would burst into tears at the idea of her daughter and Laura alone in the world.

Dear Lord, protect my babies. Keep them safe from harm Protect us from all evil.

Over and over, she repeated the prayers as the car continued to climb under a relentless barrage. Bullets pinged off the doors and roof, but

Isabelle sensed that Nate was ignoring them. Bullets were the least of their concerns. The most treacherous stretch was just ahead, and if the mercenaries had their way, they would never make it off the mountain alive.

Chapter Fourteen

"Pray, Isabelle. Like you've never prayed before."

With those words, Nate braked hard and began to swing the car into a tight arc. Adam braced himself as the tires skidded on gravel and rocks shot up at the underside of the vehicle. He ducked and pulled his jacket up to shield his head as a large chunk shattered the passenger window already weakened by gunfire. Glass showered down around him, the shards needling into his skin.

He held his breath as the car scraped the barrier, all but hanging on two wheels as Nate quickly accelerated out of the turn and roared off down the road they'd come.

Gunfire continued to pepper the vehicle. Nate's white-knuckled grip on the wheel was the only sign of the strain he was under. They passed no other cars on the way, which concerned Adam. Was there a barricade at this end too?

Nate was clearly thinking the same thing as he warned, "Isabelle, stay down. I don't think we're through yet. You should get down too," he directed Adam. "I'm wearing a vest."

"That won't save your head," Adam replied. No way was he leaving his friend to deal on his own while he took shelter.

They flew down the mountain, going airborne each time they hit a dip in the road. Adam knew it had to be rough on Isabelle, especially with her residual dizziness, but she uttered no complaint.

As the slope of the mountain eased, they rounded a curve and found the roadblock stretching across both lanes with armed men on either side.

"This is where we find out how well the new safety designs hold up," Nate muttered as he floored the accelerator. At the last moment, Adam lifted the backpack to shield them from any attack through the broken window.

The car barreled through the barricade, bullets flying at them from both sides. Nate didn't slow down until they were out of range. "Everyone okay?" he asked as the bullet-ridden vehicle coasted to a stop.

Isabelle lifted her head warily. "Is it safe to get up?"

"For the time being," Nate answered.

"You're bleeding," she cried out as she hoisted herself onto the seat where she could see Adam.

"It's just from glass shards. Nothing serious. Nate's fine too. New vehicle held up pretty well."

Nate chuckled grimly. "Don't want to think about the repair bill, but it's still running. If everyone's okay, I'm going to start up again. Somebody check on Claire. We're going to have to take the back route to her ranch, and that'll cost us time."

The atmosphere in the car dimmed as they were reminded that though they'd survived this attack, the mercenaries weren't giving up.

Adam leaned back in the seat so he could see Isabelle. "How are you holding up?"

She smiled bravely. "Okay. I said a lot of prayers," she admitted.

"You have a strong trust in God."

"How can you not? Look at the impossible situation he just got us out of."

"I guess my driving gets no credit," Nate joked.

Isabelle wasn't offended. She knew Nate's faith was strong. "God gave you skills."

"That He did," Adam concurred. "This isn't the first time Nate's done the impossible to save me." The minute the words left his mouth, he wished he could recall them. The last thing he wanted to do was to open himself to questions.

As usual, Isabelle seemed to have an intuitive understanding. She changed the topic. "So, Nate, how are you going to get us home in time to rescue the girls and Claire?"

"With your prayers and my driving skills, Isabelle."

Adam glanced at his friend, knowing he was deliberately making light of a terrifying situation. With the road blocked, they were forced at least twenty minutes out of their way. A lot could happen in twenty minutes.

"Did anyone check on Claire?" Nate asked.

Isabelle retrieved Adam's phone from the floor of the car and handed it to him. He tried calling, but the phone rang through to voice mail.

The silence made him uneasy. Claire would know that they'd be worried. She wouldn't go silent without a reason. He could only hope the reason was that Nate's deputies had gotten there to rescue them and she was busy with the girls.

Doubt gnawed at him, though it was pointless to second-guess himself about leaving the girls behind with Claire. Nate had assigned a top deputy, former military like themselves.

Suddenly his blood ran cold. Former military. Suspicions spun through his brain. "Nate, what division was Deputy Stevens in?"

Nate glanced over and Adam could see he was trying to follow the train of thought without giving anything away. Adam continued. "Is Deputy Warren also headed to Claire's?"

Nate gave a slight nod, showing he'd clued in. "Yes. Let me have them check in."

Nate radioed both men. Deputy Stevens responded first.

"Have you made it to Claire's animal shelter yet?"

"Negative that. I must have run over some glass. Tire went flat. Changing it now."

"Deputy Warren?" Nate called into the radio.

"Roger. Not there yet, sir. Approaching. Over."

"I'm calling for backup. Let me know what you find when you get there."

The radio had no sooner gone dead than Nate's phone buzzed. Nate pulled it from its holster and tossed it to Adam.

"It's Deputy Warren."

"Answer and put him on speaker." Nate made sure the radio was off, and Adam set the phone on the center console.

"Sheriff Brant here. You're on speaker, Deputy."

"Radio off, sir?"

"Affirmative."

"Don't know how to say this without seeming a snitch, sir."

"Spit it out, Deputy."

"Deputy Stevens does not have a flat tire. I parked on the back road, intending to approach from the opposite direction. He is standing at the house, talking to a man who is holding the baby. He's got a gun pointed at your friend and a young girl."

Isabelle's muffled cry pierced the deadly silence in the car.

"Talking as in negotiating, Deputy?"

"Talking as in laughing like old drinking buddies. Wait. Now he's walking with the man toward a car." His voice lowered suddenly. "He's forcing the woman and the two children into the back seat."

"Did Deputy Stevens get in the car with them?"

There was an audible hesitation before Warren spoke. "No, sir. He picked up something from the ground and sliced his tire."

"Which way did the car go, Deputy?"

"Headed down the river road. Toward the cliffs."

"I'll call highway patrol. Thank you, Deputy. Your courage is appreciated. What was the car, color and make?"

The deputy had already disconnected, so Nate asked Adam to redial. It went straight to voice mail. Nate tried the radio instead. At first there was nothing but static. As seconds ticked by, a weak voice came through.

"Canyon Road. Silver SUV. They have subjects."

A gunshot exploded and the radio went silent.

No one in the car dared to breathe for a long moment.

"Thoughts?" Adam finally asked.

Nate replied. "Not good. That wasn't Deputy Warren."

He quickly put out an alert for backup from the next county and to Colorado State Patrol.

The silence hung heavily.

"One of my deputies is bad, and I can't be sure which one."

"Stevens served under Alexander James," Adam reminded him.

Nate nodded, and Adam waited. He had his own ideas, but Nate knew his men better.

"Serving with him makes him look guilty if we jump to conclusions." He paused, clearly unwilling to jump to those conclusions, and again Adam waited for him to process his thoughts.

"Serving under him might also mean he knows why not to join him if he was as rogue as you reported."

Isabelle interrupted them. "How much farther, Nate?"

Adam could hear the tension threading through her words. She must be barely holding panic at bay, and he had to give her credit. Over and over, she had showed mental fortitude worthy of a warrior.

"Too far," Nate muttered.

"But if they are really on Canyon Road, and we're on Canyon Road headed toward them?"

"Then maybe your prayers are answered, Isabelle. Maybe. But I don't have time to get backup here, so we'll have to figure it out on our own. Best estimate, we have ten minutes, fifteen tops, before they reach us. That's if they don't turn off somewhere along the way."

As Nate was talking, Adam was quickly mapping the road and distance in his head.

"We need to set up a roadblock. If you slow down, that will give us more time and we'll be able to see what we can use. The storm that washed out the road has to have knocked some trees down. If we can pull one into the road and make it look natural, it will give us an advantage."

Adam could feel Nate's lack of enthusiasm. "You have a better idea?"

"No. It's a good plan. I just don't like having to rely on the chance we will find something."

"It's not that much of a long shot. I hike these woods. There are a lot of downed trees. We should be able to see something. Isabelle, I'll look to the front and right if you could search the left."

Isabelle was happy to have something to focus on other than her terror about Mia, Laura and Claire being in the hands of a maniacal mercenary's man. She locked her desperate thoughts away and focused her attention on the forest streaming past the window.

After five tense minutes of visually scouring the side of the road, Adam spoke up. "I see one up ahead, but I'm not sure it's big enough. If we don't see something else soon, though, we'll have to come back and make it work."

Isabelle glanced at the tree he was talking about, but she wasn't impressed. The kidnapper would easily be able to drive around it if they placed it to look natural, but if they added to it, the man was sure to realize it was a trap. She didn't want to consider what he would do then.

The minutes ticked by with pressure mounting as they continued to evaluate the trees.

"I think we need to admit defeat and make do with the one I saw," Adam conceded. "We need time to set it up, and we're running low."

Nate agreed. "We need time to hide the car too."

"I was thinking about that. Why don't you and I stay behind to create an ambush. Isabelle can drive the car out of sight."

This wasn't the time to pick a fight, but Isabelle knew she could not leave when her daughter's life was at stake. "Wait," she called as Nate started to make a U-turn. "I see something up ahead that looks like roots in the air."

Adam turned to look in the direction she indicated. "Bingo! That's perfect." He had the door open and was out of the car before Nate even pulled to a full stop. He ran over to assess the tree and quickly signaled approval.

Working together, they grasped the roots and began to pull the tree across the road, arranging it to look as natural as possible. The tree was massive, and it was a struggle that left them covered with mud and leaves, but the tradeoff was that it provided enough cover for Nate and Adam to hide in the branches to wait for the kidnapper.

Adam rubbed his hands on his pants and faced her. "I know you don't want to do this, Isabelle, but we need you to take the car and drive back along the road. Block traffic so no one else can come by."

Isabelle bit her tongue and walked back to the car.

Adam followed her to the vehicle. "I left the gun in the glove compartment. Would you know how to use it?"

She shrugged. "Not really. If I see anyone coming, I'll hide in the forest." She climbed in and put the key in the ignition before turning to him. "I don't like this, but I trust you to protect Mia and Laura and Claire. Just don't do anything that will get you hurt."

The last words were the hardest thing to say,

but she had to do this for him. She had to know that she was not putting pressure on him.

He stepped up to the patrol car's window and leaned in. "We will rescue them because this is what we are trained to do. Trust me."

Eyes brimming, Isabelle could only nod. "I do," she whispered. "I absolutely do."

Adam bent forward and kissed her cheek before stepping back. "Go," he uttered. "I'll call when it's safe."

Isabelle reversed and turned the vehicle around. For a moment, she almost considered obeying. The tears pouring down her cheeks were not only testament to her faith in Adam, but also because her heart was petrified of losing him. How could he expect her to just wait in safety with so many lives in danger?

Isabelle knew the answer to that. He expected her to stay safe so he didn't have to worry about her. Well, he wouldn't have to worry about what he didn't know.

But she knew he also had made the request because he and Nate needed to be certain of their surroundings. If she suddenly appeared back at the roadblock, she could interfere with their strategy.

Isabelle tried to comply. She drove back the

way they'd come until she passed a curve that took her out of view. The road was straight far enough ahead that she could park sideways in the middle of it to create a roadblock without fear of someone accidentally hitting the car.

She tried to sit and wait.

She prayed for their safety.

She prayed for the success of their plan.

She prayed for them to capture the kidnappers and free Mia, Laura and Claire.

And then she couldn't stand it a moment longer.

She opened the driver's door, grabbed the keys from the ignition, and jumped out onto the road.

She wouldn't risk ruining their plan, but there was no reason she couldn't hike back through the woods as long as she stayed hidden deep enough in the forest. And if she walked parallel to the road, she wouldn't risk getting lost.

Her mind made up, Isabelle set off through the forest.

The going was harder than she'd expected. Snow began falling again as she trudged through the heavily wooded area. She was grateful for the difficulty of walking because it helped keep her mind from giving in to the absolute terror that threatened whenever she thought of her precious daughter in the clutches of a kidnapper. Pain wrenched through her body at the thought, but she used it as inspiration to keep moving despite frozen feet and snow blowing in her face. She couldn't hear anything, and her imagination ran wild.

Maybe she should have stayed back at the car.

Chapter Fifteen

Isabelle eased her way through the forest until she could see the roadblock. Within minutes, the sound of an engine alerted her to a silver SUV approaching the ambush site. She buried her face in her hands, peering between her fingers and the branches, praying with all her might that Claire and the girls were safe. She saw no sign of Adam or Nate, but presumed they were waiting for the right moment to strike.

Heart in her throat, Isabelle watched the driver pull to a stop at the downed tree. He got out and walked over to it, his body language revealing his frustration even though she couldn't make out the words he was yelling. She watched with bated breath as he searched the area. It made sense that a trained mercenary would be wary of a trap. He walked the length of the tree and spent time studying the roots, which seemed to convince him all was okay. He turned and called to the other man in the SUV.

The second man joined him and they got to work trying to clear the road. Isabelle watched intently, waiting for Adam or Nate to appear, but suddenly, out of the corner of her eye, she observed Claire stealthily climb from the vehicle with Laura in her arms. Ropes dangled from her wrists as she helped Mia out, clearly ready to make a run for it through the woods. Isabelle knew only too well the desperate fear that would make Claire choose such a risky move. She had no way to know that her brother and his friend were there to save her.

Isabelle couldn't breathe. She clenched her hands against her thighs as she silently cheered them on. One step around the back of the SUV, two. One step more and they would be hidden.

Laura's wail pierced the silence.

The men dropped the tree and whirled around. As soon as they spotted Claire, they pulled weapons and shouted. Claire pushed Mia away. Isabelle watched her daughter cower behind the vehicle, and it was all she could do not to run to her, but wisdom dictated she stay hidden until Adam and Nate made their move.

Claire turned and ran down the road, obviously trying to pull the men's attention away from Mia. One man followed her. Nate darted out from hiding and jumped him, wrestling the mercenary to the ground as they struggled for control of the weapon.

Before Adam could grab the other man, he snatched Mia and ran into the woods—directly toward where she was hiding. Adam started to give chase, but a cry from Nate distracted him. The mercenary had broken loose and scrambled to his feet. He backed into the woods on the far side of the road, keeping his gun leveled at them until he reached the trees. He turned and dashed deeper into the forest.

"Go after Mia!" Nate shouted. "I'll track him."

As the mercenary dragged Mia through the trees, Isabelle could see the terror etched on her daughter's face. She had to do something to stop him from getting away with her little girl. Quickly, she scanned the ground for a branch or anything she could use as a weapon, yet found nothing she could swing without risking injury to Mia.

But she had another weapon. She didn't know how to use it, but the kidnapper wouldn't know that, and she only had to hold him off until Adam caught up. Silently, she pulled the handgun from her pocket. She'd seen enough police dramas to know that she had to release the safety if she had a prayer of fooling him, so she located that part and rested her finger lightly on it, all while keeping an eye on the man advancing toward her. Mia was dragging her feet, which slowed him down and gave Isabelle time to step into position.

When they were just yards away, she breathed a prayer for confidence and stepped out in front of the man, assuming a spread-leg pose as she boldly raised the gun and pointed it at his head. "Stop right there."

The man laughed and whipped out his own gun. "Think again, lady. If you want to ever see your daughter alive, throw down the gun and let me go."

For a panicked moment, Isabelle wanted to kick herself. What had she been thinking to imagine she could take on a mercenary?

She hadn't been. She'd been a terrified mother watching a heavily armed man kidnapping her daughter. She tried to blank her mind, to think through how to get out of this standoff and keep Mia safe.

Lord help me.

She had to keep him talking.

"If I toss down my gun, will you give me back my daughter?"

His harsh laugh in reply chilled her blood, reminding her this was a man without pity or scruples. He wouldn't hesitate to take out both of them.

She tightened her grip on the gun. Did she have the guts to try to shoot?

Out of the corner of her eye, she saw Adam stealthily approaching. She held her stance, keeping her eyes on the man while surreptitiously looking past him for a signal from Adam.

Adam made a motion with his hands that she read as *keep him talking*.

Isabelle avoided looking at her daughter, knowing that if she did she would come completely apart. "Why are you doing this? What do you want from us?"

"Look, lady, I'm not here for Sunday tea and chat. Put the gun down or I'll shoot you."

"Why?"

He looked exasperated. "So, you'll give us the baby."

Isabelle feigned confusion. "What are you talking about? I don't have the baby."

He shrugged. "My friend probably has her by now. You'd be wise to stop fighting."

Chills shivered through her at his evil tone. Adam had crept closer. Isabelle watched him holster his gun then reach down and come up with a rock. Now more than ever, she needed to distract the mercenary.

"And if your friend does have her?"

The man gave a harsh laugh that paralyzed Isabelle.

"Then you'd better hope that my boss is in a good mood."

Adam was so close now, Isabelle was terrified the man would hear him.

She let out a cry to cover him. "No! I can't depend on your boss. I don't even know him. Why would he want the baby?"

The man shot her a disgusted look. "To force her father to give us what we want. Now, put the gun down or—"

The rock coming down on his head halted whatever he had been about to say.

Isabelle dropped the handgun and charged forward, opening her arms to Mia and wrapping them tightly around her baby girl, just holding her close and absorbing her frightened sobs.

Adam glared at Isabelle. He was mad because she hadn't stayed at the car, and his feelings were justified, but she didn't want Mia to witness more anger. She angled her head to Mia and then shook it, hoping Adam would understand.

He nodded. "We'll talk later."

Adam cuffed and hogtied the mercenary. He didn't like leaving Isabelle alone with the man, but he was only semiconscious and posed no threat. "Can you stand guard over him while I find Nate, Claire and Laura? I'll come back for you."

Isabelle picked up on the thread in his voice that indicated he was not confident all was well back at the road. "Go ahead. I've got my brave girl to help me guard the prisoner."

"You have the keys to the patrol car? We need to retrieve it."

She handed them over and he loped off through the woods.

Once Adam was gone, Isabelle found a boulder to sit on. She brushed off the snow and gathered Mia onto her lap. "Oh, my baby girl." She kissed the top of her head. "That must have been so scary. You were so brave."

Mia looked up, her eyes wide. "You had a gun."

Isabelle spoke softly to reassure her. "Can I tell you a secret?"

Mia nodded.

"I have no idea how to shoot a gun. Mr. Adam gave it to me to scare off bad men so they would think I did." She hugged her daughter close. "But I promise, I would have figured out how to do it so I could keep you safe. Because that's my job—to protect you."

Mia snuggled into her arms, and Isabelle felt a huge sigh shudder through her body. She made a silent vow that when this was over, she was going to find the best child therapist money could buy to help her daughter cope with everything she had been through.

But that was later. Right now, she had to pray that Adam could rescue Laura, Claire and Nate.

Adam ran back through the woods in search of Nate, his thoughts racing as hard as his feet. Having to choose between chasing after Mia or helping Nate had torn him apart, but his training had made the choice clear. Nate stood more of a chance on his own than Mia did.

And then there was Isabelle. Adam had wanted to rage at her over her foolish actions, but in truth, he couldn't fault her. He should have known she was incapable of staying behind when all those she loved were in danger.

Did he fit into that category?

The errant thought caught him by surprise, and he brushed it quickly aside. Isabelle was grateful to him, but love didn't figure into their relationship. He was there to protect her and the children, nothing more, even if they did remind him of all that was missing from his life.

He broke through the edge of the forest onto the road. Nate was nowhere in sight and neither was Claire or Laura. Frustrated, he headed across the road to the silver SUV. A soft whimper caught his attention and he swiveled toward the forest on the far side of the road. A flash of blonde hair caught his eye.

"Claire," he called. "It's me."

His sister waved from behind a tree, but she didn't move to come forward. Fearing she was hurt, Adam dashed across the road. He found Claire huddled behind a tall pine, cradling Laura, who appeared uninjured.

"Where's Nate?"

Claire let out a shuddering breath. "He took off through the woods after the man. He told me to stay hidden here and not to come out for anything."

And his obedient sister had listened to Nate, unlike Isabelle, who had ignored his directions. But then, Claire wasn't a mother bent on protecting her child.

A crashing sound back in the woods alerted Adam and he stood guard, his back to Claire, blocking her from sight.

"Claire, it's just me." Nate ducked through some underbrush and emerged from the forest. He saw Adam and shook his head. "He got away. Had too much of a head start, and I didn't want to risk leaving Claire and Laura alone for too long with the other man at large."

"The other man is restrained."

At Nate's surprised look, Adam gave a chuckle. "Long story, but Isabelle is standing guard. Why don't you and Claire retrieve your car? I'll get Isabelle, Mia and our prisoner, and meet you back here. We'll have to deal with their vehicle, though."

Nate agreed. "I don't know who of my deputies I can trust at this point, so I'll call in the Bureau of Investigation to take custody of the SUV and our prisoners."

Adam tossed him the keys to the sheriff's car.

Nate helped Claire to her feet and steadied her. As they turned to walk up the road, he uttered a warning, "I don't have to tell you these guys mean deadly business. When we get back to Claire's, we need to find a safe house that no one knows about."

Nate's words echoed in Adam's mind as he

made his way through the woods to Isabelle and Mia. Despite his concern to reach them, the forest began to work its magic. His heart rate slowed, his breathing became easier, and he had a sudden yearning to introduce Isabelle and Mia to the peace he felt. It was just the tonic they would need after these endless days of terror.

Suddenly he knew exactly where to take them, who to ask for help. His forest therapy guide was one person he knew he could trust. Matt was a clear example of how money didn't matter in the line of fire, but it sure made the recovery process more accessible. He had built several ski chalets in the mountains and routinely loaned them to fellow vets in need. Adam could easily borrow one, no questions asked.

And maybe, since they would be deep in the forest, he could teach Mia and Isabelle how to let nature heal them.

Adam breathed a sigh of relief as he arrived at the clearing and found Isabelle sitting guard, Mia asleep on her lap. His heart broke for all the trauma this child had experienced. She needed the forest, and he would give it to her.

Chapter Sixteen

Isabelle joined Adam beside an unmarked car and watched as a speck in the sky came close enough for him to point out his friend's private helicopter. They'd chosen the hospital helipad as the natural place to unobtrusively rendezvous.

A bark to their left drew attention away from the sky, and Adam turned just in time to see a bundle of gold fur streak across the parking lot and skid to a stop at his feet. He sank to his knees and burrowed his head in Chance's fur. "How'd you get here, buddy?"

Claire came running across the lot, out of breath. "We made it. I was afraid you'd be gone already."

Adam grinned at his sister and then turned to Mia, who'd come up beside him. "Not without Chance, right, Mia?"

"Right, Mr. Adam."

Adam hoisted her in his arms as the chopper descended. "Ready to go for a ride in the sky?"

Isabelle gazed at him in amazement. How could this man continually find the reserves to be so gentle with Mia when his wounds were repeatedly being triggered?

Adam hurried them across the tarmac as soon as the helicopter touched down. They were in their seats and off again within minutes. Claire stood on the ground, waving goodbye. Isabelle hated leaving her behind in danger, but she'd refused to leave her dogs, and Nate had promised to keep her safe.

As the helicopter lifted into the sky, Isabelle sat back and breathed what felt like her first clear breath in a week. She wanted to close her eyes and sleep, but Mia had other ideas. Isabelle lifted her so they could sit, heads together, peering out the window at the mountains and marvel at the snowcapped peaks.

"Want to go sledding down those mountains?"

Mia giggled, but then her shoulders drooped.

"What is it, sweetie?"

"Aunt Jess promised to teach me to ski this winter."

Before Isabelle could summon a reply, Mia brightened. "Maybe Mr. Adam will."

The words brought a pang to Isabelle's heart. She couldn't bear to tell Mia that Adam would be out of their lives as soon as they were safe.

The sun was setting over the Rockies an hour later as Isabelle handed Mia down to Adam. She sucked in a deep breath of cold mountain air and sighed in pleasure. "This is extraordinary, Adam."

"Not my doing. Thank my pal, Matt."

Isabelle turned to the tall man she'd barely had a chance to meet as they'd loaded into the helicopter at the hospital. "I don't even know how to possibly thank you enough, sir."

"Matt. And no thanks necessary. Adam told me what you're doing for your friend. That's mighty brave."

Adam spoke up. "I've got a little girl here who seems in need of food. What do you think? Shall we go inside?"

Matt showed them into the house, a gorgeous A-frame nestled into the side of a mountain in the heart of the Rockies.

After a quick tour that included a fully stocked freezer and pantry, Matt took his leave. "I need to head out before anyone suspects where I am. I'll fly on to California to draw attention away from here, in case anyone tried to track us. Make this your home. And stay safe."

Isabelle smiled gratefully. "You've given us that chance."

Adam walked Matt out. "Thank you."

Matt brushed the thanks aside. "You all right to do this? We didn't talk about that part."

Adam responded softly. "I am because I have to be…for them. But this…" He gestured to the forest crowding the back of the house. "This gives me what I need to rejuvenate."

Matt nodded. "I thought it might. Take care now. Call if you need anything."

Adam watched his friend disappear into the night sky, and then took a moment to just stand and breathe in the peacefulness of their sur-roundings.

He was under no illusion that they were out of danger but, for tonight at least, he could relax his guard and find his balance. With one last glance as the sun sank in the west and the indigo sky began to fill with stars, he decided he'd bring Mia out here before bed.

First, he had to feed her. He headed into the living room. Isabelle has been exploring the

house while he saw Matt off, and she greeted
him with a genuine smile relaxing her face.

"This place is amazing."

Adam returned the smile. "I was about to see
what I can rustle up for dinner. What do you
think, Mia? Any chance Matt left us chicken
nuggets?"

Once they'd eaten their fill of chicken nuggets and mac and cheese, Adam carried the
plates to the dishwasher. When Isabelle followed, he asked quietly, "Would it be okay if I
took Mia out to see the stars?"

The smile that lit her face at his suggestion
kindled a fire in his heart.

"Sounds lovely. I'll settle Laura in while you
do that."

He bundled Mia into her jacket and scarf, and
took her hand. "I want to show you something
special. Let's go see the stars."

"We have stars at home. Sometimes Mama
and I look at them together."

"I often watch them at home too."

"Maybe sometimes we're looking at them at
the same time," she chirped.

Adam's heart swelled with joy. "Well, tonight
we will be for sure."

He led her outside onto the rooftop balcony

and stopped short. He'd been expecting to surprise Mia, but he found himself stunned by the magnificence.

Mia's voice was hushed with awe as she spoke. "Mr. Adam, look at them!"

Adam crouched beside her. "Do you see those stars up there, the three together like a belt?"

"That's Orion the Hunter," Mia told him. "Mama showed me him in a book and then we found him in the sky. The red star has a funny name, like a bug."

"Betelgeuse," Adam confirmed.

"If you lift me up, I think I could touch them."

Adam laughed and raised her as high as he could.

Her face fell. "I can't reach them."

Hearing her disappointment, he lowered her into his arms. "That's the beauty of nature, Mia," he said softly. "We just feel it inside even if we can't touch it." He paused. "Can you feel it?"

Mia was quiet for a long moment, and he smiled as he watched her scrunch up her face. "You don't have to try so hard. Just breathe softly and let your heart open wide."

Mia lifted her face to the stars, and he could feel her body relax as she slowly breathed in and out. He could tell the moment she let go and just let the joy fill her body.

"I can feel it, Mr. Adam," she whispered. "I can feel it."

Moisture sprang to Adam's eyes as he soaked in the peace of holding this precious little girl under the glorious star-studded heaven. In this moment, in this place, it was easy to believe in a future that held goodness.

They stood for a few minutes in rapt silence until he felt Mia begin to shiver. "I think it's time to go in, Stargirl. Take one good long look to bring into your dreams."

When Mia had done so, he turned to the door, but he stopped when he saw Isabelle standing there, watching them, her own eyes shimmering.

He handed Mia over to her. "Good night, Stargirl."

The look Isabelle shot him was part gratitude and part simmering with something he couldn't even allow himself to recognize but didn't want to lose. "Join me in the library once they're settled?"

She nodded and slipped away.

Adam took another minute to look up to the heavens and whispered a prayer. *Lord, help me keep them safe.*

★ ★ ★

Isabelle stopped in the doorway to the living room. The fear that held her back had nothing to do with the dangerous mercenaries who pursued them and everything to do with the dangerous feelings Adam was igniting in her. She couldn't do this again, couldn't let someone in who had the power to break her.

But Adam had asked her to join him, and she owed him far too much to reject such a simple request.

He had his back to her, poking at the fire, but he turned as she entered, as if her presence called to him as strongly as he called to her heart.

"Come in. I thought you deserved some hot cocoa and a fire after all you dealt with today."

There he went, thinking of her again, when his day had been every bit as stressful. When had anyone ever put her first like this? She shook away the alluring thought. "Thank you. That sounds lovely."

They settled on chairs opposite each other before the fire and, for a few minutes, made small talk about the house, the beautiful location—anything but the danger that dogged them. After a time, Isabelle broached a topic that intrigued her.

"You seem so at home in the wilderness. Did you grow up here?"

He shook his head. "Nope, I was raised a city boy."

"Wow, I would never have guessed."

Adam dipped his head and hesitated so long that Isabelle feared she'd offended him.

"The wilderness, it saved me." He took a sip of his cocoa, then stood and walked to the plate-glass window that dominated the eastern wall.

"When I was medically discharged from the army, I was a mess—physically and mentally. The physical wounds healed, for the most part. I'll have symptoms from the brain injury for the rest of my life. You've seen some of them, like the headaches." He leaned forward in what looked like physical pain as he scrubbed his hands over his face.

When he raised his eyes to look at her, the agony in them ripped through her heart. She wanted to tell him to stop talking, to spare himself the pain of reliving it, but something told her he needed to share his story.

"The emotional wounds weren't as noticeable as the ones that left visible scars, but their pain was worse. When Nate invited me to visit him here…well, there's no easy way to say it. I was broken. I had nothing to lose."

He turned and stared into the night beyond the window. "I found myself again out there. In the forest, the mountains. The quiet silenced all the noise in my head. I could just…be."

He shrugged away from the window and came back to sit across from her again. "Slowly, I began to heal. Not completely. I'll never be the man I was. But on good days, I like to think I'm someone better."

Isabelle leaned forward and reached out to touch his hand. "Obviously, I didn't know you before, but the man you are now…he's pretty special."

Adam closed his eyes and breathed in deeply. "Thank you."

She sighed. "I only wish…" The words drifted away. She didn't want to mar the evening with thoughts of Daniel.

"You wish what?"

She shrugged it off. "It's nothing."

"Isabelle," he said gently, "I bared my soul to you. What I told you, it's not something I talk about. But I wanted you to know that part of me. And I knew it was safe to tell you."

He took her hands in his. "I want you to have that safety, too, to know you can tell me anything."

She closed her eyes, and her hands fell away from his. Was that what they were doing? Exchanging pieces of their souls into each other's safekeeping? Somehow helping each other heal amid all the danger?

She raised her head and locked her gaze onto his. And the words began to pour out.

"The other morning, when you were making the pancakes, it…" She stumbled, unable to find the words.

"It triggered a memory," Adam supplied.

She nodded and looked away. "I've never told anyone, not even Jess. It felt… I guess it felt too private. But I want to tell you, so you'll…understand."

She lifted her mug, cradling it in her hands and stared blindly at the cocoa as she began. "I told you that Daniel also struggled with PTSD. But he was different than you. He wouldn't acknowledge that he needed help. His treatment came from a bottle." She paused, needing to stop the bitterness seeping into her voice.

"The morning of his last deployment, Daniel took Mia out for breakfast. It was supposed to have been father-daughter time, something they'd never had much of." She paused to take a sip of her cocoa because her mouth had gone suddenly dry at the memory.

"Based on eye-witness reports, Mia had been enjoying her favorite chocolate-chip pancakes while Adam's breakfast had been mostly liquid, poured from a flask into his coffee." Isabelle closed her eyes, remembering what had saved Mia's life. "Mia needed to use the restroom. She'd barely been potty-trained at the time. A kind waitress took her in. When they came back out, Daniel was gone."

Tremors shook her body and Adam stood and draped a blanket across her shoulders. He sat on the coffee table in front of her, took the mug from her hands and clasped them in his, giving her the strength to continue.

"The waitress called me to come get Mia." She gripped his hands hard. "I drove right by Daniel's wreck without even realizing it was his car. Apparently, he walked away and hitched a ride to the base. I was so furious with him after talking to the waitress that I barely spoke to him when he called to say goodbye. He

tried to apologize, promised he would do better. I so badly wanted to believe him. It was
only later, after he'd already left, that the garage called about the car." She shuddered. "The
back, where Mia's car seat was attached, was so
badly crushed, she never could have survived."

Tears poured down Isabelle's face, but she
had to finish. "He deployed that afternoon and
never returned."

She was trembling so badly by the time she
finished that Adam pulled her to her feet and
into his arms. He wrapped them around her
and held her close to his heart, gently stroking
her hair and whispering soothing words. They
stood like that for a long time, the fire crackling, the aroma of the burning wood edging
past Adam's fresh scent and filling her senses.
Isabelle wanted nothing more in that moment
than to stay in his arms forever, to be able to
open her heart to loving him, but the scars ran
too deep.

She pulled back and reached a trembling hand
up to cup his cheek. "Thank you. You are the
best man I have ever known."

He raised his hand to cradle her head and,
as he leaned forward, she knew he meant to

kiss her. She allowed herself a moment to gaze deeply into his eyes, but then she pulled away.

"Good night, Adam. I hope your dreams are filled with stars."

Chapter Seventeen

Adam couldn't sleep. The pain of Isabelle's story pierced his heart while thoughts of her in his arms tormented him. Isabelle, Mia, Laura, they represented all the love and the family he'd always longed for but couldn't have. Even though his arms ached with the memory of holding Isabelle, she'd been right to pull away before he'd made the foolish mistake of kissing her. He was still a broken man. He couldn't give her the healing she needed.

But he could protect her. He rose and went to the window. The sky was growing lighter, the stars that had promised such wonder dimmed by sunlight that teased on the eastern horizon, reminding him a new day and responsibilities lay ahead. Resolve tightened in his gut. He would do whatever it took to give Isabelle and the girls safety and a future free from fear. And then he would say his final goodbye.

The aroma of coffee alerted him to Isabelle's presence before he noticed her standing by the window. He indulged for a moment, just drinking in the beauty of the woman who'd captivated his heart.

She turned when she heard his footsteps and offered a tentative smile. "You couldn't sleep either?"

He shook his head, afraid what he would say if he dared to speak.

"Come, look. The sunrise is spectacular. It makes up for the loss of sleep."

He couldn't help himself. He walked slowly until he was standing beside her. Sunlight danced over the tops of the snow-laden pines in a spectacular show of glory.

"See the way the sun's rays shine down?" Isabelle murmured. "It's like God is extending His hand to the world saying, 'Look what I've given you.'" She tilted her head to look up at him. "That's how I survived, you know. I learned to trust in God."

Adam glanced back at her, at the way the rays lit her face and gilded her hair, and his heart echoed the words. *Look what God has given into your care.*

He turned away abruptly. "We need to start

go—" The words died on his lips as he noted the papers strewn across the table.

"Going through Jess's stuff. Yes, I started." She shrugged. "It seemed better than staring at the ceiling."

Adam picked up the coffeepot and filled his mug. "Should I top off yours?"

"No, thanks. I made it for you. I'm still sticking with tea. Come, let me show you what I found. I have no idea what any of it means, but maybe you will."

Isabelle had spread out the contents of the knapsack, the rolls from the cylinder sitting beside it still tightly clipped. Adam removed the clip and started to unroll the papers. "These are blueprints."

"I guess that makes sense if Nate said Jess's husband was a military engineer. What are they for?"

"I don't know yet, but I'll hazard a guess it's what the guy in the woods was talking about when he said they wanted her to force Laura's father to give them what they want."

Isabelle resumed reading Jess's journal while Adam pored over the blueprints. He had no relevant training, but between the notes in the margin and the images that took shape before his eyes, he understood exactly why the mercenaries wanted Laura.

His gut clenched as he recalled his brief conversation with Matt on the helicopter ride. Matt had maintained close ties with the military, and as he'd related what he'd known, Adam's concerns for Jess, Isabelle, and the girls had grown exponentially.

According to Matt, Alexander William James III had been a highly decorated soldier who'd become too well known for his reckless ways and ruthless actions. Reliable in getting the job done but bad for army PR, he'd put diplomatic relations at risk. He'd been censured and, when that hadn't stopped him, he'd been court-martialed. He'd vanished before the trial, and no one had heard anything until rumors arose of a man they called Silver Wolf who commanded a band of mercenaries so ruthless even the cartels were afraid of them. At first, Silver Wolf had accepted only missions in support of the United States. He'd accepted assignments the military considered too risky and beyond the pale. Nothing had been officially sanctioned, but no one stopped him. Until things went south.

Matt had said it wasn't exactly clear what was

truth and what had become myth, but Silver Wolf was believed to be James. He had severed ties with the US and now worked for the highest bidder. No one knew the exact size of his band of mercenaries, but they had a reputation as the wildest, most vicious outlaws on the planet.

Now they were after Laura. And only Adam and Isabelle stood in their way.

"Adam, what's wrong?"

Adam jerked his head up. "What?"

"I can read your body language. What did you find?"

"The reason James is so determined to get Laura." He swallowed hard. "These blueprints her father created are for brilliant designs that will enhance the mobility and reach of troops while elevating their security." He swallowed hard. "But in the wrong hands..."

He couldn't even allow himself to voice the thought, but he knew one thing for sure. James, Silver Wolf—regardless the name he was using— he needed to be stopped. Whatever it took.

The rest of the morning passed quickly as they studied the clues Jess had left. The girls, exhausted from days of adventure, slept soundly, and when they woke, Isabelle took a break to play with them. When he finished with the papers, Adam set himself to tinkering.

"What are you making?"

"I got these from Claire before we left. She uses them to track dogs that get away. I figured I'd make an anklet for you and each girl, so that in the event something happens, I'll be able to find you."

By noon, Adam had finished the trackers and made a playful ceremony of attaching one to each of the girls and Isabelle. "Special bracelets for the special ladies in my life. Now, who wants to have a snowball fight?"

Isabelle laughed. "Had enough of espionage for one morning?"

His expression sobered. "Sometimes you need to be reminded of what it's all for. Come on, Mia. You look like a champion snowball maker."

Mia's giggle warmed Isabelle's heart. Adam's attention was so good for her.

"Why don't you two play while Laura and I round up some lunch?"

"Sounds good. Come on, Mia. Let's go build us an appetite."

The music of Mia's squeals of joy peppered with Chance's happy barks provided background as Isabelle cooked. With Laura strapped to her back, she chatted to the baby and kept anxious thoughts at bay.

Until the first streaks of flame soared past the kitchen window, quickly followed by at least ten more.

"Adam! Mia?" Isabelle dashed for the door into the yard. She flung it open and raced outside.

An arm swung out and wrapped itself around her neck. The roar of a helicopter swooping overhead, shooting flares around them, drowned her screams for help.

Isabelle wrestled with the man as he tried to unlatch Laura's carrier, but she was no match for his strength. He flung her aside and took off into the woods with Laura.

Isabelle stumbled to her feet and tried to give chase, but he was too far ahead. Her roar of pain echoed through the mountains.

Adam came running around the house. "What happened?"

"He took Laura." She pointed at the woods.

Adam picked up the baby blanket that had fallen to the ground. "Chance."

The dog was at his side in a moment. Adam held the blanket for him to sniff. "Seek Laura." The dog took off through the woods. "He's not really trained in scent detection, but Goldens are naturally good at air scents. Take Mia back inside. I'm going after Chance."

Isabelle took Mia and started in, but a whiff of smoke caught her attention. She ran to the corner of the house and screamed when she saw flames racing across the lawn. Intentional or not, the flares had set the mountain on fire!

Isabelle rushed inside to call for help. From the window, she could see the helicopter hovering, no doubt waiting for the man with Laura, but the winds from the rotors fanned the flames and the fire was rapidly growing out of control. She fell to her knees and raised her voice in prayer.

"Dear Lord, protect Adam and Chance and help them find Laura in time for us to get off this mountain."

Chapter Eighteen

Isabelle glanced at her phone. It had been less than five minutes since Chance had torn into the woods after Laura, but already the flames had spread, licking along the underbrush and leaping from tree to tree on the perimeter of the property. The road was wrapped in smoke and visibility was decreasing by the minute.

Terror wound through her heart, but she tried to put up a brave front. "Mia, help me gather these things so we're ready when Adam comes back." Her lips whispering prayers, Isabelle repacked all of Jess's papers and their bags and brought them down to the garage where Matt had showed them the truck he kept for emergencies. She buckled Mia into the back, then grabbed some cloths from a stack and soaked them with water. "Keep this for your face."

With nothing left to do, she turned on the ignition and hit the remote for the garage door. Slowly the door rose, revealing an inferno. Panic took hold and, for a moment, she feared her eyes were deceiving her, but the wind shifted and she saw Chance emerge from the flaming woods with the baby carrier in his mouth, Adam racing behind him. Isabelle sank against the hood of the truck. *Praise the Lord.*

"Adam," she shrieked. "Over here."

Adam paused then veered off in her direction. When they reached the truck, he took the baby and handed her over to Isabelle, all while lavishing praise on Chance. He grabbed a towel and soaked it with water to rub over his buddy. Chance bounded into the back seat, next to Mia. Adam closed them in while Isabelle climbed into the front, cradling Laura. He ran around the front of the truck, hopped in, and set off through the fire.

Isabelle had been frightened when the men had first chased her through the woods to Adam's house. She'd been frightened each time they'd been pursued on dangerous roadways, and she'd been terrified when she'd had to fight off a mercenary holding her daughter hostage, but none of those even approached the magnitude of terror that paralyzed her now.

Flames leapt through the cloud of dark smoke

that obscured the road. Adam had the truck lights on, but they couldn't penetrate the density. Trees crackled and popped beside them, making the entire mountain feel apocalyptic. Sparks showered down upon them as flames danced across the roadway. She glanced at Adam. His expression was grim, but his hands were steady on the wheel. Had he driven through similar conditions while deployed? And then the follow-up thought—was this triggering him? Would he be able to maintain his focus?

She breathed in and said a prayer.

From the back seat, she could hear Mia. "Mr. Adam, how can the fire burn snow?"

Isabelle chuckled despite herself. "Good question. I have no idea."

"Mr. Adam, you know, right?"

Adam's grimace gave way to a smile. "As it happens, I do. Remember the fire we saw come from the helicopter? Those were flares that firefighters sometimes use to stop fires. They're strong enough to make the snow evaporate."

"But the bad men used them to start a fire instead?"

"They did."

"I think we need to pray for them."

Isabelle hadn't thought anything could make

her feel better, but her small daughter's faith did. "Yes, Mia. Let's pray for them."

The acrid smoke was filtering through every miniscule opening in the truck as Adam eased along the burning road. Laura started to cry and Mia started to cough. Isabelle's throat was burning.

"Just a little longer," Adam promised mere seconds before a burning tree crashed down on the road before them.

Isabelle choked back a shout as Adam pressed the accelerator and drove the truck over it. In her mind, she was picturing flames licking along the bottom of the borrowed vehicle. *Please, God, save us.*

Ahead, the sky began to lighten. Sirens began to drown out the roar of the flames as they finally outraced the inferno that had blazed through the forest, consuming everything in its path.

Isabelle allowed herself to relax and drew in a breath. Immediately she started coughing and realized her mistake.

"Open the window," Adam directed. "The air down here is clear enough."

Firetrucks raced by them heading up the

mountain, but Adam didn't stop until he reached the staging area in a campground.

He pulled in and was immediately surrounded by firefighters.

"What happened? Is there anyone else up there?"

"Not sure," Adam responded. "We were staying at a cabin near the summit that belongs to a friend, but I don't know if there are any other structures nearby."

"Who's your friend?"

Adam gave him Matt's full name and the fire chief nodded in recognition. "He owns the mountain and his is the only dwelling. We'll keep searching, but it's likely there's no one else."

"There were at least two other people," Adam countered. "The ones who started the fire. One was shooting flares from a helicopter. The other ran off through the woods." He lowered his voice. "They're mercenaries."

That single word triggered a round of questioning. Adam finished answering what he could and gave Nate's name as a reference. While he waited for the fire captain to speak with Nate, Isabelle had the emergency techs check the girls.

The captain returned, his demeanor solemn. "Your friend said to call him. Said it was urgent."

Adam glanced to where Isabelle was still speaking with the techs, thanked the captain, and stepped aside to make the call.

"Nate, what's up?"

"I have a suspicion how you're being tracked."

"I'm listening."

"The deputy who found Isabelle's phone. It was Warren. Check her phone. I'm thinking they loaded some sort of tracking into it, and then Warren pretended to find it in the bushes."

Frustration gnawed at Adam. Why hadn't he thought of that? But blame was useless. Isabelle's phone had been returned to her only a day into this bizarre escapade. Back when they'd had no clue how convoluted and deep this web ran.

"I'm taking her off-grid. We'll decoy the phone. I'll be in touch."

"Where do you mean off-grid?"

He hadn't noticed Isabelle come up behind him. He signaled for her to wait and then disconnected from Nate.

"Let's get in the truck and I'll explain."

"Adam…"

He hated the trepidation in Isabelle's voice, but this time it was justified. They'd been tracked everywhere they'd gone. But at least now he knew why.

Quickly he explained Nate's theory about the phone. "So, we need to dispose of it, and then disappear. I have a small cabin up in the mountains about an hour from home. No one knows about it. It's where I go when I need to be alone. We'll bring some supplies and hole up there while I finalize plans."

"What kind of plans?"

He glanced over at her. She wasn't going to like this either. "I spoke to Matt earlier. We're creating a group to take James down."

"You're mounting a mission."

"You could call it that, I guess."

"Against arguably the most dangerous mercenary on earth?"

The ice in her voice stunned him. "I'm not following."

"You can't resist it can you? You just have to take on another mission. You need to take down the bad guys."

Adam blinked, sure he'd just misunderstood, but when he glanced at Isabelle, he knew he was wrong. Her expression had hardened, and she was taking no prisoners. Still, he had to try.

"Isabelle, we have to stop them. These are the men who are holding your friend and her husband, who've pursued us for days, tried to kill you, managed to kidnap Laura twice. They won't stop unless we stop them."

"But why you? You've already been through so much. You've already risked everything."

He was quiet. There was no answer that could make her understand. This was so much bigger than them; so much more was at stake. From the moment he'd seen those drawings and known the type of work Jess's husband was capable of, he'd realized there was no turning back. If James and his men weren't stopped, no soldier would be safe from the destructive power of these mercenaries.

He wished Isabelle could understand that. But whether she could or not, his decision was made.

He looked over at her. Her eyes were closed. Whether she was actually asleep, or feigning it, the conversation was clearly done...as was any chance of them ever building a life together. A part of his heart broke for the death of what might have been. He glanced in the rearview mirror at Laura and Mia sleeping soundly. From the start, he'd insisted he wasn't interested in a relationship, but this brave little family had crept into his heart and laid claim without him even trying to mount a defense. Broken as he was, he'd allowed himself to hope.

And now that hope was crushed. If Isabelle couldn't understand why he needed to do this—not just for her, but for all the women and men he'd served with, for all those serving now and in the future, for men like her husband who had been broken beyond healing—then she really didn't understand him at all. There really was no chance for them. And that realization destroyed him more completely than any enemy weapon ever could have.

Chapter Nineteen

The mountain retreat was lovely, yet Isabelle found neither peace nor joy in it. She and Adam were now on opposite sides of a battle she didn't even understand.

On the surface, nothing had changed. He played with Mia and took the girls for walks in the woods. She never joined them. It was too painful to see him in his element, to miss the new life she'd started to yearn for.

She was standing at the kitchen window watching Adam and Mia try to build a snowman when the first vehicle rolled up. Her heart kicked into instinctive panic until she saw Adam abandon the snowman to go welcome his friend. Isabelle recognized Matt the minute he stepped from the truck. What was he doing here?

Over the next hour, several more vehicles arrived, each carrying men and women in outdoor gear similar to the camouflage Adam had worn that second day they'd trekked through the woods. Dreadful certainty settled in her gut. He was gathering a team for his mission.

She kept her distance, not willing to interfere but terrified of being drawn in. When Adam had first said they were coming to the mountains, she'd hoped for a reprieve. That finally they had escaped the mercenaries long enough to catch their breaths, maybe even to explore the feelings that had surfaced between them.

But that was all gone now, lost in a combat mentality she knew all too well.

Mia was tired from her morning in the snow, so Isabelle settled in bed with her to read a story. By the end of the third page, her little girl's eyelids were drooping and by the end of the story, she was sleeping sweetly.

Laura was cranky and in need of a bottle, so Isabelle eased away and headed to the kitchen. She stood at the same window where she'd earlier watched Adam and Mia play, but now she saw Adam alone. He was leaning against a tree, just at the edge of the forest. He was looking away, but she could see his tortured profile and knew he was in the grips of an attack.

She wanted to run to him, to comfort him,

but a part of her wanted to yell, *See what you're doing to yourself?*

The thought stopped her cold. No. He hadn't done this, at least not from the start. Shivers ran through her body as guilt washed over her. She'd done this to him. She'd brought this upon him when she'd pounded on his gate demanding he save her.

Blindly, she picked up Laura and the bottle. She needed some place private to grapple with these revelations. When she reached the end of the hall, she stopped to catch her breath and decide where to go. This house was unfamiliar and overflowing with men and women in various versions of paramilitary dress. She needed a place away from the noise and the distraction.

Mia was asleep in her bedroom, so she couldn't go there. Mentally, Isabelle reviewed the layout of the house. There was a closed-in porch overlooking the river. Maybe she could find privacy there.

The porch was quiet, which only amplified the thoughts racing around her brain. Laura started to cry and Isabelle tried to soothe her, but she wanted to cry, too. All the stress of the past days was getting to her, all the attempts to kidnap Laura, all the near-death experiences, the constant danger to her children, the growing attraction to Adam. And the broken heart that was sure to result.

It would be easy to write off her attraction as hero worship for the man who'd protected her, but she knew that it was Adam's wounded soul, his kind heart, that called to her. She'd fallen for the tinkerer, not the soldier—not that she didn't appreciate the warrior who protected children. But it was his soft side, the way he talked with Mia... She sniffled, thinking of him showing Mia the stars. Her thoughts were interrupted by the door opening.

A man in fatigues stepped out onto the porch, closing the door behind him. When he saw Isabelle, he stopped short. "Oh, sorry. I didn't realize you were out here."

"We were looking for some privacy," Isabelle answered.

Ignoring her comment, he strode toward them. "Hello, sweetie." He reached out a hand to touch Laura, and Isabelle jerked her away. Laura started to cry again.

He reached for her. "I'm good with babies. I can calm her."

Isabelle didn't want to be rude to one of Adam's buddies, but the man was getting on her nerves. "She'll be fine if you just leave us in peace."

The man walked to the door and flipped the lock.

Panic ratcheted through Isabelle. This *was* one of Adam's friends, wasn't it? Or had one of the mercenaries just blended in?

"Why did you lock the door?"

The man tilted his head and smirked. "Smart lady like you must have already figured out the answer to that." He extended his arms. "I'll take the baby now."

Isabelle backed toward the porch door that opened by the river. "I don't think so."

If she screamed, would Adam even hear her? She opened her mouth to try, but she'd barely gotten a squeak out before the man had his arm around her neck and a gun pressed to her side. "Give me the baby."

Isabelle tightened her arms around Laura. With everything she had learned about his boss, there was no way she could turn Laura over to this mercenary. As she shifted Laura, her hand brushed the bracelet Adam had made as a tracking device. Suddenly, she knew what to do. "You'll have to take me too."

He shrugged. "No problem. Two for the

price of one." He whipped a rag from his pocket and gagged her. "You give me any trouble at all, and I take the baby and leave your body behind, got it?"

Isabelle nodded. The terrifying thought occurred to her that the only reason he wasn't shooting her now was that someone would hear. She had to cooperate or he'd make good on his threat. She just had to buy some time until Adam realized they were gone.

But after the harsh words she'd spewed at him, she didn't expect he'd be looking for her anytime soon. Maybe when Mia woke...

Her heart broke thinking of her sweet Mia. She prayed as the man dragged her off the porch and onto the waiting boat.

Oh, Dear Lord, please protect us all.

Adam was trying to concentrate on the conversation and the plans they were discussing, but his thoughts kept turning to Isabelle, rehashing every detail, and wondering how things could have gone south so fast.

Matt nudged him. "You okay, man?"

Adam nodded, but he knew he wasn't. That didn't matter now. He had to lock down his heart and focus on the mission.

They'd been working on their plan for over an hour when a sleepy-eyed Mia wandered into the room. "Mr. Adam, do you know where my mama is?"

Adam glanced up then signaled to Matt to take over. He lifted Mia into his arms. "Let's go find her."

Five minutes of searching turned into ten, and he found no trace of Isabelle. Concern gave way to fear, but he couldn't let on to Mia. "Maybe your mama took Laura for a walk. Let's get you a snack, and I'll go look for her outside."

He signaled to one of the women, figuring Mia would be more comfortable with her. "Can you take Mia to the kitchen for a snack? I have to find Isabelle. Stay there and we'll come back."

Panic was threatening Adam with each passing moment, but he had to get it under control. Chance suddenly head-butted him, and Adam breathed a sigh of relief. He knelt and wrapped his arms around his friend's neck and buried his face in his scruff. His heart rate began to settle and his thoughts to clear.

The tracking devices.

He took one last moment of peace from Chance and jumped to grab his phone from his pocket. He flipped open the tracking app and waited for the satellite to retrieve the signal. Mere seconds that felt endless. The results sent him back to his knees. Both Laura and Isabelle's devices were tracking deep in the mountains. His best estimate, they were an hour away.

All the time he'd been fuming and then plotting a mission, Isabelle and Laura had been in the grip of a mercenary bent on vengeance.

Guilt swamped him. Isabelle was right. He was no better than her husband. He'd neglected his primary duty of keeping them safe in favor of an ambitious paramilitary plan. And now she and Laura were paying the price.

How had this happened?

The only possibility was that somebody had gained access. One of his buddies? Was it possible one of them had really switched allegiance?

Suddenly, Adam didn't know who to trust. Any one of the men here could be in cahoots with the mercenaries. Panic clutched his throat, spots danced before his eyes, his heart was racing hard enough that he could feel it pounding in his throat.

Chance nudged his leg, but the panic attack was too intense. He needed something stronger than his fear. He needed—

God.

Isabelle's words from the sunrise conversation came back to him. *I learned to trust in God.* Adam breathed in the memory and prayed. Slowly, his heart rate settled, his brain cleared, and he began to plan.

He would have to trust Matt because he needed a helicopter. That was the only chance they had of getting to her in time.

In time for what? His brain shut out the question. His focus had to be only on what was productive.

He uttered a prayer that he was making the right decision. He'd briefly wondered if Matt had betrayed them when they'd been located on the mountain, but Nate's discovery of the tracking on Isabelle's phone let him dismiss that thought. He would have to check with Matt and then trust his instincts.

Adam took out his phone and sent a message asking Matt to join him on the porch. It was the only place he could think of where they could talk with complete privacy.

As he opened the door to the porch, he knew instantly that this was where Isabelle and Laura had been taken from. There was no sign of any scuffle, but the back door was open and banging in the wind.

"Adam?"

Adam waved him over and Matt stepped out on the porch.

"What's going on?"

"Shut the door."

Matt pushed it shut and strode across the porch to where Adam waited by the door.

"Isabelle and the baby have been taken. I'm pretty sure this is where they went out."

"Are you sure? Maybe the wind just blew the door."

Adam held up his phone with the tracking app open. "After the attacks on the road, I created an anklet for each of them that tracks their location. You can see where Isabelle is."

Matt whistled. "That's out near Mesa Verde."

"Can you get us in there?"

Matt took out his phone to check his weather app. "Dicey, but if we go soon, we'll make it. Winds are picking up, though."

"You know these men better than I do. Who can I trust to take care of Mia?"

"After this, I won't vouch for anyone. What if we swing by home, drop her with Claire, and pick up Nate? Three of us will be better."

Adam agreed. "But don't tell anyone we're leaving. I'll get Mia and meet you at the truck. Let's take yours. Mine is blocked in."

"Okay, but before we go, I know you had to decide to trust me." He held Adam's stare. "You can."

Adam forced himself to walk toward the kitchen, but his mind was already racing ahead to the car. He grabbed Mia's coat from the rack and picked up Chance's leash. He fixed a smile to his face and walked into the kitchen. "Hey, Mia, let's go take Chance for a walk."

"Where's Mama?"

"She's with Laura."

He could sense the barrage of questions to come, so he signaled Chance, who started to nudge at Mia.

"I think he needs to go out fast." She giggled.

Within ten minutes, they were in the truck headed to the field where Matt had landed his helicopter. The winds buffeting the vehicle amped up his nerves, but Adam focused on trusting God.

Mia had been very quiet on the whole ride, but as he lifted her into the helo, she touched his chin to get his attention. "The bad men have Mama, don't they?"

"We'll get her back, I promise." Adam was aware he'd never made a more serious vow in his life.

"I know you will, Mr. Adam."

"What's that prayer you prayed with your mama? Remember, in the car?" It felt like a lifetime ago that icy streets had been the worst of their problems.

"Jesus, I trust in You."

"Jesus, I trust in You." Adam held Mia's hand and repeated the prayer over and over as the helicopter fought the winds and finally lifted in the air.

Chapter Twenty

They'd been driving for hours. Isabelle was exhausted, and Laura was fretting, so she reached for a bottle. Earlier, she'd demanded they stop for supplies. The mercenary had chosen an out-of-the-way store, and he'd held Laura, thus ensuring Isabelle's cooperation. But at least the baby had nourishment.

"How much farther?"

"What's it to you?"

"I'm just wondering how you were planning to drive all this distance alone with a baby? Do you even know how to care for her?" She was irritating him with her questions, but she needed to stay defiant or she'd give in to despair.

Satisfied after her bottle, Laura nestled into Isabelle's arms and fell back asleep. Isabelle fiddled with the anklet, wishing she could use it to send Adam some sort of message. She had no doubt that given more time he could have come up with something like that. He was so clever.

But he probably wasn't interested in what she thought of him.

Even if he did manage to rescue them, he'd never forgive her for her words. What she'd done was unforgivable. She'd taken his weakness and used it against him. She was ashamed of herself. She'd give anything to make it up to him.

But in a way, maybe she could. If she could be brave, and keep the trackers hidden, she could lead Adam right to his prey. Because he was right, such evil couldn't be ignored.

At some point she must have fallen asleep, lulled by the motion of the car and complete exhaustion. She woke as they were pulling into a compound. It was snowing, and she had no idea where they were.

Her heart sank as a gate closed behind them with a definitive clink. The car proceeded into the center of a courtyard where a garage door opened and they were suddenly inside a building. Her captor came around, opened the door, and forced her out. Armed guards stood beside the doorway. One of them phoned for authorization, and then she and Laura were quickly escorted down a long, sterile hallway into a room where they were abandoned.

Isabelle had tried to keep track of the path they'd followed, hoping against hope she would find a way back out. Now that they'd been left alone, she took the time to scope the room, looking to find something that would help them get free. Best to be prepared even though it was unlikely she'd get a chance. She knew better than to try to escape on her own. They didn't want her. Laura was their bargaining chip. They'd likely just shoot Isabelle on sight if she tried to escape.

Time crawled. Isabelle was beginning to wonder if anyone would ever come for them, or if just holding Laura captive was sufficient to their goal, when suddenly the room lit up as a wall of monitors came to life.

Isabelle nestled Laura against her chest to protect her from the sudden glare and stared at the screens, waiting to see their purpose.

The first one flickered to life and Isabelle gasped as Jess's image appeared on the monitor. She looked strained and exhausted, but she was alive.

"Jess!" Isabelle knew she shouldn't sound so jubilant. Certainly nothing in her friend's face indicated reciprocal joy. Understandable, given the circumstances and that her presence meant Laura had been captured.

The expression on Jess's face shifted and Isabelle realized a second screen had come into focus. The man whose face appeared was gaunt with marks that looked like burns. His body, though shrunken, seemed defiant at the same time, his eyes hollow, vacant—until they rested on the small child Isabelle held. There was a brief flicker of interest before they went blank again. Isabelle remembered in that moment that he had never seen his daughter before.

"Well, what do you think, Robert? Isn't she a little sweetheart?" The words were innocent, but the tone of the man's voice coming through the speakers was chilling.

"Wouldn't it be a shame if anything were to happen to her?"

Isabelle suppressed an instinctive shudder, knowing the man was probably watching for a reaction. His voice was different from that of the man who had brought her here, and she wondered if perhaps this was Silver Wolf himself.

She looked to the screens to see if his words

had had any effect on Jess or her husband. If they had, it was imperceptible.

"Hold the baby up to the screen so Daddy can see her sweet face."

Isabelle looked at Jess and her husband, both still with eyes cast down. She decided to take her lead from them and ignored his instructions.

He was not pleased.

Isabelle's eyes scanned the room trying to locate the camera he must be using to observe her. There was one directly above the monitors, which would make sense if he wanted the baby to be directly in their line of sight.

Laura was fussing, so Isabelle seized the chance to stroll around the room to try to console her. She walked to the front wall and stood beneath the monitors.

"Get back where we can see you."

Isabelle ignored him and continued to look for something she could use in defense. There was a poker by the fireplace, but he would be able to see if she picked that up. There was one way around that.

Quietly, she set Laura down on the ground. She knew she wouldn't have much time, so she inched her way toward the camera. It was too high to reach, so she pulled over a chair and climbed up. Leaning forward, she wrapped both hands around the camera and twisted. The camera came off in her hands.

She had no illusion that she was safe for long, and there was no place to hide, so she quickly scooped up Laura and hid her in the corner. "Jess, if you can hear me, tell me where you are."

Isabelle listened carefully to her friend's response as she grabbed a cushion from a chair and wrapped it in Laura's blanket as a decoy. Then she went to wait by the fireplace. She picked up the shovel and poked at the coals in the grate. When she found the hottest ones, she scooped them into the ash bucket and set it just behind her. She put the poker in the bucket, left it sitting in the coals, and stood facing the fire and rocking her pretend baby.

Within minutes, the door burst open and a tall silver-haired man entered. "Come here."

His voice was harsh, and Isabelle's instinct would have been to obey. Instead, she stared at him defiantly. "The baby is cold. I'm staying by the fire with her. If you want to talk to me, you come over here." Isabelle's heart was thumping so hard in her chest she was surprised he couldn't hear it, but she maintained an outwardly calm demeanor. She glanced surreptitiously at the monitors and could tell that Jess and her husband were listening closely even if they could no longer see.

Isabelle faced the man as he stalked toward her. "What do you want with us anyway?"

He snarled and gave an evil grin. Tilting his head at the screen, he taunted, "Why don't you ask them?"

Isabelle's body quaked, but she stood her ground. "Because I asked you."

"You think you're so smart, so bold." He advanced on her and she wrapped her arms tightly around the baby.

He was towering over her when Laura whimpered. His head swung around at the sound, but then he lunged at Isabelle. As he reached for the baby, Isabelle collapsed in a heap. He reached down, but she grabbed the poker and swung it around at his head. That set him back with an angry roar, but she knew it wouldn't stop him for long. Dropping her fake bundle, she grabbed the pail of hot coals and flung it in his face.

His bellow of pain would have given her remorse had he not been intent on such evil. Without sparing him more than a glance to make sure he wasn't following, she ran for Laura and dashed out of the room. She slammed the door closed behind her, hoping it would lock automatically, and took off down the hall, praying she could find a doorway.

Adam had hoped with the chopper they'd be able to cut off the car with Isabelle and Laura before they reached their destination, but the detour to exchange Mia for Nate had delayed them. He'd been watching the tracking device like a hawk. It hadn't moved in the last ten minutes, so either they'd stopped for some reason, or they'd arrived. Given the remote location, he suspected the latter.

Matt was using all his military training to keep the chopper flying just above the tree line, but the snow that had begun as light flurries was getting steadily stronger.

The three of them were talking on headsets, debating their best strategies and trying to create a rescue plan based on limited knowledge. Nate was in contact with local law enforcement, Matt concentrated on keeping them in the air, and Adam focused on tracking Isabelle and Laura.

"Looks like they've arrived," Adam said into his mic. "There's been no noticeable movement from the tracker in the past ten minutes. I'm looking at satellite imaging for the area and there appears to be a sizeable bunker-like structure in an open space."

"How far out are we?" Matt's voice came through the headset. "The snow is making visibility difficult, but it will also camouflage us. As long as it doesn't get too bad. I can use my instruments to land."

"They're on the move but inside the compound. Moving fast."

"Adam," Nate called. "We've got something at ten o'clock."

Adam peered out the left side of the helicopter and a mix of terror and elation lit through his veins. "That's Isabelle. Can you land, Matt?"

"Not this close. The rotor wash would blow her away. Get ready to rappel. I'll circle around and go low enough for you to descend, then I'll land in that clearing ahead."

As Matt swung the helicopter, Nate called out a warning. "Company coming around at six." He picked up the rifle Matt had shown them earlier. "I'll hold them off while you jump."

Adam didn't take his eyes off Isabelle as he quickly donned his gear. He shed his headset, replacing it with a helmet and radio, and waited for Nate to give him the signal. Once they were in position, he opened the door and began his rapid descent into a copse of trees.

Above his head, Nate was on sniper duty, and Adam watched as the lead mercenary fell. Two dropped back and ran inside, but the others kept going. Adam ignored them. Nate was a first-rate sharpshooter, and he had to trust that. His job was to rescue Isabelle and get her out of range.

The instant his boots hit the ground, Adam disengaged his harness and took off at a run. Isabelle stared at him in blatant disbelief as he emerged from the treeline. Without stopping to talk, he wrapped his arms around her and pulled her back beneath the trees. He suspected the two mercenaries had gone inside to retrieve antiaircraft weapons, so he knew they were running out of time.

"Can you run faster?" he shouted, trying to be heard over the roar of the rotors.

Isabelle didn't waste a breath on words but increased her pace. Adam took her deeper into the stand of trees, hoping that they would be less of a target. They stumbled over the uneven, snow-covered ground and paused for breath once they were behind the trees.

"Are you okay?"

Isabelle nodded.

"Laura?" He pointed to the wrapped shape in her arms.

Again, she nodded, gasping for breath.

"Matt is going to set the helo down as soon as we're in the clearing. Nate has reinforcements coming. I'll take Laura so we can run faster."

His heart eased at how quickly she handed over the baby, but when he tried to run, she tugged him back. "Jess and her husband are in that building."

Adam's heart sank.

He took her hand in his. "Let me get you to the helo, and I'll go back." He could see she wanted to protest, but he pulled her with him as he zigzagged his way through the forest, constantly aware of the gun-fighting behind and above them. As they neared the clearing, Adam glanced skyward.

Matt was circling the helicopter to set it down when Adam heard the distinctive pop of an RPG. He held his breath watching the rocket stream toward his friends, terrified he was about to see them be blasted from the sky.

Isabelle gripped his arm, and he stood frozen, listening for the explosion, mentally counting down Five…four…three…two… Then the tense moment, knowing the grenade would self-destruct in one. When the rocket exploded and the smoke cleared, Matt was ascending, having veered slightly to the left to avoid direct impact. But one of the rotors had been hit and the ship was wobbling.

Praise the Lord. Adam breathed a prayer of thanks that it hadn't been worse. Matt would be able to land safely, but it meant Adam and Isabelle were on their own until help arrived.

He motioned to Isabelle. "Back into the trees." They had no time to waste. He hated to even attempt this with a woman and child, but they would be sitting ducks if they stayed out there. Their best chance of surviving was to sneak into the building and find Jess and her husband while the mercenaries were busy trying to shoot down a helicopter that was now out of range.

They crept back, careful to stay hidden within the trees. When they were almost to the edge of the forest, he stopped. "What can you tell me about the layout?"

Isabelle closed her eyes and described it as best as she could from memory.

"Any sense of security? Guards, cameras?" It was a lot to ask of her, but he needed whatever she could recall.

She quickly recounted the details of her escape, and Adam's eyes grew wide with admiration. He was torn between leaving her hidden while he scoped out the building or taking her with him. It was an inestimable risk. Better he know where she was. He grabbed her hand and ran for the door.

Once they were inside, he stopped to take stock. The hallways seemed deserted, but there was a lot of foot traffic overhead, as if the mercenaries realized the compound was under attack.

"Do you have any idea where they're holding Jess?" he whispered to Isabelle.

"No. I asked before James appeared. She didn't know exactly, but she said she could hear a lot of running water."

"That's good. It sounds like she's on this level, hearing all the water draining through the house. We need to find the main drainpipe."

Adam searched the hall as far as he could see and found nothing, but the minute they rounded the corner, he knew they were in the right place. He could see the heavy pipe protruding from the ceiling and running into a wall between two doors. He cautiously approached the door, surprised there wasn't more security. He tried the handle. Locked.

"Is anyone in there?" he called.

A muffled response prompted Adam to force the lock. The pop was gratifying, and they cautiously entered to find Jess tied to a chair with a gag in her mouth. Adam removed the gag, then made quick work of the zip ties while he talked. "Do you know where your husband is?"

She nodded. "After Isabelle clocked James, he ran for help, forgetting that we were still on screen. We figured out Robert is just down the hall."

Noise overhead alerted Adam to incoming support just as Matt's voice came over his radio. "Backup has arrived and is engaging above."

"Tell them we're inside. I found Jess, and her husband is also here," Adam called into his radio. The last thing he needed was their allies bombing the building.

Within minutes, they'd located Robert, but evacuating him proved more difficult. Months of captivity had taken their toll. He was emaciated and weak, barely able to stand on his own. Jess ran to him, but Adam maintained focus.

"Matt, any update?"

"Bunker is ninety percent secured. James is on the run in the building. Recommend sheltering in place."

"Roger that. Radio when clear."

Adam had begun to barricade the doors when Matt's urgent voice came over the radio. "Bunker is rigged to blow. James is about to detonate. Get out now."

Chapter Twenty-One

"Isabelle, I'm going to put Robert in a fireman's hold. I need you and Jess to follow right behind until we get to the door. Once we get there, if all is clear, fan out and run to the woods."

The fear on her face could have paralyzed him.

"I need to know. Where's Mia?"

"Safe with Claire."

Her whole body relaxed with the news and Adam knew he could count on her.

He slipped his arm around Robert and lifted him onto his back just as explosions began to roll through the building.

"Scratch the plan. Run!"

The women took off ahead of him. Adam could feel the vibrations as the bombs detonated in a chain. The entire ground was rumbling, and memories of far too many similar situations in battle reverberated through his head. Not now. He couldn't give in now. They were so close.

"Adam, do it for Mia!"

He looked through his darkening vision to see Isabelle standing in the doorway, waiting for him. Her face was frozen in terror, but her eyes were defiant, calling to him, pulling him through.

As the floor pitched and split apart, he dashed the final few feet, grabbed her hand, and burst through into daylight.

Snow swirled around his head, delicate flakes dusted his shoulders, and he lifted his face to breathe in the crisp, clean air.

"We're safe. You did it. You saved them."

Isabelle's jubilant voice danced through his head.

He took her hand and pulled her into an awkward embrace. "No, we did it together."

The next hours passed in a blur as military personnel arrived to assume command. Jess, Robert and Laura were taken away for evaluation. Isabelle borrowed Adam's phone and called Mia, who told her she hadn't been worried because she knew Mr. Adam would find her.

Isabelle disconnected the call and sank against a tree. Night had fallen and stars were filling the sky now that the smoke and storm had cleared. She was reminded of that peaceful night on the mountain when she'd listened to Adam telling Mia to open herself to joy.

When had she forgotten how to do that? When had she gotten herself so tied in knots that she'd disconnected from the person she'd always been? She missed that carefree, joyous woman.

"Isabelle?"

As if her thoughts had summoned him, Adam appeared before her. "They're going to give us a ride into town. Matt's copter is damaged. We have a choice, stay in town or make the long drive home."

Ravaged was the only word Isabelle could think of to describe how Adam looked right now. Her tall, handsome hero looked absolutely ravaged. There was no way she could ask him to drive home. She summoned a smile. "Town sounds good."

They settled into a cute inn for the night. Adam saw her to her room. As he said good-night and started to leave, Isabelle called him back.

"I owe you an apology."

He smiled at her sadly and shook his head. "You owe me nothing."

She grasped his hand. "You're wrong. I owe you everything. But mostly I owe you an apology. Is there somewhere we could talk?"

He seemed to hesitate for a moment. "There's a back deck, but it's cold."

She shivered just thinking of the temperature, but she knew how much being outside revived him. "I'll bring a blanket and meet you out there."

When she walked out onto the deck, she saw that Adam had the fire pit burning and he'd pulled chairs close. She angled hers to face him.

"I'm so sorry for what I said to you…"

Adam made to brush it off, but she persisted. "I was wrong, in so many ways. You're nothing like Daniel. I've known that since we first met. But when you told me about the mission, I reacted as if you were him. I didn't understand why right away, but I've had time to think." She hung her head. "I lashed out at you because I felt guilty."

"Guilty? What did you have to feel guilty for?"

Isabelle fidgeted. "I brought all this upon you. You had treatment. You were recovering, and I dragged you right back into a battle for our lives. It wasn't fair of me to blame you for doing what needed to be done."

He started to interrupt, but she raised her hand and asked him to let her finish.

"This isn't about you or about your brain injury or your PTSD. It's about me, my failings. I couldn't save my own husband from himself. I failed Daniel, and I failed my daughter by losing myself in my own grief and guilt. I promised myself I would never do that to Mia again. But, instead, I did it to you. I failed you. I said awful, unforgivable things, deliberately giving you the wrong impression because I was scared. Scared to love again. Scared to risk a broken heart. Because when you told me you were going after Silver Wolf, I was afraid of losing you too. I'd brought this to your door, and I couldn't save you from it."

Adam buried his face in his hands and, for a long moment, she feared she'd gone too far.

Finally, he lifted his head, and his expression was grave.

"You are so wrong, Isabelle. You are the strongest woman I've ever met. You have to know, deep in your heart, that you did not fail

Daniel. War failed him. The repeated injuries destroyed him."

"But I didn't make him get help."

Adam shook his head sadly. "Daniel is far from the only soldier who couldn't seek help. That's part of what is so complicated about this. Soldiers are groomed to be strong, self-reliant, to never admit weakness. It's a mindset, and a broken brain sometimes can't see its way around that in order to seek help.

"Please don't destroy your life out of some misplaced sense of blame. What you've done these past few days, the way you fought to protect these children, that showed courage worthy of the finest soldiers I've ever fought beside."

Tears stung her eyes as she tried to process his words. "But I still failed you. I set you back. I know because I've watched you. I've seen the toll this has taken on you."

Adam rose and walked to the edge of the balcony. He stood for a long moment staring up at the sky before he turned, took a deep breath, and spoke.

"You didn't fail me, Isabelle. You saved me. Before you pounded on my gates, I was a recluse afraid to step into the world for fear I'd panic. The only place I ever felt safe was in nature. But you, and Mia, and my football baby opened my heart again. You showed me that life could be more than safe. It could be good. You took a man who was broken and helped him begin to heal—just by being you."

He came and knelt before her. "I know I'm not cured. There will be days, hours, when I struggle, but I can promise you this, Isabelle. I will never give up fighting it. I will never let it ruin your life or Mia's life. I want to be a whole man, to be the love you deserve, the father Mia needs. If I thought I couldn't be, if I thought I couldn't promise to love and cherish both of you, I would walk away from you right now, because I love you too much to hurt you."

He sighed and sat back on his heels. "I'll confess, I was not going to say this. I was going to be noble and walk away, let you and Mia have a good life without the burden of a broken soldier to hold you back."

She opened her mouth to protest, but he stopped her.

"I'm not walking away. I'm only saying that because I want you to understand that if I thought that was what was best for you and Mia, I would disappear from your lives in a heartbeat."

A chasm opened in Isabelle's heart. The idea of being without this man in her life was devastating.

Adam wasn't done. "A chaplain shared this quote from Isaiah at a very low point in my life. *But they that wait upon the Lord shall renew their strength; they shall mount up with wings as eagles; they shall run, and not be weary; and they shall walk, and not faint.*"

He leaned in and grasped her hands in his. "You say you brought danger to my door, but in my heart, I know it was God bringing you. Because we are meant to heal together, to build a life." He paused, then continued, his voice cracking, "Please say you'll give us that chance."

Isabelle closed her eyes, absorbed his words, and then pulled their clasped hands to her heart. Opening her eyes, she stared into his. "I love you, Adam. I love you so much. And if you'll have me, then yes. Yes, I absolutely accept that chance for a life with you."

Epilogue

Four months later

Adam and Isabelle emerged from the forest, arms wrapped around each other, faces wreathed in smiles. They'd left Mia and Chance at home with Claire so they could have time alone together in their favorite place to celebrate their recent engagement.

Now, as they approached the house, another smile lit Isabelle's face when she recognized the car in the driveway. "Jess is here?" Isabelle paused to correct herself. "I know, she's really Julia, but that's going to take some getting used to. Did you know they were coming? Is Robert out of the hospital?"

Adam just grinned, so Isabelle pulled away and rushed inside.

In the living room, she found her friend cuddling Laura, while a vastly improved Robert sat with his arm around them both. Isabelle stopped short as tears welled. She beamed at Adam, who had come up beside her. "You made this possible," she whispered.

Before he could answer, Mia ran across the room and launched herself at them. Isabelle caught her up in her arms and hugged tight.

"Mama, did you see? Aunt Jess finally came home. Chance found her."

Isabelle glanced at Adam and then at Jess and her husband. They all broke out laughing. She gazed up at Adam, at the love shining in his eyes, and sighed happily. "Thank you."

She set Mia down. "I'm sure Chance deserves a treat for that. Why don't you get him one?"

Mia scampered off, and Adam put his arm around Isabelle's shoulder. "Do I get a treat, too?"

She laughed and kissed him lightly on the cheek. "Will this do?"

"A little more to the left."

She grinned saucily and kissed him on the lips. "Better?"

"Only if you repeat it frequently." A sudden huskiness in his voice belied the joking tone of his words.

Isabelle laughed and shook her head. "Just

like Chance and his treats." She reached up to rest her hand on his jaw and gazed deeply into his eyes, holding on to the promise of forever that shimmered there. "Whenever you want one," she murmured against his lips.

"In that case..." He lowered his head to hers and kissed her again.

Isabelle was vaguely aware of Mia clapping, and Jess and her husband cheering, but then Adam deepened his kiss and gathered her in his arms, and all she knew was the joy of his love.

★ ★ ★ ★ ★

Romantic Suspense

Danger. Passion. Drama.

Available Next Month

Hunting Colton's Witness Anna J. Stewart
Last Mission Lisa Childs

....

Baby In Jeopardy Tara Taylor Quinn
Canine Protection Linda O. Johnston

....

LOVE INSPIRED

Montana Abduction Rescue Jodie Bailey
Showdown In The Rockies Kathleen Tailer

Larger Print

....

LOVE INSPIRED

Guarding His Secret Son Laura Scott
Hunted By A Killer Laurie Winter

Larger Print

....

LOVE INSPIRED

Deadly Ranch Hideout Jenna Night
Ambush In The Mountains Mary Alford

Larger Print

6 brand new stories each month

Romantic Suspense

Danger. Passion. Drama.

MILLS & BOON

Keep reading for an excerpt of a new title
from the Special Series series,
DOG DAYS OF SUMMER by Teri Wilson

Chapter One

So this was Texas.

Maple Leighton wobbled in her Kate Spade stilettos as she stood on a patch of gravel across the street from the Bluebonnet Pet Clinic and fought the urge to hotfoot it straight back to New York City. What was she even doing here?

You're here because you sold your soul to pay for veterinary school.

A doctor-of-veterinary-medicine degree from a top-rated university in Manhattan didn't come cheap, especially when it was accompanied by a board-certified specialty in veterinary cardiology. Maple's parents—who were both high-powered divorce attorneys at competing uptown law firms—had presented a rare, united front and refused to fund Maple's advanced degree unless she followed in their footsteps and enrolled in law school. Considering that her mom and dad were two of the most miserable humans she'd ever encountered, Maple would've rather died. Also, she loved animals. She loved them even more than she loathed the idea of law school. Case in point: Maple had never once heard of animals clawing each other's eyes out over visitation rights or who got to keep the good wedding china.

Especially dogs. Dogs were always faithful. Always loyal. And unlike people, dogs loved unconditionally.

Consequently, Maple had been all set to plunge herself into tens of thousands of dollars of student-loan debt to fulfill her dream of becoming a canine heart surgeon. But then, like a miracle, she'd been offered a full-ride grant from a tiny veterinary practice in Bluebonnet, Texas. Maple had never heard of the clinic. She'd never heard of Bluebonnet, either. A lifelong Manhattanite, she'd barely heard of Texas.

The only catch? Upon graduation, she'd have to work at the pet clinic for a term of twelve months before moving on to do whatever her little puppy-loving heart desired. That was it. No actual financial repayment required.

Accepting the grant had seemed like a no-brainer at the time. Now, it felt more like a prison sentence.

One year.

She inhaled a lungful of barbecue-scented air, which she assumed was coming from the silver, Airstream-style food truck parked on the town square—a *literal* square, just like the one in *Gilmore Girls*, complete with a gazebo right smack in its center. Although Bluebonnet's gazebo was in serious need of a paint job. And possibly a good scrubbing.

I can do anything for a year, right?

Maple didn't even *like* barbecue, but surely there were other things to eat around here. Everything was going to be fine.

She squared her shoulders, pulled her wheeled suitcase behind her and headed straight toward the pet clinic. The sooner she got this extended exercise in humiliation started, the sooner it would be over with.

Her new place of employment was located in an old house decorated with swirly gingerbread trim. It looked like a wedding cake. Cute, but definitely not the same vibe as the sleek glass-and-steel building that housed the prestigious veterinary cardiology practice where Maple was *supposed* to be working, on the Upper West Side.

She swung the door open, heaved her bag over the threshold and took a glance around. There wasn't a single person, dog, cat, or gerbil sitting in the waiting room. The seats lining the walls were all mismatched dining chairs, like the ones in Monica Geller's apartment on *Friends*, but somehow a lot less cute without the lilac walls and quirky knickknacks, and Joey Tribbiani shoveling lasagna into his mouth nearby. The celebrity gossip magazines littering the oversize coffee table in the center of the room were so old that Maple was certain the couple on the cover of one of them had been divorced for almost a year. Her mother had represented the wife in the high-profile split.

I turned down my dream job to come here. A knot lodged in Maple's throat. *Could this be any more of a disaster?*

"Howdy, there."

Maple glanced up with a start. A woman with gray corkscrew curls piled on her head and a pair of reading glasses hanging from a long pearl chain around her neck eyed Maple from behind the half door of the receptionist area.

"Can I help you, sweetheart?" the woman said, gaze snagging on Maple's shoes. A furrow formed in her brow, as if the sight of a patron in patent-leather stilettos was somehow more out of place than the woefully outdated copies of *People*.

Maple charged ahead, offering her hand for a shake. "I'm Dr. Maple Leighton."

A golden retriever's tawny head popped up on the other side of the half door, tongue lolling out of the side of its mouth.

"Down, Lady Bird," the woman said, and the dog reluctantly dropped back down to all fours. "Don't mind her. She thinks she's the welcome committee."

The golden panted and wagged her thick tail until it beat a happy rhythm against the reception desk on the other side of the counter. She gazed up at Maple with melting brown eyes. Her coat was a deep, rich gold, as shiny as a copper penny, with the feathering on her legs and underside of her body that goldens were so famous for.

Maple relaxed ever so slightly. She could do this. Dogs were dogs, everywhere.

"I'm June. What can I do for you, Maple?" the receptionist asked, smiling as benignly as if she'd never heard Maple's name before.

It threw Maple for a moment. She hadn't exactly expected a welcome parade, but she'd assumed the staff would at least be aware of her existence.

"Dr. Leighton," she corrected and pasted on a polite smile. "I'm here for my first day of work."

"I don't understand." June looked her up and down again, and the furrow in her brow deepened.

Lady Bird's gold head swiveled back and forth between them.

"Just one second." Maple held up a finger and then dug through the vast confines of her favorite leather tote— a novelty bag designed to look like the outside of a New York pizza parlor, complete with pigeons pecking at the sidewalk—for her cell phone. While June and Lady Bird cocked their heads in unison to study the purse, Maple scrolled quickly through her email app until she found the most recent communication from the grant committee.

"See?" She thrust the phone toward the older woman. The message was dated just over a week ago and, like every other bit of paperwork she'd received about her grant, it had been signed by Dr. Percy Walker, DVM. "Right here. Technically, my start date is tomorrow. But I'd love to start seeing patients right away."

What else was she going to do in this one-horse town?

June squinted at Maple's cell phone until she slid her reading glasses in place. Then her eyes went wide. "Oh, my."

This was getting weird. Then again, what wasn't? She'd been in Bluebonnet for all of ten minutes, and already Maple felt like she'd landed on a distant planet. A wave of homesickness washed over her in the form of a sudden craving for a street pretzel with extra mustard.

She sighed and slid her phone back into her bag. "Perhaps I should speak with Dr. Walker. Is he here?"

June went pale. "No, actually. I'm afraid Dr. Walker is…unavailable."

"What about the other veterinarian?" Maple asked, gaze shifting to the old-fashioned felt letter board hanging on the wall to her right. Two veterinarians were listed, names situated side by side—the familiar Dr. Percy Walker and someone named Dr. Grover Hayes. "Dr. Hayes? Is he here?"

"Grover?" June shook her head. "He's not in yet. He should be here right shortly, but he's already got a patient waiting in one of the exam rooms. And I really think you need to talk to—"

Maple cut her off. "Wait a minute. We've got a client and their pet just sitting in an exam room, and there's no one here to see them. How long have they been waiting?"

June glanced at an ancient-looking clock that hung next to the letter board.

"You know what. Never mind," Maple said. If June had to look at the clock, the patient had already been waiting too long. Besides, there was a vet in the building now. No need to extend the delay. "I'll do it."

"Oh, I don't think—" June began, but then just stood slack-jawed as Maple swung open the half door and wheeled her luggage behind the counter.

Lady Bird reacted with far more enthusiasm, wagging her tail so hard that her entire back end swung from side to side. She hip-checked June and nearly wiped the older woman out.

Someone needs to train this dog, Maple thought. But, hey, at least that wasn't her problem, was it? Goldens were sweet as pie, but they typically acted like puppies until they were fully grown adult dogs.

"Where's the exam room?" Maple glanced around.

June remained mum, but her gaze flitted to a door at the far end of the hall.

Aha!

Maple strode toward the door, stilettos clicking on the tile floor as Lady Bird followed hot on her heels.

June sidestepped the rolling suitcase and chased after them. "Maple, this really isn't such a good idea."

"Dr. Leighton," Maple corrected. Again. She grabbed a manila folder from the file rack hanging on the back of the exam-room door.

Paper files? Really? Maybe she really could make a difference here. There were loads of digital office-management systems specifically designed for veterinary medicine. Maybe by the time her year was up, she could successfully drag this practice into the current century.

She glanced at the note written beside today's date on the chart. *Dog seems tired*. Well, that really narrowed things down, didn't it?

There were countless reasons why a dog might be lethargic. Some serious, some not so worrisome at all. She'd need more information to know where to begin, but she wasn't going to stand there in the hall and read the entire file folder when she could simply go inside, look at the dog in question and talk to the client face-to-face.

A ripple of anxiety skittered through her. She had zero

problem with the dog part of the equation. The part about talking to the human pet owner, on the other hand…

"Dr. Leighton, it would really be best if we wait until Grover gets here. This particular patient is—" June lowered her voice to a near whisper "—rather unusual."

During her surgical course at her veterinary college in Manhattan, Maple had once operated on a two-headed diamondback terrapin turtle. She truly doubted that whatever lay behind the exam-room door was something that could shock her. How "unusual" could the dog possibly be? At minimum, she could get the appointment started until one of the other vets decided to roll in to work.

"Trust me, June. I've got this." Maple tucked the file folder under her arm and grabbed hold of the doorknob. "In the meantime, would you mind looking into my accommodations? Dr. Walker said they'd be taken care of, but I didn't see a hotel on my way in from the airport."

She hadn't seen much of anything from the back seat of her hired car during the ride to Bluebonnet from the airport in Austin, other than wide-open spaces dotted with bales of hay.

And cows.

Lots and *lots* of cows.

"Dr. Walker…" June echoed, looking slightly green around the gills. She opened her mouth, as if to say more, but it was too late.

Maple was already swinging the door open and barreling into the exam room. Lady Bird strutted alongside her like a four-legged veterinary assistant.

"Hi there, I'm Dr. Leighton," Maple said, gaze shifting from an elderly woman sitting in one of the exam-room chairs with an aluminum walker parked in front of her to a much younger, shockingly handsome man wearing a faded denim work shirt with the sleeves rolled up to his elbows. Her attention snagged on his forearms for a beat.

So muscular. How did that even happen? Swinging a lasso around? Roping cattle?

Maple's stomach gave an annoying flutter.

She forced her gaze away from the forearms and focused on his eyes instead. So blue. So *intense*. She swallowed hard. "I hear your dog isn't feeling well this morning."

There. Human introductions out of the way, Maple could do what she did best and turn her attention to her doggy patient. She breathed a little easier and glanced down at the animal, lying as still as stone on the exam table and, thus far, visible only in Maple's periphery.

She blinked.

And blinked again.

Even Lady Bird, who'd muscled her way into the exam room behind Maple, cocked her head and knit her furry brow.

"I, um, don't understand," Maple said.

Was this a joke? Had her entire interaction at this hole-in-the-wall practice been some sort of weird initiation prank? Is this how they welcomed outsiders in a small town?

Maybe she should've listened to June. How had she put it, exactly?

This particular patient is rather unusual.

A giant, Texas-size understatement, if Maple had ever heard one. The dog on the exam table wasn't just a little odd. It wasn't even a dog. It was a stuffed animal—a child's plush toy.

And Cowboy Blue Eyes was looming over it, arms crossed and expression dead-serious while he waited for Maple to examine it as if it was real.

Don't say it.

Ford Bishop glared at the new veterinarian and did his

best to send her a telepathic message, even though telepathy wasn't exactly his specialty. Nor did it rank anywhere on his list of abilities.

Do not *say it.*

Dr. Maple Leighton—she'd been sure to throw that *doctor* title around—was definitely going to say it. Ford could practically see the words forming on her bow-shaped, cherry-red lips.

"I don't understand," she repeated. "This is a—"

And there it was.

Ford held up a hand to stop her from uttering the words *stuffed animal.* "My grandmother and I prefer to see Grover. Is he here?"

"No." She lifted her chin a fraction, and her cheeks went as pink as the blossoms on the dogwood trees that surrounded the gazebo in Bluebonnet's town square. "Unfortunately for both of us, Grover is out of the office at the moment."

"That's okay. We'll wait," Ford said through gritted teeth and tipped his head toward the door, indicating she should leave, whoever she was.

Instead, she narrowed her eyes at him and didn't budge. "I'm the new veterinarian here. I'm happy to help." She cleared her throat. "*If* there's an actual animal that needs—"

"Coco isn't eating," Ford's grandmother blurted from the chair situated behind where he stood at the exam table. "And she sleeps all day long."

As if on cue, the battery-operated stuffed animal opened its mouth and then froze, exposing a lone green bean sitting on its fluffy pink tongue. There was zero doubt in Ford's mind that the bean had come straight off his grandmother's plate during lunch at her retirement home.

Dr. Maple Leighton's eyes widened at the sight of the vegetable.

Lady Bird rose up onto her back legs and planted her paws on the exam table, clearly angling to snatch the green bean for herself.

"Down, Lady Bird," Ford and Maple both said in unison.

The corners of Maple's mouth twitched, almost like she wanted to smile…until she thought better of it and pursed her lips again, as if Ford was something she wanted to scrape off the bottom of one of those ridiculous high-heeled shoes she was wearing. She'd best not try walking across the cobblestone town square in those things.

Her forehead crinkled. "You know Lady Bird?"

"Everyone in town knows Lady Bird," Ford countered.

Delighted to be the topic of conversation, the golden retriever opened her mouth in a wide doggy grin. This time, Maple genuinely relaxed for a beat. The tension in her shoulders appeared to loosen as she rested her hand on top of Lady Bird's head.

She was clearly a dog lover, which made perfect sense. She was a vet. Still, Ford couldn't help but wonder what it would take for a human being to get her to light up like that.

Not that he cared, he reminded himself. Ford was just curious, that's all. Newcomers were somewhat of a rarity in Bluebonnet.

"Can I speak to you in private?" he said quietly.

Maple lifted her gaze to meet his and her flush immediately intensified. She stiffened. Yeah, Maple Leighton definitely preferred the company of dogs to people. For a second, Ford thought she was going to say no.

"Fine," she answered flatly.

Where on earth had Grover found this woman? She had the bedside manner of a serial killer.

Ford scooped Coco in his arms and laid the toy dog into his grandmother's lap. She cradled it as gently as if it was a newborn baby, and Ford's chest went tight.

"I'm going to go talk to the vet for just a minute, Gram.

I'll be right back. You take good care of Coco while I'm gone," he said.

"I will." Gram stroked the top of the dog's head with shaky fingertips.

"This will only take a second." Ford's jaw clenched. *Just long enough to tell the new vet to either get on board or get lost.*

He turned, and Maple had already vacated the exam room. Lady Bird, on the other hand, was still waiting politely for him.

"Thanks, girl," Ford muttered and gave the dog a scratch behind the ears. "Keep an eye on Gram for me, okay?"

Lady Bird woofed. Then the dog shuffled over to Ford's grandmother and collapsed into a huge pile of golden fur at her feet.

"Good girl." Ford shot the dog a wink and then stepped out into the hall, where Maple stood waiting for him, looking as tense as a cat in a roomful of rocking chairs.

It was almost cute—her odd combination of confidence mixed with an aching vulnerability that Ford could somehow feel deep inside his chest. A ripple of…something wound its way through him. If Ford hadn't known better, he might have mistaken it for attraction.

He crossed his arms. "You okay, Doc?"

"What?" She blinked again, as if someone asking after her was even more shocking than finding a fake dog in one of her exam rooms. Her eyes met his and then she gave her head a little shake. "I'm perfectly fine, Mr...."

"Ford."

She nodded. "Mr. Ford, your dog—"

"Just Ford," he corrected.

Her gaze strayed to his faded denim work shirt, a stark contrast to the prim black dress she was wearing, complete with a matching black bow that held her dark hair in a thick ponytail. "As in the truck?"

He arched an eyebrow. "Dr. *Maple* Leighton, as in the syrup?"

Her nose crinkled, as if being named after something sweet left a bad taste in her mouth. "Back to your 'dog'…"

Ford took a step closer to her and lowered his voice so Gram wouldn't hear. "The dog isn't real. Obviously, I'm aware of that fact. Coco belongs to my grandmother. She's a robotic companion animal."

Maple took a few steps backward, teetering on her fancy shoes in her haste to maintain the invisible barrier between them. "You brought a robot dog to the vet because it seems tired. Got it."

"No." Ford's temples ached. She didn't get it, because of course she didn't. That hint of vulnerability he'd spied in her soulful eyes didn't mean squat. "I brought my grandmother's robotic companion animal here because my gram asked me to make the dog an appointment."

"So you're saying your gram thinks Coco is real?"

"I'm not one-hundred-percent sure whether she truly believes or if she just *wants* to believe. Either way, I'm going with it. Pets reduce feelings of isolation and loneliness in older adults. You're a vet. Surely you know all about that." Ford raked a hand through his hair, tugging at the ends. He couldn't believe he had to explain all of this to a medical professional.

"But Coco isn't a pet." Maple's gaze darted to the exam-room door. "She's battery-operated."

At least she'd had the decency to speak in a hushed tone this time.

"Right, which is why Grover usually tells Gram he needs to take Coco to the back room for a quick exam and a blood test and then he brings the dog back with fresh batteries." He threw up his hands. "And we all live happily ever after."

"Until the batteries run out of juice again." Maple rolled her eyes.

Ford just stared at her, incredulous. "Tell me—does this pass as compassion wherever you're from?"

"I'm from New York City," she said, enunciating each syllable as if the place was a foreign land Ford had never heard of before. "But I live here now. *Temporarily.*"

Ford's annoyance flared. He wasn't in the mood to play country mouse to her city mouse. "As much as I'd love to take a deep dive into your backstory, I need to get back to Gram. Can you just play along, or do we need to wait for Grover?"

"Why can't you just replace the batteries when she's not looking? Like, say, sometime before the dog gets its mouth stuck open with a green bean inside of it?"

"Because Gram has been a big dog lover her entire life and it makes her feel good to bring her pet into the vet. She wants to take good care of Coco, and I'm not going to deny her that." He let out a harsh breath. "No one is."

Maple just looked at him as if he was some sort of puzzle she was trying to assemble in her head.

"Are you going to help us or not?" he finally asked.

"I'll do it, but you should know that I'm really not great at this sort of thing." She pulled a face, and Ford had to stop himself from asking what she meant. Batteries weren't all that complicated. "I'm not what you would call a people person."

He bit back a smile. Her brutal honesty was refreshing, he'd give her that. "Could've fooled me."

"There are generally two types of doctors in this world—general practice physicians, who are driven by their innate need to help people, and specialists, who relate more to the scientific part of medicine," Maple said,

again sounding an awful lot like she was talking to someone who'd just fallen off a turnip truck.

If she only knew.

"Let me guess. You're the latter," Ford said.

Maple nodded. "I have a specialty in veterinary cardiology."

"Got it. You love dogs." It was a statement, not a question. "People, not so much."

She tilted her head. "Are we talking about actual dogs
or the robot kind?"

Ford ignored her question. He suspected it was rhe-
torical, and anyway, he was done with this conversation.
"June can show you where Grover keeps the batteries. I'll
go get Coco."

"Fine," Maple said.

"I think the words you're looking for are *thank* and *you*."
He flashed her a fake smile, and there it was again—that
flush that reminded Ford of pink dogwood blossoms swirl-
ing against a clear, blue Texas sky.

"Thank you." She swallowed, and something about the
look in her big, brown doe eyes made Ford think she actually meant it.

Maple and her big-city attitude may have gotten themselves clear across the country from New York to Texas,
but when she looked at him, *really* looked, he could see the
truth. She was lost. And he suspected it didn't have much
to do with geography.

She turned and click-clacked toward the lobby on her
high heels.

"One more thing, Doc," Ford called after her.

Maple swiveled back toward him. "Yes? Is there a teeny
tiny robotic mouse in your pocket that also needs new batteries?"

Cute. Aggravating as hell, but cute.

"Welcome to Bluebonnet."

Don't miss out!

LIMITED EDITION COMMEMORATIVE
ANNIVERSARY COLLECTIONS

In honour of our golden jubilee, don't miss these four special Anniversary Collections, each honouring a beloved series line — Modern, Medical, Suspense and Western. A tribute to our legacy, these collections are a must-have for every fan.

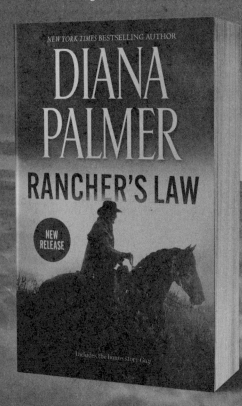